THE INN ON
THE MARSH

Also by Lena Kennedy

LENA KENNEDY

The Inn on the Marsh

Futura

A Futura Book

First published in Great Britain in 1988
by Macdonald & Co (Publishers) Ltd
London & Sydney

This Futura edition published in 1989

ISBN 0 7088 4236 4

Reproduced, printed and bound in Great Britain by
BPCC Hazell Books Ltd
Member of BPCC Ltd
Aylesbury, Bucks, England

Futura Publications
A Division of
Macdonald & Co (Publishers) Ltd
66–73 Shoe Lane
London EC4P 4AB
A member of Maxwell Pergamon Publishing Corporation plc

CHAPTER ONE

The Alianora

Joe Lee leaned lightly on the polished steering wheel of his brightly painted barge. The windows of the steering house were spotless as was all the brasswork which glinted in the late afternoon sun. As he surveyed the gleaming buckets and water cans — gaily decorated with colourful birds and flowers — Joe Lee's heart swelled with pride. His lovely *Alianora* was spick and span and easily the best-looking barge on those southern waterways.

For a moment he watched his two little sisters playing happily on the towpath and then turned dreamily back to the brown waters of the river. A light breeze ruffled his chestnut hair. With his freckled face and keen blue eyes, Joe Lee was a good-looking young man.

Down below in the cabin, Joe Lee's mother, Helga, was preparing the evening meal. She was a faded little woman whose shoulders and back were rounded from living continuously in cramped quarters. As she pottered around the shining stove, her sharp face peered out from under her grey hair, which hung down in untidy wisps. Her eyes, once as bright and piercing as a bird's, were now dull and listless. Around her shoulders, she wore a soft woollen shawl. Though very clean, it was old and shabby. Helga had spent countless hours cooking, cleaning and polishing in that little cabin below deck. Seldom did she ever relax, for she had very little time for leisure and she certainly paid no attention to her own appearance.

Joe Lee, her first son, had been born abroad the *Alianora*, as had all her children, including the ones who had not survived her. The *Alianora* was her world, for she had always worked hard alongside her husband, for the many long years they had sailed the waterways of England.

But now that Helga was sick and prematurely aged, her sons frequently begged her to go ashore, to take a cottage and to send the younger ones to school. But Helga would not hear of it. The *Alianora* was her life, she would tell them. And it had been that way since her marriage to that hefty bargee, their father.

Helga had been born to a life on water. She had come from the Netherlands and lived all her years on the waterways. And, miraculously, she had maintained a code of cleanliness and respectability for her own family. In those days, the barge people who sailed the canals and rivers of England were regarded as very low class. The barges usually carried animal manure and human sewerage from the big towns to be dumped at the dung wharf, further down the creek, where it would be filtered away by the tides. Most of the bargees piled their vessels high with filth and did not care that this attracted a vast army of flies wherever they went. And with their huge families of dirty, illiterate children, the barge people were not made to feel welcome to those who lived on the land.

The *Alianora*, however, was different. Her long hatch was always tightly covered to keep out the flies, and her gleaming bodywork put all the other barges to shame. Helga's achievement was all the more remarkable because her husband was an uncouth Geordie who had sailed the deep seas in his youth. The rough life on the salty seas had left its mark, and Geordie was now a cruel and bitter man, addicted to drink.

Yes, life had been very hard for Helga, but now that her sons were almost full grown men, they sheltered and protected her as she had never been before. And generally, the whole family depended on her eldest son Joe Lee, who was the calmest, most capable and hardworking of them all.

The setting sun glowed down on the water as Joe Lee watched a group of village women wade knee-deep into the watercress beds which stretched under the bridge. The sound of festivity wafted across the fields from the inn on the hill which stood outlined against the sky. Joe Lee squinted at the inn's tall crooked chimney and the winding path leading down to the river bank. It was Saturday night, and there was bound to be trouble at the Malted Shovel, he thought. The insular-minded inhabitants of this hamlet of Hollinbury had a particularly strong aversion to the barges — 'shit boats' they called them — and they loathed the loud-mouthed nomadic barge skippers who dared to anchor at weekends just outside their local inn.

Joe Lee now moved his gaze to fix intently on a small attic window high up on the gabled roof of the inn; he was patiently watching and waiting for something to happen.

Suddenly he received the signal. Smiling broadly, he took his arm from the wheel and smoothed his hair with one work-worn hand, before jumping lightly down onto the landing stage. Lucinda had waved to him from the window, a sign for him to meet her at the churchyard.

Briskly Joe Lee stepped out along the path, casting furtive glances to each side to make sure no one was spying on them.

Lucinda was there before him. As he came through the gate, Joe Lee caught the glint of the sun on her long golden hair which she had tied back with a blue ribbon. She was kneeling demurely over her mother's grave, her sweet doll-like face set in a serious expression as she placed a large jar of red-gold chrysanthemums beside the headstone.

In a second, Joe Lee was by her side. Catching hold of her hand, he pulled her into the shadow of a huge shady yew tree and they leaned towards each other in a close embrace.

Lucinda was small and well formed. Her high-waisted white dress was tied with a blue ribbon that matched the one in her hair and accentuated her lovely breasts. Joe Lee never met her without feeling his heart heave. Lucinda was completely unaware of her beauty, and her virginal modesty made her seem to Joe Lee all the sweeter.

'Oh, Joe Lee!' Lucinda whispered coyly. 'Not here, some-one might see us.'

Staying in the shade of the ancient church, the couple walked hand in hand towards the deep black dyke that carried the salt water over the marsh back to the sea. There, as the cool evening came in over the marshlands and the village women carried their bundles of watercress back to their homes, Joe Lee and Lucinda lay happily together, oblivious of everything except the other's presence.

Inside the Malted Shovel, the evening was beginning with much activity and bustle. Lucinda's Aunt Beatrice was polishing the pewter tankards at high speed, while Dorothy, Beatrice's sister, swept out the dirty sawdust, and put clean sawdust down on the floor, spreading it carefully where the heavy boots would tread, and around the row of spittoons which most customers invariably missed. These two unmarried ladies ran the Malted Shovel and never hesitated to broadcast their opinions to anyone who would listen.

'Dirty lot of blighters,' commented Aunt Beat. 'That's the second time today we've had to put new sawdust down. It's them old bargees from the shit boats what does it.'

Auntie Dot's loose mouth stretched into a grin that made her teeth loom out. She seemed to have too many for her jaw. 'It's a public bar,' she remarked. 'We can't forbid no one to come in. But soon they'll be traipsing all over the bar parlour.'

'Never!' cried Beat. 'Pa will not let them in *there*, it ain't right.' Her huge untidy head shook like a wet dog. 'It's not healthy having all them barges out there all weekend.'

'I can't see what we can do about it,' commented Dot, her white mop cap bobbing as she carried the cardboard sawdust box under her arm.

'Better get that girl in,' said Beat suddenly. 'Now where is she?'

'She's gone to the churchyard,' replied Dot. 'You know how she likes to put fresh flowers on her mother's grave.'

'Well, call her in,' insisted Beat. 'We don't want her mooching about in the graveyard after dark.'

Dot popped her head out of the door. 'Lucinda! Lucinda!' she screeched.

Within a couple of minutes, Lucinda came running, over the bridge, her white cotton dress clinging tightly to her trim figure in the cool evening breeze. She carried the blue hair ribbon, now rumpled, in her hand, and her golden locks looked very untidy. 'Coming, Auntie,' she called breathlessly.

'Now come in, Lucy Cindy. Let's get your Grandpa down. Whatever are you doing out there? Just look at your nice clean ribbon.' Muttering and grumbling, Dot hustled Lucinda inside. As she did so, she did not notice how Lucinda's cornflower-blue eyes shone with the light of passion. But if she had, she would not have recognised it for what it was, never having experienced love herself.

Every evening, Grandpa was brought down into the bar parlour down a home-made ramp leading from his bedroom on the first floor. Amos Dell had once been a sea captain, but was now an invalid and so grossly overweight that his clothes were bursting at the seams. His arms and legs were no longer of any use and his grey-brown beard, which had grown down to his waist, covered his bloated body like a thatch. But his voice as still loud and vibrant and within that big bald dome of a head an active brain still functioned. 'I'm still the governor here,' he would frequently remind everyone.

Each night Lucinda and Dot would heave Grandpa's huge helpless body into a rickety bathchair and together they would push and guide it down the ramp and into the bar parlour. Then, seated beside the cosy log fire, and soaking up the ale which he drank by the gallon, Grandpa was content for the evening.

The small private bar was open only to a very few privileged customers — generally, the local professionals, such as the doctor, the farmer, the smithy or the squire. There these men held long conversations about the good old days, drinking steadily, and complaining about the state of the country.

First to arrive that evening was Sam Shulmead, the smithy, still dressed in his leather cap and apron, with his shirt sleeves rolled up to reveal magnificent biceps. Sam was a hefty dogmatic man with a sour expression on his face. He

had come to the inn with his sons, Matt and Mark. They were
strikingly built boys, tall, dark and very handsome, and aged
seventeen and eighteen. At the door of the inn, father and
sons parted, with the boys heading for the public bar as their
father turned in to the bar parlour.

Hanging in a row on the low oak beams across the bar were
the shining Shulmead tankards. Each one was engraved with
its owner's name — Sam, Matt and Mark. As they entered,
Beat reached up for the tankards, filled them with strong
frothy ale, and pushed them across the counters at the men.

This would be repeated all night until closing time. No
money ever passed hands but a record of the family's
consumption of ale was kept on a big slate on the wall. The
final amount would be paid for by Sam before they all left.
With a grim face and watchful eye, Sam kept track of his sons
from the other bar, raising his huge fist in warning whenever
he considered that they had drunk enough. These two elder
boys were his right hand at the forge. He had trained them
practically from birth, and he paid them no wages for their
work but he was occasionally heard to remark that he say
'they wanted for nought'.

Some time into the evening, another Shulmead son would
come creeping into the inn through the back door. This was
poor dumb Lukey. He was thin and gawky with a mouth that
gaped and red-rimmed eyes. He was about sixteen, and with
his shambling gait he would wander around the inn collecting
the empty tankards and returning them to the customers full
to the brim again. Then out in the kitchen, he would sit to
mind the hot pies. He could not speak at all. He could only
gesticulate and mouth strange noises. Lukey was an imbecile
and would always be one, having suffered brain damage when
his brutal father beat him senseless when Lukey was a tiny
child. Lukey had never ever fully recovered his senses since then.

Auntie Beat and Auntie Dot always welcomed Lukey for he
saved them a lot of trotting about. They fed him and fussed
him and were kind to him, so their warm kitchen became an
important refuge for him.

Now in came the bargees — rugged men in caps and chokers. They always came and left in a group, and kept their own company, congregated in the public bar. There among the local farm labourers and men and women from the brick fields, there always was a tense atmosphere. And more often than not a fight would break out. When this happened, Aunt Dot would scurry away in fright, but Aunt Beat always waded in, wielding a large wooden rolling pin and a heavy pepper pot. The man who had started or was continuing the fight would get pepper in his eyes and a hefty whack on the head with the rolling pin, and he would soon retire from the fray. Thus Auntie Beat kept order at the Malted Shovel.

The inn was the centre of the neighbourhood. It was here that all the latest news and gossip was circulated. Here friends and enemies were made. The whole of life existed here in this one lonely inn beside the creek that crossed the Thames marshland.

As the noise from the bars came up through the wooden floors, Lucinda sat by her attic window and stared out across the field towards the river. She was never allowed in the bar at night and nowadays spent her Saturday evenings in this position, looking across at where her lover stood.

Down on the *Alianora*, as she lay at anchor in the creek, Joe Lee stood on deck looking wistfully back at his beautiful Lucinda. The whole summer had been like this. And both wondered where it would all end.

Drinking in the public bar on this Saturday night were Joe Lee's father, Geordie, and one of his younger brothers. Joe Lee himself did not drink alcohol and had no desire to do so. He would just wait until they stumbled back on board the barge when he would help them to bed. Within the smokey, overheated bar, a heated discussion was in progress. It had begun in the bar parlour, where a clerk from the town hall had let slip the news about a certain motion having been brought before the town elders. Apparently, a petition had been signed by the more affluent members of Hollinbury expressing their opposition to the dung barges being regularly anchored by the inn at weekends in wait for the flood tide to carry them down to the dung wharf. According to the clerk, the elders had agreed to give serious consideration to this problem. They had also, he told them, passed a resolution to go ahead with a new canal, the project which had been abandoned five years earlier for the lack of funds.

'It will pass right through the hamlet,' the clerk informed them. 'The idea is to link the Thames with the Medway.'

'Lot a good that will be,' growled Amos. 'Thames skippers sail on the ebb tide around Grain. They always have done.'

'But it will cut off forty miles of treacherous sea voyage,' suggested the clerk, a small man with the rat-like face.

'Nonsense!' roared Amos. 'Thames skippers will not use a narrow canal.'

'Who's goin' to dig it out, then?' asked the farmer. 'Can't get through them chalk cliffs, that's for sure.'

'Who else will dig the canal but them poor devils out at St Mary's?' retorted the doctor.

'What? The prisoners out on the hulks, you mean?' The farmer slammed down his tankard in surprise.

'The very same. Dying off like flies, they are, out there with the malaria ague.'

'They say they are starved,' said another. 'I saw them digging in the clay pits and it was not a pretty sight.'

'I don't pity no damn Frenchman,' roared Amos. 'They gets all they deserve.'

'But they are not criminals,' said the clerk. 'They're just prisoners-of-war, taken while defending their own country.'

At this remark Amos almost exploded. His huge face turned red and fiery. 'Don't you tell *me*, lad, because I know. And I've seen what they do to our sailor lads in *their* hell holes of prisons.'

'Calm down, Amos,' said the farmer. 'He's entitled to an opinion.'

'Then let him keep it to himself,' snarled Amos.

The clerk left hurriedly soon afterwards, but by that time his news had spread to the public bar and even to the bargees who sat in their corner puffing evil-smelling pipes. They were a hefty bunch of men dressed in shabby clothes but the largest of them all and the most voracious, was Big Geordie, skipper of the *Alianora*. He had a bullish expression on his florid face, and his faded red hair was very sparse on top. And, like Amos, he had a loud voice which carried over the bar.

The two Shulmead lads leaned on the counter and were talking to Sergeant Jock Campbell of the Scots Fusiliers, about the army, their favourite topic. An old sweat and pioneer of many battles, Jock was now in charge of the French prisoners out in the hulks. This was a soft sort of job for this army-trained bully, he loved to tell of his old exploits, and the two young brothers listened with avid interest.

Jock's only weaknesses in life were booze and women, and it was well known that he occupied the bed of Geordie's sister, Larlee, who worked in the brickfields. Larlee herself had just swaggered in to the inn looking exceptionally clean and tidy, for it was Saturday night. She wore the outfit that she saved for Saturday nights and although the dress was worn and dingy and accentuated her sallow skin, it was neatly pressed, and the pale green slip that showed through the white material revealed the trouble she'd gone to in dressing. On her head was an artfully wrapped turban that she'd created herself from some extra fabric, after seeing some of the fancier ladies come through the hamlet wearing them. Turbans had become popular after Napoleon conducted his Egyptian campaigns, and they were one of the more benign effects of the seemingly endless war with France.

Larlee was now a faded beauty but had once been a tall, dark vivacious barge girl who had married a lad from the hamlet. Soon after she had borne him two children, her husband had been pressed to go to sea and had never returned. So in order to support her daughters, Larlee had gone to work in the brick fields. Within five years she had become morally and physically dejected, and was called the local whore. Now her once sparkling eyes were dark and hard, her once lily-white teeth had gaps in them, were yellow and there were burn scars all over her face and arms. Whether she was drunk or not, her language was always blasphemous. Big Geordie could not tolerate such a sister and there was no love lost between them, so Larlee was no longer acknowledged as one of them by the barge folk. She had, as it were, gone over to the other side.

But Larlee cared little for anyone's opinion of her. She drank, smoked and swore as good as any man and anyone who took her fancy would be taken home to bed by her on Saturday nights. And nowadays she earned a good living employing young children to assist her in the brick fields.

'I'll never starve again,' she would often say, 'not while I have two hands to work with.'

The news about the new canal was quickly circulated. 'It's coming straight through the hamlet,' Beat said to Dot.

'Well,' replied Dot, 'I hope it gets rid of them shit boats at last. It's them that's brought all this sickness, with the little ones dying like flies. 'Tis brought from the town by those mucky barges.'

Then, clucking like a hen, Dot went out into the kitchen to get one of the large mutton pies that were so popular with the customers.

In the kitchen dumb Lukey sat watching the oven, mouth agape. It was his job to watch the pies, to see that they kept warm but did not get baked up. This he achieved with equanimity, spittle drooling from the sides of his mouth at the thought of a good supper that Auntie Beat would provide for him later in the evening. The argument in the bar had heated up as the bargees discussing loudly the pros and cons of the new canal.

'It will link two rivers,' one said, 'and save time. And time is money.'

'There will be a tariff, that's for sure,' warned another.

'Well, I reckon I'll stick to the estuary for I am used to it,' another replied.

Suddenly Larlee's shrill voice was heard above the din.

'Time we got them bleeding shit boats out of the creek.'

Big Geordie whirled around to face her. 'Whore!' he snarled. 'Soldiers' floozie.'

'Jock!' screamed Larlee. 'Geordie has insulted me!' She stood defiantly in the middle of the bar, hands on hips, her black hair showing beneath her now dishevelled turban, and the gold loops in her ears gleaming.

Jock slammed down his tankard of ale and swung around, swiping Big Geordie on the jaw with his fist. Geordie staggered backwards but had regained his balance in a flash. Within seconds, the two heavyweights were locked in combat, and in no time, the rest of the bargees had joined in the battle. Tumbling out of the crowded bar, the fighting raged out into the courtyard. Like two great monsters, these big men, carried away by drink, fought on as the yard outside became a mass of struggling figures. And all the while Larlee was screaming encouragement while Beat defended her bar with the rolling pin and pepper pot.

Down the road, old Charlie was dozing in his sentry box, supposedly guarding the bridge. The noise from the inn woke him up immediately and he was soon blowing his whistle to bring the soldiers running from their posts guarding the road to the fort.

The arrival of the military soon scattered the crowd. But after it had dispersed, one large figure lay still on the ground with blood oozing from his mouth. It was big Geordie breathing his last with a knife stuck in his back.

Joe Lee had heard the fight going on from his position on the barge; and he was up at the inn within minutes, as if he had had some notion that his family would be involved in the fray. The drunken sergeant, Jock Campbell, was being led off into custody as he arrived.

As Joe Lee and his brother Tom Lee carried their father back to the *Alianora*, they knew that there was no hope, for Geordie's life's blood flowed out from a gaping hole in his back. And by the morning big bargee had left this world as violently as he had lived in it. Helga knelt beside Geordie's massive body with tears coursing down her faded cheeks. He had never been an ideal husband but he was her man and the father of her children, and now he was gone.

That Sunday morning, the seriousness of the affray at the Malted Shovel had made its mark. Aunt Beat and Aunt Dot knelt with Lucinda in the old church, while the vicar rendered a long sermon on the evils of drink. And the villagers sat silent and subdued in the pews. Down on the landing stage, stood Larlee, still very drunk, waiting for the return of her imprisoned Jock and yelling insults to one and all.

Joe Lee sat out on the deck with his brother, with a grim expression on his fresh young face. Over and over in his mind he wondered who could have killed Big Geordie. It was surely not Campbell, for he had never been known to carry a knife. Guns, fists and boots were *his* weapons.

The *Alianora* was now impounded until the authorities decided where to lay the blame, for Joe Lee was not the only one to have doubts about Jock Campbell.

'It strikes me, Tom,' said Joe Lee, 'that someone came up from behind him while he and Jock were struggling on the ground.'

'But who?' asked the puzzled Tom Lee. He had been very drunk and remembered very little of that terrible night's fracas.

'The doctor has removed the blade,' continued Joe Lee. 'He says it was an ordinary table knife driven in with a terrible force. The handle is still missing.'

'Perhaps if we look we'll be able to find it,' suggested Tom Lee.

Joe Lee shook his head. 'I searched at dawn to try to find some evidence, but I found nothing.'

'What shall we do then?' Tom Lee looked to his elder brother for advice.

'Not much. You and I must go on and sail the barge and take care of Mother and the girls. It's the most we can do,' he said, thinking of Lucinda.

Later that day the other bargees came along to pay their

respects and give donations so that the family could take Big Geordie to be buried in his homeland in the north, just as he would have wished.

At the Malted Shovel, Lucinda stared desolately out of her window. She was not allowed down on the landing stage until this dreadful matter had been cleared up. Between her aunts downstairs, this was the general topic of conversation, as throughout the village. No one could talk of anything else, whether outside the church or in the village street.

That Sunday morning Sam Shulmead drove out in his pony cart with three of his sons aboard — Matt and Mark and John, his youngest, who was just twelve years old. John was a fair, pale boy whose shoulders drooped from working in the brick fields ever since his mother's death. For Sam Shulmead believed in work. This puny child would never be a man, he thought, unless he built up his muscles. So young John worked twelve hours a day carrying hods of clay from one place to another, and he had deep scars on his hands from handling the hot bricks from the kilns.

Sam was a deeply religious man. He did not hold with the church; the chapel of Zion in the village was his place of worship. So each Sunday he drove off with his three sons down into the village, while his fourth son, dumb Lukey, was allowed to stay home to mind the forge. The truth was that Sam was deeply ashamed to be seen with his idiot son. Like everyone else, the Shulmead men were all rather subdued that morning, except for Lukey, who drooled and gabbled worse than ever and seemed unusually excited. Only a swift kick to his rear from his irate father had quietened him before they left.

The inn did not open on Sundays, so after church Beat and Dot prepared their family Sunday lunch.

'It's certainly a mystery,' announced Aunt Dot. 'It gives me the shivers whenever I think about it.'

'I knew there was trouble brewing,' declared Aunt Beat. 'I could just feel it in me bones.'

The Sunday tablecloth was spread out on the table and

Aunt Beat went to get out their cutlery, precious knives, forks and spoons, a family heirloom only used on Sundays. For the rest of the week they were kept in their neat leather case in the dresser drawer in the kitchen.

'Yes, it's a complete mystery,' Beat said, shaking her head. 'But I do know that it could not have been Larlee, for I saw her still in the bar at the time, scrapping with that lowdown Wally, the herdsman. They certainly hate each other! God knows what goes on in those cottages.'

'Big Geordie was her brother,' said Aunt Dot gently. 'One never ...'

'Yes, but there was no love lost there,' returned her more practical sister. Suddenly she gasped. Before her in the open dresser drawer the beloved cutlery lay in a neat row before her. But one table knife was missing. Immediately, before her eyes swam a picture of dumb Lukey's drooling face as he had sat here in the kitchen the night before minding the pies. Quickly she shut the drawer. 'Use the old cutlery, Dot,' she said casually. 'I can't be bothered to lay up the best ones today.'

Both Lucinda and Auntie Beat were very quiet over lunch. Dot and Grandpa did try to interest them both, with conversation, but they were distant and lost in their own thoughts.

'I am of the opinion,' Amos announced ponderously, 'that those bargees did Big Geordie in themselves and are now trying to lay the blame on our hamlet.'

'Oh yes! you could be right, Pa,' cried Dot excitedly, as she picked her large teeth. Dot always agreed with her father.

Beat got up to clear the dishes, sighing a deep sigh. And Lucinda, looking quite pained, said, 'Please may I leave the table?' Without waiting for permission she dashed off to her room where she watched from her attic window.

Across the field, where a soldier stood guard over her, the *Alianora* looked so quiet and sad. There were no children playing on deck and no Joe Lee at the wheel. She felt so lonely and strangely apprehensive, as if she had had some premonition of her future.

At dawn the next day the tide rushed inland to fill the dykes and inlets, and float the barges at last. The bargees prepared to set sail, to rid themselves of their stinking cargoes at the dung wharf, before navigating down river once more.

The *Alianora*, usually the first to set sail, was now the last when the soldiers who had guarded her all night were finally called off. Joe Lee was given permission to leave and sail north to bury his father. The military had decided to hush the whole matter up. As far as they were concerned, it was just an unfortunate incident, resulting from a drunken brawl — not an uncommon happening in those unruly times. It was announced that Sergeant Campbell would be disciplined, but beyond that, as far as the military was concerned, the matter would be forgotten.

Larlee had a terrific hangover and was looking very blowsy on Monday morning, as she stood out on the road waiting for the children to join her. When the tired ragged little figures appeared they followed her in single file, plodding all the five miles over the marsh to the brick kilns, not to return home until sundown. But Larlee had tears in her eyes as she watched the *Alianora* sail away and she found herself wishing she were a child again, playing on the deck with her big brother Geordie. But Geordie was no more. He was far away from there, way up in the heavens.

Lucinda peered out of the window at the barges sailing off and then went back to bed, pulling the bedclothes around her and soaking the pillow with her tears. Joe Lee had left her.

Soon peace descended once more on the hamlet. The mist rose from the marshland. The women and children went out into the fields to work and the men attended to their affairs. They had their own lives to live and the weekend troubles seemed soon to be forgotten. Soon another Saturday came round, a damp mist still hung heavily over the marsh — a sure sign of the approaching winter. Aunt Beat stoked up the wood fire, and put a tray of hot pies into the oven. Now she gazed speculatively at dumb Lukey who sat expectantly at the table waiting for his supper. This was usually a big piece of cheese and a hunk of bread, followed by a fruit pie, which Beat would have made specially for him. Then Beat would fuss and fondle him, which he liked, and, if she was in a good mood, she would let him touch her garter. Her big frame would shake with laughter as Lukey panted excitedly letting his tongue loll out of the side of his mouth.

'He's like some old mongrel on heat,' she would remark coarsely with a loud cackle.

Aunt Dot did not approve of such frolics for she was a bit of a prude. But Beat was made of a different fibre and had had quite a few love affairs in her youth. But hard living and too much work had made her tough and her skin sallow, and her personality was now so unattractive that few men were prepared to wrangle with that wicked temper.

'Don't torment poor Lukey,' Dot would plead. 'I know he is foolish but sometimes I think he might get dangerous. He's not entirely to be trusted.'

'Oh, shut up!' Beat would snap at her. 'It's only a game.'

But tonight no supper had appeared before him and Lukey was looking concerned. This time, too, he received a smart slap from Beat whenever his hand wandered. So poor dumb Lukey just sat at the table looking very perplexed.

'Come over here,' Beat hissed to him, once Dot had left the room. She stood by the dresser and pulled out the big drawer.

'Look in there,' she said, 'and tell what you see.'

She narrowed her eyes as she watched Lukey closely. Lukey had spittle drooling out of the side of his mouth as he stared down at the open leather cutlery case. 'Where is it?' Beat hissed. 'Me best knife. Where's it gone?' The strange green eyes squinted. The wet mouth gaped. Suddenly Beat dealt him a heavy blow across the back of his misshapen head. 'Now, talk!' She yelled. 'Did, did you take it or did you not? And if not, *who* did?'

In a dazed manner, Lukey shook his head back and forth.

'Do I get me rolling pin?' threatened Beat.

Suddenly Lukey was down on his knees and clasping her solid thighs with such a strong grip that she could not move.

Then he pressed his wet lips to her stomach with tears pouring down his face as he rained kisses on her. Even through her dress Beat could feel his warmth, and some odd maternal feeling welled up inside her.

'Hush, hush, don't cry,' she crooned. 'Beatie will look after you.'

She cuddled him and guided him back to the table on which she placed a big hot pie. With trembling hands, Lukey gobbled it up almost immediately.

'Now be a good boy and don't touch nothing else,' Beat said gently but firmly as Lukey looked at the drawer in the dresser. Then she went off to the bar, her face white and strained. 'Dear God!' she muttered. 'He's done it all right. But I'm hanged if they will get anything from me,' she added defiantly.

CHAPTER TWO

The Pug Mill

The track to the Pug Mill wound past the Malted Shovel, and on over the muddy marsh to the edge of the creek where the brick works were. There it went past miles of gloomy water-logged pits where tons and tons of thick orange clay had been removed. Further along there was a long line of ugly brick kilns and wooden sheds. It was a silent and gloomy area, where only the screech of the seagulls could be heard. But through a pair of gates a trickle of small weary children plodded early in the morning and late at night to and from their soul-destroying work. On Saturdays when they were paid, each one clutched a precious hard-earned sixpence in a grimy fist, which was more often than not scarred with clay burns. Only the lowest and most degraded of local folks would allow their children to work in the brick fields, but many had no choice. And many immigrants from the north came down in droves to work themselves and their young into an early grave.

The Pug Mill made bricks, tiles and sanitary pipes which went toward the creating of new mansions for the rich, and factories to make more capital — wealth built on the bent backs of common working people.

Inside the mill, the damp smell of wet clay was overwhelming, and the sight of the filthy, half-naked women and children working at the moulding tables was enough to shock any stranger's eyes.

There at one of the tables was Larlee, her tall figure covered in a ragged sheet wound about her thin contours. It was a faded yellowy grey and caked with so many layers of clay that it was stiff. About her head a similar piece of material was wound in a rough-shaped turban, the only feminine thing about her being those loops of gold in her ears, symbols of her gypsy heritage which she never removed. Working with her hands and a large wooden spatula, she skilfully moulded the bricks from the wet clay, almost as if she were making pastry. As her strong brown hands effortlessly pushed and battered the wet clay into shape, Larlee was oblivious to the distress all around her, such as the malnourished children who staggered to the table on weak legs carrying fourteen pounds of wet clay on their heads having just made the half-mile trip from the clay pits to the moulding room. All day, a long line of them moved back and forth, listlessly supplying clay to the older women who made the bricks and who earned their money on a bonus system. For they were paid only for the number of perfect bricks they turned out. The 'pages', as these little slaves were called, waited all day on the women without a break, dropping the wet clay down on the moulding table before trotting off for more, often with a whack from the huge spatula to hurry them on. Aged nine or ten, the pages were, and both boys and girls were employed in this way. And if they survived, they would eventually rise to brick carrier.

Once the bricks were formed by the women, they were carried carefully away, six at a time, to the drying kilns where both sexes, stripped to the waist, handled the hot bricks. The morals were very low at the mill. Drink was allowed inside the drying kilns and, since there were no safety precautions, there were often terrible accidents. Once a huge pile of hot bricks tumbled down on a group of children, killing and injuring many of them. Another time there was a blow-out from the furnace which had been left uncared for while the foreman took some young virgin behind the kilns. It was a hellish existence for everyone who worked there and only the toughest could survive it.

That morning Larlee was in a particularly vile mood having consumed too much alcohol the night before. She took

out her feelings on little John Shulmead who received a few
hard blows as he carried off to the kilns the bricks Larlee had
made. He was quite used to kicks and blows, so the only thing
that really upset him was when Larlee picked on Dolly, her
own daughter. Then he would endeavour to get in the way to
protect his little friend. He watched her now as she slowly
toddled along in front of him, hanging her head in a dejected
manner like all the other tired children in the long queue.
Dolly's lovely blonde hair was grey and caked with mud and
the backs of her heels were sore and swollen with chilblains.
She had wept all the way over the marsh that morning,
complaining that her feet hurt, but Larlee had not cared. She
had walked ahead on her long legs shouting 'Get a move on!
Ain't I got enough on me plate, what with Alice getting
herself knocked up, and them two slow-witted Irish cows
starting this morning?'

Alice was Larlee's eldest daughter. She was just fifteen and
always worked almost as hard as her mother. But several
months before, on an all-night session of work, a bully boy
from the next village had dragged Alice behind the kiln and
raped her. She had fought and screamed but Larlee had been
too drunk to hear her. And John and Dolly, who had watched
as the bully had brutally taken poor Alice up against a brick
wall, had been too small to stop him. The next morning, a
sober Larlee had been like a raving lunatic, and attacked the
lad, chasing him a mile over the marsh and frightening him
so much that he had not been seen since. But now that Alice's
pregnancy was so advanced that she could not come to work,
but had to stay at home in the cottage to await the birth of
her child, Larlee had lost her most helpful worker. But the
new child, although unwanted, would be another pair of
hands for the Pug Mill before long.

The 'Irish cows' Larlee had referred to were two very thin
girls who had been waiting for them one day at the gate on
the way to the Mill. They wore ragged dresses and were barefoot with a pathetic air hanging over them. They were nine-
year-old Mary and thirteen-year-old Maggie, who were both

from a very poor Irish family who lived in a hovel down on the shore. They had no mother, Maggie informed Larlee in a thick brogue, for she had been 'drowned dead in the sea'. The father, a drunken lout, combed the shore for driftwood and sometimes, when sober, worked on the farm. Driven by dire poverty, these two children had wanted to join the slave mill and be employed by Larlee at sixpence a week. But from the beginning they had caused havoc. They could not lift the heavy loads of clay, and constantly fell over, knocking other children off balance and causing them to drop their own loads. Then the other children would turn on them and laugh at their unfamiliar manner of speech.

This state of affairs had been going on for some days and Larlee was very aggravated by their inability to cope. Little John Shulmead felt very sorry for them and, typically, felt protective towards them. Today at last Maggie had learned how to keep her balance and she began to carry the heavy loads of clay. But Mary could only help John by carrying two bricks at a time until she got used to the weight. John noticed that Maggie looked particularly pale, and she seemed distressed. He smiled gently at her but she did not respond. Instead she dumped her load of clay on the floor and stood by the wall clutching her stomach.

'Don't hang about, Maggie,' John warned. 'Someone will tell Larlee and she'll come down in a raging temper.'

Slowly Maggie picked up her load of clay again and plodded on. To his surprise, John noticed a thin trickle of blood running slowly down her leg.

'Maggie's hurt,' he informed Larlee. 'You ought to let her rest.'

But Larlee's hard eyes scrutinised the child as she wearily deposited the clay on the moulding table. 'Oh, Christ!' exclaimed Larlee. 'Come here!' she ordered Maggie. 'Is *that* all it is?'

For poor little Maggie, borne down by a heavy weight in her abdomen, had menstruated for the first time. She understood nothing about it, being uninformed about her condition.

'Come here, you silly cow!' roared Larlee again, tearing a long strip from her own filthy garment. Taking a piece of string, she bound the ends. 'Here, stuff that up yer,' she said. 'Can't see you going about like that.'

But Maggie looked up at Larlee in fear. 'Oh, I feel so ill,' she whimpered. 'I want to go home.'

'Don't be soft,' said Larlee giving her a shove. 'Just stay away from the men,' she added. 'I've had enough trouble with Alice getting knocked up.'

'But why?' asked the child with a puzzled look on her wizened face.

Larlee burst into roars of coarse laughter. 'Jesus! what a ninny!' she cried. ''Cause men are like bulls,' she cackled. 'They go mad if they see red.'

Thus little Irish Maggie received her first lesson in womanhood from the rough, clay-covered moulding queen.

Poor Maggie did not last out the year. Not long afterwards, she developed a cough which would not go away. And six months later, they buried her in the churchyard. When the father took little Mary away to the workhouse, where she lived until she was older, two village boys took the girls' places as pages in Larlee's team, and the two little Irish girls were forgotten to everyone.

John Shulmead grew taller and thinner every month now. His shoulders drooped and his back became quite bent as he worked seventy-three hours a week, walking twenty-odd miles each day carrying bricks. From the sixpence he earned, his father allowed John to keep tuppence and sometimes on a Saturday he would go down with dumb Lukey to the Malted Shovel. There he would sit at the back kitchen and treat himself to a glass of ginger wine and one of Aunt Beat's delicious mutton pies. And he liked Sundays because after chapel his father would say: ''Tis a day 'o rest, so see to it that you do nought to offend the Lord.' Then John would walk over the marsh to Decoy Farm, where the farmer had an old boat and was teaching him to sail. Once out in the estuary with the sails set high and the wind against them, John would feel deliriously happy.

'That's the life, boy,' the farmer would say, 'out on the open sea. I regret the day I ever became a farmer.'

John learned quickly and longed for the day when he too would have a boat of his own. And every night before he fell asleep, John's young head would be filled with all sorts of plans to run away to sea. But they were just idle dreams, and he knew it. He knew that he could not escape the drudgery of the brick kilns, at least not while his tyrannical father was still alive.

The renewed work on the canal project was still very much the topic of conversation in the hamlet. At the beginning of the century, when the work had originally begun, the four miles from Gravesend to the creek had been dug out, but then everything had come to a halt and for five years very little work had been done. The money had run out and the builders had come up against many hazards. The heavy wet, slimy soil was almost impossible to move in winter and the big chalk cliffs at Strood which they had to by-pass in order to reach the Medway, proved to be insurmountable. But now this new canal project had been prepared, with different ideas and new designs, and a different Canal Board had been formed by local businessmen from the various factories which had been springing up along the riverside. Now that the new canal seemed a certainty, it was the main topic of conversation in the Malted Shovel on Saturday nights.

'Them barge skippers will be here by the hundreds if the canal comes so close, hanging about, and causing trouble,' declared Amos Dell, his massive frame squashed into the wheelchair.

'And that's quite apart from the muck they transport,' replied Sam Shulmead in a gruff voice.

Usually all the men agreed with each other, nodding and grunting in unison as each gave his opinion. But tonight in the bar parlour they had strange company, a sombre-looking and well-dressed man with a beard and steel-rimmed spectacles on his nose. When he spoke it was with an accent of the North Country. 'We must give way to progress,' he said suddenly, 'but not on the backs of the young.'

Shulmead stared at him aggressively. It was not usual for a stranger to break into their conversation.

Amos puffed his pipe slowly and muttered: 'Aye, brickies and their slaves is what you refer to, sir, I presume. His tone was polite. He seemed to know the man.

'Yes,' said the stranger. 'I mean the innocents who toil night and day for very little, and whose lives are warped morally and physically from early age.'

A silence fell on the company; this was an embarrassing business. The stranger sipped some plain water and gazed around him with benevolent eyes. 'It amazes me,' he said, 'that such good-natured men as yourselves can allow such iniquities to prevail as I have just seen down in those brick fields.'

At these words, Shulmead's face grew red with anger. Did not his own little son John slave there? 'We don't go much on strangers coming here telling us how to run our lives,' he answered tersely.

'Now Sam, peace,' interrupted Amos. 'This gentleman is no stranger but George Gibbs, the brother-in-law of Farmer Wright. He is staying up at the big house.'

'I do not wish to anger your friend,' apologised the newcomer. 'But in my own area I have had much success in improving the lot of the poor children of the brick fields and of the waifs on the canal boats where the conditions are equally vicious.'

'Get moving, lads!' Sam Shulmead yelled to his boys in the public bar. 'I'm leaving, I can't enjoy my beer with these bloody do-gooders coming and poking their nose where it's not wanted.'

Aunt Beat sniffed and Dot simpered as the Shulmead boys trailed sulkily out after their dogmatic father. His other son, Lukey, with his mouth gaping open was still sitting staring into the roaring fire in the back kitchen having dozed off while minding the pies. His father did not even bother to call him. So that night Sam Shulmead left the inn earlier than he had ever been known to in the past.

Mark and Matt marched along behind their father over the freezing marsh muttering to each other. 'What's up with the devil? It's not yet ten o'clock.'

'Someone's upset him. If I had the guts, I'd upset him, all right,' muttered Matt.

They had been enjoying a long conversation about the army with a soldier lad home on leave. To these husky lads, cowed by their brutal father, the army smelled of freedom and adventure.

'I'm getting fed up with this life, aren't you, Matt?' whispered Mark.

'What the hell are we but donkeys on a string? I'd like to take the King's shilling,' said his brother.

'But you wouldn't have the nerve,' jeered Mark.

'I will one day,' Matt vowed. 'I'll just do a bunk and if you don't want to come, stay here. You can then have all his money and the old forge, for I surely don't want it.'

'You know I don't care about that, either. I shall go with you,' replied Mark, with passion.

Matt turned to him, his eyes burning with excitement. The time was right! 'They say the recruiting sergeant is in town this week,' he said. 'Let's do it now.'

'Done!' whispered his brother, clasping his hand.

They had reached their old thatched cottage next to the forge. The forge fire was still glowing and the horses in the stable whinnied. Discarding their muddy boots, the boys slouched up the stairs to bed. Sam Shulmead went to the kitchen cupboard, took out a jug of homemade wine and settled into his armchair to continue his drinking. 'Blamed parsons and what not,' he grumbled. 'They think they know everything. Never done a day's hard graft in their lives.' As he muttered, he took long swigs from the stone jug late into the night.

While he grew drunker and drunker, his youngest son, John, was at the Pug Mill sitting by the kilns all night, and turning the bricks. This was very profitable overtime for him and would add tuppence extra to his wages on the following Friday, so he was happy to while away the long hours by dreaming of sailing the next day.

At six o'clock the next morning, Aunt Beat broke the ice from the pump outside to drink some clean water. 'Better clean this mucky place up,' she moaned to herself. She poked her head into the kitchen, expecting to see dumb Lukey sprawled under the table. For Lukey rarely went home on cold icy nights, Aunt Beat's kitchen being warmer than the barn where he had to sleep.

'Now, where is that boy?' she clucked like a mother hen. 'Lukey! Lukey' She banged and rattled the bucket but there was no reply. 'Well, I never. He must have gone home, unless he fell in the creek.' She looked anxiously into the water under the bridge but seeing nothing, she went inside and got down on her knees, her big buttocks swaying back and forth, as she scrubbed the floorboards until they were snow white.

'Is that you, Lukey?' she called, hearing a movement at the door.

'No, Aunt Beat, it's John,' said a small voice. In the doorway that pale thin lad stood looking very shocked. 'Will you help me find the sergeant, please. It's me Pa. He's lying in the yard all covered in blood.'

With a deep frown on her brow, Beat quickly dried her hands on her sacking apron. 'Now, now, what is it, John? What are you babbling about?'

'I'm looking for the sergeant,' John said weepily. 'Me Pa's been murdered.'

'Dot! Dottie!' screeched Beat. 'Come here, somethin's happened!'

Within seconds Dot appeared trying to tidy up her tousled hair. 'What is it, sister?'

'Listen to him!' cried Beat. 'He says his Pa's been murdered.'

Dot rushed over to the distressed boy and put her arms around him to comfort him as he explained how he had come from the brick field at dawn and found Sam Shulmead with his head nearly chopped off and no sign of any of his brothers.

'My God!' cried Dot. 'My poor little lad!'

'Never mind the sympathy,' snapped the pragmatic Beat. 'Get over to Wally's house. He'll be up now. And ask him to go down to the fort and get the sergeant.'

Once Dot had left, Beat shook poor John very hard by the shoulders. 'Now tell me, boy, have you seen Lukey? Was he home last night?'

'Don't know,' replied John, shaking his head. 'Matt and Mark, where have they gone?'

All too soon the Redcoats arrived — the sergeant and a small party of men. Their business was to restore order whenever necessary. They shouted and stamped around on Beat's nice clean floor while Aunt Beat and Aunt Dot searched the churchyard and the barn for Lukey. But he was nowhere to be found.

And all this time Lucinda sat with Grandpa Amos, who was very upset by the news that his old drinking companion had been murdered.

Returning from their fruitless search, Aunt Beat got on with her morning chores while Dot took up a large breakfast to their father. Amos would have to be almost spoonfed, so weak and shaky were those big flabby hands. But Dot did this task with great devotion and then assisted by Lucinda, she washed his swollen body, and made him comfortable for his long day in bed.

Beat put some more logs on the roaring fire, but she stopped in her tracks as she turned and saw Lukey sopping wet and dishevelled stumbling into the kitchen. He was caked in mud and blue with cold, as water, stinking of the marsh, poured off him.

'Oh! my goodness! What a bad boy!' Beat cried. 'Quick, get inside and stand by the fire. I'll find you some dry clothes.'

She hustled Lukey inside, and shot the bolt on the back door. The Redcoats had all trooped off to the Shulmead forge and there was not one to be seen. With a big rough towel Beat rubbed Lukey's strangely shaped head until the brown hair stuck up like wire. 'Wicked boy,' she muttered. 'You've been in the creek. And where was you last night?'

But dumb Lukey only stared vaguely at her as she stripped off his shirt and trousers. The fire glowed on his nicely formed white body and as she dried him, she could not help herself caressing his private parts. 'Naughty boy,' she said. 'Bad boy.' Her voice was choked with emotion as she scolded him. 'Where was you?'

Once dry and with a hot cup of tea in his hands, Lukey mouthed words: 'Birdie fell in.'

Desperately he tried hard to speak, moving his hands to give expression.

'You fell in, did you?' Beat tried to understand him. 'Been after those cranes again? Bad boy,' she said. 'So you never went home last night. Tell Auntie Beat. Tell the truth,' she coaxed him.

As Lukey slobbered over the mug of tea, Beat stared anxiously at him, picking up his wet clothes. 'Stay there. Good boy,' she whispered, as if to a pet dog. In return, Lukey smiled lopsidedly at her, his odd-looking eyes gleaming with excitement.

Beat locked the bedroom door from the outside and went to dispose of the boy's wet clothes, for she had seen, mixed with the mud on the faded old garments, dried blood stains.

At midday the bar parlour was full as the sergeant from the fort and the civilian police sergeant from town refreshed themselves and their assistants. Farmer Knight was also there, being amongst the most honoured of the local citizens, and with him was his brother-in-law, George Gibbs. They had all been out to the Shulmead forge at the end of Bull Lane.

'Yes, by God it's the work of a maniac,' declared the farmer. 'Looks like it might have been done by his sons, for they can't be found.'

'Gone off to join the army, they have,' said old Wally the herdsman. 'They was walking about it last night.'

'They will have gone to Gravesend, then,' said the civilian sergeant. 'I will try to apprehend them there. There was no sign of a fight, and whoever dealt him that blow was very strong,' he added.

'Almost severed his head with an axe,' said the farmer. 'It was lying on the floor beside him, a terrible sight for a young lad to see.'

'Does not one of his sons work in the brick fields?' asked his brother-in-law.

'Yes, poor little devil, and he worked there all night Saturday.'

'Aye, 'tis an evil place and these are evil times,' George Gibbs said softly to himself.

While the civilians, police and military authorities placidly discussed this terrible murder and drank their beer, Matt and Mark Shulmead were marching proudly behind the recruiting sergeant as they all boarded the boat to take them to Woolwich Barracks. The boys had at last obtained their freedom.

They had made that snap decision the previous evening. The moment they had got home, they had run straight upstairs and packed their few belongings.

'We'll wait until he's really drunk, and we get out of the window,' Matt had said. 'Then it's away to the broad highway, you and me, Mark.'

Mark had always followed his elder brother. They were as close as twins in spirit and only ten months apart in age, but Matt had always been the leader in all things. Their lives so far had been hard and bitter, but they were strong, healthy lads and there was a big world waiting for them. Silently they had sat side by side on the bed waiting until the noises downstairs had subdued, the muttering and swearing, and the maudlin complaining as Sam Shulmead got drunker and drunker. Then they heard the jug crash to the floor, followed by the complete silence.

'That's it, me bonnie lad,' said Matthew. 'Come on, and go

quietly, it's almost dawn.'

Silently the two boys swung long legs out of the window and jumped down to the grass below. Then off they fled across the meadow at a very rapid pace until they reached the long lane that led over the marsh to the town. A freezing grey mist hung over the ground and the lane was wet and slippery. Suddenly they heard the pad of feet slipping and sliding, and saw Lukey wandering towards their home. 'It's that blamed fool Lukey, wandering about,' said Matthew. Not wanting to be spotted they crouched down in the ditch.

'Let him go by,' said Matt.

'But he might wake the old man,' said Mark.

'We will frighten him. That should keep him quiet,' decided Matt.

As Lukey wandered aimlessly past, they jumped out and pinned him down on the ground. Heavy hands held him, leaving Lukey paralysed with fright.

'We are going away,' hissed Mark. 'You must not tell the old man.'

Lukey wagged his head frantically.

'Let him go, Matt,' said his brother. 'Look,' he held a penny close under Lukey's nose. 'It's yours, but you must not tell because we don't want him to catch us. We'll bring presents for you when we come back home.'

Lukey snatched the penny and grinned, making it clear that he understood.

'Now git!' said Matt, giving him a push. 'And no noise. Don't wake Father up or he will beat you. He's very drunk.'

With his loose mouth gaping and his eyes rolling, Lukey lolloped away down the lane.

'That's scared him,' said Matt in a satisfied tone of voice. 'He won't go near the forge now.'

But they were sadly mistaken, far from understanding what they had said, Lukey, had misunderstood the penny to be in payment for a task he had to do. Muttering his animal noises, Lukey lopped across the meadow, slowing down cautiously as he neared the house, and listening out for sounds of danger. Sam Shulmead was violent enough when sober but when drunk, he was a maniac.

This cold dawn morning as the sun rose the steam was rising from the yellow thatch of the cottage. As it caught his eye, he heard a roar from the cottage as Sam Shulmead woke from his drunken sleep and staggered about the yard. 'Matt!' he roared up at the window. 'Get up, you lazy swine! It's near seven o'clock!'

Lukey crept past him but Sam aimed a huge boot at him, catching him in the thigh. 'Stay out, you dirty sod! Don't you come in here,' he yelled.

Lukey staggered against the wood pile, and fell against the high store of logs waiting to be split to feed the fire in the forge. Beside the logs lay a gleaming axe with a long handle. For a second Lukey crouched down covering his head with his hands as he waited for more blows to come but Sam was still shouting for his sons to rise, shaking his fist at the window of their room in the attic.

Then, suddenly, with a spring of a cat, Lukey pounced, swinging that sharp axe with a graceful clean sweep through the air.

The result was instantaneous. In a split second the large man was felled and lying squirming on the ground as Lukey continued to swing the axe as if splitting logs. Within moments, the figure on the ground was silent, his limbs and his head almost severed from his body.

Lukey dropped the axe and fled in the direction of the marsh. He ran and ran until there was no more air in his lungs and he sank breathless beside one of the well-filled dykes that flowed out to the sea.

The mud was thick beneath his feet and rushes stood tall. As he regained his breath, Lukey began to smile. There on the water a graceful long-legged bird had alighted. It was a black-and-white crane that had not yet migrated for warmer parts. With his hands held high, Lukey crept into the dyke and then lurched forward to grab the pretty bird. But, as always, it was too quick for him. On long graceful wings it flew away, safe from his grasp, and making a sound that almost mocked him for having failed yet again to catch the elusive creature.

But Lukey was determined not to let it escape today. With his arms upstretched and his eyes staring at the sky, he waded further into the water until he was waist deep in the filth and sludge. It was only the cold that forced him to give up eventually, long after the bird had gone, and at last, completely exhausted, he lay on the bank to rest. Then, cold, mournful and dripping wet, he instinctively went back to the comfort of Aunt Beat's warm kitchen where he now slept like a baby beside the fire, dry, warm and fed.

'It's a good job that poor deformed boy was here with me all night,' said Aunt Beat in a loud voice, just as the officials were leaving the inn. Aunt Dot opened her mouth to protest but Beat banged the tray down hard on the table. 'Was a devil, old Shulmead,' she said. 'I thought someone would do for him one day. And those two eldest boys done it sure as eggs is eggs.'

'Murder will out, madam, it's God's will,' replied the benevolent George Gibbs.

And Farmer Knight said, 'Well, let's all get to work. This is the second murder this year, and never been heard of before in this hamlet.'

So again Lukey was sheltered and protected from the consequences of his actions. Beat was not really sure why she looked after him like that; she just knew that she could never give him up to live in a cage for the rest of his life. Even so, there was a part of him she did fear, a part deep down inside where she could not reach. And that made her a little uneasy about keeping what she knew to herself.

By Monday the excitement of Sam Shulmead's death had died down a little and everyone went about their business as usual. Even little John went to the brick kilns with Larlee because he did not know what else to do. And he had no one to help or guide him.

The Shulmead forge stood stark and grim on the sky line, now deserted and shunned by the locals because of the horrific unsolved murder that had been committed there. All the livestock had been removed, the forge fire had turned cold and grass grew high in the meadow. According to some superstitious folk, the avenging ghost of Sam Shulmead stalked the marshland, making it a fearsome place at night.

For young John, the thatched cottage by the forge had been the only home he knew but now there was nothing to go home for and so he just stayed at the brick kilns overnight where he witnessed many scenes of debauchery that were quite unsuitable for a young lad. One Saturday night, he ventured down to visit Lukey, who was now well-ensconced at the Malted Shovel, and Aunt Beat was quite appalled by the sight of him. The little boy's blonde hair was matted with clay, his eyes were red and sore and his limbs looked wasted from the poor diet he had recently been forced to live on.

'Why, look at that little lad!' Even Amos noticed John's condition when he caught sight of him hungrily demolishing a hot pie in the kitchen.

'There is no one to look out for him, Grandpa,' said Lucinda as she pushed the heavy bathchair down the slope to the bar parlour.

'It's not right, poor little lad. At least Matt used to see he was clean,' complained Aunt Dot.

'Ought to put him to sea,' bellowed Amos. 'A bright lad like that, good clean salt air is what he needs.'

But Aunt Beat decided to do more than just observe. When Larlee came in that evening for her Saturday drink, Beat went up to her immediately. 'Before you come in here spending money these kids earn for yer,' she said, 'it'd do you more good to feed and look after the poor little devils.'

'They don't do so bad,' sneered Larlee. 'They get their wages regular. Besides, I ain't no wet nurse.'

'You, gel,' declared Aunt Beat, glaring at her aggressively, 'is nothing and less than nothing. Dregs of the earth, is what I call you, and I'm in two minds whether to serve you.'

Larlee's tall angry figure towered over Aunt Beat's small square frame as the two women confronted each other. A whisper of excitement ran around the bar as the onlookers prepared to watch the two attack each other like cats, Aunt Beat bent down and grasped her heavy rolling pin but Larlee was thirsty and she needed a drink badly. 'What's eating you, you miserable old cow?' she demanded, without advancing.

Beat pushed open the kitchen door with the rolling pin. '*That's* what is annoying me,' she hissed. Through the door she pointed to the ragged little boy who sat on the table swinging his thin legs and finishing off his pie.

'So, he sleeps by the kiln,' yelled Larlee. 'What do you expect me to do? He's not my responsibility.'

'Well, he should be,' snapped Beat. 'You take half what he earns.'

Larlee stared angrily at Beat for a few seconds but then looked away. 'All right,' she said, 'he can come and live in my cottage.'

Beat nodded. Larlee will do anything to get a drink, she thought cynically, but at least this was what she had wanted to hear.

'See that he gets his grub,' muttered Beat, slowly filling Larlee's jug with strong ale.

Larlee stared greedily at the golden liquid and licked her dry lips. 'Alice will feed him,' she said. 'She's home since she got knocked up. She is a good forager, is Alice. Kids don't do too bad with her.' Larlee held out an eager hand for her jug of ale.

'Right!' said Beat, handing over the jug. 'See to it that it is done.'

So young John moved into Larlee's cottage in an alley in the hamlet that was known as simply as the Street. It comprised four terraced cottages in a row. At one on the end Larlee lived and at the other was Wally the herdsman. Between the two lived some old farm labourers and their wives. The cottages were made up of just one large room that was entered straight from the front door. In Larlee's house, this room was divided by a curtain behind which slept Larlee and Alice, her eldest daughter, now six months pregnant. On

Saturday nights when Larlee brought home a man, Alice had
to move from the bed and sleep with her sister Dolly on a
couch in the corner.

The room had a musty, pokey atmosphere, with its low
beams and small windows. At the back there was the scullery
where there was a big stone copper, a table and two chairs,
and in one corner a grubby palliasse of straw and some horse
blankets. On this mattress slept the two little bargee boys who
now worked for Larlee — seven-year-old Kit, and his little
brother Toby. Their parents had handed them over to Larlee
in exasperation after deciding that seven children were too
many to cope with in one boat cabin. They had given up their
two little boys and sailed on up to the northern canals.

'Get a big bag from the miller,' Larlee told John, when she
led him home that night. 'We will stuff it with straw and you
can kip down beside the boys. At least now you will be early
for work and I won't have to hang about waiting for you in
the mornings.'

As John looked solemnly about the bleak home and at the
pale faces of the little boys who were to be his bed com-
panions, he wondered if this would be an improvement on
nights at the kiln or not.

'Get in the dyke!' cried Larlee, giving him a push. 'Have a
swim, you are bloody filthy.'

In spite of the freezing cold, John slipped into the icy dyke
water and re-emerged shivering uncontrollably. Then he
crouched beside the fire, his thin body wrapped in a sack
while Alice washed his clothes in the big copper.

Alice's hair was long and lank, and her dry, brown skin was
covered with scars from clay burns. Even though her belly
was now swollen with life and she moved awkwardly, she
never complained. As always she just made the best of that
which life had provided. Alice's long dress covered her ankles.
But it was taut against her front and could barely contain the
swelling of her breasts, which along with her belly, showed
how far along she was.

She was a tall, sad-looking girl who always went out of her

way to make life a little more pleasant for the poor brick field orphans her mother brought home. She scrounged oats from the fields and skimmed milk from the farm so that she could give them a hot bowl of porridge every morning. And in the autumn, she made big fruit puddings from the windfalls she collected from the orchards. And now that she was confined to the house, the 'family' ate better than ever before.

Although she rarely showed it openly, Larlee was very fond of Alice, whom she always called Lal. She seldom lost her temper with Alice, but her feelings towards her other daughter, Dolly, were quite different. Poor little Dolly, only ten years old, and Larlee could not abide her.

Dolly was as fair as her mother was dark, with sensitive skin that was often sore and raw, coming up with chilblains on her hands and feet. She was slow and, in spite of the hard grind of carrying large lumps of clay on her head for twelve hours every day, inclined to plumpness.

For John, the best part of moving in with Larlee was being close to Dolly. He loved his little blonde friend and had done since he had met her. He always petted and fussed her, and shared little treasures with her. Sometimes on Sundays the two children went hand in hand through the woods, or to the shore or even to Decoy Farm, where John would then sit and clean and paint that cherished boat with Dolly watching him with great devotion.

As he became more experienced, John was becoming a good sailor and getting to know very well all the tidal waters that swept that treacherous coast. The old farmer, who was nearly eighty and losing his sight, now totally trusted little John to sail the boat competently once the sails were up. 'Tis yours, boy, this old boat, when I go on my way,' he often told him.

And although John would be sad when the kind old farmer died, he very much looked forward to the day when he would own that beloved boat.

Spring was just around the corner. Pale shafts of sunshine warmed the bedraggled children in the early morning as they plodded to work over the marsh. A full tide filled the dykes and the migrating geese came flying back to the sandy stretches on the shore. Every morning an even more pathetic procession passed the urchins as they made their way to the brick fields, a long line of ill-clad, half-starved men, escorted by armed soldiers. These were prisoners-of-war from the hulks moored off the shore, and were marched off each day to help complete the new canal.

When little John stared at the men's lean, unsmiling faces and the ragged remains of uniforms he was always reminded of his big brothers, away now in the army. He hoped that they would not be taken prisoners and be humiliated in such a degrading manner.

One morning Larlee was in a particularly vicious temper. Earlier, Alice had gone into labour and Larlee had not liked leaving her. But she had to go to work, so an old crone from next door had been raised from her bed to sit with Alice instead. But now everyone was late for work and fines would undoubtedly be handed out by the foreman brickie. Larlee was furious, and was pushing, shoving and grousing as she urged the children to hurry. Little Dolly's legs were bad, the clay had gone into her chilblains and turned septic. As Larlee hounded the children along, Dolly held up her ragged skirt and snivelled that her legs were hurting her. With a vicious blow, Larlee knocked her across the lane.

As the child landed on her face in the dirt, John rushed to her aid. Dolly lay squirming and crying in pain, for the gravel had scraped her poor reddened legs and made them even worse.

As Larlee bellowed at her to get up, and aimed some nasty kicks at Kit and Toby as they scuttled past on up to the mill, a well-dressed man on a horse appeared in the lonely lane. He pulled up his horse and stared with amazement at the extraordinary scene. 'By the grace of god!' he exclaimed. 'What is going on?' Jumping down from the saddle, he picked up the sniffling Dolly and wiped the blood from her knees with a large white handkerchief.

'It's none of your business,' snapped Larlee. 'I can't afford to waste time. Get moving!' she screamed at John who just held onto Dolly and looked scared.

'Woman!' the man said in a voice of great authority. And he poked Larlee with his cane as if to keep her at a distance. 'Go on to your work and leave these helpless children to me and the mercy of God.'

Larlee slouched away. 'It's all right for the likes of you to interfere,' she snarled. 'It's us who have to work to make you rich.'

'Go, woman!', the man roared. 'This child's legs are septic, I am going to take her to the doctor.'

'Do that,' sneered Larlee. 'Come on, John,' she said, grabbing the boy by the arm, 'there's work for you.'

'I'll stay with you, Dolly,' said John obstinately, pulling away from Larlee's grip. The presence of the stranger had given him courage.

Swearing and shouting, Larlee backed away. She shook her fist but it was pure bravado. She knew she could not oppose this man. At last she went on her way and the man gently picked up the weeping Dolly and placed her in the saddle of his well-trained horse. He handed John the bridle and as the boy led the horse down the lane, the man held Dolly's hand and walked along beside her.

'Now, child try to stop crying,' he cajoled her, for Dolly was weeping loudly and copiously, so terrified was she by all this attention.

'You were just about to begin your day's work in the brick kilns, I presume,' the man said to John. John nodded glumly.

The gentleman looked benignly at the children through his spectacles. He had mild blue eyes set in a remarkably stern face. 'How old is the girl?' he asked John.

'She is ten and a half, sir. And I'm twelve,' replied John politely.

'You don't look twelve, I must say. You are shamefully underweight,' said the man. 'How long have you worked? And where are your parents?'

All the way to the doctor's house the man fired questions at

John which the boy answered politely and quietly. It seemed so strange to have someone talking to him as if he cared.

When they arrived at the doctor's large brick house, John was quickly reminded of his position in the world. The sight of the two brickfield children in his clean bright room was almost too much for the doctor, whose patients were usually the well-to-do inhabitants of the area. He hummed and hawed, coughed and spluttered, and looked down at little Dolly, all bloody and muddy, as if there were an evil smell under his nose. He had no calling to attend the children of the hamlet unless they died. Then he would certify them dead and receive a fee from the parish funds for his services.

George Gibbs quickly pushed aside any reasons for the doctor to hesitate. 'Help this poor child, my good man, if you will. You will be paid in full. Farmer Wright will see to the bill.'

Raising his eyebrows as if the subject of money had not even occurred to him, the doctor rolled up his shirt sleeves and set to work. In no time, he had cleaned the septic parts on Dolly's legs and bound them up.

With thanks to the doctor for his time, George Gibbs put Dolly back on the horse and the three of them walked to Farmer Wright's bright, warm farmhouse. In no time, Dolly was looking rather cheerful sitting in a well-scrubbed chair amid the shining pots and pans, while her saviour George Gibbs explained to his rather bewildered sister Jenny Wright how he came to be in charge of the little girl. And he told her how he was determined that the child should never return to the slavery of the brickfields.

'But, George!' remonstrated Jenny. 'The child's mother is responsible for her. You just can't do that.'

'I can and I will,' insisted George. 'Even if I die in the attempt, I will eventually relieve the plight of those poor children who slave in the kilns.'

Jenny sighed deeply. George was such a problem with his fanatical ways. She would feel very relieved when he finally returned to the Midlands. 'All right,' she said. 'I'll keep her

until her legs are healed, and then I'll send and ask her
mother if she can work in the dairy. Does that satisfy you?'

George smiled. 'God bless you, dear sister. Yes, it will do
for a beginning, I will now proceed out to that den of iniquity
to read a midday sermon to these poor afflicted folk.'

John had taken the horse to the stables and was hanging
about with the farm boys and enjoying a little freedom. That
evening when he returned to Larlee's cottage, Alice's new
baby had been born. It was a boy, to be called Adam, and he
was red-faced and squealing. As the infant lay in the big bed
with Alice, John stared at him in amazement. It was extraordinary that he could be here now when he had not been
there that morning, and how odd to think that everyone
starts out in life looking like that, whatever their station . . .

The birth of her grandson had put Larlee in a good mood.
She made no comment to John about his absence from work
that day and she sent him down to the Malted Shovel for a
big jug of ale. And as she sat at home that evening chatting
with Alice and admiring little Adam, it was obvious that she
could not care less about Dolly staying up at the farm.

'Silly bitch,' she had exclaimed when John nervously told
her about the situation. 'She was always snivelling. It's just as
well if they keeps her up there.'

Later, John sat beside the warm copper with Toby and Kit.
The other two boys were exhausted from their stint that day
at the brick kilns, and as John told them about his great ideas
for running away to sea, they were soon nodding off and were
fast asleep long before John had described the deep blue sea
and the desert island he saw in his dreams. John was disappointed, particularly since he himself could not sleep. He
was not as tired as he usually was, and he missed Dolly.

But at dawn the next day, Larlee was back to normal. Her
good temper had gone completely as she kicked all the boys
out of bed to march across the misty marshland to work.
'Have to get another boy,' she remarked. 'Girls are just a
bleeding nuisance.'

CHAPTER THREE

The Stranger

Although the marshland was a lovely place in the summer, green and luscious, and teeming with wild life, no one cared for it ever. Not only was it hellish in winter, bleak and wind-swept, but it was also thought to be the source of the fatal malaria ague which killed so many, young and old. The ague had been particularly widespread that year, so when the November mist settled over the flat Kent countryside, the fire in the bar parlour of the Malted Shovel was stacked high with logs so that old Amos could spend his evenings sitting cosily by the wide brick fireplace. Dot would place a knitted shawl about his shoulders and on top of his bald dome of a head, he would wear an old three-cornered naval hat.

The sisters were very fond of their father and were careful to protect him from winter chills but with the malaria so bad, they were extra careful.

The weather was also severe that month and on many nights the bar was quite empty because the regular customers were so loath to leave the warmth of their own homes and brave the wind and the cold. However, a few would trudge over the marsh each evening to drink with Amos and his cronies and discuss the war in France and the vague prospects of Napoleon ever being defeated. Nowadays they rarely thought about last autumn's incidents concerning the murders and the bargees. Besides, the bargees had disappeared for the season. In such wild weather they preferred inland work on the great northern canals to the hazards of the Thames Estuary in deep winter.

So when a stranger came into the bar one dark windy evening, Beat was more than a little curious. He wore a shiny oil-skin overcoat, and a large fisherman's hat. Tall and thin with a very dark complexion, he hesitated momentarily at the door before drifting slowly over to the bar.

Beat squinted at him suspiciously. He was not a local fisherman, for she knew them all. So he might be one of those damned smugglers, having lost his way over the marsh, she told herself. He did not remove his overclothes but just stood forlornly letting the water run off them down into the sawdust on the floor.

'Well, what can I get you?' asked Beat briskly.

The stranger placed two coins down on the counter. 'Wine,' he said huskily. 'Is that sufficient?'

'Wine from the barrel you mean? That's just about it,' replied Beat, picking up the money smartly and filling a jug with red wine.

The man took a sip and then tipped his head back, guzzling the wine greedily as he held the jug with trembling hands.

Beat got a cloth and wiped the counter so that she could get a closer look at him. 'You ain't from these parts?' she said, half questioningly.

He shook his head. 'No, just passing through,' he said. He definitely had an accent that was unfamiliar to Beat's ears.

'Walking over the marsh in this weather?' Beat sounded incredulous. 'We've got some hot pies, if you're hungry,' she added.

The stranger shook his head miserably.

'Nice hot mutton pies,' continued Beat. 'I make them myself. At two pennies each, they are a bargain.'

'I have no more money, *madame*,' the man replied in his odd accent.

'Well, you are unlucky then, ain't yer?' snapped Beat and went out to the kitchen.

There Dot and Lucinda were arranging the freshly baked bread and pies on trays. All the baking was done midweek when the bar was not usually too busy. Beat busied about for a while, and then she said. 'We got a funny fellow in the bar. I think he is a foreigner.'

Dot immediately looked interested.

'Ere!' Beat said, noticing her sister's expression. 'Take him out one of these leftover pies. He looks hungry, but he said he has got no money. Give him the pie free.'

Gleefully Dot put the pie on an earthenware plate and trotted out into the bar parlour. After a while suppressed giggles were heard as Dot tried to converse with the stranger in bad French.

'Hark at her,' sneered Beat. 'Fancies herself, don't she? Two foreign words is about all she can say, but by the sound of them out there he must be French. I had better go back out, I suppose, he might be a spy.'

'Go up to bed, Lucinda,' she said to her niece. 'I don't want you hanging about out here on your own.'

So Lucinda went up to her room and Beat joined her sister, anxious to find out more about this stranger. She found him looking better, and quite revived by his pie. He was even smiling.

'This is Jacques,' Dot informed her. 'He is a French prisoner-of-war, from out on the river hulks.'

'I thought so!' cried Beat, 'What does he want? We can't encourage them, you know, they'll keep other customers out, they will.'

'Be quiet, Beat,' her sister warned her. 'He speaks good English. He came because he would like us to buy some of the things that the prisoners make. He says they are all very hungry out there and many of his comrades are dying of the ague. He himself has only just recovered from it.'

'Poor devil,' muttered Beat. 'Well, I suppose they are flesh and blood, after all. Tell him to show us what he's got.'

From beneath the oil skins long slender hands produced a beautiful little hand-carved boat. It was made of bone and the work was exquisite.

'Oh, isn't it lovely!' cried Dot enthusiastically.

'Just ask him what he wants for it,' returned the more practical Beat.

'Just a little brandy for a friend who is very sick,' Jacques replied huskily.

Beat nodded. 'That's all right,' she said to Dot. 'Give him a quartern of brandy while I go and put this boat in our parlour. Then pack a few pies and a bit of cake for those other poor devils out there in St Mary's Marsh.'

A smile crossed the Frenchman's handsome, strained features. 'I thank you, madame,' he said politely. 'I am most grateful. And your pie was delicious.'

Beat was charmed by such good manners. She smiled back at him. 'Don't worry,' she said. 'You will be welcome here as long as you are not discovered, and I'll take any little knick-knacks you bring.'

So the tall thin man got to his feet and bowed courteously. Then, in graceful melancholy manner, he bade them good night and went out into the dark mist outside.

'Oh, he's not an ordinary soldier,' cried Dot excitedly. 'Why, he had the manners of a perfect gentleman.'

'Git back to them pies, will you, Dot?' snapped her sister. 'And stop fussing about here like a broody hen.'

Dot bustled back to the kitchen, but could not resist going to tell Lucinda all about this handsome Frenchman who was a prisoner-of-war.

Lying on her bed, Lucinda barely listened. She was missing Joe Lee so much that she thought she had no time for thoughts of other men. Of course, she was wrong.

The Frenchman began to come regularly to the inn, on those misty nights, bringing with him lovely little trinkets. There were French poodles carved out of wood, figures of priests made out of ox-tails, and many figures of the Holy Virgin and the Saints, all carved out of mutton bones. There were also often beautiful boxes either with or without bone dominoes. The craftsmanship was always exceptional. Beat always accepted these carvings in exchange for small amounts of food and drink and then she would sell them at a good profit to her customers. She quite fawned on Jacques as she made outrageous bargains for the artistic bric-a-brac he brought, and Dot giggled her head off trying to converse in French with him.

Then late at night Jack, as they had anglicised his name, would plod back through the muddy marshland to the battered old warships where his fellow prisoners were packed two or three hundred to a deck. The conditions on board were appalling. The prisoners were overcrowded and there was no privacy, and disgusting food. These were once idealistic, gallant, young men who had left their homes eager to fight for the great Napoleon. And they had ended up living in pathetic squalor dying off one by one as the ague slowly claimed them. As the months passed, the river banks became lined with rows of rough graves, dug by the British, their captors. A few small comforts could be obtained at a high price, so Jacques was able to get away by bribing a guard to turn a blind eye while he set off over the wet marsh each night.

Neither Beat nor Dot was aware of what was building up between the Frenchman and their pretty young niece Lucinda. Every evening Jack would peer through the kitchen door to catch a glimpse of Lucinda working in the kitchen, normally with her arms deep in a big bowl of flour as she helped with the baking. A lover of beauty, he was amazed by her. With her blonde hair caught up in a white floppy cap, Lucinda would gaze silently back at him and give him a shy smile. He was so dark, so handsome, and so different from Joe Lee who was big and fair. She was also fascinated by the way he spoke, and took every opportunity to listen in to his conversations with her aunts. How she would have liked to get to know him better! But there was little chance with her two old aunts watching over her all the time. So Lucinda went to bed each night and dreamed of a handsome lover who came on a white horse to rescue her. It was Jack.

And as Lucinda lay between her sheets, Jack would trudge back to the hulks across the misty marsh thinking how fine it would be to hold a clean shy girl in his arms once more. There were women in plenty to be had, but they were dirty whores who hung about down on the riverside, and Jack's pride would not allow him to consort with such types.

CHAPTER FOUR

The Philanthropist

Easter in Kent arrived with a burst of colour after the long, bleak winter. Primroses carpeted the woods and the sweet purple violets scented the air, while the hedgerows were alive with the songs of bird choristers.

In Hollinbury, as the old church bells rang out across the fields, Lucinda knelt down in the church pew next to her two aunts. There they asked God to save and protect old Amos, who could no longer rise from his bed.

As George Gibbs walked smartly down the lane from the farm, his step was light and springy. His short fair beard caught the sun's rays, and he swung his stick high in the air. But behind those steel-rimmed spectacles, he had a sad expression in his eyes. For he would have liked to be sitting in the church listening to the word of God but he had much urgent work to do. He planned to spend the Easter holiday in the Pug Mill, those darkened brick fields that lay out on the marsh. To the pigmy army of boys and girls with matted hair and bare feet, Easter made no difference. Slavery was slavery at any time of the year; they had to keep working, no matter what.

Amid this hell, George Gibbs was determined to spend the holy days of Easter. He was just twenty-five years old and done well for himself, now being a lay preacher for the church in his own village in the north. But memories of his own youth spent working in the brick fields gnawed constantly at his heart. Even if it took him all his life, he was determined to ease the pain of slavery for these tortured youngsters. He had taken the opportunity to visit his sister Jenny in Kent with the precise intention of investigating the conditions of the child labour in the south. Over the months he had penned many letters to the newspapers about conditions in the northern potteries, the coal fields and the brick fields, always begging some influential persons to take note. The letters were always the same.

Dear Sir,
The air of England is reported to be fatal to slavery. If one black slave sets foot on our shores he is made immediately free. Yet our own children are slaves. This oncoming generation are vassals of cruel masters and drunken parents, toiling from morning till night carrying loads of wet clay, back and forth sometimes as far as twenty miles a day. . . .

But in spite of the passion he continually poured on to paper, George Gibbs never received any encouragement or response.

On this lovely sunny day he walked over the marsh to the Pug Mill, knowing that he would be allowed through the gates. For to the mill owners, Gibbs was just a crazy person who read to their workers from the good book and passed out little religious texts, and they would not have dreamed of inferfere with the work of the church, for they were upright, church-going citizens themselves, whose wives indulged in all sorts of charitable work.

When George arrived, the children had just started work again after the five-minute breakfast break, having been working solidly since six o'clock in the morning. He stood amidst those squalid surroundings and read a chapter from the gospel to the little children who stood silently in a line. Some were half naked, others ragged as robins. They were all filthy and very thin. Ranging in age from five to twelve years, most were very young and very small. Then, at the blow of a whistle, they began to scramble down a steep incline to the pit itself, deep in the bowels of the earth. There, with long

knives, each child sliced out a huge lump of clay and returned
in single file towards the moulding tables with the large lump
of clay balanced precariously on his or her head. Some
marched nimbly but the smaller ones, mostly girls with short
skirts and bare legs, went more slowly. Arriving at the moulding tables, the children bowed their heads and dropped the
clay before the moulding queen who, with nimble hands,
fashioned it into bricks. Then another group of children
carried away the soft, damp, bricks six at a time, depositing
them very carefully on the floor of the kilns to harden.
Eventually the bricks would go into the fire to be baked hard.

'There is no respite. The toil goes on and on ...' George
Gibbs stood in the shadow watching this slave contingency. It
was a terrible sight anyway but made all the more vivid by the
revival of his own childhood memories. He watched Larlee, as
he spoke. She was so tall and grim, with her shapely body
swathed tight in her clay-matted sheet and a characteristic
turban on her head. The sparkling gold loops in her ears gave
the only hint of her personality, and she was so thickly
covered with clay that she might have been a clay model. Her
harsh voice chivvied on the small pages who waited on her,
and every now and then she would strike out at one of them
with a long stick. As he watched her, George shuddered and
muttered a prayer of thanks that he had saved one child from
this hell when he had taken little Dolly to work on his
brother-in-law's farm. One soul had been saved but what
could be expected of children who grew up amid this atmosphere of filth and lust?

As the day wore on the movement of the lines grew slower
and the children's heads sank lower, as their faces and bodies
seemed to merge into one mass of brown clay. Every now and
then an older girl would halt them all and throw dust over
everyone to prevent the clay drying on them. If it were
allowed to dry, then it would be impossible for the child to get
it off without removing the skin.

Outside the dark mill, the sun shone down on the marsh.
The wild flowers pushed their way up in the fresh green grass

and the birds sang their spring songs. But the little slaves were oblivious to nature's gifts. And even if they were not, they would not have time to care.

In the evening George closed up his Bible and walked back over the marsh to his sister's comfortable farmhouse. But he could not eat the nourishing mutton stew she had cooked for him, so choked with horror and grief was he after that long day at the Pug Mill.

'For goodness sake, George,' begged Jenny. 'Don't take on so. It is just a way of life, and it always has been ever since I remember.'

'But, dear sister, you did not see them. It was dreadful to watch,' George said, shaking his head.

'What can you do?' Jenny asked. 'Only advise the parents not to send their children up there.'

'That would not solve the problem, Jenny,' George replied. 'Those children have no schooling and their parents still less. The parents have to be helped so that they don't feel obliged by circumstance to send their little ones out to work like this.'

'Well, George, I'd go back home if I was you. Find a wife and settle down as a preacher, there,' advised his sister. 'It's no good knocking yourself to pieces over something you cannot alter.'

'I'll return home soon,' George informed her, 'but certainly not to settle down. I've no intention of giving up this fight until I get a bill before Parliament. I swear before God that I'll ease the burden of those poor children if it takes me all my days.'

His sister shrugged her shoulder and went on with her chores. There was no point arguing with George, she told herself, as she watched him settle down to write yet another letter to *The Times* concerning the deplorable conditions of the brick fields down in Kent.

After dark John Shulmead huddled beside the stone copper in Larlee's cottage next to Kit and his brother Toby. The smaller boys were so tired that they had nodded off to sleep as they sat waiting for their supper.

Holding her baby on her lap, Alice looked at them. 'Poor little boys,' she said. 'They are so tired they cannot eat. You had better eat their share, John.'

John sat very still, resting his filthy elbows on his knees.

'I miss Dolly, John,' said Alice, as though reading his thoughts. 'Have you seen her?'

'No,' said John, munching the apple pie Alice had made that day. 'But I might see her tomorrow. Larlee says she is taking the day off because there is a fair in the village. You know, Alice,' John added thoughtfully, 'that preacher chap was at the Pug Mill today. Most of the time he stood there just watching us and reading from the Bible. Then he weighed one boy and asked him how old he was. What do you think he's doing up there?'

'I don't know,' replied Alice, 'but I think he is a very nice man.'

'I've got my sixpence wages. Would you like to come to the fair with me tomorrow, Alice?'

'I might,' said Alice. 'Perhaps we can persuade Dolly to come too if she has finished work in the dairy.'

Later that night, the inn closed, Larlee came staggering home with a soldier who was even drunker than she. John was tucked down in the straw bed beside Kit and Toby and Alice lay with her baby on the couch in the corner of the front room. From there the girl could hear her mother and the drunken soldier as they clumsily cavorted in the bed on the other side of the tattered curtain dividing the room. Shuddering and sleepless, she had to listen to the creaking and groanings of her lustful mother as sleep would not come to her.

The next morning Alice rose early and went down the street to the end cottage where there was a communal well, and brought back two buckets of fresh water. She filled the copper and then washed and fed her baby. After lighting the fire, she put on a pot of oats to cook slowly while her lovely child with his fat sturdy limbs lay cooing and kicking in his small crib. Although she was only sixteen, Alice was an exceptionally good mother and it was a surprise to strangers that this tall, alert-looking girl could be the daughter of the debauched Larlee. Circumstances and hard living had made Larlee what she was but so far her daughter, who had already had a fair share of suffering, showed no signs of following the same path as Larlee. Alice was a clean, sober and industrious young girl.

From her bed Larlee called out for a drink. Her soldier bedmate had left earlier for duty at the fort. 'Is there a cup o' tay, Lal?' she called. 'I'm so dry.'

Tea was a precious commodity in those days and only on request were the contents of the old tin caddy on the mantelshelf used to make a brew. But now Alice obediently took her mother a cup of tea, which Larlee supped lustily.

'Get them bloody boys up,' she said hoarsely, 'and make them wash. I can't have them going around holiday time with clay stuck all over them.'

Larlee rarely took a day off from the Pug Mill but she was very fond of the annual Easter Fair in the village. All the troops gathered there and the bar was open all day and night.

So with the water left over from the baby's bath, Alice washed the two emaciated young boys, rubbing soap on to their soft skins to remove the clay. The elder was Kit, a nervous boy with a permanent stutter, while his seven-year-old brother, Toby, was a bit of a whiner, who clung passionately to his big brother. They were just poor little waifs who had been dumped from the canal boats like some stray animals no one wanted the responsibility for.

'Now you both be good boys,' said Alice, rubbing them down with a towel. 'Today you are having a holiday and I might take you to the fair.'

She patted the terrible sores on their knees and elbows very carefully so as not to knock the huge scabs off.

'We got sixpence,' spluttered Kit, indicating that they had money to spend. The boys' small faces lit up into rare smiles. They received sixpence between them each week — at least whenever Larlee remembered to pay them.

As the little boys settled down to eat the bowls of hot oats Alice had made for them, John came in to the cottage. He had risen early and been swimming in the creek. His eyes were sparkling and his cheeks rosy red from the chilled water, but he was smiling and looked very refreshed. It was never too cold for him to take a swim. He then joined Alice and the boys to enjoy his hot breakfast in front of the fire of the copper.

At midday the little group set off towards the farm. John strode ahead while Alice walked with the baby strapped to her back and two ragged but clean little boys on either side of her.

George Gibbs had crossed the meadow and just climbed the stile into the road when he saw this little band of children coming in his direction. When he stopped to greet them, they stood to attention and Alice dipped a polite curtsy.

'Well, how are we, and where are we off to on this beautiful day?' George Gibbs quizzed them breezily. He clearly did not remember having seen John before.

'We are going up to the farm,' replied John. 'We want to ask if Dolly can come with us to the fair.'

George's mild blue eyes peered back at them kindly. 'Oh, now I place you,' he said. 'You are the children of Larlee who moulds the bricks.'

John nodded, but then he added: 'Me and Kit and Toby only work for her. We are not her children, like Alice and Dolly.'

Alice hung down her head shyly and George put out a finger to the baby cooing in his blanket. 'Well, I will walk with you,' he said 'and you can explain to me how you come to be so fortunate as to get a day's release from your toil.' He surveyed the small thin boys with grave concern.

'Mother is going to the fair, as she does every Easter,' Alice told him. 'So we have the day's holiday, sir.'

'Very nice, too,' replied George. 'And call me George,' he said. 'Never sir. For we are all one in the eyes of our God — brothers and sisters.'

The children waited quietly in the farmyard amid the chickens and geese while Mr George went to find out if Dolly the milkmaid was free to come with them.

Jenny was kneading the dough for the bread when George came in to enquire. 'For goodness sake, George,' she snapped irritably, 'why have you brought all those unkempt children in here?'

'They are looking for their sister Dolly to go with them to the village fair,' he informed her.

'Well, I never, what a cheek! And that saucy little bitch who had a baby is with them,' exclaimed Jenny.

George looked shocked at her outburst. 'Sister,' he said, 'just mind your tongue! Has the devil entered into you?'

'Oh fiddle di dee!' exclaimed Jenny impatiently. 'Tell Dolly she can go, I'm just too busy to argue with you, George.'

After a few more minutes of negotiation, George persuaded his sister to lend him the pony cart for the afternoon. At last he was satisfied.

Dolly emerged from the dairy, looking very pretty. Her cheeks were pink and she wore a long white dress and cotton cap.

'All aboard!' cried George, lifting the smaller ones up into the back of the cart. Then Alice sat beside him with her baby on her lap, and they all drove off the three miles to the village.

The local gentry at the fair stared with open-mouthed astonishment, at the sight of George Gibbs in the pony cart with its passengers. Gentlemen did not do that sort of thing, they agreed. It was an outrage to ride in a cart to the fair sitting next to a slut from the brick fields and her bastard child. It was even worse to hobnob with the ragged children from the Pug Mill.

But George Gibbs did not care what they thought. He rode with the children on the round-a-bouts, knocked down some coconuts, bought them gaily coloured ribbons and brandy snaps. Never before had these children had such a good time.

Larlee was unaware of what her charges were up to. She was too pre-occupied in the refreshment area to notice a thing, and later, when they all travelled home singing, she was looking very drunk on the sea wall with a man in uniform.

As they passed, Alice held her head high, for she was very ashamed of her mother. Mr George had given them all such a good day out, and unlike everyone else, he was not judgemental. He never questioned her about the baby's father, he just joined in the fun. Oh, he was such a fine man! She never dreamed that anyone could be so kind and so gallant.

As they rode home in the twilight Alice dreamily cuddled her baby as she listened to John telling George Gibbs of his ambitions to go to sea, and of the old boat out in the creek belonging to the blind old farmer who had taught him to sail.

The sun was going down over the marsh in a splash of red gold splendour when George deposited the happy children at the cottage, and then took Dolly back to the farm.

'You know, Mr George,' remarked the pert little Dolly. 'I never saw Kit and Toby laugh before. I am glad you came to our hamlet.'

George felt suddenly sad. Tomorrow their toil would start afresh and there was very little he could do about it. And indeed, a week later, he left Kent for his home in the North. But his thoughts were still on those little children and the terrible conditions in which they lived their lives.

After the Easter crowds the next day was quiet at the Malted Shovel. Aunt Dot caught up with her chores, while Aunt Beat sat reckoning up the takings and Lucinda read out from the local newsheet to her grandfather. There had definitely been a change for the worse in poor old Amos, and another fit had dimmed his active brain. But his bleary eyes peered kindly at Lucinda as he feebly patted her hand. His slowly fading mind concentrated on the subject of a husband for his beloved Lucinda. It could not be that damned bargee, for she deserved much better than he. Amos had decided that he would provide Lucinda with a handsome dowry for, while not a wealthy man, he had accumulated a tidy pile over the years. 'Please God,' he prayed, 'allow me to live long enough to find her a secure husband.'

Downstairs Aunt Dot dashed here and there breathless with exertion as her cap all awry as she flicked the furniture and shutters with long feather duster. 'Did you hear the sound of guns last night, Beat?' she asked.

'Not me,' growled Beatie. 'I've a clear conscience, I can sleep.'

'I am sure the noise of guns came from the fort,' said Dot. 'Have you noticed that Jack the Frenchie has not been to visit us lately?' she added.

'Fancy him, don't you?' sniggered Beat, 'and you're old enough to be his mother.'

'Oh, sister!' cried Dot, 'how warped your mind is. I was only thinking that perhaps that nice young man might be in danger.'

'Well, if he is it's his own fault,' declared Beat. 'He ain't supposed to be sneaking out over the marsh a night anyway.'

Dot bustled away with a frown on her face. Beat infuriated her at times. She began to sweep and dust even more energetically than before; it helped her keep her mind off other things.

Down in the cellar sat dumb Lukey. He was supposed to be sweeping the floor but the broom lay idly beside him, as he sat on a big wooden barrel staring at that massive door in the cellar that was kept bolted and barred. He had always been fascinated by it because it was secured with thick chains and a huge padlock. Now he had picked up a long piece of wire and tried to tamper with the rusty padlock, but it was not with much success. He was desperate to see what was behind but before he could think up some other way of tackling it, Aunt Beat knocked on the floor over his head. 'Come up, Lukey!' she hollered. 'You should have finished tidying up down there by now.'

Lukey rolled the barrel back against the secret door and then climbed the ladder to the bar. Perspiring and dribbling he presented himself to Aunt Beat, who gave him a clout for taking his time and chased him out into the yard.

Five miles away, a long line of French prisoners-of-war dug

at the high cliffs, cutting and hacking at the white chalk which hung in a cloud around them and covered every bit of their bodies. Some had racking coughs with lungs already infected with the malaria ague and the cloying chalk made them much worse. There was much discontent among the prisoners, for they did not know what was happening on the other side of the Channel. It had been rumoured that the war was over and they were all about to be repatriated. Now Napoleon had escaped from Elba and was marching to gather up another army on the way. The night before several prisoners had managed to get hold of a boat and attempted to run the gauntlet of the soldiers standing guard over the big guns which guarded the river. But the attempt had failed and many of the prisoners had been trapped and shot to pieces. The following morning the river still ran red with the victims' blood, so these cold shivering prisoners were now in a dangerous and rebellious mood. The Redcoats guarding them were alert and wary.

For Jacques, life had become intolerable since he had been caught out at night after curfew and been punished by having to work on the canal. As his sore, blistered hands wielded the spade, Jacques' thoughts reached out to the gallant little emperor who was gathering another big army. Oh, how he, Jacques, would have loved to be in on that last great battle, a battle that must and would end in victory for France! Yet here he was sweating and shivering, digging deep into the bowels of the earth in this wild Kentish marshland.

Over and over in his mind, he worked out plans to escape. Not up the Thames, that was too dangerous. But on the other side of that tall cliff was another river, the Medway. It was a wide slow-moving waterway that went out to the coast in many small inlets. There was plenty of space to tie up a small boat on it. There might be a chance there, he told himself. But how could he get a boat and who would assist him? Then into his mind came an image of the beautiful Lucinda in a white dress and apron, up to her elbows in flour as she rolled out the pie dough on that well-scrubbed wooden table at the local inn. Yes, she was his chance to escape ... And he had to escape, he could bear it no more, what with one thousand men crowded tier upon tier into those tall, battered hulks, with no sanitation, and illness and corruption running riot. He simply had to get free.

As Jacques laid plans for his escape that morning, down in the hamlet of Hollinbury there was a big set-to. An infuriated Larlee with her hair hanging wildly about her shoulders and her clothes very rumpled from having slept in them all night, was screeching loudly from her cottage door. She had risen with a terrific hangover and was setting about the kids left and right. In her slow placid manner Alice had tried hard to keep order but her child was cross and squalling loudly and it was enough for her to calm him down.

'Shut that brat up!' screamed Larlee. 'And get up, you lazy sods!' Brutally she kicked little Kit and Toby from their shabby sleeping quarters beside the copper and they now cowered in the corner, trying to protect themselves from her blows.

John had already gone down to get water from the well. There he met Old Wally the cowman who lived in the end cottage. Wally always got up early to attend to his master's herd and then returned to eat breakfast. He was a jolly little man, red of face and bandy-legged. He had more affection for cattle than women and had never married. He loathed Larlee. He had been distantly related to her late husband — a decent, hard-working seaman — and her current licentious way of living offended his puritanical family feeling. Very often the two of them quarrelled and sometimes even indulged in a stand-up fight. But Wally always had a kind word for the children and gave Alice a can of milk each morning for her baby.

Today he smiled his wrinkled grin of welcome to John who stood cold and shivering in his thin rags awaiting his turn at the well. 'Morning lad, how are thee?' he asked John, who nodded miserably in return. 'Tell Alice her can of milk will be under the hedge later,' Wally added.

John smiled his thanks and rubbed his bare feet along his calves in an attempt to warm them.

'Er's in a fine mood this morning,' remarked Wally. 'All that boozing at the fair, no doubt.'

At the mention of the fair, John brightened up and stepped forward to help the old man pull his full bucket out of the well. 'We went to the fair,' he said brightly. 'George Gibbs from the farm took us, and we had a grand time.'

'Foine, foine,' muttered old Wally. 'he is a good kind gentleman and there's not many about here like him.'

'He won me a coconut,' said John proudly as he lowered his own bucket into the well.

'Now, that was great,' agreed Wally. 'I'll give thee some cake tonight, lad. Missus up at the farm always makes a seedy cake once a week.' He looked with sympathy at this neglected boy, who was so tall and so fair, but whose shoulders were already bent and whose thin legs were covered with scars from the clay burns.

'No news of thy brothers yet,' queried Wally.

'No,' said John, 'not yet.'

'That's a fine old forge lying empty out there,' said Wally. 'And five good acres lying fallow. When are they going to do summat about it?'

'I don't know,' replied John sadly. He hated to be reminded of that night when his father had been killed. And he did not want his brothers to be captured and hanged for the murder. The thought of it distressed him beyond expression.

Larlee was now screeching frantically from the cottage door, so John hurried off with his over-flowing bucket.

'What does that nosy old devil want?' demanded Larlee.

'Nothing,' muttered John. 'He only asked if we enjoyed the fair and I told him that George from the farm had taken us in a pony cart.'

'Jesus Christ!' cried Larlee. 'You mean that Alice rode into the village with George Gibbs?'

Alice was busy stirring the porridge. 'Of course I did Mother,' she piped up. 'I took the baby on my lap.'

Larlee looked very disturbed and she aimed a tin bowl across the room. 'You silly hussy!' she cried. 'Ain't you done enough to blacken your name without riding into the village with the local gentry?'

Alice looked at her mother in astonishment and incomprehension.

'You silly dopey cow!' cried Larlee in a blazing temper. 'What do you think the locals will have to say about that?'

'I fail to see why I should worry about anyone else,' returned Alice primly.

'Oh, Christ give me patience!' snapped Larlee. 'Don't you know you have classed yourself as a whore? God only knows what will become of it.'

Alice stared back at her mother with tear-filled eyes. 'Why Mother? I don't understand. I did nothing wrong.'

'Oh, for Christ's sake, let's all get a move on! Let's get to work,' snarled Larlee impatiently.

'But, Mother, the boys have not had their breakfast yet,' pleaded Alice.

'Too bleeding bad,' said Larlee, using her feet to help the little ones on their way. 'Get moving, all of yer, else we'll be late.'

So Larlee went storming out over the marshland, pushing the three little boys ahead of her.

Back to another day of slavery. It was always the same, no matter how cold or hungry they were.

Alice watched her mother go, with puzzlement in her deep brown eyes. What could she have done wrong? George Gibbs had been such an honourable gentleman and had given them all such a grand time. Whatever possessed her mother to react as she did? Yet according to Larlee's code, Alice had done wrong.

If Alice had been able to read Larlee's thoughts, she would have been touched by her strong sense of maternal concern. That Larlee herself was a whore, a low-class woman of the brick fields, Larlee readily accepted. In fact, she did not want any other kind of life. When she was young she had loved her handsome husband and cared very well for her children, only circumstances had changed all that. Now life was just a survival of the fittest and the strongest. Despite outwards appearances, Larlee was not all bad. She was very fond of Alice and had always wanted her to get a good husband and live in a comfortable home. But that lout who had raped her daughter had destroyed all chances of that now and for Alice to be classed as a rich man's plaything was a real disgrace. Even Larlee could not condone that. And it could bring plenty of trouble, for these Kentish folk were evil when roused. Larlee knew that only too well. She had spent many days and nights in the stocks being pelted with filth, and now she really feared for her naive young daughter.

This George Gibbs who hung around the brick yard, was supposed to be very respectable but as far as Larlee was concerned, all men were tarred with the same brush. After all, it had been this man who took Dolly from her, not that she really cared because Dolly was doing very well at the farm. And what if he were to come calling for Alice at the cottage when Larlee was away at work? You could never trust these so-called gentlemen. Yes, she had to get Alice back to work at the Pug Mill where she could at least keep a wary eye on her.

That evening Larlee told Alice what she thought. 'It's time you got back to work. You have been hanging about at home long enough. I've asked up at the mill and they have agreed to let me teach you moulding. With a few more pages we will make a fair living.'

'But, Mother, what about the baby?' asked Alice,

'Give him to the old crone next door,' said Larlee. 'For two pence a week she will mind him.'

'That dirty, deaf old crone who sits on the doorstep all day?' Alice was plainly shocked. 'Oh, Mother I couldn't do that!' cried Alice. 'I'd sooner starve.'

'Well we are all going to bloody starve unless you bring in some extra cash,' retorted Larlee.

'But, Mother,' insisted Alice. 'I clean and cook. I do all that is necessary in this house so that I pay for my keep.'

Larlee glared at her angrily. She was not used to defiance from her placid daughter. 'I said you had to get out of this bloody house and back to the Pug Mill, or by God I'll paste the daylights out of yer,' she threatened.

Alice picked up her child and held him close. 'I'll never leave him with anyone else,' she declared. 'He is mine and I'll take care of him.' Her voice was calm and assertive.

'Well, bloody well do then,' stormed Larlee. 'But get out, I ain't going to work my fingers to the bone to keep you and your bastard. Life's bloody hard enough.' She grabbed her shawl and flounced out to the Malted Shovel to drown her troubles.

Weeping silently, Alice gathered up the baby's shawl and garments and neatly folded them. Then she began to put a few of her own clothes into a bundle.

Young John watched her with wide eyes. 'You are not going, Alice, are you?' he asked. 'She did not mean it.'

'Yes I am, little John,' replied Alice gently. 'I know my mother, and I know that she will not rest until I am back in that hell and my child is at the mercy of that poor crazy old woman next door.'

'But where will you go?' asked John.

'I'll walk to the town and look for domestic work. I'll find a place where I can keep my child with me.'

'I think you are so brave, Alice,' said John. 'I once planned to run away to sea but I was too afraid to in case they brought me back and beat me.'

'Yes,' sighed Alice, 'it is hard, but my son and I will escape or die one way or the other. Look after yourself, young John, and look after Kit and Toby. I'll send you word some day.'

'Do not go at night, Alice,' pleaded John. 'It's too dangerous along the road at night. Why not wait till the morning?'

'No, John,' Alice answered firmly. 'Mother will be raving drunk when she returns and I cannot argue with her anymore, so I will go now.'

'Can I walk a way with you?' asked John.

'Only to the bend in the road and then you must come

back. Tell Dolly that I will keep in touch with her.'

So as the evening shadows fell, Alice set off, a tall and willowy figure with her dark hair under a white cap, her baby bound to her back in a ragged shawl, and her few possessions wrapped in a bundle. As she walked down that long dark lane she did not once look back at that dreary cottage called home. Instead, she kept her eyes ahead as she stepped out into that cold hard world.

There was no moon and the going was hazardous. The baby slept peacefully but after a while Alice was sore-footed and very weary and her courage was leaving her; the slightest rustle in the hedgerow made her heart jump. But it was only ever a small animal rising to seek food under the cover of night. 'There's nought to be afraid of,' she told herself repeatedly, and plodded on wearily.

At the big crossroads, Alice hesitated. Which direction should she take? If she took one of these roads it would surely lead to civilization where someone would hire her. She had never actually seen a town; she had only heard tales of them from others at the brickyards. Should she go to Chatham or to Dartford or even Dover?

She decided not to go to Chatham because that was too near, and she took the road to Dartford which was much further on. Had she made a different decision on that cold dark night her fate might have been very different and she could have ended up as an obscure floozie. But Alice's sights were set high. Although she had no education or religious beliefs she was intrigued by this great God that George Gibbs believed in. When he had come to the Pug Mill on Sundays and read from his good book, had he not said that this God loved everyone?

Alice looked up at the star-lit sky. Did he know and care about her and her baby son? Or did one have to have some private initiation ceremony to share this God of love? With these deep thoughts in her mind her footsteps lagged. Suddenly she heard the sound of heavy clip-clopping hooves behind her on the road. Quickly, she crouched in the hedge.

By now it was almost dawn and the air was damp and very chilly. A great cart came trundling along the road piled high with sweet-smelling hay. It was on its way to catch the early morning market at Dartford. The driver squinted in Alice's direction as the girl tried to press herself closer into the bushes.

'Whoa there!' he shouted, pulling up his team of heavy shire horses. He did not want anything or anyone darting out and scaring his horses; it took too much to halt them if they bolted.

'Who's there?' he called. 'Come out if you want a ride!'

Encouraged by his friendly tone of voice, Alice crept out and gratefully climbed up on the back of the cart where she settled down amid the trusses of comfortable warm hay. The baby had woken up and begun to cry so she placed him to her breast with a deep sigh of relief. Soon they both slept heavily lulled by the gentle rocking of the cart.

When she awoke the cart had come to a stop and there were loud noises all around her — voices shouting at each other, sheep bleating and cattle lowing, and the creaking wheels of other carts.

The driver disappeared, having gone into the inn for his breakfast and Alice was alone. After making her baby comfortable in his back sling, she slipped down off the hay wagon and began to wander around the town of Dartford. She was utterly amazed. She had never seen such tall houses or houses built so close together. She had never seen a place so teeming with life — the fruit vendors and the water carriers alone seemed so unfamiliar to her. She sat down in the middle of the square, looking at the great confusion about her. It was so early in the morning and everyone was busy with the market. It was so odd and frightening to her to see all these folk and not one familiar face among them.

There were others like her, sitting in the town square. Most were ragged and lame, and all were homeless, wrapped up in their own particular grief. Suddenly, a deep feeling of loneliness swept over Alice and she stood up abruptly. There had to be a hiring fair somewhere, she thought. Then she noticed a well-dressed couple coming into the square, a man and a woman each carrying a basket. One contained small pieces of bread and the other contained rosy red apples. As the pair paused by the fountain in the square, Alice's baby began to cry. Immediately, the woman, dressed in a brown dress and straw bonnet, came towards her. 'Are you hungry, child?' she said.

Then she offered Alice a piece of bread, Alice shyly declined.

'Have you just arrived?' asked the woman. 'I do not recall seeing you here before.' Her dark eyes surveyed Alice shrewdly.

Alice licked her dry lips and nodded as a cool slim hand reached out to her. 'Oh, come, my dear, you look so weary. We will go over to the Mission and make your baby clean and comfortable and give you some breakfast. I am Ruth Anneslee,' she said, as they crossed the square. 'Where are you from? Have you no husband?'

'Ben,' announced the kind lady to the man she had arrived with. 'This child and her sweet babe have just come into town. God willing, we will take care of her.'

Ben Anneslee with his wide hat and his benign features was a direct descendant of the great preacher John Wesley. 'Ah,' he said, with a gentle smile, 'welcome to Dartford, my dear.'

At the Weslyan Mission, Alice was fed and her child laid down in a clean crib. So she found comfort and sustenance so quickly and easily. It was as if George Gibbs' great God had known about her troubles and need after all.

CHAPTER FIVE

The Proposal

With her youthful cheeks still flushed with sleep, Lucinda turned drowsily in her bed. The sun shone through the shutters and the early spring sounds came in from the window. The blackbird sang a mating song; the robin twittered as she built her nest in the eaves.

Languorously, Lucinda stretched out her arms. She had just had such a lovely dream, about a lover who had told her how beautiful she was. Oddly enough, he had not been a bit like Joe Lee. Instead, he had been dark and handsome, with a flashing smile in a somewhat haggard face. With a soft, unusual voice he called her *chérie*.

The dream had been very real but now it was fading. Lucinda sat up suddenly and put her feet down onto the cold floor to wake herself up. Other sounds were coming up from the yard where dumb Lukey was sweeping with a stiff broom. She heard the slosh of the buckets of water being thrown on the ground and the swish of the broom followed by Aunt Beat's scolding voice. All this noise soon brought Lucinda to full consciousness. She arose and went in to see her grandfather, give him his cough mixture, and prop him up in bed. As the day had begun at the Malted Shovel, so it would continue on the same old routine. Lucinda often felt nowadays that if this pattern was to be for the rest of her life, she would never face it.

Grandpa's room was stuffy, smelling of tobacco, rum, and old age.

'May I open the window, Grandpa?' Lucinda asked.

'Just a little,' wheezed Amos. 'I have to be so careful of

draughts what with me old chest being so dicky.'

Lucinda carefully pushed open the lattice and looked out across the fields. She felt a shock go through as she saw that out in the creek was anchored the *Alianora*. She would recognise that smart clean craft anywhere. After the long winter, Joe Lee was home.

Breathing excitedly, she peered out towards the creek hoping for a sight of her lover's red-brown curls.

'Don't stand there dreaming, lass,' called Grandpa. 'Fetch me the chamber pot.'

Obediently his granddaughter brought in the pot and left. Aunt Dot would empty it because Lucinda was still considered too young for such a task.

That day seemed endless but as soon as it was dusk, Lucinda was released from her duties and went up to the attic to signal to her lover by waving her blue hair ribbon out of the window.

Joe Lee responded as he always did, and Lucinda slipped away from the Malted Shovel to meet her darling after so many months being apart. It was the first time they had met since Joe Lee's father had died and, to her disappointment, Joe Lee did not respond to her as affectionately as she had dreamed. He seemed awkward and rather shy.

Distanced by his aloofness, Lucinda suddenly looked at him with a slightly different aspect, noting with slight distaste his heavy working breeches and rough grey shirt, and the fact that there were unshaven ginger hairs on his chin. Joe Lee looked very tired and explained away his long absence by the fact that now the *Alianora* belonged to him and he had been working very hard. His mother had gone to live ashore so that his young sister could attend school, and his brother, Tom Lee, who was supposed to help him sail the barge, had got drunk and was subsequently press-ganged to sea. Thus Joe Lee had been left to work the *Alianora* alone. He now employed a boy to assist him huff the sails and load the barge, having obtained a regular contract to carry bricks from the local brickfields down the Thames to London. It was very profitable work and he had also applied for a Master's Ticket. All this he told her in a very serious manner, holding her hand and staring at her as if from a great distance.

Lucinda had been lonely for too long and was hungry to be loved, though thus far their affair had just amounted to kissing and cuddling. She sat quietly listening to his tale of adventures since he had last left Hollinbury with a great passion building up in her heart.

'But don't you love me anymore?' she suddenly asked with childish petulance.

'Oh, of course I do, darling,' Joe Lee replied. 'But first I want to talk with you because I want us to be married soon. I can now support you and for awhile we can live on board the barge.' He looked restrained as he added: 'So I will not pet you until you tell me sincerely if you want to marry me.'

'Oh, dear,' gasped Lucinda. She longed to be loved but she had not thought beyond that. 'I don't think Grandpa will let me.'

'Lucy, darling,' Joe Lee insisted, 'you really must grow up. Life is a serious business and must be treated so. We will both go to him and I'll ask his permission.'

Lucinda looked quite dismayed; she just could not face such a complex situation. 'Could we not wait awhile?' she murmured. 'Until next year, perhaps, when I will be eighteen.'

'It will make little difference,' Joe Lee replied. 'You must be twenty-one to marry without any consent.' He went down on one knee and pressed her hand to his lips. 'Lucy, I swear I'll be good to you, and I don't mind how hard I have to work for you. When I complete my Master's Ticket we will buy a sea-going ship and sail the wide ocean together.'

The words were well-meant but these plans made sheltered young Lucinda very much afraid. To have a lover was very romantic, but to leave a comfortable home and live on a barge, well, that was another matter entirely ... She put her arms about his neck. 'Kiss me, Joe Lee,' she demanded, 'and stop being such a spoilsport.'

Joe Lee kissed her passionately but he sighed. 'Oh, Lucy darling, you must grow up. I intend to ask for your hand. If it's not this trip it will be the next, for I will not be put off. I cannot afford to. I must make headway while I am young, and in this business a man needs his wife beside him.'

'Oh, Joe Lee, wait until I have talked to Aunt Dot,' Lucinda pleaded. 'Don't upset Grandpa, he is an invalid.'

'I'll wait, Lucy, but only until next time. I'm sailing with the tide tomorrow. There is so much competition on the route that I cannot afford to waste any time.'

Tears filled Lucinda's large eyes as they parted. Their longed-for meeting had proved to be so disappointing. Joe Lee had changed dramatically since she last saw him. He was so sober, and did not love and fuss her as he used to. And in her opinion, this change was not for the better. Feeling very down-hearted, she fled across the fields and over the bridge.

Towards home, as darkness fell, she saw a dark shadow in the yard watching her. It was dumb Lukey. She felt sure he had been spying on her and Joe Lee, and she ignored him as she went past but a shiver ran down her spine as she did.

Early the next morning she stood by her window watching the red sail of the *Alianora* billow out in the wind as Joe tacked his way down the narrow creek out into the open sea. In her snow-white nightdress and her flowing waist-length fair hair, she was a pretty enough picture, but tears of self-pity poured down her cheeks. How she wished at that moment that her mother was living or that she had a close friend to confide in. And it would have been nice to have had a sister to talk to. But she loved the two old aunties who had been so kind to her, and she thought the world of Grandpa. But at this moment her need was a jumble of confusing thoughts and she was quite sure that none of them would understand her predicament. Letting out a deep sigh, she climbed back into bed and wallowed in her misery.

At eight o'clock Aunt Dot came breezily along the landing, humming. Her voice trilled away, 'Fol de de, fol de da,' and her white cap bobbed and her white teeth flashed as she appeared in Lucinda's bedroom door. 'Now, Lindy, come on, dear, time's passing.'

'I won't be long, Auntie,' called Lucinda from under the bedclothes, her voice hoarse with crying.

'Got a cold, dear?' asked Aunt Dot anxiously. 'You had better lie in. I'll bring you a hot drink. *And* I've got a nice surprise for you,' she added, as she disappeared again.

Lucinda sighed. Aunt Dot was so nice and kind. It did seem a shame to upset them all as she was sure Joe Lee was going to.

Within ten minutes, Dot returned with a cup of hot milk for Lucinda. She handed it to her niece and sat on the bed. 'Look what I've got for you,' she cried in her dramatic manner, handing Lucinda a little packet. Lucinda unwrapped the present and gasped as she pulled out a beautiful crucifix carved in bone. It was attached to a white silk ribbon so it could be worn about the neck.

Excitedly Dot lifted Lucinda's heavy mane of hair and tied the cross about her neck. 'Oh, it looks lovely,' she cried. 'It's really quite beautiful.'

'It's very nice, Auntie,' said Lucinda gratefully. 'But where did you get it?'

'It's from, you know who ...' Dot's voice dropped to a conspiratorial level. 'Jack, the Frenchie.'

Lucinda recognised the man of her dream the night before, the dark eyes and the strange voice calling her *chérie*. 'How strange,' she murmured, staring out of the window.

'What's strange?' asked Aunt Dot. 'You know who I mean. He's a prisoner out on the hulks. The one Aunt Beat makes cakes and pies for.'

Lucinda nodded coyly. 'Yes, I know him,' she said. 'But does he carve these lovely things himself?'

'No, some of the other prisoners make them. Jack sells them for extra food,' replied Aunt Dot. 'It's pretty grim out there on the hulks, so they say. And I bought the ribbon myself,' she declared excitedly as Lucinda rewarded her with the big hug and kiss she had been waiting for.

Dot cuddled Lucinda and fussed her, tucking in the bedclothes. 'Now dear, you have a nice rest. I'll see to Grandpa this morning. Then, humming her tune again she scuttled off like a lively puppy.

Lucinda lay back on the pillows idly dreaming. As she admired the little crucifix she knew deep in her heart that it would be very hard to leave the warm home she had grown up in, and tender care of the two aunts who had taken on the task of bringing her up when her mother died in childbirth.

At that moment, some miles away, Joe Lee was battling his way around the Isle of Grain into the Medway, red sails flying in his effort to be ahead of the other barges. For in his world it was first come, first served, with many bricks waiting to be transported to the big towns, now that the era of prosperity and property had arrived.

Near the town were long lines of dejected men swinging picks and wielding shovels as they dug a deep tunnel through the chalk cliffs for the new canal to flow through it. These were all prisoners-of-war, fine young men who had marched to glory with Napoleon. Once they had been proud youths. They had sweated in Spain and frozen in Russia, but now they were worn-down and beaten, standing day after day in cold clammy clay and sleeping in old warships under appalling overcrowded conditions. It was no wonder that they were often rebellious and that armed soldiers had to stand guard over them.

The news reaching the prisoners that morning was making them more than ever depressed. In their own tongue, they muttered together about the threatened return of the hated Bourbons and the abdication of their great hero, the Emperor Napoleon.

Back at the Malted Shovel, mid-week Jack, as he was now known to the family, sat in the warm back kitchen. Of late he had been looking even more handsome to Lucinda, for, thanks to her aunts, he had been well-fed and had filled out. And in spite of the patched faded uniform that he continued to wear, he even had an air of arrogance about him. 'The war is almost over,' he said, 'and, as always, my poor country is on the losing side.'

'Not to worry,' Aunt Beat consoled him. 'That also means you will be going home soon, doesn't it?'

'No doubt, *madame*, but when?' he replied. 'And do I wish to return to a country that is ruled by the hated monarchy?'

'Have you no wife awaiting you?' asked Dot, ignorant of political machinations at home or abroad.

'Indeed, I have, *madame*,' Jack replied in his polite manner. 'And a son I have never seen.'

'Well, then,' declared Beat. 'It's time to go home and get some more.'

Lucinda was rolling out the pastry and she suddenly blushed at her aunt's coarse remark. But Aunt Dot giggled, and Lukey sitting in the corner, seemed to leer.

'Are you sad tonight also, *chérie*?' Jack asked Lucinda.

Lucinda placed the rolling pin on one side and turned to look at him. Her dimpled elbows were covered with flour. Jack's expressive dark eyes seemed almost to caress them and before wandering up to those firm breasts beneath the loose apron.

Lucinda felt a hot blush run across her face and neck. 'No, no, Jack, I'm quite all right,' she stammered. 'And thank you for the cross. It is quite beautiful.'

'Yes, a very old man carved that,' Jack said with a charming smile. 'He saves the bones from what little meat he gets and turns them into things of beauty.'

'Oh, how sad but how lovely.' Lucinda sighed once more and Jack looked at her with interest.

Aunt Beat bustled off to serve in the bar while Dot sat with her elbows on the pine table, listening dreamily to that cultured voice of the Frenchman.

'I have a touch of England in my veins,' he was saying. 'My grandmother was an English woman and I received some of my schooling here. But I love my country France, and I was proud to fight for the little Emperor. But now great ambition and treachery have defeated him. It is a very sad time for me.'

Dot nodded her head vigorously. 'Pity you did not stay on our side,' she said.

'*Madame*, you are exactly right,' said he, mistaking her meaning. 'We should have allied our cause with England. Then how great we would have been! Dutch, Russians and Prussians — between us and our Bonaparte we could have defeated all!'

'I just don't understand,' said Dot, 'why men have to kill each other. We don't ask a lot of life and it does not last all that long anyway. So why do these dreadful things have to happen?'

Jack smiled and kissed her hand. '*Madame*, how wise you are. Let us pray that the next generation will be more enlightened.'

Lucinda watched the two of them, feeling quite envious of Aunt Dot, of the ease with which she conversed with this handsome young man and thoroughly enjoyed his attention. Perhaps it might be better or easier to be ugly and old ... This terrible thought suddenly flashed through her mind: suppose she never married and remained here at the inn to become an old maid just like her aunts. Goodness, it might be better to marry Joe Lee just as a way of escaping out into the world.

All these depressing thoughts seemed to overwhelm her as she pressed out the pastry and cut it into small rings for pies. When Joe Lee returned next week she knew she would have to face up to her problems.

'I may not be coming here much more,' Jack was saying to Dot. 'The nights are getting lighter and there is much trouble in the camp. Several men have been shot recently trying to escape.'

'Oh, dear, that's terrible,' said Dot. 'You must not take chances,' she smiled and pressed her hand on his. 'Whatever happens, Jack, it's been nice knowing you,' she said warmly.

'Well, it has been fine knowing you and your honoured sister,' returned Jack gallantly. His dark eyes turned to

Lucinda. 'And I'm not forgetting you, *ma chérie*,' he said, 'I shall always remember your lovely fair English beauty.'

Thrilling shivers went up and down Lucinda's spine, but she dropped her gaze quickly. 'Goodbye, then, is it, Jack?' she said quietly.

'No, let us say it is *au revoir*, which means that we may meet again.'

That night Lucinda pressed the bone crucifix close to her heart, 'Oh, please, God, forgive me, I must not think such wicked things, but Jack is so fine, so gallant. Why can't Joe Lee behave in that way?'

On Saturday evening Joe Lee returned, but oddly enough, he made no attempt to contact Lucinda. And when she signalled in her usual way from the window, he did not respond. Then suddenly he appeared walking right up to the inn looking very spruce. He was dressed in his Sunday suit and his hair was smoothly brushed. Walking with a very determined air, he came straight over the bridge and where she could hear Grandpa's bellow. 'What do you mean, young fella, me lad, walking in here? The public bar is open. This is private.'

'What I have to say to you, sir, is private,' Joe Lee answered quietly and firmly.

'Well, well, what is it?' asked Amos impatiently.

'I seek the hand of your grand-daughter, Lucinda. I have come to ask for your consent.'

Amos let out a roar like an enraged bull. 'Bloody saucy fellow! You're off one of those shit boats, ain't you?'

Joe Lee nodded. 'But we love each other,' he added quickly. 'I am my own master and will be able to support her.'

'Dottie! Beattie!' yelled Amos. 'Come in here and get this bloody bargee out of my house!'

Both aunts came running as Lucinda crouched miserably in the dark passage.

'What is it, Pa?' stammered Dot.

'Who's upset you, Pa?' cried Beat. Then she saw Joe Lee.

'Hey, what's he doing in here?' she demanded.

But Amos had gone purple in the face and was clutching at his chest and gasping for breath. The two sisters ran to help him.

Joe Lee turned to Lucinda who was beckoning him from the doorway and went to her.

'Quick, come out into the yard,' she whispered.

Once outside, Lucinda began to weep. 'Oh, Joe Lee, I warned you, didn't I? Poor Grandpa.'

'Poor Grandpa, indeed!' mocked Joe Lee. 'What about me? He has had his life and mine is just beginning. Either you want to share it with me, Lucy, or you don't. I feel very bewildered at the moment but I am not beaten yet.'

Lucinda threw herself into his arms. 'Oh, Joe Lee, I do love you, and I do want to marry you,' she gasped, 'but not yet. You must give me time to get them all used to me leaving.'

Joe Lee held her close. 'Darling,' he said, into her golden hair. 'For all the time I've loved you, I have never harmed you or taken advantage of you, though, God knows, I have wanted to. But you are still as sweet and pure as the day we met, and your folk have no reason to reproach me. I know they think I am the dregs of humanity, the son of a bargee off the shit boats, so it's up to you now, Lucy, to put them in the picture. Tell them I have regular runs and that I am getting my Master's Ticket. You must tell them, Lucy, for I can see they will not listen to me.'

'Yes, Joe Lee, I will,' Lucinda said forlornly. 'I'll tell Grandpa myself when he is feeling better.'

He kissed away her tears. 'Oh, I love you, Lucy! If I lose you I will be finished, for then nothing will be worth working for.'

'Lucinda!' Aunt Dot's screeching voice was calling from the back door.

'I must go, Joe Lee,' whispered Lucinda, pulling herself away. 'Grandpa might be worse.'

'Tell them, Lucy,' Joe Lee urged as she fled inside. 'Tell them.'

'Lucinda,' said Aunt Dot in a shocked voice. 'You were talking to that boy out there, that dreadful bargee who has upset your poor Grandpa. I've sent for the doctor and Grandpa has been put back to bed.'

'Oh, don't go on so, Aunt Dot,' said Lucinda, as tears of self-pity ran down her cheeks. 'Please leave me alone.'

Aunt Beat was filling up a stone warming pan in the kitchen. 'Is that you, my girl,' she called. 'What have you been up to?'

Feeling very forlorn Lucinda crept up to her room sobbing as though her heart would break. How was she to get the family to agree to her marriage with Joe Lee? Anyway, did she really want to marry him and live on one of those long narrow squalid barges for the rest of her life? Barge life would be quite a change for a young girl who had had such a sheltered upbringing.

The next day, Grandpa Amos was worse. He had slipped into a coma brought on by another stroke. The two aunts were very solemn and stared accusingly at Lucinda.

'What did that boy want?' demanded Aunt Beat. 'Don't never encourage them bargees in the private bar.'

'The saucy fellow, I've never seen him in the bar before,' replied Aunt Dot.

'Joe Lee is a steady fellow,' Lucinda defended her lover. 'And he does not drink.'

Dot shook her head. 'I don't care,' she said, 'They are a low-class bunch them canal folk, with no schooling, and no religion. They live like a lot of Beat's hens, they do.'

Lucinda remained silent. She knew it was no use trying to convince them. She looked out of the window and across the fields but the *Alianora* has already left her berth and was far out on the estuary. Again all decisions would have to wait until his return. She sighed. And to her amazement she realised that she felt a tremendous sense of relief.

CHAPTER SIX

Old Wally

The lanterns were lit in the Malted Shovel and the sisters pattered about serving an occasional customer. The familiar smell of baking came from the kitchen as the black night had settled down on the marsh.

The bar parlour was completely empty Amos' friends had stopped visiting him for he no longer left his bed and his mind wandered as he lay there with his swollen belly still demanding his rum ration. He would sing sea shanties in a loud tone or just mumble away to himself as his mind travelled back to his youth through jumbled thoughts of pirates and smuggling and old comrades of the sea. His daughters and grand-daughter still tried valiantly to cope but it was becoming increasingly difficult.

On this particular night there was such an air of sadness about the place. Earlier in the evening, Beat and Dot had words and were not speaking to each other. Aunt Beat still felt very bitter about the young bargee whom she held responsible for her father's collapse. And she had cursed Joe Lee when she saw his barge anchored again in the creek, when he had just returned from a long voyage up and around the coast.

But Aunt Dot had been more tolerant and had tried to reason with Beat. ''tis nonsense, sister, to blame that boy,' she said. 'Father would have deteriorated in the end. The doctor always told us that his illness would eventually reach his brain.'

'Don't argue with me,' snapped Beat. 'All that worry of the shit boats and them fighting and swearing uncouth bargees brought his illness on, there's no doubt about it.'

'Oh, don't be so bigoted,' sniffed Dot. 'It was God's will, and remember that Father is of a great age.'

'But a mighty man with a great brain,' retorted Beat. 'I cannot bear to think that that fellow destroyed him.'

'Don't then,' said Dot. Then she grimaced. 'Dear sister, don't let us quarrel,' pleaded Dot. 'Let's just pray that he will soon find peace of mind.' Tears poured down her cheeks and her loose lips trembled.

'That's it, cry!' sneered her sister. 'Soft as shit, you are.' As she abused Dot, she turned to see a wind-blown Lucinda creeping in at the side door. She had earlier secretly left the inn to visit her lover and was now returning, cold, shivering and very down-hearted.

Beat was furious! With an unearthly screech, she lunged at Lucinda and dealt her a hard slap across the face. She grabbed her by the arm and would have continued to beat her. 'You bitch!' she yelled. 'You have been out there to see that bargee, haven't you?'

The blows were as hard as they were unexpected. Lucinda had never been hit before. She held her hands protectively to her face and cowered against the wall.

Dot had rushed forward and grabbed Beat, knowing how violent her sister could be. But in return Beat grabbed Dot's untidy hair and the two women struggled together, scratching and spitting like two angry cats.

'Oh, please don't! Don't!' cried Lucinda, appalled at the sight of her beloved aunts fighting.

Then suddenly, a figure appeared through the side door and a strong arm thrust the two sisters apart. 'Ladies, ladies,' a voice said. 'Whatever is the matter?'

It was Jack.

Dot ran to Lucinda and they both fled up the stairs. Beat was left behind, her hair sticking out as she waved her fat fist defiantly.

Jack put an arm about her shoulders. 'Calm down now, *madame*,' he said gently.

Beat stared at him and forced a smile. 'It's just a family set-to,' she said. 'Nothing to worry about' she smoothed down her hair and held out her hand. 'It's nice to see you again,' she said. 'Come, Jack, into the kitchen.'

In the kitchen, Lukey was hiding under the table. Beat gave him a sharp poke with the pointed toe of her boot. 'Go and watch the bar,' she ordered, and he slunk out.

Taking down a jug, she poured wine into a beaker. 'Take a drink, Jack,' she said, 'while I get myself together. What a set-to. My poor father is so ill and Lucinda is so disobedient and that stupid sister of mine doesn't help much by encouraging her.'

As Beat poured out her tale of woe, Jack listened quietly and respectfully as he quietly sipped his wine. Beat got up to take a pie from the oven and put it on a plate. 'Here you are,' she said. 'Put that inside you, you look like you need it.'

Jack smiled wanly. The bones in his cheeks stood out and he was so thin that the skin stretched tightly over them. But his dark eyes twinkled merrily as he watched this belligerent old woman.

'Have you brought anything?' asked Beat, feeling fully recovered at last.

'Yes, I have,' replied Jack. 'A wall plaque.' He produced a lovely picture composed of a religious theme — saints with halos and flying angels. It was cleverly created with shells from the shore, feathers from wild birds, and little pieces of bone and clay from the riverside, all materials obtained from the environs of the prison ships.

'Oh, it's lovely. Did you do it?' asked Beat.

'No,' said Jack. 'It was made by my old friend and compatriot who in peacetime is an artist.'

'How much do you want for this?' asked Beat, determined as ever to get a bargain.

'Well, two sovereigns if it can be arranged,' replied Jacques. 'I am only sorry not to be able to give it to you, *madame*. But this time it is necessary to arrange a proper deal.' He did not say so, but Jacques had begun to plan his escape, so he needed money to bribe his captors. The last spell of punishment had been intolerable and it would go on indefinitely now that Napoleon had escaped.

'Well, I expect I can manage it,' Beat replied, thinking of one of her customers who would undoubtedly buy it for his wife so that Beat would make a profit in the transaction. 'Rest yourself, Jack, while I get the cash.'

Jacques relaxed by the fire and turned his mind to the beautiful Lucinda. What could she have been up to to distress her beloved aunts so?

Minutes later, Lucinda appeared in the kitchen with traces of tears on her cheeks. She ventured in timidly to make a hot drink for Aunt Dot who was still weeping her heart out in the bedroom.

'Good evening, Lucinda,' said Jacques. 'Are you well?'

Lucinda nodded dumbly, her lovely eyes still full of tears.

He held out her hand to her. 'Please don't cry. Can I help you?' His voice was soft and gentle.

'No, it's all right,' Lucinda said, shaking her head. 'It's just that life is so depressing what with Grandpa being so ill and my aunts quarrelling.'

Jacques stroked her smooth white arm with his long sensitive fingers. 'The trouble will pass,' he said slowly with his eyes resting on her fair bosom and the little carved crucifix that rested there.

Lucinda's hands went to her neck and she held the little carved cross in her palm. 'This is so pretty,' she said with a little smile.

'Yes,' replied Jacques. 'The old man who made it is very skilled and his work is unique.'

'How sad that he is shut up in prison,' Lucinda murmured.

Jacques sighed. 'Yes, it's no life for any of us,' he said, 'just wasting away so far from our homes.'

'Oh, poor Jack!' Lucinda exclaimed as tears that had been held back suddenly escaped and rolled down her rosy cheeks.

Jacques put out a gentle finger to catch one of them and put it to his lips. 'Lovely pearl,' he said softly. 'No one has shed tears for me for many years.'

'Oh, Jack,' cried Lucinda, blushing to her ears, 'you are so romantic.'

'And you are so beautiful, my English rose,' he murmured, placing her hand to his lips.

At the sound of Aunt Beat's footsteps, they drew apart and Lucinda quickly made the drink for Aunt Dot. Beat snorted suspiciously as Lucinda hurried out of the kitchen with a mug of hot milk.

'Little minx,' grumbled Aunt Beat. 'What has she been saying?'

'Very little,' replied Jacques.

'Got herself involved with one of them shit boat fellas,' explained Beat. 'But I won't allow it. I'll beat the hide off her if she don't stay away from him.' She carefully wrapped up the picture and gave Jacques the two gold coins.

Jacques' eyes glinted. At last he had something to help him obtain his freedom! 'She is still young,' he said, 'but possibly she does need a husband.'

'I am sorry,' said Jacques, 'but be gentle with Lucinda, she is so lovely.'

Beat narrowed her eyes suspiciously. 'And you can keep your thieving eyes off her,' she suddenly snarled.

'*Madame*, I have so many troubles of my own,' declared Jack calmly, 'I hardly want to indulge in any more.'

Beat sniggered as she realised that she had reacted rather rudely. 'Get off with you,' she said. 'And mind how you go — we don't want you to get caught near here.'

Jacques pulled his old ragged coat about him and bowed low. '*Au revoir, madame*,' he said. 'I wish you and your family well.' With that he swept out of the door and into the night.

Aunt Beat went back to the bar giving Lukey a severe clout as she went and chasing him down into the cellar. 'Get down there and tidy up, you lazy good-for-nothing,' she yelled at him.

Old Wally was still sitting in his corner in the bar. He had witnessed the earlier fight between the sisters and was still pretending not to notice anything that went on. But his eyes and ears took in everything that went on in that inn, though he kept very silent when Beat re-filled his jug before serving two thirsty farm labourers who had just come in.

Moments later a very tipsy Larlee staggered in. Her hair was wet and her clothes all muddy, and she looked extremely agitated.

'Quartern of gin,' she gasped, placing a florin on the counter.

Beat stared at her suspiciously; Larlee usually only drank gin when someone else was paying. Larlee gulped the fiery liquid down quickly and then went to sit by the fire. So looked so dejected that Beat was quite concerned. 'What's up with her?' she whispered to Wally.

'Alice ran off,' Wally whispered back, 'took the baby. I saw her go, last night after dark.'

Beat's mouth dropped in surprise. She knew that Larlee was surprisingly fond of Alice, her firstborn, and Alice had always seemed to be fairly close to her mother. Beat could remember when they had lived happily in that cottage in the Street with Larlee's sailor husband. 'Why did she do that?' she asked. But Wally just shrugged.

Aware of the whispering, Larlee called out: 'You can all mind your own bloody business and get me a jug of ale.' She had walked all the way to town and back in search of Alice, unable to believe that her daughter had really gone. What little human feeling that was left inside her was all for Alice and her baby. She had not meant it when she told Alice to get out, she had just been trying to protect her from the wiles of men. But now Alice was gone, and her grandchild too. Wallowing in her sorrows, Larlee sat swilling ale until her money ran out. Then true to form, she attached herself to a lone soldier from the fort and staggered home to bed with him.

Later that night young John lay awake wondering where Alice and her baby were, and listening to Larlee as she argued drunkenly with her escort. John was hungry and his belly was rumbling. There had been no meal at all that night. He had scrumped turnips from the field and tried to cook them but they had still remained hard and uneatable. Kit and Toby had sat on their bed of straw and gnawed at the turnips like young animals but had gained no nourishment from them. John had looked at the two tired little boys huddled up together and wondered why nobody cared about them. How could their mother have abandoned them? He felt quite sick at heart and wished, not for the first time that day, that he had the courage to run away.

All these jumbled thoughts went through his young mind in turmoil. Then he began to think of Dolly, fat, fair, affectionate Dolly, and he was so glad that she had escaped from this hell. She was so happy and well cared for up at the farm. On Sunday he would ask the old farmer to let him take out his boat and perhaps Dolly would be able to get the afternoon off and come with him ... Finally able to ignore the creaking and mutterings coming from Larlee's bed, John closed his eyes and peaceful sleep took over. And in his slumber that night he dreamed of an island where the skies were always blue and there were no brickfields.

On Sunday morning, as little John trudged over the marshland down to the shore, old Wally dressed in his best straw hat, went about his duties as assistant verger in the church. He escorted the congregation to their seats and went around with the collection plate. When the service was over, he stood outside gossiping to old friends, spreading the tittle-tattle from the hamlet around into the surrounding farms and villages. His chief topics this week were the errant Larlee and the conflict going on amongst the ladies in the tavern. Bonnets waggled and the ladies whispered and exclaimed in unison. Accompanied by her aunts, Lucinda felt quite uncomfortable as deliberate glances were cast in her direction.

Aunt Beat snorted loudly, digging her umbrella down viciously into the path. 'Look at them all,' she sniffed. 'They're chattering away like a lot of sparrows. It's that nosey little Wally who's behind it, I'll be bound.'

Aunt Dot was not so tough. Her eyes were still red with weeping and she hung her head miserably as Lucinda held her arm tightly.

But it was actually Larlee whom Wally was most incensed and worked up about. ''Tis disgraceful,' he said. 'That woman's a harlot, and she drove that young lass and her baby out into the cold.'

The respectable citizens from the neighbourhood agreed with him and some went so far as to say that Larlee should not be allowed to employ the small children in the brick fields at all, that she was not fit to do so.

Meanwhile, young John, unusually happy was skipping along across the fields, his fair curls bouncing in the breeze. He was off to meet Dolly down by the farm gates, for she was getting the afternoon off once the chores in the dairy were over. Every time John saw his beloved Dolly he was more amazed. She had grown tall recently and filled out. Her cheeks were rosy and her clean cotton dress and white bonnet suited her to perfection.

They met and joined hands, running across the meadow as free as young lambs in the spring.

John was small for his age. Hard work and undernourishment had stunted his growth. He was suddenly conscious of this fact. 'Why, I do declare, Dolly,' he said. 'You have outgrown me,' he said.

'I expect it's all the good food,' said Dolly. 'How are you doing now that Alice has gone?' she asked, 'and poor little Kit and Toby?'

John shrugged. 'Oh, we manage, and sometimes Wally gives us rabbit stew.' They had slowed down to a walk and John put his arm on Dolly's shoulder.

'Oh dear,' Dolly sighed. 'I wonder where Alice and her dear little baby are now.'

'Don't you worry about Alice,' said John. 'She knows what she's doing. She was going to get herself a nice job, and I bet she does. She did not want to work in the Pug Mill, and I don't blame her. Alice will be all right.'

In the old borrowed boat from John's friend the farmer, John and Dolly sailed out to Motney Island where they had much fun scampering around the deserted rock in the middle of the estuary. Afterwards they lay on a patch of sand talking of the things they would like to do when they grew older.

'I'd like to marry you, Dolly,' declared John. 'We could sail away in this boat right over the horizon.' He waved his arm in the direction of the setting sun.

Dolly blushed. 'I'd like to go with you, John,' she said quietly. 'I'd never be afraid. But first I'd like to stay at the farm and learn to read and write properly. I've been having lessons — look, I can write my name!' With a sharp stick she slowly wrote in the sand. The letters stood out sharply: DOLLY.

John stared in wonder. 'Is that what your name looks like?'

Dolly nodded proudly.

John was full of admiration. He could navigate a boat, and tell the changes in the tide, but he had no idea of how to write his own name. That would have been a great achievement. 'Let me try,' he said, taking the stick from Dolly. Concentrating hard, he slowly traced a 'D' in the sand.

'That's right,' said Dolly. 'But your name begins with a 'J'.' She took back the stick and traced a 'J' in the sand.

For a while they made letters and shapes in the sand and laughed and romped about the island until they noticed the tide was ebbing. They could not get stranded, or it would be four hours before the tide flowed in again. John dashed to the boat and pushed it into deep water completely missing his step. In a flash he was into deep water completely up to his neck in water but giggling with joy.

Dolly laughed back as she struggled to the boat, holding up her skirts to show her fat podgy legs as she lifted them over the water.

'Oh, it's been a lovely day!' sighed Dolly, as she settled into the little boat. 'I hope I can often get Sunday off like this.'

'Yes, it would be fine to have days like this to look forward to,' said John reflectively. The wind whipped up the tide and the golden rays from the sun floated on the water. It was idyllic out there.

On Monday morning, young John was back at the Pug Mill, one of that long desolate line of small slaves urged on by their task-masters. It was such a contrast to the glorious day before. Now thirty pounds of cold wet clay struck a chill to his head as he walked along to lay it before the moulding queen, then off again for another load without respite.

Larlee was in a foul mood and a very angry frame of mind. She worked like a fiend, screaming at little Kit and giving Toby such a violent shove that he slipped and twisted his foot causing him to limp for the rest of that weary day.

John coped with his aching back and numbed legs by keeping his mind on higher things. He thought of the blue seas, the salt spray in the air and little Dolly in a pink cotton dress, barefoot laughing and giggling as she was when she fell in the boat.

At last, at six o'clock the shrill whine of the factory hooter announced that at last the long day was over. Then John trudged back over the marsh with the other two boys to the cold deserted cottage, for Larlee had stayed behind at the kilns with her bottle and her new lover, the brick foreman.

Outside his cottage, Wally sat and watched the children arrive, noting that the smallest boy was limping badly. 'Come lads,' he said kindly. 'I've got a nice bit of stew for you. Why don't you join me for supper?' he said.

So in Wally's warm and cosy cottage the young boys ate a hearty meal and enjoyed a rare moment of relaxation, laughing and chatting, and listening to Wally talk of his own life as a boy. He had been born in this very place he told them, and had worked on the farm since he was a boy. 'Hard work don't kill no one,' he said 'but it's good grub you need and clean air. Yer get nought of that in them old brick yards.'

However, old Wally did more than just work at the farm, he thrived on several occupations, as verger, herdsman, and gravedigger. 'Got a heavy day myself tomorrow,' he informed them as they got ready to leave. 'Got to dig a grave for old

Amos Dell tomorrow. Funny to think that my father dug a grave for Amos' father and his wife. Yes, many good folk reside in that old churchyard.'

With a nice bit of cake wrapped in paper to take with them, the boys went home feeling very happy and without complaint. Tucking themselves into the straw bed beside the fireless copper, they huddled close to keep each other warm. And John lay there for a while before closing his eyes and thought about Wally's parting remark. He vowed there and then that he would leave the hamlet a long time before he was ready to be buried in a graveyard.

CHAPTER SEVEN

Larlee's Curse

All the most important people in the district attended the funeral of Amos dell. In his later years he had been well respected in the neighbourhood as people chose to forget the fact that he had been engaged in many smuggling ventures in his wild youth. Now at last his massive body was laid to rest in the little churchyard beyond the inn in a grave next to those of his beloved wife and daughter.

Weeping loudly and heavily veiled, the ladies had left the churchyard after the funeral and made their way back to the inn where a breakfast was laid on for the guests. Most of these had travelled from outlying farms and villages to pay their respects to Amos.

As the procession headed for the Malted Shovel, Joe Lee stood on the deck of the *Alianora* with the wind blowing his chestnut curls. He was feeling quite elated. At last, Amos was dead! The one remaining obstacle to his marrying Lucinda had been removed. Lucinda was his! He would wait until the mourning was over and then she would have to marry him ...

As the funeral procession made its way, a long line of prisoners from the fort were marched past the churchyard on their way to dig out the new canal. Catching a glimpse of Lucinda's golden hair under her heavy black veiling, Jacques wished that he could be walking beside her, consoling her and helping to dry those jewels of tears.

Aunt Beat stood there looking so grim and stern, while Aunt Dot wept copiously unable to control her grief. And dumb Lukey frisked and gambolled about like a spring lamb. The excitement of seeing all these strange faces was almost

too much for him. Wally was there, too, his big ears ever-
alert, standing on the path with heavy traces of brown clay on
his breeches, evidence of his recent grave digging. He
frequently touched his cap to these prominent citizens who
came to mourn the old inn-keeper.

When the will was read later that day it contained no
surprises, except for one clause which left a fine legacy to his
grand-daughter, Lucinda, to be used as a dowry when a suitable husband of Christian belief was found for her. Any possible suitor had to be approved by both Amos' daughters,
Lucinda's aunts. Aunt Beat and Aunt Dot had jointly been
left the inn.

Although work in the fields all over the small hamlet
almost came to a halt the day they buried Amos Dell, this
did not, of course, include Larlee or her little slaves. She still
stood as queen of the moulding table, furiously and speedily
turning the clay into bricks with the use of a flat wooden
spatula.

Little Toby was still limping. His leg was very painful but
no one cared except his brother who eyed him anxiously but
was unable to help. And Larlee certainly did not care.

'Get moving, you lazy sods!' she cried, whenever the boys
lingered to talk.

John's fair curls were bathed in sweat as he took his turn
placing the newly made bricks on a trolley before wheeling it
into the fiery hell of the drying and firing kilns. For it was
here that those lumps of clay were cooked until they were
hard and golden — gold dust for the manufacturers and
beauty for the new London buildings. These bricks were also
being used to build the ever-expanding railways and their
stations.

The sun rose high over the marshlands and the cattle lay in
the shade as the geese and wild fowl out on the muddy water
floated gracefully in the cool dykes. Even the farm labourers
took their rest in the shades but there was no respite for the
little children out in the brick fields. On and on they plodded.

The haze of the hot afternoon rose amid the deep clay holes and the long line went back and forth with the huge lumps of clay perched on their heads. In the other direction went the long crocodile of little brick carriers, carrying their loads under thin arms and then placing them carefully in rows ready to be stacked in the ovens. The heat of the ovens glowed white hot and was almost unbearable to any human. Whenever they approached the kilns, the little ones closed their eyes tightly for fear of having them burned out, so fierce was the fire.

Toby limped along behind his big brother, holding the cold wet clay to his belly. Little tears crept down his cheeks. 'My leg hurts, Kit,' he whispered.

'Take it easy, boy,' returned Kit quietly. 'Don't fret. I'll ask Larlee again if you can rest.'

They lagged behind the rest of the line beside a deep water-filled clay hole. Toby suddenly slipped as his bad leg gave way and he went down into the pool of slimy yellow water. Immediately, Kit dropped the lump of clay from his head and ran to his young brother's aid, reaching out his arms as Toby slid down the steep bank. 'Help! Help!' he called. 'Toby has fallen in!' He had grasped hold of Toby's small hand and was hanging on as best he could, trying to keep his brother above the water. But slowly he too was beginning to slide down the slippery banks. The other children started running to get help.

When young John learned what was happening, he dashed from the kilns, jumped into the clay hole head first and managed to grab Toby just as his head was sinking under the water. With a few swift strokes John swam to the bank pulling Toby so that Kit would then help to haul him out. Lying exhausted on the bank, Toby was scared, wet and whimpering just like a half-drowned pup.

Suddenly they heard Larlee's shrill and angry voice. 'Where are all those bleeding boys?' she demanded. 'What's going on out there?' She had not moved from her position by her table for she could not afford to stop working, even for one second. She had set herself a target that day and would get a good bonus based on the number of bricks she turned out.

'Toby fell in,' cried the other children

'Stupid sod!' she sniffed. 'Put him down here. He can carry bricks to the kiln, that will dry him out.'

So the little boy was brought along to Larlee and there he crouched shivering in the corner while he coughed up the filthy water from the clay hole. And it was filthy, for everyone urinated in this hole and rubbish of all kinds was dumped in it. Now little Toby had his young lungs full of this liquid and no one was concerned.

With a grim face, John returned to his task at the kilns where the fierce heat soon dried his clothes. And half an hour later, little Toby, pale-faced and still wobbly on his legs, came carrying his quota of bricks to the kiln. Despite his ordeal he was back in the slave line once more.

That evening the huge gates swung open and the tired little ones came out slowly, walking zombie fashion, stiff-legged and unseeing. The sun hung low over the marsh and a warm glow flooded the landscape. Birds sang cheerfully as they settled in their nests but those weary little ones neither saw nor heard the beauties of nature around them; they drifted off to their poor comfortless homes.

Young John sped home carrying Toby on his back. 'Come Toby,' he had said. 'I'll give you a piggy back.' And his lithe young body, toughened by all the hard work, bore the little boy home two miles over the marsh. At least they did not have to put up with Larlee that evening. She was spending the night at the kilns with a gin bottle, because she was in charge of the youngsters doing overtime turning the bricks through the night.

From his cottage window Wally watched the sad little group arrive and he went out onto his porch to greet them. 'Hallo, lads, what's the matter with Toby?' he asked.

'He fell into the clay hole,' replied Kit.

Wally gently lifted Toby down from John's back. The little boy's body was very hot, and his ragged shirt and breeches were as stiff as boards where the brown clay had dried on them. A dry cough racked his tiny frame.

'Poor little soul,' murmured Wally. 'He's got pneumonia. Had a horse once with that,' he added. 'Let's get him inside.' Wally cut off Toby's stiffened rags and bathed him with a hot sponge. Then he wrapped him warmly in a blanket. Toby's lips were now blue and he was shivering violently.

'Here, lad, a nice drop o' me elder wine.' Wally gently held the cup to the purple lips but as soon as Toby swallowed the liquid, he vomited.

Wally shook his head. 'It's bad, bad as can be,' he declared. 'I'll put him in my bed. Now, you, young John, take a sup o' that hot milk on the stove and eat one o' them oat cakes. Then get down to the Malted Shovel and ask ol' Beatrice to tell the doctor about Toby when he goes in for his pint. He might just come by and see the little lad.'

'You can stay here with me, Kit,' he said to the other boy. 'Don't go in that cold place tonight.' He paused as a thought came to him. 'And where was the ol' witch Larlee when all this was going on?' he demanded.

'Working,' said Kit. 'She don't stop for nothing when she's working, and tonight she's minding the kids at the kilns.'

'Bloody damned whore!' muttered Wally. 'I know what she's really doing up there all night.'

When John was refreshed he went down to the Malted Shovel where the ladies of the inn, still clad in their black mourning clothes, had got back to their usual routines. Beat served over the bar and Aunt Dot, helped by Lucinda, baked their famous pies in the kitchen. A group of Amos' old cronies sat in the bar parlour exchanging anecdotes about their dear departed friend and finishing off his best port. Dumb Lukey sat outside the back door hugging himself tight. A sinister, secret smile lingered on his face.

John greeted his brother. 'Hallo Luke.'

Lukey grinned and put his strong arms around John's neck.

'Give over, Lukey,' cried John, wriggling free from this

rough embrace, 'you'll throttle me. Where is Aunt Beat?'

Lukey pointed down at the two cellar flaps, through which the brewer's men rolled the barrels of beer and took away the empties when they came.

'She's not down there, you silly fool!' said John impatiently.

But Lukey jabbered excitedly as though there were something he wanted John to see down there. But John was not in the mood. 'Blamed if you ain't gettin' worse, Luke,' he muttered as he walked past him and into the kitchen where Lucinda was rolling out pastry.

With her lovely hair tied up under a white cap she looked very pretty. She smiled sweetly at little John. 'Hullo, darling, get yourself a pie,' she said. 'It's free. They are left over from the funeral breakfast. There are some sandwiches too, and I'll pack some for Kit and Toby in a moment when I get my hands free.'

John gladly took a mince pie and munched the sweet pastry. 'Toby's sick,' he said, with his mouth full of crumbs. 'Fell in the clay hole, he did. Wally asked me to ask Aunt Beat to tell the doctor.'

'Poor little boy,' Lucinda murmured. 'Aunt Dot will be here in a minute, she will tell Beat.'

To get the doctor to visit any of the cottages in the street was no easy matter. He was a professional man and expected to be paid for his services and there was little money to be had from the poverty-stricken hamlet. However, if Beat asked him, he would go, because she would always guarantee his payment. So after several negotiations with the sisters the doctor eventually came into the kitchen to talk to John.

'What is wrong with the boy?' he asked. He was a tall, white-haired man with red cheeks.

'He's coughing and all blue,' explained John.

'Why wasn't he given medical attention up at the Pug Mill?' demanded the doctor. His blue eyes glared and his beard twitched angrily.

Little John felt very afraid of him. 'I dunno,' he stuttered.

'Larlee did not report it. She just made him keep working.'

The doctor shook his head and made disgruntled sounds.

'He could easily been drowned,' said John. 'I dived in and got him out.'

The doctor's expression softened and he looked quite kind as he patted John's head. 'You are a brave little lad. Get Lucy to give you some of that ginger pop and I'll pay.'

The doctor got into his little dog cart and rattled away over the bridge to Wally's cottage.

Back in the bar parlour, many rude remarks were made about Larlee and her exploitation of children who earned money just for her to drink. In the kitchen John consumed his ginger pop and had a fine time being fussed over by Lucinda and her aunts.

'Let that Larlee come in here tomorrow and I'll give her a piece of me mind,' declared Aunt Beat with her fiercest expression.

'She certainly is a monster,' said Aunt Dot.

Lucinda plied John with goodies and wept for little Toby. 'He's so alone,' she cried. 'Surely he has someone somewhere who cares for him ...

That night Wally sat up watching Toby fighting for his breath while Kit and John lay on the rug covered by blankets in front of the roaring fire. The doctor had told him that it was touch and go for Toby because his lungs are full of filth. But he would do whatever he could to help him.

At four o'clock the quiet dawn silence was shattered by the sound of an explosion out at the brickfields. This was followed by the shrill warning siren which only went off in time of emergency.

Woken from their sleep, the villagers rose from their beds and peered out of their windows to see a thick black column of smoke rising up over the marsh.

There was a lot of confusion and shouting but no one knew what had happened until the duty sergeant from the fort rode bareback into the hamlet to rouse the doctor and the vicar.

'Kids all buried,' he hollered. 'There's been a big blow-out up at the Pug Mill.'

Old nags were saddled or harnessed to carts and then urged down the winding lanes as the villagers set out to rescue the children.

It was a terrible scene at the Pug Mill. The kilns had exploded and crashed down on the group of young children asleep beside them. Hot bricks were everywhere and many children were trapped and buried under them. The men ripped the skin off their fingers in their desperate attempt to rescue them.

The explosion had happened because the brickie foreman, a young married man from the village, who was responsible for checking the temperature of the ovens, had been lying out in the marsh with Larlee. No one had been there to check the sudden rising heat of the ovens which could not be contained.

Many of the tiny children had been injured or maimed. Five were dead, crushed under the fatal bricks. Grown men wept as they carried the bodies out.

By early morning crows waited outside the gates and watched the farm carts take the bodies away. Tension ran very high as they demanded to know why this accident had happened. It did not take long to find out, and when the brick foreman tried to escape they pounced on him, beat him up and marched him down to the magistrate's house in the village.

Now it was Larlee's turn. Amid the crowds there were some strong determined women, one of whom was Aunt Beat. When Larlee staggered drunkenly out of the mill, squinting into the sunshine, the women grabbed her, tore off her clothes and rolled her in the muddy lane. Larlee screamed and fought as they then pulled her along tied to the tail-board of a cart and pelted her with refuse until they reached the church. Across the road from the church were the stocks. Into the holes, they thrust Larlee's head and legs and locked her in it. Everyone in the crowd had brought bad eggs and rotting vegetables — any rubbish they could find to aim at Larlee. This they did with gusto all day long until Larlee was almost covered with a pile of stinking refuse. Then the mob went on to her cottage where they proceeded to batter down the door and break the windows. Once inside, they smashed the meagre bits of furniture and threw them out into the street.

A few doors away, Wally sat bathing Toby's hot brow. 'Serves the bitch right,' he commented bitterly. 'She's got her dues at last.'

Little Kit was terrified by the blood-thirsty sound of the crowd's cries, and young John watched amazed and astonished by the hatred and violence of these people.

At dusk the vicar helped release Larlee from the stocks. Shouting and cursing she staggered to her cottage and picked up a few belongings. 'To hell with the bastards!' she screamed, tying everything into a bundle. 'I've worked bloody hard to get a living and now this is my reward. Curse you all. May you all end in hell, I've finished with this stinking hamlet. I'll never come here again.' Then, without a backward glance, Larlee staggered off down the road in the direction of the town.

CHAPTER EIGHT

Waterloo

The tragedy at the Pug Mill appalled many prominent and influential local dignatories and letters of protest flooded the newspapers for days. News of the disaster was printed in papers and broadsheets alike, and floral tributes came from far and wide. A special fund was raised for the parents of the injured and the dead, and a large communal service and burial was held in the parish church in the village.

At last that section of the brick kilns at least was declared too dangerous to work in. It was temporarily closed down and the children were all sent home.

Soon afterwards, a well-known methodist magazine published a long article written and signed by one George Gibbs. It read as follows:

From time to time I have endeavoured to bring to the attention of our goodly reader the fact that there are in our brick fields, from twenty to thirty thousand children, ranging from the ages as low as three and four, slaving in them, undergoing a bondage of toil and the horrors and devils it carries with it. Loudly I claim the protection of the law for these children whose tasks compare with the children of Israel, whose lives were made bitter in hard bondage in mortar and brick. I pray you God-fearing people will listen to the cries of our own afflicted children.

But in fewer than two weeks, the fuss had all died down. That section of the kiln was reopened and the long crocodile of little children returned over the marsh to work once more in the Pug Mill. Thus life went on in the village and its adjacent hamlet of Hollinbury as always.

The disaster at the Pug Mill was soon overshadowed by the news from Europe where everyone knew that Napoleon was rebuilding his army. That took precedence over all else.

On the other side of the river, the fort at Tilbury was a hive of activity as men, mounts and ammunitions were loaded aboard the warships headed for France. While just outside the town, the French war prisoners continued to slave with picks and shovels at the tall chalk cliffs in their forced efforts to build the new canal.

In the Malted Shovel, the regulars debated these events as though for the first time.

'What do we want a canal for?' demanded Aunt Beat. 'The creek is darned nuisance enough with them old shit boats always anchored out there.'

'That's true,' replied her customer, 'but we must give way to progress.'

'More factories going up every day beside the river,' said another.

'I don't see how they are going to get the canal over them cliffs,' intervened Aunt Dot vaguely. 'Why, they must be forty feet high.'

'They won't go over the top of them, that's for sure,' sneered Beat sarcastically.

As usual Dot came out the loser in any sort of discussion.

'Well, can't say I like the idea,' continued Beat. 'We will just get more poverty-stricken folk off those canal boats.'

So the debate went on as dusk came down on the marshland and Lucinda, wrapped in a blue knitted shawl, crept furtively out of the back door to visit Joe Lee. The *Alianora* barge was lying out in the creek with its sails unfurled.

Unnoticed by Lucinda, but stalking along a good way behind her, was dumb Lukey. He had a wild look in his eyes and his mouth drooled as he watched her slim shape half-running, half-walking over the field looking furtively behind her every now and then as if in fear of being followed.

Just under the bridge Joe Lee was waiting. He placed his strong arms around her and hugged her. 'You came to me, darling. How I prayed that nothing would prevent you!' he murmured as he kissed her lips passionately. 'Let's go aboard the *Alianora*. No one will disturb us there.'

They walked slowly along beside the deep dyke which led to the creek, and Joe Lee tenderly helped Lucinda aboard. In his cabin below deck he proudly showed her all the changes he had made. 'I've bought a new modern stove, new cooking pots and blankets. This is going to be our honeymoon chamber.'

Lucinda's forget-me-not blue eyes were wide in amazement. 'But Joe Lee the date has not been fixed yet. And I still have to get my aunts' approval.'

Joe Lee crushed her to him. 'Darling Lucy, tonight you will be my bride, then tomorrow we will face them together.' He picked her up bodily and lay down on the bunk with her, smoothing her hair, and kissing her lips. Unable to resist his passion Lucinda responded as sweet feelings of love overwhelmed her.

'Oh, Lucy, darling, be brave,' Joe Lee urged. 'If we miss this chance I feel sure I shall lose you, and then I will die.'

'Oh, don't be silly,' she murmured back. 'Be patient with me, Joe Lee, for I am so very scared.'

Joe Lee slid his hand down the neck of her dress and his lips sought her young firm bosom. 'Tonight, darling,' he whispered huskily. 'We will make the child that will hold us together forever.'

Lost in passion they tossed and turned on the narrow bunk. He kissed her everywhere and his hand caressed her thighs. Lucinda had closed her eyes and succumbed. She did not care any more, the indecision, the ache inside her, would all be gone.

In his gentle manner Joe Lee prepared Lucinda for that final stroke of love, for she was a virgin and he knew he had to be patient with her.

Lucinda moaned and slowly opened her eyes to look at her lover's kind face. But over his shoulder she suddenly caught sight of dumb Lukey leering down at them through the tiny porthole. His face was more distorted than usual as he stared with his tongue hanging out like some old mongrel on heat.

Lucinda sat up and screamed, pointing towards the porthole and gasping.

Instantly, Joe Lee ceased his love-making, and grabbed his pants to chase up the gangway after Lukey who had by now run off, hopping and jumping like a jack rabbit.

When Joe Lee returned, Lucinda had pulled her dress down but was weeping uncontrollably. All efforts on the part of Joe Lee to get her back on the bunk were to no avail.

'No, no,' she cried. 'Please, Joe Lee, leave me alone, I could never do that again.' The image of Lukey's ugly face swam before her eyes.

'But darling,' he protested, 'we are going to be married.'

'Well, let us wait until my aunts have given their consent,' she said, feeling more in control. 'I am sure I will feel more confident then.'

Joe Lee suddenly lost his temper. 'How naive can you be, Lucinda? They are already lining up a husband for you and it won't be me. No you will be wed to some oaf you do not love and just because your grandfather left you a dowry.'

Lucinda gazed apprehensively at him and pouted her lips. 'I'll never allow that,' she declared firmly.

Joe Lee sighed and caught her tight in his arms. 'Listen, my love, I have planned that we run away together. I'll not ask you to do anything you do not want to do, darling, but go gather a few possessions and sail with me when I return with my cargo in three days' time. I beg of you, Lucinda, make this decision, because I know if I sail away without you, you will belong to another on my return. If that happens,' he added with terrible passion, 'I shall kill him or myself and that will be the end of this love affair.'

Lucinda's eyes filled with dismay. 'Oh, don't Joe Lee. Please don't say such terrible things.'

'But I mean it, Lucinda. Sometimes I feel that you do not love me enough.'

'Oh, I *do* love you,' she cried, clinging childishly about his neck. 'But I am so afraid of everything.'

'Well, grow up, darling,' he said gently. 'Be ready and meet me at the other side of the bridge after dark tomorrow. Then we will sail away to happiness.'

Lucinda pondered for a while. If she stayed here at the inn she might never marry anyone or worse be tied to someone she did not love. She had no desire to live on that wretched old barge but she knew that she had to make a decision. 'I'll come with you,' she announced suddenly.

Joe Lee smiled and knelt before her. 'Oh, my love,' he said, 'I'll do all I can to make you happy. I am saving to buy a bigger ship which will sail the foreign seas and together you and I will dicover the treasures of the world.'

Content at last with her promise, Joe Lee walked with her to the bridge.

'When I catch that damned Lukey. I'll break his neck for what he did,' he jested.

Reminded of Lukey, Lucinda shivered and looked about her. She was really very afraid of him for he was so strange and was continually spying on her, often suddenly appearing as if out of nowhere.

With a swift embrace and another promise, Joe Lee and Lucinda parted. She ran swiftly over the bridge causing its rickety wooden boards to creak loudly in the dark night. At last she reached the inn. She crept in at the back door and ignoring an unusual commotion in the bar, ran up to her room on the second floor. Removing her crumpled dress, she sat down at the dressing table to brush her hair. She took one look in the mirror at her startled tear-stained face, and suddenly began to cry heart-brokenly, laying her head down on her arms. Suddenly, a little noise behind her made her jump and look round as the curtains in the bay window moved.

'Come out of there, Lukey!' she cried impatiently. Grabbing her hairbrush, she began to beat the curtains. There was a loud yelp as the brush struck home and there, from behind the curtains, stepped out Jack the Frenchie.

He caught her arm quickly and placed a finger to her lips.

'Hush, Lucinda, don't make a noise,' he whispered. 'The Redcoats are down in the bar searching for escapees. There was a mass break-out this evening and if I am caught here I will be shot.'

'Oh dear,' cried Lucinda looking about the room. 'Get under the bed, Jack.'

Lucinda was struck dumb and stared at the Frenchman in astonishment as he crawled under the pretty cretonne frill that decorated her bed. There he lay, his long shape very still, while Lucinda opened the door and peeped out into the passage.

Along the corridor bounced Aunt Beat with two armed Redcoats behind her. She was frowning and gesticulating angrily. 'There's no need to search up here,' she was grumbling. 'Why should I harbour those foreign devils here?' Then spotting Lucinda she cried: 'Inside your room, dear. I'll lock the door because you can't come out with all them bloody military fellas knocking about.'

The old soldier grinned but stood at the top of the stairs while Aunt Beat pushed Lucinda inside her room and locked her in. Inside, Lucinda stood for a moment looking amazed. Then she started to giggle. From under the bed, Jacques stuck out a foot and wiggled his toes, just to let her know that he thought it was funny too.

The noise downstairs in the bar continued for a while. Then everything went quiet, apart from the occasional musket shot out in the marsh as the Redcoats rounded up the escaped prisoners.

Dressed in a white camisole with pink ribbons and a long, white stiffly-starched petticoat, Lucinda sat on her bed. About her neck hung the little carved bone crucifix that the French prisoner had carved.

'This is so pretty,' she said, touching it gently. 'I always wear it.'

Jacques looked down at her small rounded breasts and desperately wanted to fondle them. But he controlled the urge to take Lucinda in his arms. 'I still cannot leave here,' he whispered 'for if I am caught out on the marsh it will be just as dangerous.'

'Go up in the loft,' said Lucinda. 'There is a truckle-bed up there and you can sleep till it's daylight.'

Jacques hesitated and smiled. 'You won't be afraid of me, little Lucinda?' His gaze was hot and inquiring.

'Why should I be afraid of you, Jack? We are friends,' Lucinda replied so innocently.

Jacques looked deep into her eyes and held them with his. 'Why were you weeping earlier,' he asked.

Sadly Lucinda lowered her gaze. 'I don't know if I can tell you,' she murmured.

'Ah, a secret lover!' he exclaimed.

'Yes, it's Joe Lee, the bargee,' she confessed. 'We have been courting a long time but Grandfather would not allow us to marry. He thought Joe Lee wasn't good enough.'

Jacques placed an arm about her waist. 'Do not worry, *ma chèrie*, with your beauty you can still find another lover.'

'Do you think I am beautiful, Jack?' Lucinda asked with childish coyness.

'I know you are!' Jacques rubbed his rough chin on her bare shoulder.

She shivered with excitement. 'Oh, don't!' she cried. 'It tickles.'

Jacques moved closer and gently caressed her bosom. When she pouted her rosy lips, he pressed a swift hot kiss on them.

Lucinda suddenly blushed and pulled away. 'Oh, dear,' she cried, 'I feel so wicked. You know, tonight I nearly let Joe Lee make real love to me.'

Jacques shrugged and smiled teasingly. 'I don't see why,' he said. 'It is a very honourable state to be in and it makes a man need you more.'

'But you know, Jack,' she said confidentially, 'I don't want to be a virgin, yet I could not let Joe Lee do it to me. Why?'

'Perhaps it is because he is an Englishman,' Jacques replied with a misty look in his eyes.

'Why, is there a difference?' queried Lucinda.

'Oh, very much so,' said Jacques as he pressed Lucinda down on the bed.

Lucinda struggled momentarily and then gave in to her passions which had been lying dormant within her, waiting to be roused for so long. Jacques was an expert at lovemaking. He made her feel wonderful: he guided her and reassured her.

Afterwards Lucinda lay back pacified while Jacques was very apologetic. But Lucinda put her arms around him and hugged him. 'Oh,' she cried, 'don't say sorry, Jack. It was the most wonderful experience. I'll never be afraid again.'

Jacques looked rather shame-faced and embarrassed at having taken advantage of this sweet innocent girl. 'Now Lucy,' he said, 'where is this attic? I'd better not stay down here in case one of your aunts arrives.'

As quietly as they could, they climbed the step ladder to the attic. The little room under the roof was very crowded. There was a rocking horse and lots of toys and an old cabin trunk full of old Amos' belongings. In the corner was a small bunk bed. Lucinda pointed to it and handed Jacques a candle so that he had some light. Holding the other candle, she turned to leave the attic. Jacques put out a gentle hand and held her. 'Well, little Lucy,' he said 'we have got all night now. Would you like some more lessons in love?'

Lucinda's heart jumped and she leaned towards Jacques' lean hard body. 'Oh, I feel so terribly wicked,' she sighed, as she subsided into his arms.

When dawn came bringing with it the birds twittering in the creepers outside the small window in the roof, the sun shone down on the lovers' naked bodies as they lay close together on that narrow bed. Entwined in each other's arms, they talked about the future. Jacques told Lucinda of his plans for escaping out of the country. 'I must get back to France to fight again,' he said. 'I must be there at the victory.'

'But are the French not our enemies?' enquired Lucinda.

'No one is *your* enemy, my beauty,' said Jacques, kissing her passionately.

'Is it possible that I did not ever love Joe Lee?' asked

Lucinda, a strong sense of guilt was beginning to nag her.

Jacques shrugged. 'It's possible but not likely,' he said with a laugh. Then he kissed her again. 'As sweet as you are, Lucinda, we might never meet again because I am determined to escape to France.'

She turned to him in dismay. 'But I am sure that it is *you* I love, not Joe Lee. Do not leave me, you cannot leave me,' she pleaded.

Jacques shook his head. '*Ma chèrie*, I must, but nevertheless you will not forget me.'

'I'll always remember you,' said Lucinda sadly. 'This morning I feel that life is still worth living, and I have been sad for so long.'

'Good, good,' Jacques fussed her as he might a child. 'Now, Lucy, you must help me. By now I have been posted as missing, so I'll not get back into the camp. And if I am caught out on the marsh they will not hesitate to shoot me down.'

'Oh, poor dear, what shall I do?' cried Lucinda.

'You must help me,' he said.

'But how?'

'If no one comes up here, I can hide for a few days until you find some means of getting me to the other side of the river. Then I can mingle with the troops embarking for France.'

'Is that possible?' Lucinda asked, very puzzled.

'We will make it possible,' he replied.

'But, Jack, I don't want you to go,' she said urgently.

'Lucy, dear, you must marry your Englishman,' he said wisely. 'My path lies in another direction. Now promise me you will help me escape.'

So Lucinda agreed. When Aunt Dot came to her niece's bedroom later that morning, Lucinda was lying in her own bed, the picture of sweet innocence.

'Come, Lucy, dear, there's work to be done,' beamed Aunty Dot as she bustled about, pulling back the curtains. 'Did you sleep well, dear? I do hope all that confusion last night did not worry you.'

'I'll be down soon, Auntie,' said Lucinda. She dressed

hurriedly and went down to the kitchen where she went about her chores singing very cheerfully.

'Happy this morning, ain't she?' remarked Beat. 'She's not usually so cheerful.'

'Be kind to her, Beat,' said Dot. 'She is such a baby.'

Out in the backyard Lukey was sitting on the ground snivelling. Earlier Beat had given him a good larruping with her slipper. 'As if I ain't got enough trouble,' she grumbled. 'Lukey goes missing, and then I discover he's opened the cellar door that leads to the old tunnel. No one is allowed to go in there. Father forbade it and now so do I.'

Lucinda pricked up her ears at this bit of news. 'Where does the tunnel lead to Aunt Dot?' she asked.

'Right out to Shulmead's Forge,' replied Dot. 'It was used for smuggling years ago. The monks built it when Wright's Farm was a priory.'

Then Lucinda recalled the door in the cellar which was always bolted and barred. She had a faint recollection of going through with her grandfather when she was a very small child, but she could not remember much about it. Now Lukey had found his way through the tunnel back to his old home which still lay empty. No wonder he managed to disappear so quickly.

Lucinda began to have an idea about how to help Jacques. If she could get him through the woods to the river and find someone to ferry him over it would be comparatively easy for him to escape. But whom could she trust?

While polishing the pewter pots her mind turned over all sorts of schemes until her thoughts were interrupted by a small voice at the back door. 'Could we have a pen'worth of ginger beer, please, Lucy?'

It was young John and with him was Kit. Both were dressed in ragged old pants and nothing else. They wore no shirts and no shoes.

'Oh, come in, dears,' cried Lucinda. 'Come and sit by the fire while I find something nice for you to eat.'

She hacked off some lumps of fresh bread and slapped

some butter on them. 'Now get on with that while I get your ginger beer,' she said kindly.

The two little boys sat tucking into the new bread, and when Lucinda returned with two cups of ginger beer,' and some stale cakes, their faces shone with gratitude.

'How is Toby?' Lucinda asked

'He can't walk,' John told her. 'He's living in Wally's cottage.'

'Where are you now? Back at the mill?'

They nodded. 'We got a new moulder. It's a man, but he's not so bad. We sleep in the cottage and Wally gives us food.'

'Poor little lads,' murmured Lucinda.

'John is going to take me to sea in his boat out on the saltings,' announced Kit proudly, his mouth full of food.

'How nice,' replied Lucinda, then a sudden thought flashed through her mind. Why, of course, little John was a born sailor. He had sailed the estuary all his life. 'When you come back, John, I want to see you alone,' she whispered.

Later that same evening she made plans with young John. 'This is a deep secret which you must keep. But I want you to take a friend of mine across the river at night. I will pay you for it, of course. Do you think you can do that?'

'With my eyes shut,' replied John. 'And I don't want to be paid, Lucinda. I am very glad to do something for you in return for your kindness to us.'

'No one must know, mind,' she warned.

'Your secret is safe with me,' returned young John in a very adult manner.

Lucinda was sure she could trust him, so that night she smuggled food and wine up to Jacques who was still hiding in the attic.

'This old tunnel, is it clear?' asked Jacques when Lucinda had told him about it.

'They say dumb Lukey has been in and out of it for some time.'

'I'll need some civilian clothes,' he informed her. 'Or I'll be spotted instantly.

Lucinda opened the old cabin trunk and produced some old thick breeches and a reefer jacket that Amos had worn in his sea-faring days, when he had been a lot thinner than he was at the end. They fitted Jacques well enough.

They spent that night in the narrow bed, again, and both shed tears of love.

'It is not going to be easy to part from you, Lucy,' Jacques said with real feeling.

'Oh, please come back when the war is over. I'll wait for you,' urged Lucinda. She was so full of love that the rendez-vous with Joe Lee was temporarily forgotten.

They made the last minute arrangements for Jacques' escape. It was to be the next evening at nine o'clock at high tide, when both the aunts would be busy in the bar.

At a quarter to nine on that fatal evening, Lucinda and Jacques crept down the stairs to the cellar, carrying a lantern.

'Stay here now, Lucy, I'll find my way,' he said.

Lucinda shook her head. 'No, Jack, I'll come with you to the end of the tunnel,' she said. 'If I remember correctly, it branches off at the end. One way goes on to Wright's Farm and the other goes to the Shulmead Forge. I went along there with my grandfather when I was little. I must come with you in case you take the wrong turning.'

Timidly she came up close to him and they crept slowly through the dusty tunnel towards freedom.

Out in the creek young John was waiting in his boat. The little craft was bobbing up and down on the rough water as the high tide came rushing in. Dark storm clouds floated on the high wind which was whipping up to a strong gale force. John tied up his boat, and lay down under the oilskin cover and waited patiently.

At the same time the *Alianora*, with sails flapping in the wind was also anchored in the creek. Joe Lee stood momentarily out on deck looking anxiously up at the changing sky before wading ashore to keep his rendezvous with Lucinda under the bridge.

He strolled along the edge of the dyke looking towards the

Shulmead Forge. The dark building looked very grim, and its tall, cold chimneys stood out starkly against the evening sky.

Then, to his astonishment, Joe Lee saw dumb Lukey running excitedly across the marsh towards him.

Joe Lee frowned. 'That swine! What's he up to now?' he growled. 'Tormenting Lucy, I'll be bound.'

As Lukey's panting figure approached, Joe Lee caught him by the scruff of the neck, Lukey's eyes were crossed, and he was foaming at the mouth, pointing and gesticulating in the direction of the deserted forge.

'What the hell's the matter?' demanded Joe Lee, releasing him. 'Where is Lucy?'

Lukey crouched on the ground, mouthing strange panic-stricken noises.

A terrible sense of foreboding washed over Joe Lee. Without a moment's hesitation, 'My God,' he muttered, 'something has happened to Lucy.' He began to run towards the forge and its outbuildings.

Suddenly Joe Lee stopped in his tracks. For there standing in the doorway of the barn spotlighted by the rising moon, was his darling Lucinda in the arms of another.

Leaning close to each other and quite oblivious to anything else, Jacques and Lucinda made their last farewell. The tunnel had led them out into the Shulmead barn and this was where they had to part.

'I'll never ever forget you, Jack,' whispered Lucinda.

The words had no sooner left her lips when a large figure, hurled itself at them mouthing some swearwords, and grabbing Jacques about the neck. Jacques literally was hurled away from Lucinda and fell to the ground, while Lucinda, terrified of the rage on Joe Lee's face, dashed back into the barn.

Jacques stumbled to his feet and started to run but Joe Lee was quickly on his back, a dagger in his hand. Grunting loudly, the two men rolled over and over in the grip of death, while their terrified lady love sped back along the tunnel towards home and safety.

But the candle in the lantern had burned down and it flickered precariously as Lucinda crept along the tunnel's uneven floor. It cast a poor light and Lucinda was so intent on watching where she trod, for fear of falling, that she did not notice Lukey's huddled figure lying in wait for her. He was upon her in a flash, his mouth foaming, his eyes wild, as he pulled her to the ground with superhuman strength and began to tear at her flesh. Dumb Lukey's sexual instincts were running amok.

Lucinda screamed and struggled in blind panic. The lantern fell to the floor and the candle was extinguished leaving her at the mercy of this monster in total darkness.

But neither of her lovers heard Lucinda's bloodcurdling cries. They were both too busy trying to murder each other as they fought and rolled over and over on the rough ground. Joe Lee's dagger pierced Jacques' side and wet blood soaked the grass beneath them, but with a last terrific heave, Jacques managed to drive his foot into Joe Lee's groin with tremendous force. With a mighty yell, Joe fell backward over the bank, struck his head hard on the thick root of an old oak tree, and lay still.

Jacques pulled himself to his feet and staggered off into the woods clutching his side and leaving a heavy trail of blood behind him. Desperately he battled against the rising wind in his last bid for freedom. Struggling to find his way down to the shore, he lost the way to the path and lost his fight. In the distance he could hear voices and the baying of bloodhounds on the trail of his blood. The Redcoats knew he was out there and would make sure that there were no more escaping prisoners in the woods. Within minutes the hounds were upon him, dragging him down and mauling him viciously. Jacques' untimely but by then welcome end came from the musket of an over-zealous private, who finished him off.

The Redcoats then dragged Jacques' blood-soaked and mutilated body back to their camp and buried him in the communal grave with the rest of his compatriots who had met their deaths out on that wild marsh.

Joe Lee's body was found early the next morning. His neck

had been broken. He was carried back to the hamlet, his young face looking quite serene; he had given his life for love, just as he threatened to do.

It was when news of Joe Lee's death reached the inn that Aunt Dot went up to see how Lucinda was and found her bed empty. The sisters panicked.

'Oh my God!' cried Beat, 'I warned her about that fella. She must have gone out to meet him.'

'Hush,' declared Dot, trying to control herself. 'Whatever we felt about him, we must not speak ill of the dead.'

'Oh, be quiet,' snapped Beat. 'Anything might have happened. She could have been murdered,' she wailed.

As word got around of Lucinda's disappearance, a search party was organised. But with no result. No one had seen her. They searched the house and the marsh all around for hours until admitting defeat and giving up. Then early the next morning, Dot suddenly heard a sound coming from the cellar. She rushed down to find Lucinda lying in the entrance to the tunnel. With almost her last ounce of strength, she had managed to drag herself along the tunnel and push open the heavy door. With her clothes ripped and her face and hair filthy, she now lay groaning on the floor. Aunt Dot fainted with fright but Beat, who was behind her and made of sterner stuff, instantly picked up her niece and carried her upstairs to bed. The doctor was called and, after he had examined Lucinda, announced that a maniac had raped and savaged this innocent girl.

'Oh dear God,' wept Dot. 'Will she live?'

'Probably,' the doctor replied 'but I would not like to predict whether she will ever be the same again. An animal, a positive fiend, has attacked her, madam. The scars on her body will heal with time but not those on her mind.

'She must be kept very quiet and no mention of this terrible happening must be made until she is fully recovered. And don't let her look in any looking-glass for the sight of her mutilated face, which was once so lovely, will be enough to shock her all over again.'

That evening in the bar, the customers were baying for blood. 'This maniac must be caught and brought to justice,' one man said, emphatically.

The others agreed. But who was to blame? Not Joe Lee, for they knew that he had died defending his love.

'They said an escaped French prisoner killed Joe Lee,' someone said. 'Then the Redcoats shot him, and a good job, too.'

And so it became the general opinion of the locals that, it was that French bastard, Jacques, who had brought such tragedy to the hamlet. And the questions raised were debated everywhere, from the inn and the farm to the cottages and back again.

And the horrors of the previous night were added to when it was discovered that young John Shulmead was missing as well. When Kit was questioned about the whereabouts of his friend, the lad knew nothing except that John had taken the boat out that evening. The stormy night had surely ensured the boy's death. Certainly neither he nor the little boat were anywhere to be seen. It was concluded that he had been swept out to sea and drowned.

So the next day in the Malted Shovel this additional tragedy of John Shulmead was discussed, and everyone mourned for that lively little lad as well as for Lucinda who still lay upstairs unconscious, with Aunt Dot sitting anxiously by her side.

Later that day Beat noticed that dumb Lukey had not done his chores, and she went looking for him. After about an hour, she found him lying down in the dyke covered in mud but with an extraordinary expression of joy on his face. It made her spine tingle. Beat got hold of a hefty stick and beat Lukey all the way back to the inn. She made him change his clothes and get back to work. Whatever Beat thought, no one else had reason to suspect that dumb Lukey had anything to do with that dreadful night's work.

The excitement of that stormy night in June had scarcely died down when the news of a big battle in France swept through the hamlet of Hollinbury. It was to be the testing ground for the defeat of Napoleon who had gathered together another army and stood opposing the might of England at Waterloo. The locals all liked to natter about it but it made little difference to their everyday lives. All they cared about were their opinions. Otherwise it was all business as usual.

Upstairs at the Malted Shovel, in her neat little bedroom, Lucinda still lay pale and silent. The bruises on her face and body had begun to heal but she was tormented by memories of that terrible night. The doctor was right; it was doubtful that she could ever fully recover psychologically even after the physical scars had gone.

Under the strain, the two aunts were constantly at loggerheads with each other. Aunt Dot blamed Beat for her severity with Lucinda, while Aunt Beat retaliated by insisting that it was all Dot's fault for having filled Lucinda's head with a lot of romantic nonsense.

But Lucinda never heard any of these frequent rows. She just lay in her bed like a sick child, always silent apart from a few pathetic weeping fits when she was persuaded to take nourishment.

Night after night, Aunt Dot sat beside Lucinda's bed watching anxiously as her niece tossed and turned, moaning unintelligibly in her sleep. Then one day, hoping to rouse Lucinda from her lethargy, Dot put her into Amos' old bathchair and pushed her out along the passage. Dumb Lukey had been sweeping the landing and was now crouching at the top of the stairs. At the sight of him, Lucinda let out an ear-splitting scream and twisted helplessly in the bathchair in a frantic effort to get away.

Aunt Beat came running upstairs to find out what was wrong, Lucinda flung herself on the floor, covering her face with her hands to shut out the sight of Lukey, who had by now fled.

'Whatever frightened her?' asked Beat.

'I don't know, it was only Lukey,' replied Dot, very puzzled.

The two women carried Lucinda back to bed. 'That Lukey's enough to frighten the bloody devil himself,' declared Beat. 'Wait till I get my hands on him. I've told him time and time again that he is not to come upstairs.' Even though Beat suspected Lukey of many things, they did not include attacking her beloved niece.

Lucinda was eventually calmed and the mystery of her attacker remained a deadly secret. But Beat sometimes eyed dumb Lukey in an odd way as though she were thinking of past incidents. But she quickly dismissed any suspicions. After all, Lukey was scarcely a man, and what had happened to Lucinda had been a sexual assault. According to the doctor it was entirely possible that Lucinda was pregnant. So who was the father, if this was so? Was it Joe Lee or a strange Frenchman from the prison camp. Jack the Frenchie had not been around recently but he had often looked longingly at Lucinda, Beat thought. And Beat was no fool. She saw what went on about her. Had there been something between Jack and Lucinda? Had it been a love tangle? Oh, one could never tell, Lucinda was so pretty but so impossibly naive in the affairs of the world. Perhaps it was their fault that they had sheltered her so much, but they had really had to, what with her mother having been so very wayward.

The Battle of Waterloo was won and, like the rest of the country, the hamlet celebrated the victory over the French down in the public bar. The Redcoats were also there so Beat took the opportunity to ask questions of the sergeant who was off duty from the fort. 'Was it you who found Joe Lee's body?' she asked.

'No, my men brought him in. I was out in the woods rounding up the prisoners. We got one fellow who was already wounded but one of my men finished him off. Goodbye to bad rubbish, I say,' he sniffed.

'Did he have a name?' asked Beat.

'No, only a number, but the funny thing was that when we brought him in he was wearing a reefer jacket and an old-fashioned pair of breeches. I can't think where he got them from. He must have planned his escape well. Still, it did not work and it's too late now anyway, France is finished. Napoleon won't fight again.'

That night, on a hunch, Beat climbed up into the attic and looked into the cabin trunk. Not surprised with what she discovered, she went down to Lucinda's room and stared down at the sleeping girl.

'You was up to something, girl,' she murmured. 'Darned if I know what it was, but it looks like you got to face the consequences, poor little soul.'

Then Beat went in search of Lukey, who was sitting on his bed down in the cellar playing with his penis until it stood stiff and upright.

'Why, you naughty boy!' cried Aunt Beat, grabbing a copper stick and beginning to beat him.

Lukey grovelled on the floor and moaned ecstatically. To Beat's horror, he seemed to enjoy his beating. His hand slipped up under her voluminous skirts and he tried to grab her between the legs.

'Why, you devil!' exclaimed Beat, leathering him soundly. 'God in heaven, what am I going to do with you?'

But now Lukey was lying back on the bed exhausted. With a worried expression on her face, Beat went up the ladder to the bar and poured herself a stiff glass of port. 'Glory be to God,' she whispered. 'It could have been him after all. What am I going to do?'

The heat was terrible that summer. The cornfields lay shimmering in a hot sun and the workers sweated as they laboured to bring in the harvest. The victory celebrations had long passed and the toll of the battle was now known as each day relations were notified that a son or husband would return no more but would lie buried forever in a foreign field.

The news that Matthew and Mark Shulmead had been amongst those to fall at the battle of Waterloo was a terrible shock to the hamlet, especially after the sad death of young John.

'Dear God, what an unlucky family,' remarked Aunt Dot.

'As ye sow, so shall ye reap,' quoted Beat in a grumpy manner.

Wally was now back as a regular visitor to the Malted Shovel, having nursed young Toby back to health and obtained jobs for him and Kit on the Wrights' farm. They now lived with him in his cottage and Wally was very fond of his boys.

'T'was a pity about young John,' he remarked. 'He was a fine boy, the best of the bunch, was John. But what he was doing out in that boat in a storm, only God knows.'

'Well, they are all gone now,' said Beat, busy as always wiping the counter and collecting the tankards. Then she suddenly stood still. 'Except for dumb Lukey, that is. He is the only survivor,' she said.

'I often wonder what will happen about the Shulmead property,' said Wally. 'It's fine arable land and the forge is strongly built. I wonder what will be done about it.'

'Well, it must belong to dumb Lukey,' declared Beat. 'It must do. Why else have they left it lie fallow? Them city lawyers was waiting for Mark to turn up. The old man did not leave a will and Mark was the eldest.'

'But Lukey's potty,' said Dot. 'The property will not be any good to him.'

Beat turned on her furiously. 'Why not? Lukey's got rights, ain't he? And besides, who has fed and cared for him this past year? Why, *I* have, and I think I must be entitled to some compensation.'

'Don't know as how that his inheritance will be worked out,' pondered Wally. 'If Lukey is not fit enough to claim it, it will go into chancery and then the law will get it, I suppose.'

'Not while I am able bodied,' declared Beat. 'If Lukey's got an inheritance, he will claim it. I shall see to that.'

So Aunt Beat talked the matter of Lukey's inheritance over with the curate who in turn negotiated the case with a lawyer.

It was suggested by the two men that the property be sold and the proceeds turned over to some institution which would take care of Lukey for the rest of his life. But for reasons of her own, Beat did not like this idea and she fought tooth and nail against it. Eventually she persuaded the village doctor to write a letter declaring that Lukey Shulmead was quite capable of handling his own affairs.

By the time the heat of summer had died down and the chill winds had begun to blow over the marsh, Lucinda could now sit at her bedroom window with a shawl about her shoulders. A fresh blue ribbon was tied in her hair which hung down over her tummy, now swollen with life.

Dumb Lukey swaggered about the hamlet in the new tweed suit and brown boots that Beat had bought for him. Lukey was now a person of considerable means in the hamlet. He owned forty acres of farmland and a workable forge. There was also a cottage which Aunt Beat persuaded him to let out to a family of horse traders while the land was leased to another farmer.

Dumb Lukey himself did not seem to be aware of this change in his circumstances but the fact that he now shared Aunt Beat's bed some nights certainly pleased him very much indeed.

When Aunt Dot learned of these goings on, she was very shocked, 'Beatrice!' she commented, 'I am disgusted at you.'

'Shut your mouth!' retorted Beat. 'He's a man, ain't he? Ain't he got some feelings? Besides, I still ain't too old.'

'We all know that it's dumb Lukey's legacy that is most interesting to you,' Dot said tartly. 'All I can say, is that let's hope some good will come of this terrible business.'

Beat sniffed. 'It might surprise you to know that I am going to marry Lukey after Christmas when he is twenty-one,' she said defiantly. 'And you can put that in your pipe and smoke it.'

Shaking her head disapprovingly, Dot went upstairs to sit with Lucinda. Next to the young girl's listless shape, Dot sat crocheting a shawl for the baby who was due in the spring.

CHAPTER NINE

The Methodist

Alice was as long and thin as a bean pole. Her skin still had a yellowy tinge from the ravages of the brickfields, and there were clay burn scars on her long swan-like neck. Yet she was not unattractive. She had her mother's thick black gypsy hair, a pair of large dark brown eyes and a wide quick smile. And although her teeth were yellow from the effects of the clay, they were also straight and very strong. Her only disconcerting feature was a rather knobbly nose which was possibly inherited from her father.

'My, Alice, how thin you are!' declared Ruth Anneslee at the Mission. 'We must feed you up a bit and put some flesh on those bones.' Then Ruth took hold of Alice's thick mop of hair in her gentle hands and cried. 'Well, for the love of God, what are we going to do with these unruly tresses?'

Alice flashed a charming smile. 'Cut it all off,' she said gently. 'I don't care.'

'No, I couldn't do that, it would be such a pity,' declared Ruth. So she brushed it flat and wound it round Alice's head in a tight knot and placed a small bonnet on her head. 'Now, dear, see how tidy you look? Cleanliness is next to godliness,' she gusted. 'Here is your own soap and face cloth, and a toothbrush, which will bring up those nice teeth lovely and white.'

Alice was amazed. Soap had been a rarely seen luxury in Larlee's cottage and one face cloth did for all the inhabitants.

Now dressed neatly in her straw bonnet and a brown serge dress, Alice went each day with Ruth to the mission hall, while her baby stayed at the Anneslees' home, tucked up clean and comfy, and cared for by the jolly cook-housemaid, who loved him on sight. So Alice was free to set out each morning with Ruth walking around the town giving solace to the poor and hungry and encouraging children from the back alleys to come to Sunday school. Ruth would say to them kindly: 'You must come clean and tidy, but Jesus will be there to love and comfort you.'

So on Sundays the little ones would come and sit wide-eyed as Ruth explained the rudiments of her religion to them, and Alice led them in singing simple hymns such as, 'Jesus loves me. Yes, I know for the Bible tells me so.' Then afterwards, Alice would stand at the door as they all left, giving each one a boiled sweet from out of a large tin. And to the very ragged little ones, Ruth would whisper: 'Come around to my house tonight, dear, I've got a nice dress that will fit you nicely.'

In the evenings Alice and Ruth sat sewing and sorting out the old secondhand clothes bequeathed by Ruth's numerous friends. Alice would sew, wash and iron these garments with infinite patience, for she was happiest when she was most busy and so she took to the environment of this Methodist family easily and readily. The past and its unhappiness were very soon forgotten.

Ben Anneslee was well-known in that area as a Methodist preacher. He also ran a night school, to help educate the illiterate working class for whom there were very few free schools to improve their minds. Many of them could not read at all but worked very hard and there were several who reached great academic heights having first begun their education at night school. Ben was an enthusiastic teacher and gave wholeheartedly his knowledge of religion to his pupils and taught them the rudimentary elements of reading and writing. Like his ancestor, John Wesley, he lived only to improve the lives of the socially deprived, considering it to be his duty and the lot of God's workers. Alice also attended this night school and was making good progress.

It was in this pleasant hard-working atmosphere that Alice thrived. Nowadays no one would have recognized her as that poor little drab from the brick fields. She was bright and cheerful and now full of self-confidence. But always deep down in her heart she had an overwhelming feeling of compassion for the less fortunate, those who had no chance of escape as she had. To her this clean orderly life was wonderful. It was so different from her own poverty-stricken background, where most of the money, so hard-earned in the brickfields, went straight into the tavern.

Her lovely little boy Adam could now stand up, walk a few steps and say 'Mama,' and he was a joy to have around. The Anneslees had a little girl called Faith, who was six months younger than Adam. Faith was a very sweet-natured baby and was fair and pretty next to Adam, who was dark and sturdy.

Ben and Ruth, Alice's surrogate parents were as kind as anyone could be to her. Every morning, with his mop of frizzy brown hair and his bushy beard, Ben sat reading out aloud from the daily paper. Ruth sat next to Alice, her neat blonde head bowed and her eyes cast down as she listened to the news patiently. This was the daily breakfast routine. First Ben would read the newspaper's glorified accounts of the victory at Waterloo. There was never any mention in them of the many bodies still lying unburied on the battlefield, or any mention of the widows and orphans left behind, nor of the dire distress and poverty they lived in. There was just an ode to England, a great and glorious country and an account of how pleased the Prince Regent was at the success of his regiment, even though he had never even seen a battleground.

'Oh, dear God,' sighed Ruth, when Ben had ended his long narrative, 'how sickening is human society. The fact that one man must kill another never ceases to amaze me.'

'It is often the case of kill or be killed — even the Old Testament explains that.' Ben, replied a trifle pompously.

'Nevertheless, I am very much against war,' replied Ruth firmly.

'Ah, blessed is the peacemaker,' murmured Ben with a soft smile. He turned back to his newspaper and was silent while he perused it. Suddenly he cried out. 'Well, well, listen to this long letter about the children who slave in the brick fields. Apparently there has been an accident out in the marshes. A kiln blew up, burying some of the children.'

Alice glanced up with fear in her eyes. She knew what Ben was going to say next.

'It's at a place called Hollinbury,' he said, 'down near St Mary's Marsh.'

'I know the place,' said Ruth, with a sad nod of her head.

Tears were now flooding Alice's eyes but she said nothing more.

'Well, well,' exclaimed Ben. 'This is a surprise. The author of the letter is my old friend and colleague, George Gibbs.'

'The one you were at the Academy with?' asked Ruth. 'I can well believe it is he. He was a born campaigner. His sister lives in Kent. I remember that she married a farmer.'

Once more Alice's fine eyes looked up. Her mouth quivered but she made no sound. Her heart fluttered in her breast as she recalled her trip to the village fair, the reason for her mother's anger and subsequently her departure from home. No, she was not sorry, she had no regrets at leaving that grim home. But an accident at the kiln . . .

'Well, read out the letter, Ben,' requested Ruth.

Ben cleared his throat and began to read in a loud voice.

Dear reader,

I have recently returned from the brickfields in Kent where several children lie dead with many others injured. Rather, if you are a father in comfortable circumstances, imagine if you will, your own little boy, still scarcely old enough to go to boarding school, eight or not yet nine, compelled to rise at five o'clock each morning and prepare for thirteen hours work. Think of him toiling under the blazing sun, carrying that heavy load of clay on his head. Think also, dear reader, of that weary little worker hurried on by savage acts, angry words and cruel blows. Then when at last the toil-worn day is over the little ones almost too weary to walk, to crawl home to bed to sleep and rise again to face another toiling day. Such is the fare of the little brickyard boy. Also, I have seen half-naked girls carrying heavy clay loads, remorselessly hurried on to keep pace with an ogre who fashioned the bricks, repeatedly asking for more. Instead of staggering half-nude with such burdens, these young girls should be at school or be trained at home.

This matter cannot be allowed to continue. We must have a Parliamentary Commission to inquire into this whole dastardly business.

I beg you, Christian people. Listen to the cries of our small brickyard child slaves.

George Gibbs

When Ben had ended his reading, Alice took out her handkerchief and wiped her eyes. But Ruth sprang up as if in a fierce temper, the colour mounting in her pale cheeks. 'Oh, Ben, it's monstrous! It's heathen! We have to *do* something about it.' Her voice was urgent and strong.

'There's not much we can do,' explained Ben. 'It is not illegal. It's the law of the land.'

'But surely something can be done to prevent the employment of the young,' insisted Ruth.

'There are a few religious bodies anxious to help but their hands are tied,' said Ben. 'George Gibbs is a fine fellow and the one most likely to be able to do something. Write to him, Ruth, and ask him to come and dine with us next time he is in Kent.'

Ruth had noticed Alice's distress. She placed a gentle hand on Alice's arm and smoothed those deep unsightly scars on her face. Ruth had never probed into the girl's background, but she had a pretty clear idea of what terrible experiences Alice had had in the past. 'Now, Alice,' she said gently. 'Do not weep. God will provide the means and we will have justice for all those forgotten children.'

Alice kissed Ruth softly on the cheek but still remained

silent, keeping her heartbreak all wrapped up deep inside.

With such warm compassion Ruth and Ben continued their good works, Ben teaching evening classes to anyone who wished to learn to read and write, and Ruth caring for the children of the district and spreading the religious teachings.

Each month in the Anneslees' newspaper was a long letter to the editor from George Gibbs appealing to the church, the British worker and anyone else who might listen to his demands that children should not be employed in the brick-yards. Every letter was carefully cut out and kept by Alice, who stuck them into a scrapbook to re-read at her leisure. In no time at all she had learned most of them by heart and could quote the lovely phrases he used such as 'From early morn till late at night these tiny Amazons rush hither and thither with the burdens of clay serving a boss who is as insatiable as the grave,' and 'the beggars and thieves have their champion,' or 'but who will champion those little slaves of clay?' All these fine words were digested by Alice's fertile mind until she felt as if she shared herself with George Gibbs.

As England slowly recovered in the aftermath of those long years of war with France, the soldiers began to return, ragged and tired, their bodies often covered with festering wounds. They joined the general population of the homeless and hungry, who would congregate in the market square, Dart-ford being a centre point between London and Dover. The swelling numbers of needy kept Ben and Ruth very busy, and Ruth would be busy ten hours a day with perspiration oozing from her fair skin as she set about her tasks. By the end of the day she would be so weary and wan that she could barely stand, but great faith and determination egged her on.

It was in this atmosphere that Alice's character was moulded. With her enormous amount of energy, no task was too heavy as long as it helped Ruth. The lame, the lousy, the helpless and the hungry, no one was too much for them. 'Only God knows what it must be like in the big towns,' Ruth would sometimes remark. 'At times I think we are wasted here.'

Alice seldom spoke unless it was absolutely necessary but

she would look up at Ruth with those soulful eyes and Ruth would murmur a passage from her testament: 'Whither thou goest, so will I go.' So sure was she of the love and loyalty of Alice.

One day Ben announced that George Gibbs was coming to the town soon and would join the Anneslees for dinner. Ruth's clear grey eyes lighted up at this news and her small mouth gave an amused twist. 'Well now, Alice,' she said, 'I do believe that our good Lord will forgive us if we indulge ourselves a little on this festive occasion. I have a mind for a new dress. Would that be approved of by you, dear husband?' she asked, turning to Ben with a smile.

'My dear Ruth,' Ben jested, 'if you are in mind for a new gown, I am sure my displeasure will not stop you.'

'There now, listen to him, Alice, one would think I was a wayward woman. But we will meet our guest in proper manner. Now,' pondered Ruth, 'I wondered if my best lawn dress could be altered to fit you, Alice, dear. You *are* such a lanky specimen that I shall probably need several yards of material to lengthen it. But we will take a bit of time off and go shopping.'

The shopping trip to the centre of town was an exciting adventure for Alice, who had never been into shops before. Timidly she followed Ruth's trim shape bustling along looking for the cheapest store to buy material for her new dress. Alice was amazed by the display of hats and bonnets all trimmed with gaily coloured feathers and flowers. She stared aghast at the lace trimmings and long leather gloves, and other luxuries she had never even known existed.

Ruth was appalled by the prices. 'Dear God!' she whispered. 'One pound for a pair of gloves? Who on earth can afford such extravagances when others are dying of hunger?'

Eventually Ruth bought several yards of pink-and-white spotted muslin for her new gown, and two yards of plain blue silk with which to lengthen her own dress for Alice. Then, feeling pleased with their purchases, and still with some change from a sovereign, the two women went happily back home.

Later that evening, when the affairs of the mission were all in order and their children safe in bed, Ruth and Alice sat sewing their garments. They cut and fitted Ruth's dress, and Alice sewed the seams with a neat stitch while Ruth made buttonholes. They added tiny rosettes and an indulgent posy of pink ribbon that nestled on the shoulder. The soft folds of white muslin swept the floor with a soft rustle as Ruth paraded in her new gown.

'My, my,' mocked Ben from behind his newspaper. 'Such sinfulness, woman, you know that vanity is one of the worst of the deadly sins.'

Ruth stood still as the colour flashed her cheeks, 'Oh, Ben, don't jest,' she stammered. 'I feel such a deep sense of guilt. I am sure that I should have made do with my old dress.'

Ben rose and put his arms about her. No words were uttered. The quick gentle caress was all Ruth needed for re-assurance.

'Thank you, dear husband,' she murmured, her eyes down-cast. Then she brightened up and smiled. 'Well, now, dear Alice, why don't you put on your new dress and allow my husband to comment on it.'

Alice held the white lawn dress over her arm. A deep blue frill had been added and tiny rosettes added to the lengthened sleeves. 'I'd rather not,' she said shyly. 'I'd much prefer to wait until the evening your guest arrives.' She spoke so quietly her voice was scarcely audible.

'It's all right, darling,' said Ruth. 'We were only playing. Let us go and look to our lovely babies.'

Together they left the room, arms linked, to visit the nursery where fat and bonny Adam slept peacefully beside Ruth's angelic fair little girl, Faith. Alice's heart swelled with happiness. There was such love in this home, combined with a deep humility.

The day that George Gibbs came to supper was indeed a special day. There was a joint of lamb to roast and sweet cakes to make, in addition to the usual chores. Their special guest was due to arrive at eight o'clock. By seven, the parlour table was laid with the best silver and glass, and Ruth was dressed in her pretty new gown and putting the finishing touches to her floral decorations. Ben had gone to the coaching inn to meet George Gibbs.

Upstairs Alice brushed smooth her long dark hair and placed a blue comb in it. Her tall lean figure was set off by the close-fitting gown. The dress had two deep frills at the hem in a pretty shade of blue which contrasted nicely with the white lawn. When she was ready she went downstairs and stood shyly in the doorway waiting for Ruth's opinion of her appearance.

When Ruth saw her, her reaction was spontaneous. 'Oh dear,' she cried, 'why Alice, you look absolutely lovely!'

Alice's velvet brown eyes filled with tears. She had never been admired before.

A noise in the hall told them that the men had arrived. Alice stood, as still as a statue, as the gentle George Gibbs greeted her courteously. He looked a little curiously at her and seemed puzzled as though he wasn't sure if they had met before or not. Alice said nothing to enlighten him, she just stared momentarily into his grey eyes, and then turned modestly away.

'Alice is my wife's companion and our dearest friend,' announced Ben.

'I am most honoured to meet you,' George Gibbs murmured.

Alice's heart jumped high as her mind travelled back to the village fair and the pleasant young man who had knocked down coconuts just to please small Toby. But still not one word did she utter.

Dinner was a very relaxed affair and while the men were left to their port, Ruth and Alice withdrew and whispered together, agreeing that George Gibbs was certainly a very nice gentleman. Alice's mind felt very alert; it had been the most stimulating evening of her life.

'I sincerely hope you will honour us with another visit soon,' said Ben, as George was preparing to go.

'I will indeed,' replied George gravely. 'I do so little socialising. My time in the Midlands is spent with the poor folk. Some change must certainly be made in our social systems. Currently the conditions that human beings live in are a disgrace.'

'I agree, sir,' said Ben. 'We are a little better off down south, there is such dire poverty, it is no wonder that people forsake God.'

'I am most concerned with the treatment of our youth,' said George. 'We work them to death or starve them into crime. What future is there for a country that treats its coming generation in that way?'

'What can we do but pray and try to feed those in need?' returned Ben.

George's eyes seemed to burn fiercely. 'I intend to change matters, even if it takes me all my life to get the government to intervene on behalf of the brickyard children. Such immorality and degradation exists in these places. Even if he lives to maturity, what chance does a child have of becoming an upright citizen?'

'But thank you, my friend, for a most interesting evening,' said George warmly grasping Ben's hand. 'By the way,' he asked, as he turned to the door, 'is your friend Alice from these parts? I feel I have met her before.'

Ben shrugged. 'Ruth and I do not probe into others' lives,' he said. 'Alice is a grand person yet so very sad. It's as if something were eating at her very heart.'

'Give her my regards, Ben,' said George as he set off into the night. 'And tell her I hope to meet her again.'

CHAPTER TEN

Weddings and Epidemics

Farmer Wright's trees were in full bloom. The cherry trees scattered pink flowers over the green grass and its fragrant perfume filled the air. At the end of the lane, in the parish church at Hollinbury, a strange scene was being enacted as the hamlet's idiot was married to an elderly spinster.

Farm labourers stood and stared, barely able to believe their eyes, as the wedding procession came down the cobbled path to stop by the lych-gate to receive congratulations from the congregation.

For on this day, Beatrice Dell, spinster of this parish, aged forty-seven years, was joined in holy matrimony to Luke Shulmead, bachelor, aged twenty-one years.

The wedding was the talk of Hollinbury hamlet for many years. And what a sight they made — Aunt Beat in a flowered dress and bonnet, and dumb Lukey all dressed up in a new woollen suit! There was poor dumb Lukey, who could not speak, let alone read or write, and who had to sign the marriage document with an 'X'. There he stood, with a huge red carnation in his buttonhole, standing simpering and giggling beside Beat who held him firmly by the arm and looked grimly at the onlookers.

'Well,' declared old Wally, 'I've yet to see the like o' that.'

'Oh dear,' giggled the fair milkmaid Dolly. 'I wonder how he will manage on his first night!'

Kit, now a tall fair cowman, frowned down at Dolly as though he thought her remark rather unmaidenly.

Dolly smirked and leaned on the farm gate to gape. Her fair bosom under her cotton dress rose and fell rapidly with the excitement of it all. Kit's heart warmed as he looked at her and forgave her everything. Beside him, was Toby, his small brother whose leg, since the accident, had grown bent and stunted. As a result his body had a slightly grotesque shape but his lovely hazel eyes were clear and bright and his smile was charming.

'I think this is very sad,' said Toby. 'Everyone knows, that old Beat is only marrying Lukey to get her hands on the Shulmead property.'

'Aye, you are right there, lad,' butted in Wally. 'But there will be free drinks in the inn, so what are we hanging about for?' So in his long smock and straw hat, Wally made his way to the Malted Shovel to claim his share of the spoils. And with him went his two unofficially adopted sons, Kit and Toby, while Dolly retired sulkily back to the farmhouse, knowing that she would never be allowed in the tavern.

Jenny Wright had done a good job in rescuing Dolly from the slavery of the brick fields. Almost sixteen, Dolly was an excellent dairy maid. She was well-mannered and could even read and write — rare talents in those days.

High up in the attic in the Malted Shovel sat Aunt Dot. She had refused to attend the wedding. Her hair was now silver and her face a mass of tired lines. In her lap she rocked and crooned to Lucinda's son, pressing his black curly head against her breast as she sang him a lullaby. Three-year-old Percy Amos snuggled up close, his bright eyes full of mischief. Aunt Dot was butter in his small hands, he could do practically anything he liked with her.

Percy's mother, Lucinda, now lay in her grave, between her own mother and her beloved grandmother. The birth of that lusty babe had proved too much for her. On that terrible night when he had torn his way out of her young body, she had whispered her last words. 'I am here, Joe Lee.' With that, she left this sordid world behind.

Aunt Beat had surveyed the newborn child with a grim expression. 'He is a Shulmead, if ever I saw one,' she muttered. 'He looks just like the old smithy himself.'

Aunt Dot took the motherless babe in her arms, and from that moment, all her love for poor Lucinda was now poured into Lucinda's son. 'Let him be called Percy after the poet Shelley,' she said, her romantic streak asserting itself.

Beat sniffed. 'Father's good name is good enough for him,' she argued fiercely.

So after much debating, the child was given both names and now, at three years old, he ruled the roost at the Malted Shovel.

Now on this particular day Aunt Beat had kept her word and married dumb Lukey to keep him safe and to secure his legacy. Already there was quite a bit of money, for Beat had accumulated wealth by letting out the forge and the surrounding farmlands that went with the house. The folk in Hollinbury were astonished. Aunt Beat was a much respected member of the community, yet she had married Lukey for what they saw as purely materialistic reasons. But their surprise and disapproval did not stop them from joining in with festivities as the inn gave out free beer and Aunt Beat got drunk and danced the hornpipe with a sailor home on leave. Hollinbury, it was decided, could live with such an odd matrimonial match.

A few weeks later, young Dolly watched the sun rise over the marsh behind the golden clouds which were swept along by a stiff wind. In the distance she could see the silver strip of the Thames and the faint shadows of the barges as they sailed down on the morning tide. Dolly stood dreaming by the farm gate. This was no special morning, and she barely noticed the beauty that surrounded her, having risen at dawn for a number of years now, ever since she had left the squalor of her mother's cottage, and the hard labour of the brick fields.

She would be seventeen in August and she cut a fine figure. Her breasts were high and her waist trim. Long golden hair was tucked under a snow-white cap. As she waited for Kit to bring in the cows for milking, the rest of the milkmaids giggled and gossiped in the milking shed. But Dolly was in a serious mood; she wanted to think clearly about her future.

The night before Kit had lain with her in the sweet-smelling hay loft and passionately declared his love for her, his dark brown eyes shining with sincerity. He told her that he wanted to marry her that harvest time, when he was eighteen. They would both be very young, he knew, but people in service did marry young. The masters preferred it that way. Kit was now a labourer on Farmer Wright's farm and their master would probably provide them with a cottage and promote Kit to herdsman. Dolly hoped that they would be given a cottage because she could never live with Kit in old Wally's cottage. Just the thought of it repelled her. Wally drank like a fish and chewed tobacco in a revolting way. And he would keep jawing on about the years ago. It seemed that Wally had really disliked her mother, Larlee, and enjoyed telling tales about that irresponsible errant woman who had been put in the stocks for all the folk to throw muck at.

Dolly found the details quite difficult to digest. Her small nose would wrinkle as she thought about the rumours that her mother had slept with lots of men. No one was going to use *her* that way. A gold ring would be on her finger, Dolly decided, before any man took liberties with her.

Her gaze swept down the river towards the creek where the *Alianora* still lay with its sails in tatters and its hull deep in mud. What a dreadful story that was, she thought, the skipper had been murdered and his love had died of a broken heart. Yes, one must be very wise and careful how one approached this certain time of life. But Dolly reckoned that she was too sensible for anything so disastrous to happen to her. Mistress Wright had given her a good training and advised her well on that account.

Along the muddy lane, lumbered the huge brown-and-white cows, lowing painfully as their udders hung low over-flowing with milk. Farmer Wright was rightfully proud of his herd, which was made up of pure-bred Kentish cattle, of the kind that had trod this muddy lane for centuries.

Kit was accompanied by lame Toby as he herded the cows through the gate. With a coy smile, Dolly picked up her milking stool and, swinging her hips, made for the milking shed.

Once the last cow had meandered past, Kit carefully closed the gate, while Toby went off to feed the pigs. Then Kit prepared the churns that would be filled with the fresh creaming milk for him to deliver about the neighbourhood later that morning.

'See you tonight, Dolly,' he whispered. 'Same place.'

Dolly sat astride her small wooden milking stool, the cow's soft udders in her hands. She nodded assent to Kit and produced a fruity chuckle that rippled along the old beams of the cow shed. Dolly dreamily thought of being kissed with soft kisses, and of arms around her pressing her close. Dimly in her mind a face appeared. It was not Kit's, but a fair smiling face surrounded by lots of curls. And in her ears she heard a happy voice saying:

'When I grow up Dolly, we will sail away to a desert island, you and I.'

It was young John Shulmead she recalled so clearly, he who had been swept out to sea one stormy night. Dolly sighed. It was no good looking back, she told herself. She was secure, she had a good situation and a young man of her own. What more could she possibly want? Then, for no apparent reason, she wondered briefly about her big sister Alice, who had never been heard of since she ran away, all those years ago, and she wondered how Alice had fared.

At exactly the same time, miles away, in Dartford, Alice had risen early and gone out into the garden to say her morning prayers. She had always felt that much closer to God when she was out in the fresh air amid the tall hollyhocks and rows of pansies that Ruth had planted. It was such a pretty place, and Alice knew that she would like to own a garden like this one day. But then she could never marry, so how would it ever be possible? As she looked up at the pinky golden cloud that had drifted inland over the marsh, the fresh green meadows of her old home came to her mind and she remembered gathering mushrooms in the early morning or picking up the windfalls in the orchards. Momentarily she was back in Hollinbury hamlet and fair fat Dolly was weeping because her chilblains hurt. Larlee was shouting and cursing as usual, and driving those boy slaves from their wretched bed. Alice drew a quick breath as if in pain at the memory of that lout who had pushed her against a wall, pulled up her petticoats and rammed his filthy body into hers. How she had screamed and fought but to no avail. Her mother had been too drunk to hear her. Alice's knees went weak at the return of this traumatic nightmare and she clasped her hands in prayer. 'Dear God, take these wicked thoughts from my mind,' she whispered. 'Please let me find peace and happiness here with my child and my good friends. Do not let me look back, dear Jesus. Allow me to look forward and I'll promise you my life in your service. I'll live to aid afflicted humanity as you did, dear Lord.'

With this pathetic prayer sailing up into the clouds, Dolly's elder sister struggled to forget that haunted hamlet.

Soon Ben and Ruth had risen and breakfast was served in the usual fashion.

'I see our friend George Gibbs is making headway with his campaign for the brickyard children,' he said. 'There is another article here by him in *The Times*.'

'Thank God, I am well pleased,' murmured Ruth as she fed her small daughter with hot porridge. 'Now, dear,' she coaxed, 'eat it all and God will love you and make you strong. Look what a good boy Adam is. He has eaten all his porridge and is now on to his bread and jam.'

Alice looked at her sturdy son with jam all around his face and smiled. She loved him with all her being. Sometimes when she saw a mischievous look in those deep blue eyes, she was reminded of Larlee, and Alice hoped that it was purely her imagination. She did not want Adam to inherit any genes from her poor afflicted mother. Alice wondered if her mother was still working at the moulding table, banging away with that long wooden spatula and harassing those poor little children. It was strange, she thought, that George Gibbs never mentioned Larlee.

Ruth's sweet modest tones suddenly interrupted her thoughts. 'This morning, Alice, I am going across town to the mission hospital. They say there is much sickness there. The nuns and the soldiers are unable to cope and have asked for volunteers. I will take Jasper and his son with me to help.'

'And I,' said Alice.

'No, no dear,' Ruth reduced her voice to a whisper. 'There is talk of smallpox there, and that is highly contagious.'

'Whither thou goest. ...' Alice muttered piously.

Ruth shook her head. 'My dear, I have served in overseas missions and have already had smallpox, so I am immune to it now. But you cannot go.'

'Please, Ruth,' pleaded Alice. 'Do not leave me out. Allow me to do the work with you.'

Ruth put an arm about her and sighed. 'As you wish, dear, but remember to do as I bid you. If the illness is confirmed we must have no contact with our babies until it is safe. Now promise me that.'

Alice looked over at Adam and nodded gravely. Then, at midday in a cart loaded with medical supplies they set off, driven by Jasper a big husky man, with his thin gangling son sitting beside him. These were the Anneslees' two loyal servants.

They travelled in the rickety cart to the other side of the town where the soldiers' barracks were situated right by the crowded lower class district bordering on the river. As they drove along, people swarmed past them carrying bundles and leading animals. All around there were carts full of children.

'It's an epidemic, as I feared,' muttered Jasper.

Ruth looked worriedly at the distressed folk hurrying out of the town. The air was loaded with a sense of furtive activity. The soldiers returning from foreign climes had brought this dreaded disease with them and it had hit the unhygienic side of the town within days.

In no time, Ruth was at work attending to the stricken patients, giving them water and saying a prayer for the dying.

As she hurried herself, she forgot all else but the needs of the sick humans. But she made sure before they started that she bound a mask soaked in spirit around Alice's face, and produced white linen gloves for her to wear. 'Do not touch anyone's skin,' she instructed her. 'And never remove that mask.'

So all that long day the two women nursed the sick, washed the dead and consoled the bereaved and all day the long line of strangers in the hospital corridors grew longer. Alice grew weary but Ruth, urged on by some hidden fervour, toiled endlessly. Women were not usually allowed in his hospital, since it was owned and run by the military, but because this was an epidemic, any help offered was welcomed.

After two days and nights Alice and Ruth were completely exhausted and were given a place in a convent to rest. Ruth sent Jasper back home with a message to Ben to remove the children from the town as the disease had reached such proportions that it was likely to spread all around.

The humid heat of those last weeks suddenly built up that night into a terrific thunder storm that rolled back and forth across the weald of Kent, flooding the small towns and flattening the ripening corn. The next morning a man in a long riding cape and flat black hat alighted from the stagecoach. He had travelled all night and was wet and cold. He strode briskly down the main street in the direction of the town centre where beggars lay huddled in dark doorways, and ran lightly up the steps of the half-timbered house facing the main square. Quickly he pulled the bell which jangled loudly, and then he waited patiently with an eager smile on his lips, quite expecting to see the door open to Alice's serious face.

To George Gibbs' disappointment, the door was opened by Ben Anneslee himself looking very tired and somewhat harassed.

'I am mightily pleased to see you, George,' said Ben, holding out his hand in welcome. 'Step inside.'

'I am truly sorry to bother you at such an early hour,' George said as he removed his long cape and wide hat in the sparsely furnished hall. 'But it's Alice I really called to see.' He spoke in an uncharacteristically embarrassed voice.

'Come into my study,' urged Ben. 'It is warmer in there.' As they walked into the book-lined room, he motioned his guest to a chair. 'I am afraid that neither Alice nor Ruth is here,' he said apologetically. 'I expect you have heard that there is smallpox on the other side of town.'

'Yes, I did hear a rumour when we changed horses at Watling Street,' replied George.

'It is most upsetting. Ruth volunteered her services and has taken Alice with her. There is no one to care for the mission and the children are alone but for one old nurse, I am at my wit's end.'

George murmured sympathetically. 'Well, can I help you Ben?' he offered.

'Ruth and Alice will not now return until the quarantine is over. Ruth asked me to take the children from the town and I now realise that it is more serious than I thought.' Ben poured out his woes to his friend. 'And where to take the children, I simply cannot think.'

'That's where I can help,' declared George. 'I am on my way out to visit my sister Jenny. I only called in for a quick word with Alice, so if you will allow me, Ben, I am sure the children will be given a good welcome out on the farm and be safe in isolation out there.'

'That is certainly most kind of you, sir,' said Ben relaxing a little. 'And how are affairs between you and Alice?'

George shifted uneasily on his feet. 'Well, sir, quite well,' he said. 'We have indulged in a long correspondence these last few months, and Alice sent me copies of her poems about the children in the brickyard. I must say, I thought they were excellent.'

'Perhaps we have a budding genius in our Alice,' jested Ben.

'I do hope the ladies take good care of themselves,' murmured George. 'It's a deadly illness, this smallpox.'

'Please God,' muttered Ben piously. 'What would we do without our women?

'We will partake of a light meal while the nurse prepares the children for your departure,' suggested Ben. 'Then I must be off to the mission. There are still the hungry and needy to look after.'

Later that day, in a small hired dog cart, George drove Adam and Faith out of town away from the dreadful pestilence. The children sat close together with the bulky shape of the old nurse beside them, a basket of her possessions on her wide lap. The nurse looked quite grim. She had not wanted to leave the shelter and comfort of Ben's house at all, least of all to go to some farmhouse in the wilderness. In her sixty years, she had never left Dartford and she felt that she was too old to start now.

Through the misty lanes the little cart rattled, while George sang cheerful hymns to the children in an effort to make them feel less disturbed by this abrupt change in their peaceful existence. The old nurse rocked to and fro and groused loudly about her old bones being shaken to bits.

After an hour on the road, they at last approached the hamlet of Hollinbury. Long lines of wagons passed them loaded high with blocks of white chalk dug from the high white cliffs at Strood. A large gang of workmen continued the work on the canal that the French prisoners, now repatriated, had left unfinished. The new canal would soon be through the hamlet and emptying off into the creek.

As he watched the activity George thought about the canal that now ringed the north bringing with it the appalling conditions in which large families had to live. Yes, this was another subject that had to be tackled — the waterways, the canals.

The little dogcart passed through the hamlet and on into the wide open farmlands. High on the hill was the fine farmhouse which, before the Reformation, had been an old abbey. Remains of the old buildings still remained — strong stone walls which still withstood the elements as they had for hundreds of years. It was an impressive piece of property. Acres and acres of yellow wheat and green meadowlands rolled over the hill and down to the riverside. In the fields lines of women wearing a variety of coloured sun bonnets, industriously picked peas and beans. As they drove on, George noted the long avenues of hop poles supporting the fruit ready for picking in the autumn, and as he watched the cherry pickers busily working in the orchards, George reflected on how prosperous this farm was. And it was all owned by one man, his brother-in-law. It did not seem fair somehow. All God's children were entitled to a fair share of this wealth for the little time one spent on earth. George sighed. How much would he be able to achieve during his short time here?

Jenny Wright was disconcerted to see her brother arrive with two small children and an old nurse complaining that her legs were as stiff as pokers. But she emerged from the stables to greet them as though she were expecting them all. She was a tall, comely woman with an attractive manner. Her dark hair was wind blown, and her skirt always muddy at the hem since she spent most of her time around the stables with her horses. Now she stood in the yard with sleeves rolled up and a grooming brush in her hand.

'Well, dear brother,' she said with a smile, 'what orphans have you brought us this time?' She surveyed the little children with a warmth in her eyes while Adam and Faith held hands and gazed up at her in awe.

'They are not orphans, dear sister,' said George, 'just fugitives from the fever that is so prevalent in the town.'

Jenny looked alarmed. 'Now George,' she said. 'Was that wise?'

'Do not worry, sister, these are the children of my close friends, and they have had no contact with the illness.'

Jenny stiffened impatiently. 'Then why did you not say so immediately?' Her heart had melted and she now knelt down to fuss the children. 'Come in, darlings, I've got a nice slice of cake for you,' she said, taking each one by the hand.

George smiled. They would be safe and well cared for here. Her husband and son were travelling abroad but Jenny was a home lover and rarely left the farm.

'Will you stay with us a while, George?' she asked.

'No, sister. I have to leave early in the morning. They need all the help they can get in that infested town.'

'Don't go, dear brother,' Jenny pleaded. 'Death has no mercy. It takes good, bad, rich and por.'

George shook his head. 'No, my mind is made up. Ruth Anneslee and Alice are already working hard to nurse the sick, and that is why I brought the children here.'

'Alice?' Jenny said. 'Who's Alice?'

'The boy's mother,' George replied quietly.

'But I thought they were brother and sister.'

'Well, you were mistaken, dear Jenny,' George answered abruptly.

Jenny smiled. 'Why, George, do I detect a secret in your life?'

George tried to cover up his embarrassment. 'No, I have no dreaded secret to hide, unless it is my love for that child's mother.'

'Oh, George!' Jenny gasped, truly shocked. 'The boy is not yours!'

He laughed. 'What nonsense. But he will be mine when I marry her. Then I will be his father.'

'Then she is a young widow,' said Jenny. 'Well, good for you, George, it is time you settled down. Don't worry about these babes. They will be quite safe here with me. But take that old nurse back with you. She does not want to stay, and has done nothing but complain since she arrived. I will bring a young girl from the dairy to help me with the children.' She paused. 'Believe me, dear brother, I cannot but simply adore them.'

The morning came and George left with the nurse who wept loudly, torn between her desire to escape from this God-forsaken hole and her guilt at leaving her little charges in it. But once the nurse had gone, a lovely young girl came in from the dairy to look after Faith and Adam. The children took to her immediately.

'I hope you don't mind, Dolly,' said her mistress, 'but I'd

like you to take care of my brother's wards. It will be a good opportunity for you to learn some childcare. Since I have heard a rumour you will wed Kit after the harvest.'

Dolly blushed and curtsied. 'Thank you, mum, I'll be pleased to mind the darlings.'

So, unknown to Dolly, she was to be nurse to her own sister's child, her nephew. She loved and fussed him without hesitation. 'Adam,' she said. 'That's a fine name. We once had a baby called Adam.'

In the days before vaccination smallpox was a deadly killer, taking the lives of old and young alike. Families were easily decimated as their loved ones were struck down one by one. The disease was highly contagious and it was extremely difficult to find volunteers to help. Although it struck at rich and poor alike, it was always the poorer classes, living in cramped conditions, who paid the highest toll.

It was always members of the deeply religious societies, who braved the threat of death and stepped in to help the authorities cope with a smallpox epidemic. So when George Gibbs turned up to help at the military hospital in Dartford, neither Alice nor Ruth was unduly surprised to see him. He immediately went out to the poor shacks huddled by the riverside to bring in the sick and organize some merciful quarantine.

Alice went quietly about her duties at the hospital as she always did, her face serious behind her mask and her lips moving as she muttered prayers for the Lord's mercy.

Unshaven and unkempt, George Gibbs often greeted her as he passed. 'God bless, you, Alice,' he would say, and she would give him a pious answer in return. But neither stopped to talk, for uppermost in their minds was the care of the sick and dying.

On one particular day the heat was terrific and a long line of stretcher cases lay in the corridor. A large tent had been erected in the grounds and soldier orderlies were very busy caring for the less sick patients. As Alice returned from a well-earned rest period, she walked past the line of moaning patients and felt quite overwhelmed by the sight and the smell of sick humanity. Tied about her face was the mask that Ruth had provided for her and she wore white linen gloves on her hands. None of these provided very adequate protection from such a dreaded disease. But as she walked by, a skinny hand rose up and a hoarse voice cried: 'Lal!'

Alice jumped, her heart beating quickly as if in fear. Only one person had ever called her Lal, and that was her mother. Turning back, she knelt down beside the figure under a red blanket and found herself looking at a thin, pock-marked face under a mop of untidy white hair. There was the unmistakable face of Larlee, her own mother.

A thin, claw-like hand grabbed wildly at her sleeve. ''Tis my gel,' Larlee gasped. 'Take me out of here, for God's sake,' she pleaded.

Alice was speechless. Immobilized by shock, she gazed at what had once been beautiful wayward Larlee.

Busy at her duties in the corridor Ruth suddenly noticed Alice kneeling down as if in prayer. She came over to her. 'Get up, Alice. The orderlies will bring these people in when they have been thoroughly cleaned up.' She looked down at Larlee. 'This poor woman is off the streets. I should leave her for a while.'

Still Alice did not get to her feet but she reached out and took Larlee's skinny hand in her own to hold it tight.

Larlee's cracked voice cried out: 'I've found my gel, and I've been looking everywhere!'

Ruth's eyebrows arched a little but she said nothing more before ordering Larlee's stretcher to be brought into the Receiving Ward. Between then, Alice and Ruth cleaned Larlee's filthy body without a word being passed between them. Finally, Ruth said: 'Poor woman, she has lost consciousness. There's not much hope for her, I'm afraid. Not only has she got smallpox but she seems to have some other disease too. The sores on her legs look syphilitic to me,' she sighed. 'Poor soul. But God does not forsake the fallen. Let us kneel and pray for her, Alice.'

With tears streaming down her face, Alice knelt. 'I'd like to stay with her for a little while, Ruth,' she whispered. 'Do you mind?'

Ruth looked perplexed but did not object. 'Be careful, Alice,' was all she said before leaving her alone.

With cold water, Alice sponged her mother's fevered brow. To her amazement, Larlee eventually returned to consciousness. When she opened her coal-black eyes they seemed to be the only living parts left in that emaciated body. 'Goodbye, Lal,' she whispered. 'Give me a kiss.'

For a second, Alice hesitated, but then she pulled the mask from her face and touched Larlee's hot dry lips with her own. 'Thanks, Lal,' gasped Larlee. 'Please forgive me.' Then with a shudder which shook her thin body from head to foot, Larlee passed out of the world, leaving Alice staring down at her, her head a jumble of confused thoughts and emotions.

For the next week Alice worked like a Trojan from morning to night. Finally Ruth told her to be careful. 'You must ease up, Alice, you do not look at all well.' Indeed, Alice had bags under her eyes and her skin was tinged with grey.

That final night they slept, as usual, in the narrow confines of the convent where they had been so kindly accommodated. Alice tossed noisily and restlessly in her bed and Ruth, hearing her, arose, lit a candle and looked down at her. 'Oh dear God,' she muttered. 'Not my Alice!' For the red spots glowed out clearly on that pale face.

Ruth slipped on her cloak and went quietly out into the night to the tents in the field where George Gibbs and his followers were camped. 'I must speak with George Gibbs,' she informed the sentry.

Roused from his slumber, George finally came out, very sleepy-eyed. He was most surprised to see Ruth.

'It's Alice,' she murmured. 'Alice is sick and you must help me, George. I will not allow her to remain in this pest-house.'

'But, Ruth, you cannot break the quarantine rules,' begged George.

'No one knows yet,' Ruth replied determinedly. 'I will take her home and nurse her in the little room over the Mission Hall. If you love her, George, you will assist me.'

Very quietly in a hired cart, George and Ruth drove Alice back to their own mission. The early morning streets were now completely deserted since most of the population had fled from the epidemic.

Barely able to move, Alice lay placidly in George's arms as he carried her up the narrow stairs at the Mission Hall.

'Here we will stay,' declared Ruth, 'and I will take the necessary precautions. I will nurse her myself. I hope that they will not miss me at the hospital. But anyway, the worst is over and I have done my share. God willing, I will pull Alice through.'

So Ruth installed herself and Alice in that tiny room above the Mission Hall and each day would lower out of the window a basket along with a list of supplies she required. The door of the room was sealed with protective blankets of disinfectant as Ruth fought alone for the life of her true companion and friend.

At eventide, her husband Ben and George Gibbs walked about outside looking up anxiously at that small attic window, and listening to Ruth's sweet tones as she sang hymns to the feverish Alice and bathed those terrible body sores.

Then one night, about three weeks later Ruth was singing as usual:

'Fight the good fight with all they might,
Lift up thine eyes and see the light ...'

Suddenly the two men heard a weak voice joining in:

'Lay hold on life and it shall be,
Thy joy and crown eternally.'

Ben and George clasped each other tight. 'It's Alice!' they cried in unison. 'She has recovered.'

Ruth came to the window and waved at them. Her sweet smile assured them that all was indeed well.

From then on Alice grew stronger. The marks on her face distressed her but Ruth tried to make her accept them. 'It was

God's way of letting you see that life is important no matter how you look,' she said gently.

Once the convalescent period was over, Alice returned home and was soon able to take the classes at the Sunday school once more. There the depleted size of the groups depressed her.

'Where is little Minnie?' Alice asked one tousled youth, she knew to be Minnie's brother.

' 'Er dead and buried, along wiv me baby bruvver,' replied the lad.

'Oh, Ruth, how many little ones did we lose?' Alice asked that evening.

'Many, many, I am afraid dear. All angels now with God in his heaven. They never had sufficient food inside them to withstand the infection.'

'Are our own little ones safe do you think?' asked Alice anxiously. She missed Adam dreadfully, not having seen him for weeks.

'Yes, quite safe and well. They are being well looked after.'

Until now, Alice had never known where George had taken the children to safety. And she was shocked when she learned of their exact whereabouts that evening.

'George took them out to his sister's farm in a place called Hollinbury,' Ruth informed her. 'They have been very well and happy. We will collect them after the service on Sunday. How I am looking forward to seeing my darling Faith!'

The effect of this conversation on Alice was dramatic. As Ruth spoke, she paled noticeably and even staggered slightly.

'Dear Alice, are you all right?' cried Ruth. 'You look terrible,' she rushed towards her with deep concern on her face.

'Yes, yes, I am fine,' murmured Alice. 'It's just a dizzy spell. I'll go and rest.'

When she had gone, Ruth confided in Ben. 'I worry about Alice. I think the fever has weakened her heart.'

'Nonsense,' said Ben. 'She will be all right, she has great courage, our Alice. Wait until the children come home and then all will be well, I can assure you.'

For the rest of the week, Alice remained quite withdrawn and she even excused herself for not taking the trip out to the hamlet to collect the children.

That Sunday afternoon as the little pony carriage sped through the green lanes, Ruth thought about Alice's behaviour and tried to puzzle out some answers. 'I wonder if Alice came from this hamlet on the marsh?' she pondered out aloud. 'I also feel sure that she knew that poor destitute woman who died in the pesthouse.'

'Do not probe into her past, Ruth,' Ben warned his wife. 'It has always been our policy not to do so and we must not start now,' he added, somewhat sternly.

'Well, I suppose you are right,' replied Ruth. 'But I so much want our Alice to find happiness.' She smiled and added: 'I feel sure that George is trying to gather up enough courage to propose to her.'

'It will be a good match,' said Ben, 'but then we will lose our greatest asset in dear Alice. I know that George is planning to return to his home in the Midlands. He has been offered a resident post near the big potteries in the Black Country, and they say that poverty and child slavery is even worse in those industrial towns than they are down here. So he will have plenty of work to do, and Alice will be an ideal wife in such circumstances.'

'I have a strong feeling that Alice will refuse him,' argued Ruth. 'And I feel sure that it concerns her feelings over the child. She never mentions Adam's father. There was some tragedy there, I'll be bound.'

The conversation ceased as they drove through the gates of Wright's Farm. The dogs came tearing down the path, barking furiously to herald the approach of visitors.

George Gibbs was already at the farm and he and his sister came to the door to greet them. Behind them came a lovely fair girl carrying the two clean, contended-looking children. Adam and Faith struggled down and with shrieks of delight ran towards Ben and Ruth. Then Adam hesitated and frowned when he saw that his own mother was not with them.

'Where is Alice?' asked George in a disappointed tone.

'Still convalescing, you know,' replied Ruth, 'but she sends her regards.'

Tea was soon served in the comfortable farm parlour and the children full of chatter, told of their three-month stay in these lovely surroundings. Although they announced vehemently that they did not want to go home, when it was finally time for the party to leave, Adam and Faith were waiting with their belongings by the door. And the Anneslees drove back to Dartford, knowing that Alice's reunion with her beloved son would be a joyful sight to behold.

CHAPTER ELEVEN

Return of the Sailor

Friday night at the hamlet witnessed the harvest supper held in the big barn. There was much ribald talk and guzzling of country cider. The long table was laden with good food and the local inhabitants stuffed themselves while Farmer Wright, fit and tanned, and back from his travels, told them of the strange land of Canada where he and his son had just visited and where there were so many miles of grazing land that Wright's Farm would be lost within it.

Dressed in his best smock and straw hat, and accompanied by Kit and Toby, Wally was enjoying himself, eating and drinking, heartily, in spite of his age.

'Meself, I don't go much on foreign parts,' he announced. 'Me own uncle was ate out there by them Indians.'

Kit and Toby laughed. They were in good moods, particularly Kit, who was leaving the warm comfort of Wally's home the coming Sunday morning, when he was to marry his beautiful Dolly and live in a cottage on the marsh, provided by Farmer Wright. Now he watched his Dolly dancing with all the young lads and lasses, her young healthy body spinning across the dance floor and swinging to and fro. Kit's heart swelled with pride. Dolly was the sunshine of his soul. He positively worshipped her and could hardly believe his luck.

At ten o'clock Wally was so much the worse for drink that he had to be taken home. Toby and Kit guided him down the lane to his cottage where Toby volunteered to stay with him so that Kit could return to the festivities to keep an eye on his lovely bride-to-be.

As Kit headed back for the barn, he saw a dark figure

coming down the lane towards him. He carried a heavy pack on his back and walked slowly and wearily. Kit gazed at this traveller with curiosity, wondering where the husky youth was bound, for there were only four cottages in the street. But the young men passed each other without comment, and without recognizing each other.

After years of wandering, John Shulmead had decided to return to the hamlet of his birth and here he was. Almost seven years had passed since he had been washed out to sea on that stormy night. But he still recalled the rough voices and gentle hands of the sailors who had hauled him aboard the big warship, as they rescued him from the perils of the deep sea. He had been drifting for a week and had lain half-dead in his little sailing boat until his rescue.

John had immediately taken to the life aboard the big battle ship. After all, it was something he had always dreamed about. But now, after many long adventurous voyages all around the world, he had suddenly wanted to return home. With a pack on his back and little else, he had trudged the Kentish lanes towards his old hamlet. He felt strange as he passed the marshlands across which he could just see, as darkness fell, the misty shadows of the brick kilns, where once he had been a young slave. He put down his pack beside the water well, pulled up the bucket and passed the refreshing cold water to his parched lips, recalling how on many a frosty morning he had stood bare-footed awaiting his turn at this well while Larlee raged and screamed at him to hurry up. John had always wondered what had happened to everyone else, and above all, how little Dolly had fared.

Continuing on, he passed someone in the lane but he did not stop until he came to the little row of cottages where he had once lived. A broad grin spread across John's face as he heard singing and recognized Old Wally's unmelodious tones.

Indeed, Wally, very drunk, was sitting up in his bed and shouting out all the tunes he knew. 'We plough the fields and scatter, the good seed on the lands. ...'

Wally must be getting on a bit, John thought as he came up

to Wally's cottage. He pushed open the door and shouted: 'Avast there! You are still in fine voice, Wally.'

Wally turned towards the brawny man at the door and stopped singing. Who on earth was this fellow with the cheery grin and mop of fair curls?

'Don't you know me? I am John Shulmead,' John cried.

'Glory be!' said Wally, grabbing him by the hand, ''tis our John! They always said you was a gonner, boy.'

'No, Wally, here I am, and fighting fit.'

'Toby! Toby!' Wally cried. 'Come you here. 'Tis our John come home.'

Warm arms encircled John as Toby limped in, and the two boys were joyously reunited. Then they sat beside Wally on the bed talking of old times until the old boy dozed off to sleep.

'We will have a bite to eat,' said Toby. 'Kit will be home soon. He will be so surprised and delighted. You are back in time for his wedding.'

'What wedding?' asked John.

'Why, to Dolly,' exclaimed Toby excited. 'You remember Dolly, don't you? We all worked together in the Pug Mill.'

'Yes,' said John, feeling his heart sink. 'I remember Dolly well.' A strong feeling of disappointment threatened to overwhelm him but he fought it off by reasoning to himself. After all, he told himself, he had not seen Dolly since she was a child. How foolish were all his wild dreams about meeting her again!

While Wally snored in the corner, Toby and John sat in that one room which served as a bedroom and dining-room. Toby provided John with a supper of fresh home baked bread and cheese washed down with beer. After all those years of wandering John felt that he had returned home at last. He was very full of himself and his adventures and wanted to recount everything that had happened to him since that night when he was washed out to sea, and of the great world outside of Hollinbury hamlet. For Toby had been to no other place since he had been dumped from the canal boat in which he had been born.

But as John informed Toby of the war, death and destruction he had seen, of the treachery and rape of towns, cities and women, Toby's thin faced paled. 'Don't tell me any more, John,' he said. 'I have no interest of what goes on outside the hamlet.'

'That may be,' argued John. 'But it's not been so bloody grand here. Have you forgotten the old days in the Pug Mill?'

Toby eased out his crippled leg in front of the fire and stared down at it. 'How could I forget?' he said sadly. 'I am left with a diseased leg bone and scars that will never heal. We can only trust in God.'

'Don't tell me you got religion,' crackled John.

'I have great faith in my maker,' murmured Toby.

'Don't worry so much, son,' John felt suddenly very contrite, wishing that he had not mocked this ugly little fellow whose skin was sallow and whose body was bent through no fault of his own. 'It all comes out in the wash,' he added, swallowing his jug of ale. 'Fill it up, lad,' he said, holding out the jug, 'and have a drink yourself.'

'I take barley water,' said Toby. 'I never touch alcohol.'

John stared at Toby incredulously for a moment, and then continued with his monologue. 'Still, it's not all bad out there, you know. You can find beauty and damsels and miles of wide open seas. Mind you, it can be lonely. There were times when I longed for the sight and sound of old Wally coughing and spluttering in the Malted Shovel.'

'Now, tell me,' he said, 'what's happened to everyone? Is dumb Lukey still living at the inn?'

This line of conversation Toby could cope with and he perked up, but just as he was about to launch into the details of the comings and goings in Hollinbury over the past few years, Kit suddenly arrived. He looked concerned when he saw his brother with a stranger but realizing who it was, was soon hugging John. 'It's grand you are returned from the dead,' he cried.

'Still alive and kicking vigorously,' jested John. 'Now what's this I've been hearing. You are going to marry our Dolly?'

'On Sunday,' replied Kit, thinking uncomfortably back on the hour he had just spent with Dolly and the anxious moments she had given him.

When Kit had got back to the party, all the old men were overcome with drink and had begun their journeys back to their outlying farms, and their wives were hurrying up their lovely daughters just in case they were snuggled down in the hay by some amorous young man. Serving women were clearing up the debris and Dolly and Kit had wandered hand in hand towards the duck pond where huge willow trees trailed their branches on the water.

The ducks gave a sleepy squawk as the wandering lovers disturbed their rest. Together they had strolled into the apple orchard where a silver moon illuminated the gnarled tree trunks, painting the rough bark like old silver.

Dolly gazed up at the full moon surrounded by its brilliant convoy of stars and sighed softly. She felt so good inside, so romantic having drunk much of the home-brewed cider at the party. 'Oh, Kit,' she murmured, 'it was such a good party, so much fun. I nearly danced my legs off. Let us sit down now, I am so weary.' She snuggled up close to him, and Kit, from his tall height, gazed down at her tiny five-foot figure. She was so fair and so lovely, with those wide-spaced blue eyes and full, rosy-red mouth. And she looked so sweet and pretty in that full white dress. His heart lurched in his chest and tears came into his eyes, so great was his love for Dolly. But he was bothered by what she was now suggesting.

'Let us wait,' he said. 'It's just two more nights to our wedding day.'

Dolly pushed out her lower lip sullenly, but continued to press herself close to him, her young body hot with love. Their lips clung tight together.

'Oh Kit!' she cried. 'Why not? Everyone else does it.'

'No, darling,' Kit replied firmly. 'You will be my virgin bride when I swear to love, honour and protect you before the altar. So it must be the truth.'

'Oh, blow, dash and bother,' Dolly cried childishly. 'I don't understand. Other men are not like you.'

Kit leaped to his feet. 'What other men?' he caught her arm and pulled her tight and shook her.

Dolly tried to pull away. 'Oh, don't start, Kit,' she said, shaking him off irritably. 'I only know what others have told me,' she said wistfully. 'It's something I have never done and I don't think you have either.'

Kit looked forlorn. 'That's correct. I am saving myself for you, darling.'

'Well, what bothers me is how will I know if we like it if we don't try it beforehand?'

Kit suddenly began to laugh. 'Oh, Dolly, Dolly, why are you so eager? It's a natural happening. Surely you know that having been brought up on a farm ...'

'That may be, but it don't stop me wanting it,' muttered Dolly.

'Now, don't be naughty,' Kit petted and fussed her. 'Come on, let's see you home. We will be in our own bed soon enough.'

At seventeen, Dolly had left the dairy and been promoted to work in the house. When Jenny Wright had visitors for tea, Dolly would serve them graciously, politely handing round the silver platter containing freshly baked cakes. She was very popular and over the past few weeks there had been much interest in Dolly's wedding. Presents had begun to arrive from all over the countryside.

'Oh, how lucky I am, ma'am,' exclaimed Dolly the day before her wedding. 'I am so grateful.'

Jenny was quietly arranging fresh flowers in a silver bowl. 'I am very pleased to see you wed, Dolly,' she said, 'and settled comfortably. You have been a great asset to me particularly in helping to take care of Adam and Faith.'

Dolly smiled. 'But I love them dearly. How could I have looked after them otherwise?'

Jenny had finished arranging the flowers. She wiped her

hands and collected herself. 'Right now,' she said. 'Let's get this grand wedding on its way.'

That same morning, Wally's cottage was buzzing with activity. Earlier, Kit and Toby had been up at dawn with the cattle while Wally had sat up in bed in his striped night shirt and red cap, coughing and wheezing. John had got up early to go to the well. He came in now, wet and dripping, having thrown buckets of cold water over his head.

'Brrr!' shouted Wally. 'Come in and shut that door! And don't shake water all over the place! Always was fond of water, you was, young John.'

Soon Toby and Kit came in from the fields to eat huge bowls of porridge from the oatmeal that had simmered in the pot on the stove all night. They had brought in fresh milk to pour over it.

As the cottage warmed up, John opened his sailor's bag to produce a wealth of treasures — all kinds of knick-knacks he had collected on his travels, such as a small mother-of-pearl Italian concertina which Toby took a liking to immediately. For Wally had taught him how to play his old harmonium and Toby loved music. His talent was a gift born in this crippled lad who had quickly gone on to play the church organ.

'Right!' cried John generously. 'It's yours, Toby. Now, give us a tune!'

Toby squeezed out a sea shanty while John danced the hornpipe. From his chair Wally cackled at the sight of them until he lost his breath and had to be thumped hard on the back to ease his chest. For his presents, Wally chose a model ship in a bottle and a large roll of black tobacco for chewing. 'Well, well,' he said, 'all the way from the West Indies, is it?' He proudly placed the model on his mantelpiece amongst the debris of candles, bottles and bits of brass.

Kit was silent as he admired a white ivory elephant.

'I was going to keep that myself,' said John. 'But no matter, you can have it as a wedding present. I'll give this nice snake bracelet to Dolly. It's gold and these are real precious stones in the snake's eyes.'

As they all gathered around to admire the bracelet, Kit stroked the smooth white back of his elephant with sensitive fingers. 'Are there really animals like this,' he asked softly. 'I've never heard of them.'

'Of course, you haven't,' cried John, rather tactlessly. 'That's because you have never been out of this poor old hamlet, isn't it?'

Kit did not reply, he glanced away and looked a little hurt.

Toby was a knowledgeable chap who liked to read. 'But the real elephants are in India,' he said brightly. 'And they are grey. I don't think anyone has ever seen a white one. They are believed to be unlucky.'

'Lay down, Clever Boots,' growled Wally. He understood how nervous Kit was and did not want him worried.

'Toby is right,' said John. 'Elephants are grey and a terrific size. They work them like we do horses. I did hear that white elephants are supposed to be unlucky but I am not superstitious. Anyway, some old salt told me that it's all right so long as you keep the elephant's trunk pointing towards the door.'

'Well, I never!' cried Wally. 'What do you think of that?' Everyone started to laugh, so thus good humour was restored.

Toby and Kit had the rest of the day off from work to prepare for the wedding. Wally had his own plans for the day worked out. 'We all go down to the barber,' he said, 'and then it's off to the Malted Shovel.'

Stag nights in the hamlet as anywhere else, were always a very drunken occasion. Late that afternoon, the nervous bridegroom-to-be and his friends entered the inn in jolly moods — and Beat, now looking quite haggard, served them with their first tankard of ale.

At first she stared suspiciously at the stranger in the party — a good-looking lad who chatted so familiarly with old Wally. But when he came to the counter to put down some coins he clutched at her dress and muttered: 'Money or your life. . . .'

'Stop that!' screeched Beat, reaching for her rolling pin.

But she immediately recognized the natural, wide grin that appeared on his face. 'Good God!' she cried. 'Why, it's young John Shulmead!'

'The same one, Aunt Beat. Back from the grave.' John beamed at her.

Beat looked too shocked to move, and she could not utter a word.

'Is Lukey still here?' John asked.

Suddenly, from a shadowy corner sprang Lukey, throwing himself at John, muttering and jabbering. Clambering all over him, he kissed and cuddled him, chattering unintelligible words of affection.

"Old 'ard, matey!' exclaimed John. 'Steady there.' He calmed his brother down and Lukey sank to the floor, weeping like a small child.

Beat called out to the kitchen. 'Come out, Dot, there's a surprise here for you.'

Moments later, Dot emerged. She had grown thin and frail, and her hair had turned snow white. Her loose mouth trembled with emotion and tears filled her eyes as she greeted John.

'Well, well,' John jested. 'Here's a pretty kettle of fish, both weeping, you and Lukey. Now, let's all cheer up and give poor Kit a good send-off. I've plenty money and I'm about to spend it.'

So began one of the most memorable nights in the history of the tavern. News spread and locals came hurrying in. Toby played his concertina and all the popular songs were sung as the beer flowed like rain. It was all agreed that John Shulmead was a fine young man, and he was to remain a popular figure for the rest of his life.

Dolly's wedding day dawned fair, as those late autumn days often do — Little Saints' Summer, the locals called it, when the temperature rises suddenly into the seventies, and the sun shines down from the blue, cloudless sky. So, in the heat of such a day, Dolly walked down the aisle on the arm of Farmer Wright in the little parish church of Hollinbury. This church was dedicated to All Saints but known in the community as Lily Church in honour of a plantagenet princess who was buried there.

Dolly's best white dress was trimmed with lace and clung in soft folds about her young healthy body. Freshly gathered rose buds framed her face. The long expanse of veil that trailed the floor had been lent by Jenny. 'I've no daughter,' she had said, 'and my son is a wanderer. The veil might as well be used.'

Our Dolly sailed down to the altar like a young queen. The church was packed. There were the hamlet inhabitants filling the pews but many people from miles around, who had walked to the village to see this momentous wedding.

Kit stood fine and upright with his sailor friend John by his side as best man. Toby had originally agreed to be best man but at the last minute had backed out, too embarrassed by his unwieldy shape.

As the bride and groom joined hands and most of the congregation sighed romantically, old Wally commented rather loudly. 'Can't see much good a-coming of this. Her mother was a flighty bitch.'

'Hush, be quiet!' commanded the women about him, nudging him in the ribs. For no one wanted to hear old Wally's gossip or predictions. This was indeed a special day when little Dolly, who was once a poor slave at the brick fields, could now be getting married, dressed all in white and looking like a society bride.

The service was over. The bride and groom kissed and then the best man kissed the bride. Some might have said that their lips clung a little longer than necessary, and the jewels set in the snake bracelet on Dolly's plump arm gleamed wickedly.

With his eyes downcast, Kit fidgeted nervously, hoping that no one else had noticed.

But it had not escaped Wally's sharp gaze. 'Going to be trouble there,' the old man muttered, once the confetti throwing and congratulations were over.

A light meal was served in the farmhouse and then Dolly and Kit were escorted to their new home in the traditional manner. The locals followed the young couple thumping a big drum and Toby played his concertina. Then they serenaded Dolly and Kit in a rowdy noisy fashion until midnight.

Kit felt very nervous and his legs trembled as he and Dolly went up to bed amid the shouts and jeers from the wedding guests. The drunken voices and singing seemed to merge and pound in his head as he undressed and began to caress his plump and expectant new bride. But his body let him down. And Dolly could hardly hold back a look of bitter disappointment. It was a look which was to haunt Kit for the rest of his young life.

The morning after the wedding, Toby left early for work and Wally stirred the porridge. John had been for a swim in the creek to get rid of his hangover.

'Perhaps you will settle down here. . . .' said Wally hopefully.

John rubbed his blond curls vigorously with a towel. 'I'm not sure about that,' he replied.

'Could do worse, lad, and there's plenty of room here for you now Kit has gone.'

'What is there here for me, Wally? Farming? The brick works? Neither appeals to me. I've had me taste of freedom, matey, and I can't be anchored down now.'

'There's a home for you here, lad, whatever you decide,' said Wally.

'What happened to the old forge?' John asked suddenly.

Wally nodded thoughtfully. 'I was wondering when you would ask about that,' he said slowly. 'Beat got her claws into that. She always said it was a nice property. A bloody gypo's got it now. He breeds piebald horses — what bloody good are they?'

'But how did Beat come to buy it?' asked John sternly.

''Twas never sold. Beat married Lukey when he was twenty-one. Your two other brothers went down at Waterloo, and you was missing, believed dead, so the forge was inherited by Lukey.'

'Beat did what?' cried John. In all the excitement of his return, this piece of information had not yet reached his ears. He was appalled and astonished. 'She married Lukey? Whatever for?'

'For the property, lad,' Wally grunted. 'That Beat always were a greedy old cow. Your pa had plenty of cash hid up there, and no one knows what became of that either.'

John shook his head in disbelief. 'It's disgusting. What good is old Lukey to anyone? He is most disturbed.'

'Money solves many problems,' muttered Wally. 'Nevertheless, young John, you are entitled to something. Your pa would have given you a good marriage settlement, I am quite sure of that.'

'Whatever can I do about it?' John looked very distressed.

'Well, your best bet is to talk to old Beat herself,' advised Wally.

'Yes, I think you're right,' said John slowly.

'Wait a bit and I'll come with you,' said Wally. He grabbed at any opportunity to go down to the inn, just in case there were free drinks to be had. He began to potter about getting into his wide smock and placing his straw hat on his head at a jaunty angle.

By midday the two men had established themselves in the public bar. Beat stared rather suspiciously at them, while Lukey, his face grim and hands wet from mopping the floor, came to kiss and fuss his brother John.

'Git on with that floor, Lukey!' yelled Beat, and the lad fled back to his mop and bucket.

Wally nudged John hard. 'See that? Lukey is only a skivvy. Some say she do beat him mercilessly.'

John's firm lips tightened. 'Any chance of a quiet word with you, Beatrice?' he asked loudly.

Beat had been expecting this confrontation with John and her keen old eyes assessed him as she prepared to do battle. 'Come out to the kitchen,' she said.

Aunt Dot was sitting in the kitchen with Lucinda's boy, Percy, on her knee, now a bonny lad of about six years old.

'Go and play,' said Beat sharply to her great-nephew. Percy stuck out his tongue but nevertheless did as he was told.

'Mind the bar,' Beat said to Dot. 'I want to talk privately with John.'

As Dot edged out of the room, Beat poured John some wine from a jug on the dresser. John looked about him. Very little had changed. The place looked much the same as it had when he used to come cold and hungry to the back door and lovely Lucinda had fed him with stale cake and ginger beer. And now poor Lucinda lay in her grave. . . .

'Well, John, what is it you came to discuss with me?' Beat's tone was brisk. 'Is it about the forge?'

'Yes, that's the idea, Aunt Beat,' John answered respectfully, as he had always done. For Beat commanded obedience.

'Well,' Beat said defiantly. 'It's let out. Anyway, it was only a leasehold property.'

'I did not know that,' John answered quietly. 'Father was very close about his affairs.'

'Well, the majority of land about here belongs to the church, but the property came to Lukey, and, because he is not responsible enough to handle his own affairs, now it's all mine.' She looked at him aggressively.

'Well, if you say so, then it must be true,' John answered mildly. 'But seeing as I have returned from the dead, the inheritance question is not so clear-cut. The law might make a few concessions.'

Beat's steely eyes flashed angrily. 'There's no need to get sassy, young John,' she warned. 'I have taken care of Lukey for all these years. I prevented him from being shut up in a cage. Had I not protected him as I have, all the money and property of the Shulmeads would have been confiscated by the law and very little would have been left once that had happened, I can assure you.'

John looked cowed. 'I agree, I agree, Aunt Beat, but I shall probably be on my way soon so I suppose it's of little regard to me anyway.'

'Right, John,' Beat said. 'Now we all know where we stand, don't we?' She eyed him shrewdly. 'Of course, if you are short of some ready cash while you are ashore. I can always oblige.' She offered the olive branch.

'I am not yet broke,' replied John. 'I've got some money that will last awhile.'

'Good, now I must get back to work,' announced Beatrice. 'I am pleased we have had this talk and cleared the air. You have always been a very straightforward lad, John, don't let that old Wally poison your mind,' she warned him.

John left the kitchen with a strong feeling that he had been outwitted.

'Damn fool,' grumbled old Wally, when John told him what had been said. 'Didn't you ask how much ready cash the smithy left behind? Your father was heavily involved in smuggling with old Amos, years ago. Made a mint of money, they did.'

'Oh, forget it, Wally,' pleaded John. 'It's back to the briny for me soon.'

Wally was chastened by this news. He had hoped to hang on to John now that Kit had gone. Having the boys around kept him feeling young.

John Shulmead hung about the hamlet for a few more weeks frequently visiting Kit and Dolly in their new home, getting boozed nightly at the Malted Shovel, and going down to the village to take a tour of the other taverns. Returning one day, he walked along the muddy banks of the creek which had been built high to withstand the winter tides. Today the tide was out, leaving the mud flats dry. Skeletons of old crafts stuck out forlornly from the great mud.

John paused as he recognized the wreck of the *Alianora*. Quickly he took off his boots, slung them about his neck, and waded out into the mud to take a closer look at her. She was still a majestic lady, even though her paint was cracked and dry, what was left of her sail was tattered and torn, almost to nothing. And she listed to one side. He climbed aboard and spent the rest of the afternoon on the sloping decks trying to fathom out his future. It occurred to him that he might try to do something with this craft. She was still basically in sound shape, and he wondered who owned her now. With a refit he could get her working and sail her up the Thames once more. Thinking about the cost he wondered if old Beat would finance him. It would certainly be worth a try. In this way he could still stay in touch with his friends in the hamlet, and possess a home of his own. Brimming with enthusiasm, he broached the subject to old Beat.

'The *Alianora*?' Beat screwed up her face in horror at first but then thought deeply. 'Let's see now,' she said. She belongs to the cement works, I think. Joe Lee had a big mortgage on his barge, so they claimed it. The boss comes in here for a drink sometimes. Yes, I'll get the hulk cheap for you, just you leave it to me. After all, you was born and raised in this hamlet and if anyone is entitled to that old boat, it's you. I'll supply the cash for a refit — a loan, of course.'

Well, Beat had turned up trumps. John was thrilled. 'Thank you, Aunt Beat. I'll work her profitably, I can assure you.'

'I am sure of that, boy, otherwise you get nought from me,' she answered. And she meant it.

Within a month the old *Alianora* had been towed into town to the shipyard for a complete refit and John, with Beat's help, got himself a contract. He was now the proud skipper of a Thames barge.

Thus his fate had been decided: John Shulmead would soon be an important figure in Hollinbury hamlet.

CHAPTER TWELVE

Alice in Love

Life at the mission in Dartford settled back to normal once the terrible smallpox epidemic had passed. Alice still lived with Ben and Ruth Anneslee and helped them with their good work. She took the children's Sunday school class, assisted in the house and in her very few moments of spare time, she wrote her poetry. These poems tended to be long, sad epistles about the plight of the brickyard children, and she always hid them away carefully. Only George Gibbs ever saw them when she wrote to him at his own home in the Midlands.

Ruth was still puzzled by Alice's attitude to her husband's friend, as she had been the day they had brought the children home from their stay in Hollinbury to escape the smallpox.

'George Gibbs was disappointed that you did not come to his sister's farm to collect the children,' Ruth had informed her on their return. 'I feel sure that in some way you must have offended him.'

Alice had continued with her sewing, her eyes downcast.

Ruth suddenly felt angry. 'For goodness sake, say something, Alice. Make *some* comment, even if it is an adverse one. You do frustrate me with your long silences.'

'I am truly sorry, dear,' apologized Alice, 'but what is there to say? George Gibbs has his own life away in the middle of England.'

'Oh! I felt sure that he was about to ask for your hand, after your illness,' complained Ruth.

Alice smiled slightly. 'Well, then it is just as well he didn't. He would have been wasting his breath, for I have no intention of ever marrying.'

'Oh, how foolish you are!' exclaimed Ruth. 'You are not yet twenty and you have the rest of your life before you.'

'Have you forgotten, Ruth, that I also have an illegitimate son?' Alice's eyes looked at her steadily.

'That's entirely your own business,' replied Ruth. 'I never probed. As far as Ben and I are concerned, you are a young widow.'

'Nevertheless, it is true,' persisted Alice. 'How am I to explain that to George Gibbs, or to his family?'

Ruth came tearfully to her side. 'Alice, dear, please don't flay yourself like this. You are so young and any sin you may have committed you have atoned for with your good works and your wonderful unselfish attitude to God. If ever I knew an angel, Alice, it's you.'

'They say there are more sinned against than sinners, so you may be right, Ruth,' murmured Alice with unusual irony. She turned away and then said, in a remote, cold voice. 'I was pushed against a wall by a drunken lout and raped.'

'Oh, my dear!' Ruth's arms went around her. 'I have always suspected that there was some dark secret in your past. My poor darling child. Let this confession release your soul of it, for it will never be revealed by myself.'

'It is not so important now, Ruth,' said Alice. 'I have God's good work to do, but you must realize that marriage is not for me.'

'No, I cannot agree with that,' cried Ruth. 'It's not good to live alone and George will be a good father to your son as well as a fine husband for you.'

'It's impossible,' replied Alice. 'I like and respect him and wish to help him in his fight for the brickyard children, but it would be unfair. He deserves someone better than me as I am not of his class. And I simply could not endure that experience again. It would be impossible to be wife to him,' she cried passionately.

Ruth knelt beside her, 'I do understand, and I pray for you, dear, to soften your heart before it is too late. Love has a way of removing all obstacles.'

'I sincerely wish I could feel that way,' sighed Alice, 'but I have made up my mind to devote my life to God and my son.'

'Think carefully on this matter,' Ruth warned. 'Adam is still an infant, but later on he will ask questions. There is also the need to educate him. Financially you will never be able to cope.'

'I realize that life holds many problems for me, dear Ruth,' said Alice, 'but the good Lord will provide. And when you and Ben no longer need me I will apply for a post as a governess and support my son.'

'Ben and I will always need you, Alice,' replied Ruth, 'but there will be changes for us soon. There is a great need for preachers in the East End of London and Ben has been approached by the parish to take a post there. We are God's people and must go where we are most needed. They tell me that the poverty and sin is terrible in that part of London. Life will be very hard and our children are of a tender age, but if it is God's will, then go we must.'

'Are you telling me that I shall not be needed?' asked Alice quietly.

'No, darling, certainly not. I was trying to point out that it would be better to secure yourself by a sensible marriage than to campaign with us amid such adverse conditions.'

'Hard times will have little effect on me,' answered Alice. 'So far I have survived so much,' replied Alice.

'Well, I'll not discuss it any further. Let's be happy, dear, with the little that God gave us.'

That night Ruth recounted this conversation to Ben and told him of her concerns for Alice's future.

'It's strange that Alice will not talk about that hamlet,' said Ben. 'It's obvious from the scars on her arms, that she once worked in the kilns. Those brick fields out on the marshes are well known for their decadence and the corruption of the young. George seems to have managed to squeeze some sort of concession from the owner of the brick yards to see that the children went to school part time. There is another long piece about it in *The Times* this week.'

'I'm a little disappointed that he never proposed to Alice,' Ruth confessed. 'I was sure he was fond of her.'

Ben peered over the top of his spectacles in an amused manner. 'Cease this match-making, woman. No good will come of it. God willing, a man will always find his own mate.'

Ruth nodded but did not look entirely convinced by her husband's words. Then the subject was dropped.

Several weeks later Alice received a letter in the morning post. Ruth was beside herself with curiosity when she saw whom it was for and held it out for Alice with a triumphant smile on her face.

With a puzzled frown, Alice took hold of the letter timidly. She was quite afraid to open it.

'Well, open it up, Alice,' cried Ruth excitedly.

Alice slowly broke the seal and opened the letter, reading its contents without comment. She then passed it over to Ruth:

Dear Alice,

Forgive me, dear lady, but I must tell you of my feelings. I cannot work or rest until I receive your answer. I respectfully ask you to consider me in the light of a partner so that we two can work together for those distressed little ones. In unison we can do much for humanity.

This may not seem ideal as a marriage proposal but I am sure you will know that comes from the innermost feeling of my heart. Like yourself, dear Alice, I find it most difficult to express myself but I will be a good husband to you and father to your son. I love you and have done since we first met, I will be coming to see you at Christmas when I visit my sister Jenny. So I beg you, dear Alice, to give me the answer I seek.

Yours always,
George Gibbs

'Oh,' Ruth smiled joyfully as she finished reading the letter, 'this is wonderful for you, Alice,' she said.

Ben nodded. 'Good old George,' he said. 'So he's found the courage at last.'

'Congratulations, Alice,' they said in unison.

But Alice took back the letter and stared at it grimly. 'Please excuse me,' she said in a choking voice before fleeing upstairs to lie on her bed and weep heartbrokenly into the pillow. How could she possibly marry such a fine good man? How could she ever tell him about her child, her background, her mother? Oh, she loved him but it was better to refuse his hand in marriage because the terrible memory of that rape would never be erased.

Downstairs, Ruth and Ben looked sadly at one another, knowing that they should say no more about the matter to their beloved Alice.

Soon the chill of winter descended on the countryside. Frost gleamed on the grass in the meadows and the birds disappeared, leaving only the tiny robin to stay on, his red breast glowing against the white snow as he hopped on to the nursery window sill to pick up the breadcrumbs placed there by Adam and Faith.

Both children were healthy and strong. Adam with his black hair, tawny skin and soft brown eyes, was so different from the blonde Faith. But both were good-natured and sweet, full of tenderness and affection for the little bird hopping about in the snow.

And when they romped together, Adam was always kind and gentle, careful not to hurt his little friend, despite his robust way. For these were God's children, happy and protected, brought up to have love for the good Lord and his creations, and to love and respect their parents. Above all, they had been taught to have compassion for the poor unwashed children who came in from the street to their parents' Sunday school.

The years following Waterloo were very hard. Bad harvests and the Corn Laws had made the price of bread so high that it was almost beyond the reach of the working classes altogether. And still hunger and pestilence abounded even in the small country towns such as Dartford.

Every day Ruth and Ben collected donations for the poor from the prosperous middle classes. And on Friday nights hot soup was given out free. The poor families gladly queued outside the mission to receive their supper of a jug of hot soup and a small piece of bread.

Ruth and Alice worked as hard as ever to feed the hungry crowds and once a week they would ride out to the nearby farms to beg for old vegetables, chicken and meat bones, anything that would make a nourishing hot soup to warm the small bellies of the poor children. And Ben would then cajole the poor into chapel to pray for better times.

When the December snow came down and tiny hands and feet looked frozen, Alice distributed the small mittens that she had made from the sleeves of old woollens sent in by the better-off well-wishers.

Not far down the road from the mission was the Crown Inn where many of the children's parents spent their last penny on gin while their offspring queued for a free supper. Ben and Ruth were very conscious of this, as they were of the youngsters who fell down in the street dead drunk, having been supplied with a pen'orth of gin for some odd job they might have done.

'Drink is the demon,' announced Ruth one day. 'It must be abolished. No one shall take alcoholic beverage in my house any more.'

Ben had always enjoyed his after-dinner port, but now he obligingly gave in to Ruth, as he knew that they had to practice what they preached.

There were many chapel goers in the town who did not approve of the horde of unwashed humanity Ruth attracted to God's premises. The Wesleyan Church had changed considerably since it had been founded and was now essentially middle class. The respectable folk came to church on Sundays, dressed in their best, to hear a good sermon preached by Ben. But many of them began to complain to the

Church Council that Ben was too concerned with the lower classes and spent too much time and money on them instead of looking after the needs of the *true* members of the church, as they liked to think of themselves.

This was why the Anneslees were to move to London. A decision was made by the elders in the church to send Ben and Ruth down to the London slums where their pioneering works with the poor would stand them in good stead. With this move the Anneslees would have to leave their comfortable home with its long garden and conservatory, to seek a place to live in the poorest part of London slums.

'I don't care,' said Ruth. 'Why preach to those who want to go to church? After all, John Wesley went out into the fields and highways to preach to those who did not want it. I'm afraid that the whole of our religious concept has disappeared under a cloak of pious respectability.'

'You must realize that a certain amount of money is needed to run the chapel, Ruth,' said Ben. 'Otherwise how would I receive the small stipend that I get? It is not the poor who give us the wherewithal,' said Ben, 'so we simply have to cultivate those who do.'

'I don't agree,' replied Ruth. 'Our Lord welcomed sinners and lived in poverty. Sometimes I think I am no longer a Methodist.'

'Ruth, dear, what are you talking about?' Ben was truly shocked by his wife's remark.

'Well, I think the movement needs reform,' she argued.

'Now, Ruth, it is not necessary to be so militant. A woman's place is in the home, but I give you plenty of freedom so do not abuse it,' he warned her, trying to assert himself.

'Hoity, toity,' sniffed Ruth. 'Why are you so sure that a woman is the weaker sex? I am sure that we are equal to men in every way.'

But Ben had had enough and was not in the mood to argue. As he opened his newspaper in front of him, Ruth sighed noisily and stomped out of the room.

All through this Alice sat quietly in the corner making little rag dolls and re-covering old story books for her little ones at the Sunday school. Snow was piled up outside the front door and huge logs burned brightly on the fire. In two weeks it would be Christmas and George Gibbs was still expecting an answer. So far Alice had made no comment on the subject.

Ruth looked out at the snow and remarked: 'I doubt if our friend George will visit us this Christmas. The travelling will be too hazardous for him to come such a long way.'

There was just a stony silence from Alice.

'Anyway, I shall prepare his room, just in case,' murmured Ruth, loud enough for Alice to hear.

On Christmas Day, as the women changed for dinner there was a rap on the door. Ben was heard down in the hall welcoming George in a loud voice, as the visitor stamped the snow from his boots on the step.

'He has come!' exclaimed Ruth. 'Oh, he must love you, Alice, to have travelled through a blizzard like this.'

Alice sat plaiting her long hair and tears coursed down her face. She had to refuse him for all the reasons she had. Now she prayed to God to give her the strength and courage to do so.

'Make yourself look nice, Alice,' cried Ruth as she left the room. 'You can borrow my cashmere shawl if you wish. I'll go down and welcome our guest.'

Christmas dinner was a merry affair that day. There was no expensive poultry, just roast mutton and caper sauce, but there were plenty of vegetables and an enormous plum pudding. George had brought presents from the farm for the children from Dolly and Jenny and after dinner they all played games. But although the atmosphere was warm, Alice remained cold and aloof from George, after the initial courteous greeting.

As Ruth hurried the protesting children up to bed, Ben announced that he wanted to go to his study to put the finishing touches on his sermon for the next day. Thus Alice and George were left alone.

A nervous tension filled the air as Alice, panic-stricken, gazed at George with a wide terrified look from her seat on the sofa.

George held out his hand. 'Alice, my love, do not look so afraid. Come, take my hand, we will walk into the conservatory.'

Almost in a trance, Alice obeyed. It was cool, dark and pleasant in the conservatory amongst the potted palms and hanging baskets of ferns. There the couple sat on a low wooden bench.

George looked at her earnestly. 'Alice, my love, put me out of my misery. Is it to be yes or no?'

Alice cast down her eyes and clasped her hands as if in prayer. 'I am truly sorry, sir, but the answer is definitely no.' She was surprised by the firmness with which she spoke.

George looked crest-fallen. 'Have you a reason?' he asked quietly.

Alice rose to her feet and paced the floor. 'There are many reasons, sir,' she said in a very controlled voice. She had rehearsed these words so many times. 'The chief one is that it's impossible for me to be a wife to any man. The thought of it is fire to my brain. I beg you, sir, do not press me.' Then she lost control. She put her hands over her face and burst into tears.

Gently George took her hands and held them tight. 'Look at me, Alice, and tell me you hate me, that you can't abide the sight of me. Only then will I accept your answer and be content.'

'No! No!' she wept. 'I have strong feeling for you but I cannot get away from the past, no matter how hard I try.'

'Then I must help you,' he said. 'You have no secrets from me, Alice. I have known you since that first day in Hollinbury when we went riding to the fair.'

Alice looked up at him with a gasp. 'You have known about me all the time?' she asked in amazement.

George nodded. 'Yes, and every day I have loved you more. I need you, Alice. I need your ability and your love of God.

That you do not wish to be my wedded wife does not bother me. I want to care for you and your darling son. Please, dear, think about it carefully. Do not throw away this precious thing we have found.'

'I have wanted you to know about my past,' she wept.

'Then my mother, you know about her too?'

George's arm went round her waist, and Alice's head rested on his shoulder.

'Your mother was buried with proper Christian rites, God rest her soul,' he added piously. 'She is not in a pauper's grave, I saw to that.'

'Oh, George,' cried Alice. 'How can you still want me when you know my background? I bring no dowry, I bring nothing except an illegitimate child.'

'That will soon be remedied,' he said firmly. 'Now Alice, dry your tears and let us make our announcement.' He pressed her hands to his lips. 'I swear to love, honour and protect you all my life. Now, let me hear you say yes.'

Alice hung her head shyly. 'I don't deserve you but I'll love and honour you until I die.'

Later, the Anneslee house was in a festive mood to celebrate the latest news. Ruth got out glasses and a bottle. 'It's only sarsaparilla,' she apologized. 'But we must toast the health of our beloved friends.'

It was a cold and silent night outside but in Ruth's parlour the fire blazed and they sat around it, four close friends talking of old times and planning for the future. It was a Christmas they would all remember, one of great happiness and joy, their last one in that comfortable home in Dartford.

That night, in soft mellow tones George told them of his past. 'I was born in the Midlands where my folk were fairly comfortable. My father was a master builder, which meant a lot in those days before our part of the country became revolutionized and large mills and potteries were erected. Most of the poor came to slave in those mills, and men with skills were not needed any more. So Father invested his savings and lost them. The disaster killed him, leaving my mother practically penniless. Luckily, I was the last child. My sister Jenny was already married and very comfortable. Then a relative came to my mother's aid and set her up in a small haberdashery business. I went with him to work in the brick fields.

'I've no wish to condemn him but like most of his class he thought that kicks and blows formed the best means of obtaining the maximum amount of work from a young lad. At nine years of age, I was carrying forty pounds of clay on my head from the clay heap to the moulding table for thirteen hours a day, often having to stay there all night. After my day's work, I then had to carry a thousand bricks from the hardening floor to the kilns, walking in one night a distance of nine miles. And for all this labour, I received sixpence a week.

'So you see, dear Alice, I am not unfamiliar myself with what goes on in the brickyards. Most grown-ups were in utter ignorance of how the children were treated and turned a blind eye to the fact that youngsters toiled from morning until night and became prematurely old.

'I relate this personal experience to you, dear Alice, because I want you to see that we are equal and that you and I both yearn for less preaching of the dead past and more sympathetic practice for the living present. What I endured all those years ago has not altered at all. In fact, conditions have even worsened by the poverty of our times. God helping, I shall not rest till the wrongs done to the brickyard children are redressed.'

'Hear! Hear!' muttered Ben, when George had finished.

Ruth sat silently for a few moments, contemplating George's words, and then she sprang to her feet. 'Why are we all so solemn on this Christmas night? Let's have a sing-song.' She sat down at the piano and they all sang Christmas carols into the night.

The next morning as George was leaving, he pecked Alice on the cheek. 'Make arrangements for our wedding, dear,' he said. 'I'll be back in a few weeks.'

Earlier he had talked a little of how they would live. 'I am not a poor man, but I am not a rich man, either. I own a shop and cottage and I am a part-time preacher, so we will be able to live fairly comfortably. The haberdashery shop came to me by my mother and the Wesleyan Council provided the cottage, I am sorry to have to take you away from your friends Ben and Ruth but we can still visit them and they us.

'I hope this is all agreeable to you, dear Alice.'

Alice was quite overcome by it all, and just nodded her head in silent assent.

It was early spring when Alice and George married very quietly in the central Methodist Chapel in town. Ben and Ruth were the witnesses. Alice was dressed soberly but very smartly in a silver grey gaberdine suit that she and Ruth had made. On her head she wore a navy-blue bonnet with a tiny bunch of artificial forget-me-nots at the side.

Alice was indeed a blushing bride. Her brown eyes shone with tears of joy as George slipped the ring on her finger and she pledged herself to him for life. It was her supreme moment and she suddenly felt that she really belonged to the world.

The evening before had been a little uncomfortable when George had suggested that they visit his sister out in the hamlet. But Alice had shied away from the suggestion like a young pony.

'Oh, no,' she cried. 'I would not.'

George's gentle hands restrained her. 'Alice my love, what is wrong? There is nothing to be afraid of.'

'Oh, please! Do not force me to go back there. I beg you, do not make me return.'

'But my dearest, you have a young sister at the farm and my sister wants to meet you so badly.'

'Dolly does not know of me or even need me. But there are many in the hamlet who will remember my mother and me. Please, George, please allow me to start life afresh. It is all I'll ever ask of you.'

'Well,' George consented, 'as you wish. We will travel home

tomorrow, so there will be no chance to visit the hamlet again.' There was a disappointed edge to his voice.

'I do not care,' cried Alice with unusual passion. 'I swore I would never go back, so don't ever ask me to George.'

Adam was sad to be leaving Faith. He stood looking very glum, cap on his black curls, holding his little friend by the hand. Tears streamed down her chubby cheeks.

'Don't cry,' Adam said manfully. 'I will come and visit you, and you can come and stay with us.'

'I don't want you to go,' Faith whimpered. 'Who will I play with?'

'You are going to live in London,' he informed her soberly. 'There will be lots of new things to do. But I will miss you, too, Faith.' His voice was choked.

So, as the adults said their goodbyes, Adam was lifted into the stagecoach.

'Goodbye, God bless,' they called, and Adam waved goodbye out of the window to Faith until her image became blurred with his tears.

So on that fine spring day, after the wedding ceremony, the Gibbs family left for their home town in Leicestershire.

CHAPTER THIRTEEN

Retribution

Down at the Malted Shovel, dumb Lukey swept the yard with a long handled broom made out of twigs. Every now and then his eyes squinted out towards the estuary of the wide river, as if noting that his brother John had gone off sailing once more.

Lukey was not feeling very happy. The night before, John had got very drunk and he had brought Lukey sweets and ginger beer. But Beat had got cross with him because he had become too excited.

'Leave Lukey alone,' Beat cried. 'Don't torment him.' John had given Lukey his pipe to puff and Lukey had coughed and spluttered loudly before getting very violent and bashing his head against the wall.

Lukey had ended up falling to the floor in a fit. But John had been too drunk to care. Surrounded by his new-found friends, for whom he constantly bought drinks, he danced, sang and generally made a fool of himself.

'I'll be bloody glad when he sails out in the morning,' Beat complained to Dot. 'And I'll bet he's been with that dirty little bitch, Dolly, all afternoon. That I'll be bound. What's bred in the bone comes out in the flesh, that's what I always say.'

'Hush,' whispered Dot. 'Someone might hear you.'

'I am not sure that I care,' declared Beat. 'It's time someone put that fool Kit wise to the fact that he is being cuckolded.'

Dot shook her head sadly and stood young Percy up to the sink and washed his face. Then she combed his black curly locks. She was preparing him to go to the new school which had been built in the village next door to the church.

Times were certainly changing in the hamlet. A manufacturer from the big town had moved in to the neighbourhood and he was very free with the money he had earned from his workers' slave labour. He had donated money for this new school which was to be run by the church. It was not free, though the fees were low, but mostly only the middleclass children attended, for the cost was still way above the reach of the poor working-class children most of whom still toiled at the Pug Mill.

But Dot was a great believer in education and Percy was the be-all and end-all of her life.

'Lack of the schooling never stopped me counting me own money,' scoffed Beat, but she still generously provided money for the fees and schoolbooks so that her young nephew would not be deprived.

The other major change in the hamlet was in its population since the navvies had come to work on the canal. Most of these were Irish or Italian, a rough, uncouth lot imported from the overcrowded industrial towns of the north country where a large-scale canal system was already in operation. These people built shacks along the wayside, and those of their poorly clad, hungry children who did not slave in the brickfields, roamed the street scrumping for food in the fields and orchards.

Beat was not unduly worried about this, as she was making a good profit, and the coins rattled down into the wooden drawer in the counter sounding like music to her ears. But Dot looked askance at the hordes of unwashed children who played in the yard, and she was terrified that they might pass some strange disease to her Percy.

'Don't worry so much,' remarked Beat. 'Once the canal is finished those buggers will move on. In the meantime, it's business and very good business at that,' she added gleefully, counting the money.

But Dot kept Percy under a tight rein and would not let him out to play. So from the same attic window which his mother had looked for her lover, Percy would longingly watch the other children at play.

The Irish and the Italians hated each other and grabbed every opportunity to fight. But if they tried it on in her bar, Beat was always ready to break them up with the rolling pin.

Outside, every day, the huge crevice that would soon hold the water of the canal grew wider and deeper, winding over the marsh towards the river. The new canal was nearly finished.

And every day, poor dumb Lukey, with crazed eyes, would chase the Irish children who liked to torment him, mercilessly. But he never managed to catch them. So, with that witch's broom he would relentlessly sweep the yard as the children ran and clambered all over the place, just out of his reach.

One evening as it was getting dark, a particularly pretty young colleen with long ginger hair and wearing a ragged dress, was carrying home a jug of beer to her father who now lived in Larlee's old cottage with his big family. Lukey was sitting on the wall watching her when suddenly he reached out and grabbed her long mane of red hair. The jug of beer crashed down into the road as the girl's shrill scream echoed over the bridge. Lukey was still hanging on to her hair when the brawny Irishman dashed from his cottage, crossed the bridge, and brought his boot crashing into dumb Lukey's contorted face. Blood spurted out everywhere and Lukey fell backwards over the wall and the Irish navvy gathered his daughter up in his arms. But Beat was there dashing to Lukey's aid before the rest of the men set about him.

'Be Jesus!' bawled the Paddy. 'Keep that crazy fool away from my children or by God I'll finish him!'

'Keep yer bloody kids out of me yard,' snarled Beat as she hustled the dazed and bleeding Lukey inside.

In the safety of the kitchen, Beat bathed his face, fussed and kissed him so that he wept and laughed alternately. Beat looked at him anxiously as she remembered Lucinda and the others — Joe Lee and even Lukey's own father, the husky blacksmith. Was Lukey still homicidal? Beat felt very worried. For some years now Lukey had been so much more docile but she could never be quite sure, could never quite trust him. From now on she would have to keep a watchful eye on him. For should the residents complain, Lukey might be shut up in a cage, and Beat had no intention of allowing anyone to do that to him. In a strange way Beat was fond of Lukey. Although she beat him often, she also loved him at the same time. Lukey replaced both a child and a lover in Beat's barren life.

She put Lukey to bed and gave him Lucinda's teddy to cuddle. 'Good boy, Lukey, be a good boy for Beattie,' she murmured.

In the adjoining room Dot listened fearfully and hugged little Percy closer. She had really become quite afraid of dumb Lukey in recent years.

Out in their cosy cottage, some way over the marsh, lived Kit the herdsman and his plump fair wife, Dolly. The snow had left the meadows and the fresh green of the grass contrasted with those mature old timbers, interlaced with Kent ragstones. In the front garden, primroses had begun to poke out fresh young shoots and the brown earth was freshly dug ready for Kit to plant in the spring. Inside the cottage itself, everything was bright and very clean. There were the neat cretonne chair-covers, and little bits of shining brass around the brick fireplace. On the mantelshelf sat an old clock — a wedding present from Wally, and also, in all its majesty, with its trunk upraised, there stood the white ivory elephant.

But all was not well in Marsh Cottage. Kit now sat moodily beside the fire, still dressed in his muddy work clothes and clay-clogged boots. He had just returned home from work to find his little wife missing. Her red cape had gone from behind the kitchen door, and her shopping basket had disappeared from its place on the kitchen larder shelf. Kit rubbed his unshaven chin irritably, and then got up and moved the white elephant around so that its trunk faced the door. He wished that Dolly would be more careful. Every day when she dusted, Dolly would turn the elephant round and Kit did not like it. He was very superstitious and firmly believed that as long as the white elephant faced the door his luck would hold out. But his luck was not holding out in his marriage. Dolly was rarely at home nowadays, and was always out gossiping or visiting. He finished work early these days, for he was now a foreman, but Dolly was never there.

Now he removed his boots a little wearily and placed them under the dresser. Dolly was so youthful in her ways. It was a pity to reprimand her. But currently Kit had been feeling extremely unhappy about his sexual prowess. Or lack of it. He was incapable of completing the act of sex. From the village doctor he had obtained herbs and medicine to help him but none of these had proved to be of any use.

'You had a kick when young which has damaged your testicles, I should think,' the doctor had informed him.

Kit believed him. After all, he had so many kicks and blows throughout his childhood — both from the rough men in the brickyards and from his own family on the barge where he had been born.

'It might come right,' the doctor said reassuringly. 'Don't lose heart. Just keep trying.'

So night after night Kit made a play at sex, but he never managed to accomplish much and his lovely Dolly, so hot and sensuous, and ready for love, had long ago lost her patience with him.

'Get off,' she would say crossly. 'And don't start again. I'm damned fed-up with this business. You can't satisfy me, and I'd sooner do without.'

But of late she had begun to neglect Kit. He did not blame her for it. She was young, after all, and this cottage was very isolated. A young woman needed company. It was a pity that the Wrights had emigrated to Canada leaving Dolly without a job. Gloomily, Kit pondered over the long winter just past. By now he should have got Dolly with child. Twelve months they had been married and only twice had he ever managed to get anything like an erection. Then a horrible thought crossed his mind and his hands grasped the arms of the chair nervously. 'No, no,' he muttered. 'Surely not my Dolly. She would never do anything like that. . . .' The devil came in his subtle way to taunt him. 'Her mother Kit, you surely remember her mother. She was a whore.' The words echoed around his head.

White in the face, Kit got to his feet and stood at the door of the cottage looking out over the marsh towards the setting sun. Long red streaks of colour were lined with gold as the flowing Thames went out at full tide to join the sea. On the high water line Kit spied the familiar red sails of the *Alianora* lying at anchor. He stepped back inside the cottage and slammed the door shut. Then he sat at the well-scrubbed kitchen table with his head in his hands and began weeping real tears.

This was just how Dolly found him later when she came bouncing merrily in, carrying a few eggs in her basket and some herbs she had just gathered. Her red cape was crumpled and her white cap askew on her head. Lovely Dolly was radiant with happiness and good health. 'Oh, now, Kit,' she said. 'You are depressed again.' She spoke in a motherly fashion. Placing the basket on the table, she came forward and put her arms around him. 'Oh, dear, don't cry, Kit. I'm sorry I am late. I walked over to the farm to get some fresh eggs for breakfast.' She held him to her breast tenderly. 'Dear me, what am I going to do with you? Why do you get so upset?'

Kit knew that she was not telling the whole truth. The cape she wore smelled strongly of the salty sea and he knew that she had been down to the shore.

'Come now,' she cajoled him, 'I'll put on these nice warm slippers, and get a log for the fire. Then we can have our supper.'

She bustled about the kitchen and Kit, still red-eyed and full of silent misery stared at her from his thin harassed face.

On Dolly's podgy arm the snake bracelet that she always wore seemed in the glow of the fire, winking a wicked green eye at him. Dolly had a lover, he was sure of that, and who could it be but John Shulmead? It had been obvious from the beginning that they had fancied each other.

'Oh, dear God, give me courage,' he prayed that night in bed. 'What shall I do?' Beside him, Dolly lay serene in sleep. She never used to. When first were they married she used to toss and turn all night so dissatisfied had she been at his sexual performance, and her highly sexed nature had overcome her. But now her body seemed at peace each night.

In the morning the sky line was clear. The *Alianora* had sailed away once more. Kit breathed a deep sigh of relief as he kissed his sleeping wife tenderly on her brow before setting off to work once more. For a while, at least, his mind could be at rest.

All along the main road to the village new red brick houses had been built. Slowly the little hamlet was being sucked into the village and would soon be indistinguishable from it. Its personality would be gone; it would exist no more.

Aunt Dot pondered on these sad thoughts as she stood outside the church waiting for the wagon bringing the children home from school. Religiously, each day, she met that cart to greet Percy on his return from school, just as she put him on it each morning with his school books and his packed lunch. Percy would give a saucy grin as she kissed him tenderly and gave him precise instructions not to play about in the wagon in case he fell out. But once Aunt Dot was out of sight, Percy played up merry hell, tormenting the old driver and all the small girls, whose legs he would pinch. And any boy who tried to protect his sisters got a good punch from Percy.

Percy was as hard as nails. His body was big and sturdy and his temper very uncertain.

'He's the worst of the lot,' complained the old wagon driver, who felt quite battered on certain days.

But the village school-teacher was indulgent about him. 'Of course, our Percy is a trifle over-strung,' she would murmur. 'But he has good brains.'

Dot would not listen to anything about her Percy unless it was something good. He was the apple of her eye, just as his lovely mother had been. The fact that this big sturdy lad was so full of pranks that he was slowly wearing her down, was something she would never admit. Her face was wizened and her gait was much slower. She often had to stop half-way up the stairs when dashing up from the bar to attend to Percy when he screamed for a drink or the chamber pot. She always did this even when the bar was very busy.

Beat did not approve. 'Tan his bloody arse really hard, I would,' she groused one particular Saturday night when the bar was very busy and Percy was being obnoxious. 'I need you to help down here, Dot. Don't keep running up the stairs to that boy. Send Lukey to play with him.'

'Oh no! Not Lukey!' exclaimed Dot breathlessly.

'Don't be such a fool. Lukey won't harm him. He's only sitting in the bloody kitchen wasting his time. Lukey! Lukey!' she screamed. 'Go up and stay with Percy until he is asleep.'

Lukey immediately rose and looking very pleased with himself, went up those forbidden stairs to Percy. 'Oh, no!' cried Dot, visibly trembling.

'For Christ's sake, woman, relax!' roared Beat irritably. 'Young Percy is quite big enough now to take care of himself.'

So Dot gave in, she always did to her dogmatic sister, and thus began a strange, secret, relationship up in Percy's playroom.

The attic high in the roof, where his mother had hidden her lover, was now Percy's playroom, containing, as it did, every conceivable toy that a child could wish for. It was here that Percy directed Lukey on that first day. Right from the beginning Percy was the boss of the two, and Lukey did everything Percy told him to do. Lukey was allowed to ride the rocking horse only if young Percy gave permission, and he never dared touch any of Percy's fine wooden soldiers unless the little boy had told him he could. But they played so well together — soldiers, sailors, anything would keep them happy for hours. And always Percy was the one in charge.

So in this way Lukey and Percy became pals and fellow conspirators. In the middle of their games Lukey was sent downstairs to pinch cakes and ginger beer for them to consume in privacy. Once, under Percy's instructions, soap was put into the cheese sandwiches prepared for the customers at the inn and another day, a dead mouse was slipped in to one of Aunt Beat's famous meat pies. There was no end to the mischievous ideas that young Percy thought up.

As they grew older the friendship became stronger. Poor Lukey was devoted to his little friend and was much happier with Percy than anyone else. His presence seemed to calm him down, even though Percy slapped and ordered him about mercilessly. Everywhere that Percy went, dumb Lukey limped behind him like a faithful dog. At night they clambered out of the window and romped over the marsh, trapping bull frogs. Percy enjoyed pulling off their legs to see if they could still hop.

There was a very cruel streak in young Percy. His aunts were aware of it but as long as he did not make too much of a nuisance of himself, they allowed him to pursue his mean, depraved ways.

Over the years Aunt Dot had become much less active, until eventually she tended to spend her days just sitting quietly in a rocking chair and saying very little to anyone. She often read out aloud from the Bible and frequently went to church to talk to the old curate. The curate had quite a lot of time on his hands nowadays as his congregation had dwindled enormously in recent years as more folk were attracted to the fancy Methodist chapel in the village.

One day in 1825, there was a deep, dull roar and a loud long rumbling sound as the new lock gates were opened for the first time. The new canal, awaited for all these years, was open at last! As the water from the creek drained into the uniformly shaped crevice of the canal, the Hollinbury inhabitants came out to watch and cheer. But some, like old Wally and Beat, stayed back, standing outside the Malted Shovel looking very cynical.

'Told ye so,' said old Wally. 'They will divert that creek,

and that will run dry, then there will only be flats out there and no cattle will be able to graze.'

'Well, what with the time and money they have spent on it, let's hope it will pay for itself,' announced Beat.

'I can't see that myself.' Old Wally had become very feeble of late, but he still managed to fumble his way over the bridge each night to the Malted Shovel. There he would sit in the same warm corner beside the open fire and accept drinks with a magnanimous gesture from anyone who wished to treat him. Although his frame was weaker, his faculties were all there. Those large grizzled ears stuck out from his old head and he never missed a sound — a comment or an aside muttered within earshot. He would always claim that he came to the inn every night in order to escape from the noisy Irish family next door to his cottage but really it was loneliness that drove Wally down to that public bar in the hope that he would bump into John Shulmead. For John was still a grand favourite of his, since Wally felt that Toby had deserted him somewhat.

Toby still lived with Wally but was always out and about these days. Like the rest of Farmer Wright's staff, he had received a small stipend from the generous farmer before he and his family left for the Colonies. Toby had invested his money carefully. He had grown tired of pigs and cows and had apprenticed himself to the village barber, and was doing well. A religious man, at the weekends he would walk into town to attend the service in the new Wesleyan chapel.

Wally did not like this at all. 'Toby's got blamed religion,' he grumbled. 'Them Methodists got him. He don't drink and he don't even smoke, like he used to. I don't hold with them foreign religions, I don't.'

Wally often fell asleep in his warm corner and at closing time Beat would rouse him and get someone to escort him over the bridge to his cottage. Some nights Kit would come in and sit beside Wally for a while. But he was always silent, drinking his beer with a preoccupied expression on his pale face.

'He ain't a lot o' company now,' Wally would complain. 'Not since that Dolly got hold of him. What I said I still stand by. She be no good and will bring plenty of trouble, that Dolly will.' The old man's words were truer than ever he knew.

The early summer corn, a fresh green was an inch high, and an invigorating fresh salt breeze blew over the marsh as Dolly lay in her lover's arms in the small cabin below deck on the *Alianora*.

'I am really worried, John,' she said. 'I'm sure that I'm with child.'

John Shulmead looked concerned, wrinkling his fair brow, he stared down at the sturdy bare limbs of his Dolly. She was a husky wench and would make a fine mother, he thought, but how would Kit react to the situation? He had been so moody lately that John had felt a little sorry for him. 'What will you do, Dolly?' he asked.

'I'm blowed if I know,' she replied. 'I suppose I could blame Kit. After all, he is my husband!' She giggled nervously.

'Cuckold him?' grinned John. 'Well, it's often been done before.'

Dolly's mouth assumed a petulant droop. 'Oh, I wish we could be together all the time, John. Why can't you take me with you? Let us sail away from this hamlet, like you used to tell me we would, to a desert island, just you and me.'

John sighed. 'It's not that simple Dolly,' he said. 'I still owe money for this barge. You know that I am indebted to old Beatrice, and I can't run out on her. Besides, I am not even sure that I want to. I was born in this hamlet, it is my home.'

'Ah well,' said Dolly resignedly, 'it will all sort itself out in the end. I suppose I'd better go before it gets too dark.' She rose languidly from the bunk, pulling down her dress. Suddenly there was a noise outside and she saw a small figure standing on the gang plank, short, distorted shape wearing a leather cap and a short travelling cape which billowed out in the wind to create a bizarre silhouette.

'It's Toby,' said John, looking through the porthole.

'Oh my,' gasped Dolly. 'What does he want?'

John ran lightly up the gangway to greet him but Toby just stood where he was. 'Send her out, that Jezebel!' he yelled. 'I know she is in there! My God forgive you, John, you are committing a mortal sin. I pray nightly for your redemption. Send her home to Kit, my poor afflicted brother. I have already warned her that her husband is near to a breakdown.'

Hearing this, Dolly puffed herself up and flounced out on to the deck. 'You mind your own business,' she yelled back at him. 'Hop it, you ape!'

'Dolly, Dolly, I beg of you,' continued Toby. 'Ask forgiveness for your sins and return to Kit. My brother needs you!'

'Your brother?' sneered Dolly tossing her pretty curls. 'Why, he is not even a man. And you, you ugly bugger, you're just like a bloody old Toby jug. What's it to you what I do?'

Toby looked stunned. He had always been so fond of fair Dolly, but now she was showing another side of her nature.

'No, don't be unkind, Dolly,' John remonstrated with her.

But Dolly's temper was up. 'Well, tell him to git. Send him packing, that bloody Toby jug,' she jeered.

'I have warned you that your Kit has reached the end of his tether. Now it's all in God's hands,' Toby turned and his odd little shape limped away forlornly into the rising mist.

John frowned. 'That was not very nice, Dolly,' he said.

She sniffed loudly. 'Serve him right for poking his nose into other folks' affairs,' she said tartly.

'Come, I'll walk along the shore and see you on your way,' said John.

When they parted, Dolly said: 'I've decided to tell Kit the truth tonight, come what may. And if he don't like it, he knows what he can do.'

'Mind what you are up to, Dolly,' warned John. 'You know how they gossip in this hamlet. Perhaps you and I had better separate for a while.'

Dolly threw her arms passionately about his neck. 'Oh no, John! I can't live without you, I need your love.'

He petted her and looked so solemn. 'But Dolly what about

this child?' he asked.

'Oh, I'll find a way,' she said confidently and tripped off into the darkening night toward the light of her cottage which stood alone on the misty marshland. She hurried along feeling a little afraid now that John had gone. When she reached home, she pushed at the front door but it would not open. It was locked. Kit must have gone out to the inn.

'Damn!' she muttered. Bending down to peer through the window in the rapidly disappearing light she saw, to her amazement, a chair propped up against the door. Running against it and ramming it with a strong shoulder, she gave the door a hefty shove causing it to give way. The chair behind it fell over. Grumbling loudly, she stooped over and picked up the chair. Fumbling about, she managed to light a candle to cast some light in the little cottage. As she turned around, candle in hand, she bumped into a pair of feet swinging just at eye level. There, with a terrible creaking sound, was Kit's body swinging to and fro from the old oak beam. Dolly screamed again and again, the piercing sounds ringing out across the marsh. But no one came to her aid. Between screams, all she could hear was the eerie sound of the creaking rope against the beam as Kit's body swung slowly to and fro.

Panic-stricken, Dolly rushed out of the cottage and fled down the land towards the lights of the Malted Shovel.

Beat was just calling time when Dolly fell in through the door, screaming and jabbering that Kit had hanged himself. Aunt Dot comforted the hysterical girl while the rest of the men present went off to cut Kit down from the beam.

Only old Wally sitting in his corner was unmoved by the commotion. He sat in his corner staring at the fair, distressed Dolly with a malevolent look in his rheumatic eyes.

Beat handed Dolly a stiff brandy, her shrewd eyes surveying her sharply. 'Don't suppose we need to ask if yer were at home when it happened, gal. Out a-courtin', I reckon. Still, God pays his own debts. He don't need no money,' she added with an ominous tone to her voice.

CHAPTER FOURTEEN

Ruth's Kitchen

Ben Anneslee's new living was in a mean back street off the Mile End Waste. Having been a Methodist minister for many years now, he was not unused to poverty but the appalling conditions of the East End of London truly shocked him. From the Hackney Marshes to the old Roman City gate at Aldgate, there had once been three rural villages — Bethnal Green, Bromley-by-Bow and Stratford. Now they formed the worst slums in London and were packed tight with a dirty, drunken, squalling population. In this mile-long wasteland bordering the main road, were many gin shops. One shop in three sold alcohol and everywhere flaring oil lamps illuminated wrestling booths, cock-bird gambling pits and brothels. It was here that the population cavorted. It was here that the rich came to do their slumming and it was here that the poor spent their leisure. The narrow streets were lined with eel stalls, hot potato carts, opium vendors, matchsellers, and flower girls, all whining and shouting as they proffered up their wares. Men and women shrieked, swore and fought each other. They urinated in the gutter, copulated openly in doorways and were beyond control of the law. There was no law to control them.

Ragged, filthy children trotted about at night until long after midnight, begging or fetching errands. They gathered outside the pubs to watch the men fighting; they escorted soldiers and sailors to the nearest brothels for a penny, which they then usually spent on gin. There were often five-year-olds lying in the gutters the worse for drink, and every gin shop had its own small box for the mites to stand on to reach the counter in order to obtain their penn'orth of gin.

The area was packed with many immigrants. There were bearded Jews, Poles, Russians, Italian organ-grinders and German traders, all mixing with the local population of costers in green corduroy jackets and bright neck scarfs, saucy prostitutes in low-cut blouses and many ragged women and children.

'My God!' Ben had cried on that first day in London as the family had ploughed their way through the rowdy mob to reach the Methodist chapel.

Sensible, pious Ruth had been unalarmed. 'These must be the world's greatest heathens,' she said philosophically. 'We are really needed here.'

They had rented a house in a very mean little street which faced the back of the London Hospital. It had three storeys and was almost derelict.

'It's too large,' Ruth had declared. 'Why on earth do we need such a big house when others are living in squalor? Still, I shall do what I can to make it more comfortable.'

There were dreary stone steps going down to the basement, and more dreary stone steps leading up to the front door. The front of the house was hemmed in by grimy iron railings. The smoke-blackened facade of the house rose up to a deep slate roof under which there were large attics. Whoever had inhabited this house before had neglected it very badly indeed. It was filthy. There were bugs squashed on the walls, grimy wallpaper, and broken windows were patched up with wooden boards.

''Tis best that we make ourselves comfortable in some small part of it,' suggested Ben. 'We can afford neither the time nor the expense to redecorate it. I am deeply sorry, Ruth, to bring you to such a home, and I will ask the Central Council to find us a more suitable one.'

'Indeed you will not!' Ruth declared in her high-handed manner. 'I married a minister of the gospel and I am prepared to do my duty. This place will be made wholesome and we will spread the word of the Lord to these poor distressed people. Did not your ancestor, John Wesley say: "Go out into the fields and highways"? Well, it's possible he also meant these slums, for these are where most of the sinners are. But, oh dear, God, it's a terrible sight to see small children lying dead drunk in the street.'

'Ruth, dear,' said Ben gently, 'You are an angel. I only wish I had as much faith in human beings as you.'

'Trust in the Lord, dear, and it will all come to pass,' Ruth said with a confident smile.

So, with a little help from their faithful chapel-goers, Ruth and Ben began their good works in the East End of London. Faith was sent to a little dame-school run by a Methodist widow, and Ruth organized her own Sunday school. But her most difficult task was going out along the waste on Saturday nights, when the rowdyism of the crowd was at its height. There one would talk to the ragged children and give them sweets in an effort to persuade them to come to the mission on Sunday afternoon. Slowly but surely Ben and Ruth gained ground. They raised money with collections and appeals to any local manufacturer who was a philanthropist, they stabilized this poor living and increased their congregation at the chapel. But it soon became apparent that they still only had a middle-class congregation, made up of those who possessed a good Sunday suit and a 'best' hat. The very poor who thronged the streets still did not attend.

'It's as clear as daylight to me, Ben,' said an exasperated Ruth, 'that desperately poor people do not attend because they are afraid to be seen among the respectable chapel folks. So what good do we do, I ask you?'

'Oh, dear Ruth, do not probe into something that can never be solved,' argued Ben. 'We are doing what is required of us and that is all we can do.'

''Tis not enough,' his wife insisted.

When Ben went to the chapel, Ruth often stood by the high window in the front room which looked out across the narrow street at the dim lights of the London hospital. From the bleak buildings she would hear the cries of the sick and the

dying and during the day queues of people would assemble
outside for treatment — the maimed, the old, and the incur-
able. And Ruth would feel galvanized into action. This was a
very depressing place but it presented a tremendous chal-
lenge. She felt as though a flame glowed inside her, giving her
a renewal of her faith and uplifting her.

Although she loved her work, her deep regret was that the
women of the movement were not made more busy. Men
preached the sermons and men served the sick. Surely women
could do as well. Indeed, they were more steadfast and, Ruth
believed, more reasoning went on inside the female brain.
What a pity they were not allowed to use their talents when
there was work to be done.

Ruth was in the middle of one of her deep reveries when
the old manservant, who did odd jobs for them, went down
into the coal cellar to fill the scuttle. Ruth watched his tottery
figure go carefully down the steps, then heard him slide back
the cellar door. Then she heard him shouting and cursing and
could see him waving the coal shovel in a threatening manner
at a group of grubby ragged figures who dashed up the steps
and made off down the street.

Ruth opened the casement window and called out: 'Whatever is the matter?'

'It's them varmints,' the old man complained. 'Sleeps in
this 'ere coal cellar, they does.' He poked the long shovel into
the darkened doorway. 'Come out you devils, come out, I
say!'

As he shouted, a small whimper came from the coal cellar.

Her curiosity aroused, Ruth went down to investigate and
found, crouching down in the long dark cellar, amongst the
large lumps of coal, a small girl holding a squalling baby close
to her.

'Come out, dear,' said Ruth kindly. 'I won't hurt you.' She
reached out gentle hands and saw that the girl was only about
ten years old. She was thin and ragged, and her eyes were full
of pus. Her clothes were a dirty mass of rags and the baby
seemed to be in an even worse condition.

'We only want to stay 'ere till the morning,' the girl whined. 'Our muvver's gorn in the 'orspital and she ain't come aht.'

Ruth took the wet, crying babe in her arms and ushered the little girl inside the house.

'Ought to be careful,' grumbled the servant. 'Yer never knows what they got. And it could be catching.'

But Ruth ignored him. She laid the baby on her clean kitchen table and proceeded to remove its filthy wrappings to examine it. 'Sit by the fire and get warm,' she told the girl. 'Now, what is your name?'

'It's Nelly,' the girl replied. 'And that's me bruvver. I fink 'es been crying 'cos he's got the measles. I just got over it, yer see. Me muvver said to keep him in the dark but now she's gorn in the 'orspital and she ain't come aht,' she repeated dolefully.

'Well,' said Ruth as she stripped the baby. 'The coal cellar was certainly dark.' She washed the fevered little body. 'Yes, your brother has indeed got the measles,' she told the girl. 'I'll make him comfortable.'

With swift cool movements Ruth dried and powdered the little babe and wrapped him in a clean shawl. She heated some milk and tried to feed him from a spoon. But the little boy clearly had a temperature and he resisted, rocking to and fro and crying loudly in her arms. Ruth gave him a soothing mixture from her medicine store and gradually he calmed down and slept peacefully so that Ruth could then attend to Nelly. She bathed her sore eyes and found some clean clothes for her before serving up some good-smelling hot soup. Then she deloused Nelly's hair. 'Where do you live?' she asked the child.

'Well, we don't live nowhere,' replied Nelly flatly. But gradually she became quite chatty. 'Me and me bruvver and me muvver walked abaht for days and days. Then me muvver felt poorly so she went over to the 'orspital and she ain't come aht.' Her lips quivered, and her sore eyes flickered as if trying not to cry. Ruth smiled and hugged her gently.

Later that evening when Ben returned he discovered that there were two additions to his family, installed down in the basement next door to the kitchen.

'You cannot keep them, Ruth,' he informed his wife. 'Better to hand them over to the right authorities.'

'To the workhouse, you mean, Ben?' Ruth asked in a sharp tone. 'Both you and I know the conditions of these work-houses in a good town. God only knows what it is like in crowded conditions such as these.'

'Well, it is for you to decide, dear,' Ben said, already giving in, 'but it does mean two more mouths to feed.'

As time passed, many more waifs found a haven in Ruth's kitchen. Nelly was the first and stayed the longest and her little brother, who was called Gobbler, recovered well and was eventually adopted by a Methodist family in the country. Ruth had made enquiries about the children's mother and found that she had dropped dead in the long queue waiting for attention at the hospital and had already been buried in a pauper's grave.

Nelly was intelligent and very hard working. She escorted Faith to school and helped Ruth in the house, for which she received very little payment apart from her keep. She was always cheerful and never complained.

After she realized that her coal cellar was a refuge for homeless children, Ruth began to look out for them and then invite them into her home. There she would clean and feed them and give them a bed for the night. Often they robbed her, and some mocked openly when she prayed over them. But with her sweet infinite patience, Ruth would ignore their ingratitude and press on with her endeavours to save and sustain those tiny derelict souls.

The sewing bees and the charity bazaars began to be neglected as Ruth became increasingly involved in her work for the hungry, the sick and the aged. She thrived as the poor began to know her and where to find her. Women came to her house with long tales of woe, and drunken husbands would hammer at the street door late at night accusing her of harbouring their wives and children. But brave and loyal as always, Ruth stood up to them and protected the weak from the bullies.

That year London was particularly smelly. The Thames stank of sewage and the riverside was choked by an excess of filthy pollution. The river was so filthy that it was stagnant. The muck never got away to sea, instead it hung on the river bank, a huge pile of vile stinking excrement spreading terrible diseases to the City's poverty-stricken population.

For the country-bred Ben, the millions of smokey chimneys and the smell of the unwashed humanity, had become a health hazard. He wheezed and coughed and developed a heavy chest catarrh which made him exceedingly irritable. Life became quite difficult and far from peaceful, but in spite of it all, both Ruth and Ben clung persistently to their faith in God, and their strict Methodist principles.

Everyday Ruth would be seen in the street dressed in her plain grey skirt and black cape, her hair tucked neatly under a drab bonnet. On her arm there would be a basket containing some small treats for any lost child she might meet. She would hold up her long skirt and daintily pick her way among the market stalls stopping to bargain for each cheap cut of meat, some slightly off, vegetables or fish, anything to feed the horde of children she had collected. Cool, calm and unafraid, Ruth bartered with the traders and soon earned their respect.

Poor Ben with his wide black hat, greying beard and sombre suit would hold his handkerchief to his nose as he hurried along to the chapel, trying not to imbibe the stench of bad fish and rotting vegetables as he went. The numerous ragged urchins would run beside him jeering and chanting some doggerel they had made up.

Ben, Ben the methodist man
Come and catch me if you can ...

Every day whatever precautions he took, they would steal

his spare handkerchief, making Ben very angry. For handkerchiefs were becoming extremely expensive items. Since they had moved to the Mile End, Ben had lost many handkerchiefs, several valuable watches and many purses. Unlike his wife, he had no love and little patience for these little thieves as he plodded on daily to the chapel to give morning service. And once in the safety of the chapel, he would drop down on his knees and ask God to give him the strength to go on with his calling.

One evening, when returning at dusk, a noisy gang of small boys dashed past him. Then, without warning, a stone came sailing through the air and struck him on the forehead, catching him just between his brows and causing the blood to gush out down his face. He staggered home mopping up the blood as best he could.

The first Ruth knew of the incident was when she heard Nelly screaming and calling out: 'Oh, oh the master's bin 'urt,' and she scooted about on her skinny legs like a flustered hen until Ruth calmed her.

'Be quiet, Nelly,' said Ruth. 'Go and get hot water and dressings ready.'

With great dismay, Ruth examined the gaping wound in Ben's forehead. It was directly between his finely marked brows. She cleaned the wound as best she could but she was worried about it. 'I'd better get you over to the hospital,' she said. 'This is very deep.'

Obstinately, Ben refused to go. 'Leave me, Ruth, just place a good clean dressing on it. Now that the blood has stopped, I'll go up to bed.'

All night long Ben tossed restlessly. In the morning he got up and reached out to pick up his trousers. As a red mist appeared before his eyes, he sank unconscious to the floor.

Little Nelly was immediately sent over to the hospital to get someone to take a look at Ben.

A young medical student called Tom Barnard, a fine, well-bred young man from Wales, often came to give Ruth a hand with the soup on Fridays. He was a great admirer of Ruth, so when Nelly ran panic-stricken to his lodgings just down the road, he came immediately.

'It's concussion, I am afraid,' Tom told Ruth. 'And he is in danger of losing his eyesight. I'll see if I can get him over to the wards. I cannot treat him professionally as I am not yet fully qualified, but I'll do what I can,' he promised.

For many days Ben lay unconscious over in the hospital. A temporary preacher was appointed for the chapel and Ruth, although very distressed continued with her charitable work. With the other students, Tom Barnard, protected Ruth from the mobs that hung about outside the hospital. They helped her in her kitchen and also helped her feed the hungry children who would gather on the front steps of her house awaiting sustenance.

At the top of the first floor steps was a large placard which read: 'Suffer little children to come unto me'. There was a painted crucifix, and an arrow showing the little ones the way to Ruth's kitchen.

It was about this time that Ruth began her ragged school with the help of Tom Barnard. Tom was in his early twenties, and a big giant of a lad. He had a ready smile and a mop of brown curly hair. He was a great asset to Ruth and enjoyed the meanest chores. In his fine Welsh voice, he told the children tales of folklore, but he was not a good Christian.

'Madam,' he would say to Ruth, 'if I could swallow all that stuff, I'd be happy. But I cannot, my education has destroyed all that.'

Ruth would shake her head sadly. 'It's God's will, Tom,' she would say. 'One day you will need him.'

'That may be,' Tom replied. 'But at the moment all these sick people need me. I am prepared to do what I can, and if that is enough, Ruth, you are welcome to my services.'

Dressed in a large cap and a white apron, Ruth industriously stirred the big pot of soup that they would soon ladle into tin cups for the hungry children. She could hear the buzz of young voices as they waited outside.

'I am exceedingly grateful to you, Tom,' she said. 'What

would I do without you and your friends?'

One day Ruth, after a rather trying Bible class session, declared: 'It's pointless to try to teach these little ones the Bible. How can they have any understanding of the good book when they cannot read.'

'Well, teach them,' said Tom. 'I know just the fellow who might help you in that task. I'll try to persuade him. He shares my lodgings. He is from a good family but they threw him out because of his licentious ways. And he is very fond of children.'

Ruth thought that Tom added this last remark with some irony but soon forgot it.

So it was that Wilfred joined Ruth every afternoon and endeavoured to teach the illiterate children of the district to read. He was a pleasant young man with an effeminate manner. He was always well dressed, his hair was handsomely curled. He used perfume and wore an elegant monocle attached to a long ribbon. He proved to be a very fine teacher with a great deal of patience for these uneducated ragged children. He fitted in with the unusual establishment Ruth kept, although she and Ben did not always understand his perverse humour and dry witticism. At times he had a terrific sense of humour which went down well with the folk at Ruth's kitchen. He also liked to spout poetry at any time of day.

Ruth like him enormously and forgave him for his religious attitudes. 'He admits to being a heathen,' she said, 'but he gives his services freely and generously to this poor community, so perhaps our dear Lord will understand.'

Blind since his accident, Ben would now spend much of his day sitting by the window listening to the sounds of the household and of the street outside. His blindness had sharpened his other senses and in some ways he seemed at peace with himself and a much happier man. He had even stopped agitating for Ruth to give up this idea of a freelance mission which was supported only by voluntary contributions. His main activity was to accompany Ruth and her helpers to outside meetings on Sunday evenings, where in a loud voice he would preach those precious Wesleyan sermons he knew by heart. The fact that most of the congregation came to jeer did not bother him. With Faith to guide him by the hand and burly Tom Barnard to assist him, he had few problems.

It was Ruth who carried the burden of this poor living on her sturdy shoulders. Her fair hair turned a dull grey and she always kept it tucked up tidily in her sombre bonnet. Not only did she have her work with the population to do but much time was spent fighting the church bodies who did not approve of her methods of spreading God's word.

But despite the opposition, Ruth's methods were working. Among the distressed folk many converts were coming forth to adopt a new way of life; alcoholics, prostitutes, thieves and just the derelict homeless all found help and sustenance at Ruth's mission in the East End. In the last eight years Ruth had formed a lifeline particularly for girls who wanted to be helped. Some she sent up to the Midlands to Alice Gibbs, seamstresses who owed their training to Alice who was only too pleased to take them on in the workshop in Coalville.

Alice still corresponded regularly with her old friend Ruth, but had not been down south since her marriage. Both she and Ruth led such active lives that it was impossible for them to get away to visit each other.

In the large first floor room of Ruth's house the little children gathered for a meal and a prayer. Any who wished to, could stay on. Then from a large blackboard they learned how to read words and how to write them down themselves. They enjoyed the work and their progress proved that the scheme was a grand success.

Both Tom and Wilfred poured their own money into the venture and had enjoyed seeing such good results from their efforts.

Meanwhile Ben was making fair progress. He was much stronger but unfortunately his sight had not returned. The doctor informed Ruth that he would be permanently blind.

This was a dreadful blow. On her knees, Ruth asked God what they had done to be punished in this way. The deep faith that had seldom wavered before was very shaky on the day that she was told the prognosis. Now Ben, once a tall, fine gentleman, had to be held by the hand and guided everywhere, every step of the way. It was Faith, their long-legged, dark-eyed daughter who was Ruth's saviour. With her serious face and her dark sausage curls, she was always at her father's side, reading to him or just sitting keeping him company at his knee beside the fire, while Ruth went on with her charitable works.

One day the Anneslees received a visit from the Elders of the Chapel. There were three of them, looking rather like gloomy bats in their long black cloaks. Having had to force their way through the ragged throng that waited outside the house, they now cast their critical eyes around the sparsely furnished dwelling. To Ben they were exceedingly kind and wished him well, but to Ruth they were positively hostile. And their news was harsh. They informed them that Ben had to retire and that the small stipend he had been receiving as a preacher would be withdrawn.

Ruth was very angry and in no uncertain tones demanded to know what they were supposed to live on. She had nothing to lose and she had always disliked their pompous middle-class manners.

'It will be necessary for you both to retire,' they informed her. 'Perhaps you could move to some place in the country. You, madam, could possible become housekeeper to another minister of the church. This could be arranged if that is what you desire.'

'No, it is not,' Ruth replied sharply. 'I am badly needed here among these poor derelict people. I have no intention of leaving.'

'As you wish,' the spokesman said haughtily, waving a bony finger. 'But remember that you are no longer supported by our council, so be it on your own head.'

'I will survive without your charity,' replied Ruth coldly.

'Good day to you, sirs.'

As the long black shapes swept out, Ruth muttered to herself: 'Well, now, I've done it. But they will not deter me. From now on, we are an independent mission.'

So it was that Ruth became a reformer, begging donations from every source she could think of. Every Sunday she went out into the street with an old harmonium and her loyal followers surrounding her. She placed herself in the square outside the Blind Beggar Inn and preached the sermon while Faith, holding her father's hand, went around with a little velvet bag to collect donations from the onlookers.

Sometimes there were very bad days when all they got were jeers and rude cries from the crowd who jostled them and tried to break up the meeting. From time to time they were even pelted with rotten fruit and bad eggs. But Ruth ignored such abuses, holding her little band together, their voices raised in song. She sang those great hymns of John Wesley in a fresh strong tone, encouraging the drunk and the hoodlums to join in. Eventually, they did and this little godly band became one of the regular features of that long wicked wasteland of the Mile End, becoming as accepted as the cock-pits and the wrestling booths, the gin shops and the drunks. Even young society bucks, out on a Saturday night slumming, would join in with the singing, though they would often scoff and jeer, substituting their own rude words for the great Wesleyan hymns. Ruth, however, did not care, as long as that little velvet pocket was filled with coins by the end of the day. Soon Ben regained his confidence and in a strong voice, would preach those sermons he knew by heart. He was no longer afraid of the rowdy mobs, particularly while his young daughter was at his side.

Outside Ruth's kitchen there hung a new big notice: 'This mission is run entirely on voluntary contributions.' The money poured in and Ruth fed the hungry, gave aid to the sick, and soon could afford to rent another house for the homeless. Lost, rejected children remained her special interest.

As her family of waifs and strays grew larger, Ruth was

often weary but she was always in fine form and, at God's command, pressed on and on. She received help from the most unlikely places, including the local factory owners, and even the Catholic Church. The Catholic priest would often visit her to discuss the fate of some child or other who was of his own persuasion. And so, in this way, the East End Christian Mission was established by the energy of a small band of good people.

In this strange pious atmosphere, young Faith grew up, accepting day by day the ugly poverty that surrounded her. She rarely smiled and always wore a sad, melancholy expression on her face. And she seldom held a long conversation with anyone except with her beloved father, the kind, gentle blind man whom she adored. With Ben she would sit and read long passages from the Bible or *The Pilgrim's Progress*, a book that was dear to his heart.

Ruth was always too busy to show the interest she should have shown her lovely adolescent daughter but, like a rose in a garden of weeds, Faith still bloomed and flourished in a quiet steady manner.

On Saturday evenings there would be a special service followed by a supper of stewed mutton with dumplings. This dish had become very popular with the hungry children who started to queue outside for it early in the afternoon.

On one particular night, Ruth looked out into the street and saw a dark shape huddled all alone in the darkened doorway. Immediately she left her cooking, and went out to cross the road. There she ferreted out a pathetic bundle of a boy who swore at her and fought like the devil to get free from her hold, but Ruth grasped him firmly and hauled him down into the basement of her home. Inside, she saw that she was holding a very tiny boy, so black and covered with soot that it was difficult to see if he was hurt. With Nelly's help she forcibly bathed him and put some soothing balm on the large septic sores on his elbows and knees. When the dirt had been finally removed there emerged a lovely fair head of curls but they could also see that the thin, emaciated boy was covered with bruises.

'Blimey! If he ain't a chimney boy!' cried Nelly. 'And look aht' 'im he ain't arf had a bashin'.'

When the boy realized he was amongst friends, he told them that his name was Jim and that he had run away from the sweepmaster.

'Yer won't let 'im catch me, will yer?' he begged Ruth.

Ruth fondled the lovely head and smiled kindly. 'No,' she said. 'We all trust in our good Lord. He has delivered you to us from that cruel master so we will care for you.'

So Jim was yet another orphan to be installed permanently in Ruth's kitchen. He was very helpful in the house cleaning shoes, peeling potatoes, running errands and generally making himself useful. Jim was like a little angel. He was so bright and fair and so willing. He sang the hymns in a sweet high-pitched voice and took to reading like a duck to water. Wilfred was overjoyed with the boy's quick receptive mind. He loved to teach him and he fussed him and bought him sweets, as Jim quickly became the pet of the mission.

The next to arrive was Flo, a friend of Jim. One Saturday night Ruth caught Jim passing food out of the window to someone outside.

'What are you up to Jim?' asked Ruth, leaning out of the window to look.

There down below stood a thin young woman. She was very dirty, and had a face which looked very battered. She was gnawing ravenously at the meat bones which Jim handed out the window to her.

'Come inside, dear,' Ruth called. 'You are welcome to a meal.'

But the girl looked startled and then shook her head and ran away.

Tom Barnard knew her. 'She's a street walker,' he said. 'I've seen her hanging around the inns.'

'She won't come in because she is afraid,' said little Jim.

'Afraid of what?' asked Ruth.

'Of Jesus, because she is a great sinner,' Jim explained.

Without more ado, Ruth put on her cape and went out to

look for Flo. She did not have to look far, for Flo was sitting on the front steps weeping.

'Come in, dear,' cried Ruth. 'This is a shelter for the homeless. Inside you will find food and bedding. Our dear Lord has guided you here so you have nothing to fear. Come on in.'

'I can't,' wailed Flo, with tears flooding her eyes. 'I'm a sinner. I goes wiv' men.'

'Nonsense!' said Ruth. 'You are now repentant and God will hold out his arms to you. You will be washed clean of all your sins. Come now, dear,' she cajoled. With gentle hands she guided Flo inside the mission and thus Ruth had made another conquest.

It turned out that Flo had been sold to a brothel a long time before she was a mature woman. She had then run away from that house of sin only to find that her sole means of survival was to walk the streets.

Now, safe from such evils, Flo became Ruth's most ardent convert and her most loyal persistent follower. She seemed perfect in every way except for her language. In her young life she had learned the most dreadful obscene words from the streets she had walked and it was not always possible for her to control them. But she was a great asset to Ruth's mission. With her wispy brown hair, her large mouth and battered features, every day she did the washing out in the back yard, scrubbing the sheets and blankets and the second-hand clothing that Ruth had managed to scrounge. Even now she worked very hard and still swore very hard, no matter how she tried not to.

But as she worked, she swore. Sitting in his window seat, Ben would cover up his ears whenever he heard Nelly annoy Flo, for he knew that any retort from Flo would contain the sort of language that was painful for him to hear.

Nelly annoyed Flo quite a lot because there was extreme jealousy between the two girls as they vied with each other for Ruth's favours. But Ruth loved them both equally. Once Flo had been medically checked for venereal disease and given a clean bill of health, all was well, as far as Ruth was concerned. And the fact that she had been a prostitute did not bother her one bit. Flo was just one of God's creatures in need of help.

So through those very bad years of the early 1830s, the small independent mission made a significant impact on London's poor.

Beat was on her usual high horse. 'Well, if you call it progress, I don't,' she would complain to the customers in the Malted Shovel. 'Those bloody barges coming through that new canal, makes the place stink worse than ever. It is what we always said would happen.'

John Shulmead sank his pint. 'Well, Beatrice,' he said, 'we must give way to progress. But I am inclined to agree with you, that there canal is a dead loss.'

The last five years had matured John. He was now big and broad of shoulders and still retained his swinging sailor's gait and mop of lovely red-gold hair. He was now installed with his fair Dolly out in the cottage on the marsh, with poor unhappy Kit now only a faint memory.

Dolly and John now had a little girl called Emma, with long black hair and unusual green-grey eyes. This child was the light of John's life. Every day she would come running down the lane to meet her sailor Daddy and, he would sweep her up into his strong arms and cover her face with kisses.

Dolly in her contentment had put on a lot of weight. Her plumpness had now turned to obesity but Dolly did not care, she lived only for John and her lovely daughter. Sadly, there would never be any more children. For in the second year of their marriage, when John had been hoping that Dolly's second pregnancy would produce a son, Dolly had climbed up the apple tree to pick some fruit, had fallen down and miscarried. The child had indeed been a boy but the doctor said that Dolly's injuries were so severe that she would never bear another child. This news added to the loss of the child had been a terrible blow to John and he had not yet fully recovered. Nevertheless, he was quite happy with Dolly and there was always additional pleasure to be had in the dockside taverns while he was away on a voyage.

As always John was a popular person and a fine figure of a man. He was now chairman of the Waterways Company and owned several other barges. He worked up and down the Thames, transporting bricks and cement to the new industrial towns and bringing coal and cattle fodder back to the hamlet. He still clung on to the old *Alianora*, remarking: 'I just can't let the old lady go. She has been very lucky for me.'

When ashore he would be installed nightly in the bar parlour in the same spot that old Amos had occupied. There, his friends and associates would gather about him and they would all discuss matters of importance such as the state of the country, the Reform Bill and the repeal of the Corn Laws.

The new canal had indeed drastically changed the face of the hamlet and affected it in many ways. A wooden bridge, for instance, had replaced the old landing stage outside the Malted Shovel, for barges were not now able to tie up there.

Old Wally was the first casualty. His sight had become so bad that he found it a hazard to cross the bridge, so now he had to be content to sit outside his cottage dreaming of the past.

Beat had protested loudly at the loss of his custom but the Canal Company was formed of businessmen from the town who had no interest in the hamlet whatsoever.

Beyond the Malted Shovel, the canal took a sharp turn over the marshland down to the shore near to the newly formed factories that had been built there. And just before this there was a big lock with a brand new house containing a couple of foreigners who never mixed with the residents.

Many of the old barge skippers did not even use this new canal because they made too slow a progress down that long tunnel with its one-way system. Boys had to be employed to huff the sails, and the dues and the fines crippled their finances and lowered their profits.

So it was that many of them, including John Shulmead, stuck to the old route around the Isle of Grain, preferring forty miles of choppy sea to being stuck in that long dark tunnel awaiting the lock-keeper's signal. And on top of that, the old flat-bottomed dung barges still continued to come through the canal from the town to dump their muck out on the marshland at a spot called the dung wharf. This, of course, was a subject of Beat's constant complaints.

Beat was as hard a nut as ever. Her skin was so wrinkled and brown it looked like parchment and from beneath those bushy grey eyebrows her shrewd eyes shone as brightly as before. 'That canal ain't paying its way,' she informed John Shulmead one night. 'Didn't think it would. I heard a couple of those company men discussing a new railway now. It goes by steam and will run through here down to the south coast. They reckon it will come this way in the next few years.'

John was very interested. 'That does not surprise me. It's a good quick way to travel. I've seen the great stations they have built up in London. There must be a lot of money in that venture.'

'But if they do, where will they put it?' asked Beat.

'There's only one place they can build their railway,' returned John. 'Where the canal is.' he stroked his blond beard. 'If the railway buys the Canal Company out, someone will make a lot of money,' he reflected. 'It sounds like good sense to me. They are losing money on that canal, that's for sure, and it might well be wise to buy some shares now in the Canal Company,' he said.

Beat was always open to a good business deal. 'Well, I have always trusted you over business and so far you haven't never let me down. So see about this. Perhaps we will invest a bit together ...'

So began the good days for John when he made the decision to invest his savings in the Canal Company, and added Beat's investment to his.

Percy was now a hulking great lad. He attended a private school to which he wore a tweed knickerbocker suit and a big straw hat. But as soon as he came home at weekends, he would put on his old woollen dungarees, and take his gun out on the marsh where he would fire at the wild fowl which he seldom missed. Lukey loped everywhere after Percy like a gun dog, retrieving the kill as it fell screeching to the ground. Both men enjoyed the sight of blood and the wild bird struggling in its death throes. They got great pleasure from this pastime. When they weren't shooting, together they would terrorize the neighbourhood, especially the little girls. Percy would catch them and trap them and then let Lukey touch their hair. Lukey only wanted to touch and fondle them. 'Stand very still,' Percy would warn the terrified victim. 'If you start screaming Lukey will go berserk.'

Beat was constantly bothered by the irate mothers to whom their daughters had complained about the treatment they had received from Lukey and Percy.

'Leave the girls alone,' Beat would order Lukey but it had litle or no effect on him, and made no difference at all to Percy. This was his kind of fun and no one was going to spoil that.

Dot had become more and more withdrawn and kept apart from the furious battles that went on between Percy and old Aunt Beat. Aunt Beat was tough, yet in the end it was young Percy who finally ruled the roost.

Perhaps the loneliest person in the hamlet these days was Dolly, for a rural hamlet is an unforgiving sort of place. Whenever she went down to shop in the little store, women turned away to gossip about her. The fight had left Dolly and she would hang her head low and hurry on with her shopping. Then she would try to forget what had happened, and rush back to her isolated cottage on the marsh to her darling Emma and her fine husband.

Old Wally died one day while sitting outside his cottage in the midday sun. Toby was there when it happened and was heartbroken. He had loved kind old Wally and felt very responsible for him. For a long time after the tragic death of his brother Kit, Toby had longed to leave the hamlet behind him. Now that Wally was dead, he was free to go. He had a good trade with which to support himself for he was a skilled musician. So, in spite of his grotesque appearance, Toby Jug, as he was called, had much to offer the world. But the people of the hamlet were cruel and afraid of him. If any of them came upon Toby in the country lane they would cross themselves and mutter a quick prayer.

Some people did feel great sympathy for poor Toby and his plight. The youth's skin was still sallow from the ill health he had suffered as a child, and his slim body, with its twisted limbs and uneven features, was jarring to come across. His only attractive physical features were his large clear eyes. They were like the mirrors of his soul. Honesty and loyalty shone from them.

Toby always wore a flat black cap which buttoned under his chin, a short travelling cape and long leggings. On his shoulder he carried a canvas bag which contained all the tools of his trade. Seeing him in the dark, his outline was ape-like. Locals would swear that they had seen the devil as they wended their way home very drunk after a night's joviality at the inn. But it was, of course, our Toby Jug.

But after Wally's death, Toby left the hamlet, and limped out into the world to be a travelling barber. He would stop at village fairs to get up his pitch and there he would cut hair and shave his customers. It was an extremely hard life with a varied existence, but one day Toby found himself in the big city of London.

He walked wearily along the Mile End Waste one Sunday evening and outside a very shabby inn called the Blind Beggar, he saw a curious sight. A tall woman in sombre clothing with a lovely fair face stood reading the Bible. Beside her, a lovely-looking teenage girl was holding the hand of a bearded man. He wore a big wide-brimmed hat and appeared to be totally blind. In the centre of the group sat a husky lad who pumped some strange contraption up and down with his feet while the lady ground out a tune. Suddenly, the little band of followers all burst into song. A crowd of people came out from the inn and, in a festive mood, drunkenly joined in the singing. All around ragged children dashed in and out of the crowd picking pockets but their victims barely noticed, so much did this little band of religious folk hold the attention of their audience.

Toby squeezed himself up to the front of the crowd looking on in amazement. The lovely young girl calmly led the blind man around the crowd and coins were dropped into the velvet bag he carried. Money was thrown into the ring by the drunken students. On the front of the harmonium was a sign: 'This is the East End Christian Mission, run entirely by voluntary contributions. God bless you and keep you all. Thank you for your help to those in need.'

Suddenly everything became a little hectic as fighting broke out on the edge of the crowd. The young girl's face was expressionless as she did not seem to hear the foul words that came forth. Then the soldiers arrived and broke up the crowd as the little band calmly folded up the harmonium and in a lordly manner moved on.

So intrigued was Toby by this scene that he fell in line and marched with them until they reached Ruth's kitchen where a crowd of ragged children had already begun to queue outside. 'God bless you all,' called Ruth as she greeted them.

'God bless you, Ruth,' they returned in one voice.

Then they all went down the stone steps into the big kitchen where thin, scraggy Nelly stirred the soup and laid out the trays of tin cups. The children went in a dozen or so at a time. They sat around a long table and a cup of soup and a piece of bread were placed in front of them. Ruth stood at the head of the table, tall and dignified, clasping her hands together. 'For what the good Lord has provided this day, let us be truly thankful. Amen.' Then in a greedy rush, the hungry children ravenously dipped the bread in the hot soup and devoured with relish. And so it went on until the last little one had been fed.

Toby stood outside the house looking through the railings down into that big kitchen which was filled with humility of the Lord. Never in all his travels had he seen such a marvellous sight. Soon Ruth came out into the air to breathe and remove her bonnet. The light shone on her dull hair. 'Are you hungry?' she asked Toby, thinking from his shape that he was a small child. 'If so, come in, dear.' She held out her hand kindly. 'If you are hungry, come in and eat. This is the house of God.' She saw now that he was an adult. 'Once the children are fed others are welcome,' she said, turning to the house. 'Nelly, is there some soup left?' she called out.

Toby hobbled down the steps into the kitchen and sat down at the long table. The place was clean and very bright, and the workers chatted cheerfully as they cleared up. He found the soup hot and nourishing.

'Have you a bed for the night, young man?' asked Ruth. 'For I presume you are a traveller.'

'I am a travelling barber, madam,' replied Toby. 'I only arrived this day in London.'

'I will give you a note to go to our hostel,' she told him. 'Don't worry, it is not the workhouse,' she assured him.

The poor were afraid of the workhouse. Everyone knew that once you entered those uncharitable portals, your life was never again your own.

Ruth handed Toby a small slip of paper with her signature on it. 'You will need this when you go to the hostel. It is not entirely free. If you can afford it, you will be expected to give a small donation to the mission, but you can, if you wish, stay for three nights. After that, I will review your situation.'

Toby smiled and his expressive eyes lit up humorously. 'This is very kind of you, madam, but I can indeed pay. I am not destitute but I will accept your kind offer nonetheless.'

'By the way,' Ruth asked him, 'where are you from?' She threw him a shrewd look.

'I come from a remote hamlet called Hollinbury on the marshland of Kent.'

Ruth raised her eyebrows in surprise. 'How strange,' she said. 'I know of someone else who came from such a place. I wish you well now. Nelly will direct you to the hostel.' She paused and then said. 'Come and see me again before you leave, young man. I'd like to hear more of your hamlet. In an odd way it keeps turning up and haunting me.'

The hostel was further down the road. It had been a donation to Ruth's organization from the father of one of the hospital students who had helped her some nights. It was on a leasehold, and fairly run-down, but it was perfectly acceptable for Ruth's purposes. And the old rambling house proved to be a great asset. Fifty years before it had housed nobility and the once grand garden contained a well — a much sought after feature in an area where water was in short supply.

The population at large went down to the riverside to bring back buckets of water for domestic use. Grateful for her good fortune in having this well, Ruth had installed a bathhouse some way from the house to enable the weary homeless, traveller to get a good bath before he got to his bed at night. 'Cleanliness is next to Godliness,' Ruth would say piously. And the bathhouse was looked after by an old soldier who had lost a leg at Waterloo.

So huge barrels of hot water were provided for the guests at the hostel. They could have their clothes washed and dried and then go on their way refreshed, providing they left at least a small donation. So far it had worked very well indeed.

When Toby arrived he was persuaded to stay a while and carry on his trade of hair-cutting, shaving and shampooing. He was offered a clean room of his own and the comfort of Ruth's kitchen. In this way he continued to do his work and was happy to have found the religious haven he had always been searching for.

Nelly had giggled hysterically when he told her his name.

'Cool!' she said to Ruth, just out of Toby's earshot, 'looks like a blooming Toby Jug, he does.'

Ruth shook her head. 'Handsome is as handsome does, Nelly,' she said. 'We are all God's children.'

Flo in her deep voice said: 'Oi like 'im, he's very jolly.'

'Oh!' cried Nelly. 'She'd like anyfing as long as it was a man, even if he *is* a freak.'

'Now, girls, stop squabbling,' warned Ruth. 'We all have jobs to do, so let us get on with them.' Thus in her practical manner, Ruth marshalled her followers like an army major.

'So we progress with God's help,' she would frequently remark.

There was much warmth and happiness down in Ruth's kitchen but when work was ended and she retired upstairs to her own apartments, the atmosphere was cold and constrained. Ben was always sitting in his usual spot by the fire, while Faith sat on a stool at his knee reading to him.

Ruth was usually still full of energy, even after a tiring day, and would want to make conversation, but she received very little response from her family. It was as if they lived in a world of their own, one completely different to that of her own. As she battled with Faith's starchy coolness and Ben's withdrawal from the world, Ruth wondered how it was that she failed them. They had all the comforts of living — heat, light and good food — so why should she feel so guilty? Faith was receiving a fair education at a private school and Ben had his daughter's constant attention. What did they want? Tonight she told them of the arrival of the odd little man from the same hamlet that Alice had come from.

Ben sighed at the mention of Alice. 'Ah, they were good days in Dartford,' he said.

But Faith did not respond at all. So Ruth sighed and began to scrutinize her housekeeping book which she kept in good order. She was certainly more content down in the kitchen that in her own sitting-room.

The next night when boisterous Tom Barnard put an arm around her waist, Ruth paused to wipe the sweat from her brow. She had been standing for two hours dishing out hot soup.

'Ruth, dear,' said Tom. 'Take a rest. We can't have you cracking up after all.'

His embrace was gentle. He was always so affectionate with that Ruth guessed that Tom was in love with her. How nice it would be to be young again and to be held in the strong arms of this virile young man! As her thoughts wandered dangerously in that direction, she removed his arm abruptly. 'Now, Tom, no time for frivolity,' she said lightly. 'There's still plenty to do.'

'Don't you ever relax?' he asked.

She smiled. 'Yes Tom, in my work with my poor unfort-
unates. And that is quite enough for me.'

'Well, that is what I supposed,' muttered Tom. 'I will be
leaving the hospital at the end of the year. I am going to study
surgery in France but I will never forget you, Ruth.'

'I should think not,' she scoffed. 'But I will miss you, Tom,'
she added sadly.

When Tom eventually left, it was Toby who replaced him
as Ruth's right-hand man at the mission. Then Wilfred
returned to the business of his family, taking young Jim with
him. They arrived back on a short visit one day in a smart
carriage and with a basket of sweetmeats for the pupils at the
ragged school. Young Jim looked quite superior in the elaborate outfit of a pageboy as he handed out the treats. Wilfred
seemed even more effeminate than ever, sniffing his
perfumed handkerchief and pretending to shed a tear or two
as he waved his silver knobbed cane. 'Oh dear, I was sorry to
desert you, Ruth, but family affairs you know ...'

'Without you and Tom, I may have to drop the afternoon
school for a while,' Ruth told him.

'But, my dear, don't worry,' Wilfred laughed. 'I have
already put a word in the right direction for you. I know a
chappie in parliament who is really keen on educating the
poor and all that. I think he is coming down to see you.'

Ruth smiled. She had never taken Wilfred too seriously. 'We
shall miss you,' she said 'and thank you for all that you have done,
particularly for little Jim, who seems very happy with you.'

'I promise you, old dear, that I will get something done,'
said Wilfred, as he pranced away.

As time passed, the mission flourished. But there was new
hostility towards it as the newly-formed police force broke up
Ruth's meetings and refused to allow her to hold them in the
street. 'These meetings incite trouble,' she was informed.

'It's them what causes the trouble,' announced Nelly, 'goin'
around hittin' folk with them bloomin' great truncheons.'

But Ruth could not risk the dangers of open meetings and

in the end she had to content herself with an evening service down in the kitchen while Toby played his concertina.

Then one day in October when the evenings were drawing in and a mob of children queued for a meal, one little boy lay down in the gutter and retched. He was too weak to rise. Toby was sent out to look at him, and returned to report that the lad looked extremely ill.

'Get him upstairs to the schoolroom,' said Ruth. 'I'll come and look after him.'

But when she arrived to look at the child he was dead and his body was covered with red spots. 'I don't know what it is. We must get some advice.' So she wrapped the little body up in a blanket and carried it over to the hospital.

At the sight of the spots, the hospital staff panicked, dashing off with the boy's body to an isolated spot.

'It's cholera,' the doctor informed Ruth, 'and it's very contagious. That's the twentieth death this week. It's hitting mostly children.'

Ruth's heart almost stopped. Not another epidemic! She could hardly bear the thought. And in this poor distressed place. It would wreak havoc. An epidemic was something she had always feared.

The cholera hit Ruth's East End community hard. The filth and shortage of water made this inevitable. From October to January hundreds of children and young people died, having no resistance to the infection at all. Ruth was knocked by every death but particularly that of poor Flo. Ruth fought to save her but lost. She sat by that death bed thinking about the poor girl — only twenty-five and with so much tragedy in her short life. 'Ah well, she has paid for her everlasting peace,' Ruth murmured to herself. Then the face of her own lovely daughter rose before her. Faith! She must be sent away from this danger, and so must Ben. They could go up north where Alice would care for them. Then Ruth would be free to fight this terrible epidemic, giving herself freely as she had done before in Dartford.

As she knelt to pray for poor Flo, Ruth's mind constantly

wandered. Death was such a final thing. She recalled how Flo had loved bright finery. 'Anything wiv' beads and fevvers,' she had once said as she rummaged around in the donated clothes Ruth had collected. In her mind Ruth could see Flo at the outdoor meeting dressed in an embroidered skirt and a hat with an old broken feather sticking out of it, and she recalled the brash exchange between Nelly and Flo, when Nelly had suggested that the feather would be very useful to 'stick up Flo's backside and fly her home'.

Ruth had been truly shocked and lectured the two girls quite severely. And how Flo had wept then, thinking that Jesus, her new-found friend, would be cross with her. She had had such simple faith, and had been such a colourful creature.

Now as poor Flo slept in the bosom of her friend Jesus, Ruth dried her eyes and went about her daily chores.

Once she had persuaded Ben and Faith to go and stay with Alice and George, Ruth went out into the dark alleys with the Sister of Mercy from the convent to find the sick children and separate the living from the dead. As the cholera epidemic struck the East End, it was her finest hour when the hospital and the hostel were full. Only the sick poor went to the hospital because the better-off relied on home nursing and regarded hospitals as infernal establishments. And indeed, the standard of hygiene in those places was such that people often died of diseases that they caught while staying there rather than from whatever illness had brought them to hospital in the first place.

There were no female staff employed at the hospital apart from the domestic helpers, but with the Sisters from the convent, Ruth washed the dead, consoled the relatives and tried desperately to save the lives of the children. The sickness caused her own group of children to dwindle particularly since the Peelers still would not allow any of them to congregate in the street. The children would hide in poor dark hovels allowing the disease to take its toll.

After Ben and Faith had gone, the house felt cold and lonely. But still Toby and Nelly stuck loyally at her side. Toby Jug worked in the city barber shop in the day but gave his services freely at the weekends and evenings. At work, he cut hair and shaved unkempt faces, giving new looks to their owners and renewed hope of life when drink and poverty brought humanity down low.

Nelly was as hard working as ever, and bright and alert. She cooked and washed for their little charges with great energy, but her chief concern was to look after her mistress.

As usual Ruth was concerned for others rather than herself. 'Don't stay if you don't want to,' she urged. 'If you get sick, I shall feel responsible.'

The epidemic was at its height but Toby said: 'I am perfectly happy to stay with you, Ruth. Diseases do not seem to affect me. I always feel that I have borne such pain in my youth that I have become immune to any outside harm.'

'It's possible,' Ruth replied. 'And I too feel that I am immune but nevertheless we must take all precautions. Cleanliness is very important. They say that illness came from the foreign boats who dumped rotting fruit at the riverside which the poor hungry children then devoured. We must use plenty of carbolic, as they do over in the wards, I'll try to get hold of some.'

Ruth got the medical students to bring her a huge tub of disinfectant which she used in the bathhouse on the floor and in the washing and anything else that came into contact with the children.

As the summer turned to autumn, and the weather cooled, the cholera began to abate. By now, the word had spread of Ruth Anneslee's tireless efforts on behalf of the poor and under-privileged sick folk of London's East End, and many wealthy interested parties sent large donations to her. The working-man's hostel run on voluntary contributions could now begin to pay for itself and financially, at least, Ruth felt more secure. Sadly, her Sunday school had dwindled. The children who remained looked distressingly poorly because diarrhoea, one of the acute symptoms of cholera, had left them all thin, yellow and very weak. These little ones tended to come for help at Ruth's house. One by one they came under Ruth's wing. She would feed them with hot milk and arrowroot to improve the conditions of their bowels until they were once more back to good health.

By now much notice had been brought to the government authorities of the adverse conditions that existed in the East End of London and several moves were being made to relieve and reform these ills. *The Times* newspaper, that long-time champion of the man in the street, published long articles about the poverty and distress that existed there and the hordes of homeless children who rampaged through the filthy gutters. Many articles praised the various religious bodies which, all alone, had valiantly tried to combat the cholera in those overcrowded slums. Then there began long debates in Parliament itself about the financing of the ragged schools which had been struggling on unaided in their efforts to educate the poor of the big towns.

As donations poured in, Ruth was able once more to establish her day classes which taught her flock how to read.

As life settled down in London again, Ruth could turn her mind to her husband and daughter who were still up in Coalville staying with Alice and George. She had received a letter from Alice at Christmas inviting her to spend the holiday with them but at that time Ruth had been much too busy with her work to be able to leave. She did hope to come up and join them in the spring and then perhaps Ben and Faith would be ready to travel back with her then if London was totally free of the sickness once more.

So it was that in February Ruth began to make her plans for a trip to Leicestershire leaving Toby and Nelly in charge of the mission.

How wonderful it would be to see Alice and George once more after all these years, and to bring her husband and daughter back to their own home again!

But two days before Ruth was about to leave a letter arrived from Faith. Recognizing her daughter's handwriting and sensing that something was wrong, she opened the envelope with trembling hands and a fast-beating heart. Her worst fears were realized: 'Come at once,' she read. 'Father is dying. Faith.'

CHAPTER FIFTEEN

When Paddy came to Town

After receiving the news from Faith, Ruth ran around panic-stricken, trying to get organised for her journey and worrying about how the mission would go on in her absence. Toby and Nelly assured her that all would go on as before and that it was safe in their hands. Nelly packed Ruth's case and Toby got her a hackney carriage to take her to the stagecoach terminal at Aldgate pump. By nightfall Ruth was travelling north praying to God that she would not be too late. But in the early hours the next morning, when she stepped down from the stagecoach and saw George's face, she knew that she was.

'I am deeply grieved, Ruth,' George said, embracing her. 'But there was little we could do, Ben caught a bad chill and it developed into pneumonia. But thank God he was happy to the last and did not suffer.'

Ruth clasped her hands together and prayed to God to give her courage. She was grateful that her tears were not yet able to fall. 'I know you have done your very best, dear friend,' she said quietly to the woeful-looking George. She noticed that he was now quite silver-haired but his steady blue eyes still shone with that loyal fervour from behind the steel-rimmed spectacles.

When Ruth saw her lovely daughter for the first time in two years, she could hardly believe her eyes. Faith was quite beautiful. Her nut-brown hair was sleek and shiny, around her face with long curls. But her large violet eyes had shadows under them and her mouth was drawn grimly tight across that pale, oval face. Faith gazed coldly at her mother and showed no sign of welcome or even friendliness. Ruth felt as if a knife had been thrust through her heart.

Then Alice came forth, her dark hair twisted into a tight bun on top of her head and her uneven features wrinkled in grief. She held her old friend close. 'Oh, my dear Ruth,' she cried. 'That we could have met in happier times!'

Ruth gazed down at Ben's smooth, pale face as he lay peacefully in his coffin in the parlour. There was acceptance written on those cold still features; Ruth knew that he had gone to meet the master he had served so faithfully.

Ben was interred in the local churchyard in that small Midland town. Apart from Ruth and Faith, only Alice, George and their son Adam attended.

Adam was a tall, good-looking youth, with very dark, solemn features. He was about to go down to London to start his medical training there. Ruth noticed how tenderly he handed Faith into the carriage and in the evening she watched them sitting together at the round table in the centre of the room. The heavy oil-lamp shone down on their serious youthful faces as Faith sewed and Adam studied his books. They had always been very fond of each other, Ruth reflected. They had been like brother and sister, almost. It would be a good match now if they fell in love.

Ruth pondered on this for a while but then thought that perhaps it would be better for Faith to return with her to London. But when Ruth was packed and ready to leave for home, Faith stood in the bedroom looking at her mother with an expression of defiance on her face. Her eyes blazed with fury and hate. 'I've no intention of returning with you to that filthy place,' Faith informed Ruth who was astonished at this outburst.

'But darling, it's your home,' Ruth pleaded.

'Home!' scoffed Faith. 'What kind of home is that, overrun by all the rag-tag and bobtail of the streets? I'll not go back.'

'But, Faith, dear, it's God's wish that we help the poor. Did our Lord forsake those in need? Have you forgotten your own Methodist training?'

'Bosh!' cried Faith. 'As far as I am concerned it's all hypocrisy. You, mother, made beggars of my father and me. He was blinded in that filthy slum and yet we walked the filthy streets begging for your charities. And now I have lost him. It is because of you that he did not leave that dirty place but he hated it. Do you think I am such a fool that I did not see what went on about me?'

Ruth pressed her hand to her brow. She simply could not believe that her lovely child was actually condemning her. 'My dear, you are overwrought and you are so wrong. Calm down,' she begged her. 'I will wait another day before I leave.'

'You might as well leave now, Mother,' Faith replied icily, 'because I am not going with you.'

Hearing the raised voices, Alice came blustering into the room.

'Alice,' demanded Faith, 'you know my feelings. Kindly inform my mother of them.'

'Hush now, don't you quarrel, darlings,' cried Alice. Turning to Ruth she said: 'Faith is young, and it has been a big shock losing her father.'

Ruth recovered her pride. 'She may stay if she wants to,' she said sharply. 'I am only amazed by her attitude to her religion. She seems to have lost all sense of duty.'

'Goodnight and goodbye, Mother!' cried Faith rushing from the room.

Alice went to Ruth and held her tight. Suddenly, all Ruth's courage seemed to desert her as she wept like a child.

'My dear, do not let it worry you,' Alice said gently. 'It's all this modern teaching. It will pass, be assured of that. Ben was happy here, so let Faith stay awhile. She will be safe with me.'

So a lonely and unhappy Ruth was escorted to the stage by George. 'Don't worry, dear,' he said. 'Faith is in God's hands with Alice. She will change her attitude when she has recovered from her deep loss, I do not doubt that,' he reassured her.

But Ruth was not convinced. She felt that she had failed miserably in her duty as a wife and mother. She had been so taken up with the needs of others that her own close family had drifted away from her. These facts were very hard to bear. She had never had the slightest inkling that Ben had not shared her enthusiasm for lost humanity. When they had married so many years before, both had been ardent Methodists. Their religion had been the essence of their lives together. How happy they had been at Dartford! Undoubtedly it was the East End that had defeated Ben with all its terrifying poverty and sinfulness. She should have realised how much he hated it.

Sitting in the corner of that stuffy stage coach as it rattled and rambled down the country road, Ruth contemplated bitterly, alone, as she thought how different everything might have been.

On reaching Aldgate, to her relief Ruth found herself feeling once more her own bright busy self. She knew that this was her cross and that she would bear it with dignity and humility as the dear Lord had carried his to Calvary. When she reached ths Mission, Ruth found Nelly bursting with love and loyalty as she greeted her home, and small grotesque Toby, always so willing and affectionate. All was not lost when one had such friends as these.

Within an hour, Ruth was ladling out soup into cups to feed the ragged children who had waited so long outside her kitchen. Dressed in a long white smock she was back where she belonged. And she pushed the pain Faith had caused her deep into the back of her mind.

During the next year conditions among the poor did not improve much. In fact, drunkenness and vice became more prevalent in the big city which was now swarming with newcomers — Irish, Italians, Welshmen and Scots — who came teeming into the metropolis to take advantage of the offer of employment in this new age of prosperity.

The factories and improved transport, the canals and railways, had indeed provided more jobs but the wages were very low, and food prices high. So it all just made the poor poorer and the rich richer. And still young children slaved in the mines, the mills and the brick kilns as they always had.

As a result of these conditions, there was much unrest in

the streets, with the Anarchists calling upon the working man to free himself of the capitalist yoke as he had done in France. All around small militant groups rose up. But still a man could be hanged for stealing a loaf of bread to feed his family, or rot away in the debtors' prisons while his children wandered the streets homeless and starving, or were work apprentices to hard taskmasters who ill-treated them.

Many voluntary religious bodies such as Ruth's mission still struggled on to help the poor and did what they could to teach and feed them. In Parliament long debates took place as more enlightened men fought to change the laws that suppressed the working classes. Some, like George Gibbs, had after years of campaigning for the children, at last gained the ear of some influential politicians and had his papers read out in Parliament, stressing the need to raise the age that children could be employed, to reduce the hours of work and make schools compulsory and state-aided.

George wrote to Ruth to inform her of his small succes but, he told her, it was only the beginning. He intended to press on and on. He also informed her that Faith was now studying at a teaching academy and Adam was in London waiting to enter medical school and would shortly visit her.

It was about this time that another youth made his way to London to study at the new university. His name was Percy Amos Dell and he came from that wild hamlet of Hollinbury out on the Thames marsh. He was only eighteen but was six foot two with frizzy hair as black as the night. Thick muscles bulged from beneath his spotlessly white shirt and when he smiled his teeth shone white and even beside those full sensuous lips.

It had taken Aunt Beat a lot of time and money to get Percy tutored to the high standard needed for medical school. He had originally announced that he was going to be a sailor, and had always been happiest when sailing with John Shulmead abroad the *Alianora*. In fact, it was on that old barge that he was travelled up the Thames to London and alighting ashore, he swaggered along the edge of the Thames looking around him with excited admiration for this enormous city which he had never seen before. He looked up at the white buildings and at the river crowded with big ships and small boats. He was amazed by the population that hurried past him — hansom cabs, and great carriages, convey the ladies in huge hats and beautiful gowns. Yes, this was a fine city, so he might stay after all. His intention had been to hop off to sea once he had got away from old Beatrice's grasp. But perhaps he would stay here after all; one could have a good time here. Yes, he would go to that medical college that Beat had blackmailed the village doctor to sponsor Percy for . . .

So Percy joined the London College of medics in training and was almost immediately a great success. He was a popular student, mad about sailing, gambling and most of all, women. In no time he had been given the nickname of Paddy as his initials were P.A.D. He never seemed short of ready cash and was often over-generous, throwing his money around to obtain special favours. He had no intention of studying or obtaining any degrees; in fact he was just a good fellow out to enjoy himself. Where he came from and what his background was no one was really sure. Paddy had told the most fantastic tales of the thoroughbred mounts and the county parties, so there was no need actually to ask him if he came from a good country estate for it was quite obvious that he did.

The tall Georgian houses in the back streets off Mile End housed the overflow of university students during that time, so the Mile end wastes became their romping grounds. There, every Saturday night, they played up merry hell.

Paddy was not popular with everyone. The very severe-looking but exceedingly handsome Adam Gibbs, who was reading medicine very seriously, found Paddy to be a general source of annoyance. Paddy lived in a room above Adam's in the same house and he made so much noise while entertaining his friends at home that there were times when the sober Adam had occasion to complain. But in return he received only threats, sneers and violence from his neighbour and decided to ignore him as a bad lot.

Unlike Paddy, Adam was very serious about becoming a

doctor. He was hoping to qualify and then go back to his own folk in Coalville, back to little Faith and a country practice.

The streets of London's East End were as filled with vice as ever. The presence of an organised police force had not diminished the amount of crime or vice but instead had driven it underground, into the booths and taverns. Hell holes still swarmed with ragged children and adults sodden with with drink, and crowds of homeless children slept out in the market under the stalls, or in dark alleys and doorways, where the prostitutes plied their trade, paying the toughs to protect them from the police. Pickpockets still did what they pleased and dirt, squalor and misery were everywhere.

Ruth steadfastly carried on with her mission that year. Again and again she had applied to the police for permission to hold her outdoor meetings once more, for she knew that the only way to fight the demon drink that was destroying humanity was to tackle it out on the battlefield itself. But again and again, her requests to hold her meetings outside the Blind Beggar Inn were turned down as the police feared an eruption of violence as had happened in the past. But finally, after many appeals, Ruth won the right to preach outdoors in a place that was allotted to her off the main street, in an old burial ground that had once belonged to the Quakers.

So it was that every Sunday evening at six o'clock a little crocodile of women and children would leave the mission and set off for this patch of land. Leading the way were Nelly and Toby who carried the portable harmonium, and the banners that they had carefully prepared during the week. All the little children from the Sunday School also waved placards above their heads, with the messages spelled out in large letters. FIGHT THE GOOD FIGHT. SLAY THIS DEMON DRINK. COME UNTO US AND THE LORD WILL BE WITH YOU. JESUS WELCOMES SINNERS.

With her head uplifted and a holy light in her eyes, Ruth would preach a sermon on the evils of drink. Then she would call on the audience to go down on their knees and pledge their souls never to take another drink so that 'God will fill your hearts with happiness and peace.' The Wesleyan hymns were sung with Toby pounding out the tune on the harmonium and out into the night, where there lurked murder, robbery and rape, drifted the sweet sound of singing echoing along those dark alleys.

Sometimes Ruth would win converts but usually she did not, earning only laughter and having her meetings broken up by hooligans. But she never gave up. To her this mission was a Holy Grail for which she pressed on and on. Since losing her husband and the love of her only daughter, Ruth had hardened to become immensely strong in every way.

Whenever Adam returned from a vacation at home, he would bring news of Faith, of her devotion to Alice and of her vocation for learning. She had, Adam informed Ruth, become quite a blue stocking and was now studying French and Latin. And she was always top of her class in the academy for ladies for which Ruth provided the fees.

But Ruth never received a word of gratitude from her daughter for anything. In fact, her daughter Faith ignored her almost completely, though occasionally a polite note arrived with Alice's long letters. But Adam was Ruth's link with her daughter, and she got much pleasure from his help and company. He was a fine genuine lad, admirably religious and studious, and would clearly go far in his profession. He would come to the Mission on Fridays to help with the soup hand-out, and if the subject of Faith came up, he often made excuses for her, for which Ruth forgave him because she knew that Adam was in love with her daughter. Theirs would be an excellent match when Adam had finished his training. And when they had settled down as a married couple, perhaps Faith would soften towards her mother.

With this fervent hope in her heart, Ruth soldiered on. But her cross often became very heavy and then even with her usual energy and her great faith in God, she was inclined to stumble, but she always rose again with renewed faith to carry her cross to Calvary.

Now Adam had returned from his summer vacation and he

stood shyly before her. He always addressed her as Aunt Ruth, which she appreciated. Towering over her small grey shape dressed in a shabby dress, he said: 'Mother sends her regards,' he said. 'And Faith does too,' he murmured. 'I would particularly like you to know that Faith has promised to marry me when I finish my studies.'

Ruth smiled warmly. 'Oh, my dear, I am so pleased for you both,' she cried.

'I would like to ask your permission for your daughter's hand in marriage,' he said stiffly.

Ruth grasped his hand impulsively. 'Oh, Adam, you know that that's something we have always wanted.'

'There is more good news, Aunt Ruth,' when Adam smiled his face lit up and the corners of his eyes crinkled in a charming way. He was such a fine lad, thought Ruth, and would make a good husband. Secretly she hoped that Faith would prove worthy of him.

'Mother and I have persuaded Faith to come home for awhile,' Adam continued. 'Mother thought that now that Faith has qualified as a schoolteacher she might be very useful in your little ragged school. Also,' he added shyly, 'we might see a little more of each other.'

Ruth's lips twisted in a suppressed smile. It was so obvious that he was in love with Faith, and having won her promise to marry him wanted to keep her within sight. 'Oh, that is wonderful news!' she cried. But in fact, she was not really certain of her feelings about that piece of news.

'Mother and Father are coming up to London next month,' said Adam. 'Father has at long last gained attention of a member of Parliament who is making progress in obtaining a bill for the brickyard children.'

'Ever since I knew your father he has been fighting for those poor little slaves,' Ruth said. 'He really deserves to win at last.'

'Yes, Aunt Ruth. Both my father and yourself are very courageous people. I only wish that I were as persistent.'

'It will come dear, just trust in God,' Ruth said piously. Then, with a lighter heart, she went about her chores telling herself that now that her daughter was expressing God's great gift, true love, she would perhaps find kindness in her heart for the mother who bore her.

On a wet and windy day in November, a carriage brought Alice, George and Faith to the door of the mission. Ruth send down the steps to greet them and Alice was overwhelming in her generous greeting.

Faith, however, said coolly: 'How are you, Mother?' Then she gave Ruth a cold peck on the cheek.

Immediately Ruth knew that nothing had changed. She was only being used by her daughter to be nearer her future husband until the end of the university term. But she had to shrug off the pain. This was her home and her prodigal child had returned. For this, at least, she thanked God many times.

In no time Alice and George were sharing memories of the old times with Ruth and of the happy days in Dartford. They could only stay for the day but before they left Ruth took them down to her kitchen to see the long tables with the tin cups all laid out ready to be filled with soup.

The murmur of the children already lining up outside, could be heard through the window.

'This place is so badly needed,' Ruth explained. 'It was just play that we did in Dartford. Down in this poor place I am really needed. You have never known such poverty and depravity as there is here in the East End of London. It's here the soldiers of our Lord are fighting a losing battle all the time.'

'I agree,' said George. 'We are living in very unenlightened times but lately I believe that I can see a light at the end of this dark tunnel.'

'Oh, pray God that it is so,' muttered Alice, her hands folded demurely in front of her. Her sharp eyes scanned the room and her gaze halted in the doorway. There stood Toby for a brief moment. Hesitating at the sight of the visitors, he then turned and hobbled away.

'Who is that man?' Alice asked.

'That's Toby, my most devoted loyal helper,' replied Ruth. 'I don't know why he has gone away. By the way, I believe he came from the same hamlet you came from Alice.'

Alice seemed to wince but did not comment. She just kissed Ruth and Faith farewell and rode away with her husband George.

Ruth took her daughter's arm and hugged her affectionately. 'Oh, how lovely it is to have you home again, dear.'

Faith was staring forlornly after the departing carriage, then she said: 'What is this strange hamlet Alice came from? I never heard her mention it.'

Ruth shook her head. 'Oh, I don't know,' she said evasively. She thought it unwise to say too much about it.

Immediately a coldness came between mother and daughter. Already they had got off on the wrong foot.

For the remainder of that year, while Adam finished his studies, life ran fairly smoothly. Faith kept Ruth's living rooms very tidy and cosy and would sit sewing her trousseau but she refused to take part in the charity hand-outs or the religious meetings. She did, however, condescend to spend some time in the afternoons teaching the poor children the English language. Their dreadful Cockney jargon grated on her ears and she became anxious to improve their manner of speech.

The ragged school was held daily in the large living room on the first floor. Ruth now received regular donations from certain welfare societies, in addition to help from Lord Ashley who was endeavouring to draw the government's attention of the need to educate the poor. So now she was fairly well equipped with books, pens and a blackboard, and quite a regular class of pupils managed to arrive clean and tidy and sit around the big fire — a luxury to those who came from the dark hovels in the back alleys.

Adams would call in the late evening after his lectures and Ruth, for the sake of propriety, would sit with him and Faith in the parlour. Then Nelly would remark to Toby: 'Coo wouldn't 'arf upset me 'aving to play gooseberry every night.'

'It's the custom,' Toby informed her. 'The upper classes have a different attitude to courting.'

'Yer don't say,' jeered Nelly. 'But Faiff treats us all like dirt.'

'Well that's the way of the world, Nelly,' said Toby philosophically. His thoughts turned to Alice. Yes, that tall lady he had seen in the kitchen so haughty and proud, had certainly been her. In his mind he recalled that pleasant young girl who had worked with him in the kilns and foraged food for him and his poor brother Kit. Then he wondered if old Beat still ruled the hamlet and whether Lukey still lived or John Shulmead still sailed the estuary. It was so long since he had left the hamlet.

'Well,' Nelly's squeaky voice broke in, 'it'll be just as well when that Faiff gets married to the young doctor and goes back up norff. Then the missus will be 'appy again. I'm fed up wiv 'er lookin' so sad.' Having said her piece, Nelly began to hand the pots and pans about as she stacked them. Toby did not say anything but basically he agreed.

It had become a regular thing for the hospital students and the young men from the university to volunteer their services to help at the Mission on Friday nights when a special supper was prepared. Then on Christmas Eve they gave a great party and a parcel of treats was given to each child.

That year, with his bride-to-be beside him, Adam stood at the door giving out the parcels. Faith was now a very lovely young woman with rosy cheeks and soft hazel eyes. Love and devotion to Adam had matured her but often her full lips hung down discontentedly and her thick lashes were lowered over her eyes so that no one could see how much she really hated this life and despised all the poverty and the do-gooders. How she longed for lovely silk dresses and society teas! Her mother, of course, was too busy with her works of charity to cultivate her daughter's interest in the outside world in the way that Faith would have liked.

So on this Christmas Day there was the party for the neighbourhood children. A large Christmas tree stood in the corner of the kitchen purchased with money collected by the medical students. The students were in a good mood and played happily with the children. There was one rather hefty young man with frizzy black hair who gave them all rides on his back and lolloped around the room. He seemed a little drunk but Ruth ignored this as it was Christmas and these boys were really giving her children a good time.

'That's Paddy,' explained Adam to Faith. 'He lives in my lodgings. A wild boy, is Paddy, but he offered to come today to help. I was surprised but he is quite harmless, I assure you.'

Faith raised her heavy lashes and gazed straight at Paddy. He immediately came forward and kissed her hand with a gallant bow.

'So, this is your betrothed,' he said. 'Why, Adam, you lucky man, she is beautiful.'

Faith blushed and her hand trembled in Paddy's grasp. The smile faded on Adam's face as he hissed: 'Desist Paddy! This is not the place for horseplay.'

But in that brief second, Cupid had aimed his dart. From that time on it was very hard to dislodge Paddy. He would turn up at the Mission at all sorts of odd times, and usually when Adam was busy with his studies. Paddy would accompany Ruth to the shops and carry her basket, or would sit in the schoolroom while Faith was correcting children's books. He was very sweet and charming to Ruth and frequently dropping hints of the big legacy he was to inherit and of the huge manor house in the country. And he casually dropped important names in an effort to impress her. Ruth listened but did not like him or trust him. She was too shrewd for that. But she was alarmed to see that her daughter seemed to be taken in by his big talk. Ruth begged Faith to be a little discreet, not to walk along the street with Paddy, and never ever to encourage him. He was, she told Faith, the kind of man who could try to take advantage of a young lady.

Faith however was extremely annoyed by such a suggestion. 'Exactly what are you implying, Mother?' she demanded. 'I am well able to conduct my own affairs. I'll not be troubling you for much longer but kindly stay out of my business in the meantime.'

Ruth was deeply hurt by her daughter's remarks but she knew that she had to just leave her alone and let the girl make her own decisions. She only wished that Ben were still alive so that he could give his daughter some advice she would listen to.

CHAPTER SIXTEEN

Disillusion

John Shulmead sat by on his own fireside with a thoughtful expression on his face. It was not often that he lazed about but now he sat pondering and idly watching the flames roar up the wide chimney. He still sailed the *Alianora* around the coastal waters but in these days it was mainly for the pleasure of conquering the dangerous choppy estuary and to feel the salt breeze ruffle his still thick mane of red hair. The new barges he now owned were much swifter than the old *Alianora* and, being able to carry more cargo, were certainly very profitable transporting the vast amounts of building materials from the quarry and kilns of Kent to the big industrial towns. And he felt that he was entitled to a little leisure now, having worked very hard to obtain so much, but he did work hard still. Between voyages he was always at business meetings or meetings of the Waterways Company to discuss the training of river pilots to guide foreign ships down the treacherous tideways into the Thames and Medway.

Yes, it was an extremely busy life these days, but tonight John sat peacefully at home. On the arm of his chair, perched his much-loved daughter Emma, now almost a young woman, and facing him in the rocking chair, her fat legs resting on a foot stool, was his wife Dolly who rocked placidly to and fro, knitting without pause.

Dolly was still fair but her face was very white and flaccid, her limbs fat and solid. Her blonde hair tonight was tucked into a loose snood and her rosy lips puckered up as she sucked sweetmeats. She now weighed about fifteen stone and her movements had slowed down considerably. Still on her plump arm, though now digging into her flesh, was that snake charm bracelet which John had given her years ago the day she married poor old Kit. Dolly would never let go of that bracelet, in spite of the efforts of John to remove it, and her daughter's concern that it would stop the circulation if it grew much tighter.

John's keen blue eyes roved over Dolly and up to the mantlepiece where that white ivory elephant still reared its trunk, then on to his lovely daughter who clasped her arms about his neck. 'Oh, it's wonderful to have you home with us, Papa!' exclaimed Emma.

As John pulled her on to his knee, her lovely green-blue eyes lit up with love for this teddy bear-like Daddy who gave in to her every whim.

'How long have we lived in this cottage, Dolly?' John suddenly asked of his wife.

Dolly paused in her knitting, her round eyes stared and her mouth gaped. 'A very long time,' she said slowly, and then went back to her knitting.

John sighed. He never expected to get a long conversation from Dolly, she was never one for small talk. He turned his attention to Emma who chimed in: 'We have lived here almost sixteen years,' she said brightly, 'and I was born here.'

Dolly looked up and gave an apathetic sigh, her gaze resting on the white elephant.

'Well, darling,' John addressed Emma. 'I think it's time we moved on.'

Dolly dropped the knitting into her lap and looked mournfully at him. But Emma clasped him about the neck and cried: 'Oh, yes, Papa! Let us move to a great big house with stables.'

He gave her an indulgent smile. 'You would like that, eh?'

'I certainly would.' Emma smiled cutely at him. 'I get so sick of that Fiona Barrington boasting about her hacks.'

'Well, my love,' said John, 'that is what you shall have. We will see that you have the best horses and the biggest parties in the area. We will see that you have those country folk know that we are somebody. Yes, the Shulmeads have come to stay.'

'I don't want a big house,' grumbled Dolly. 'I can't even manage to keep the housework down in this cottage.'

'Woman!' roared John, giving her a good thump on her knee. 'You shall have maidservants, there's no need to worry.'

'Have you come into money, Papa?' asked Emma, as she coyly caressed John's red-gold hair.

'Well, darling not quite,' he replied affectionately. 'But any day now I am likely to. No, it's been in my mind to build you a fine house for a long time.'

'Where will you build it?' she asked.

'Out at the old forge that belonged to my father. That is, if I am lucky enough to acquire it.'

'I'll never live up there,' broke in Dolly. 'Not in that creepy old place ...

But no one took any notice of Dolly.

Emma squealed delightedly. 'Why, it's ideal, and high up, with a lovely view of the Thames and the Medway. But above all, it has lots of lovely meadowland for our horses. Oh, darling Papa, do get it for me and I'll really love you,' she cried excitedly.

Dolly grunted disapprovingly but said no more. She knew that her husband's desire was to please his daughter, not herself, and resignedly accepted the fact.

Two hours later John was installed in his usual seat in the Malted Shovel. From behind the bar, Beat served him his ale. She wore a modern auburn wig and a black silk dress. There were not many familiar faces in the bar these days, just a couple of barge skippers, and the new young doctor who occasionally dropped in for a pint. But he was a very conscientious man and never stayed long.

Dumb Lukey trailed in and out of the bar parlour collecting the empties with little energy. He had become quite subdued recently, particularly since his pal Percy had left for London. And since Percy had gone, Beat had treated him more like a servant than ever before.

When the bar closed, dumb Lukey was sent to bed that night while Beat entertained her friend and business acquaintance John Shulmead. Together they finished off a bottle of rum which seemed to have little or no effect on either of them.

'I have almost completed our deal with the railway,' John informed her. 'All I've got to do is go up to London next week to complete the final details to the papers.'

'Good,' said Beat. 'Don't drop the price, boy, see that they don't rob us,' she warned.

'No, Beat,' John assured her, 'we both come out of this deal very well, especially since we did not pay a lot for the Canal Shares.'

'Right then, lad,' Beat replied briskly. 'Remember, money is power, so don't let them toffee-nosed sods fool yer.'

John smiled. 'What will you do with your share?' he asked.

'Don't you go a-worrying about me. I always know how to take care of me own money,' Beat cackled.

'Oh yes, I am quite sure of that,' laughed John, 'but I wonder if you might not invest it in something else — gold mines for instance. There's been a lot of talk about a gold rush lately. I expect you got a bit put by for a rainy day.'

'If I have, that's my business,' Beat replied, suddenly angry. 'That bloody Percy robbed me right and left. I've not got much now but this will come in handy, thanks to you, John.'

'Well, I need a favour of you, Beat,' John said as tactfully as possible.

'Ah well, out with it,' said she eyeing him with the utmost suspicion.

'I want the Shulmead Forge and all the land attached to it.'

'You can't,' she replied quickly. 'It's leasehold and belongs to the church. And anyway, it's dumb Lukey's legacy.'

'I'll pay a good price,' argued John. 'And the church lease is renewable.'

'What do you want it for?' Beat demanded sharply.

His eyes gleamed. 'I am going to build a big house up there, a really fine house high up on that hill so that it can be seen for miles all around.'

Beat grunted and raised her eyebrows in approval. 'It's a good idea,' she said. 'The old place is in ruins now and I have not been able to let it for years. And I certainly don't get a lot from those gypo farmers for the grazing.'

John's hopes were raised. 'Well, Beat, is it a deal?' he asked.

'No,' she said quickly. 'It belongs to Lukey. He is the eldest living son and while Lukey lives, yer can't have it.'

'Now, now, Beatrice,' he said. 'Both you and I know Lukey will never get a look in. And he can always come and live with me if he likes.'

'No, no,' Beat shook her head emphatically. 'Lukey stays with me.'

John held Beat's wrinkled wrist very firmly. 'Beat, old gel,' he said, 'don't try to fool me. I know how old you are. What about Lukey when you have passed on? Who will take care of him then?'

'You cheeky sod!' Beat yelled, pulling her arm away from his grip. John thought he saw a glint of tears in those old grey eyes. 'All right,' she said. 'Let's get it signed up. It will just be another load off my mind.'

'That's it dear,' John said soothingly. 'We must all put our houses in order, as time soon flies past.'

'Emma, darling,' John said the next morning. 'I've bought you the land so now we will build that grand house.'

'Oh, Papa, can I help?'

'Please let me use my own ideas,' she cried, overwhelmed with joy.

'If you want to.' he said indulgently. 'But within reason, of course. First, what will you call it?'

Emma gazed out at the green fertile hill and almost breathlessly cried: 'Riverview, Papa, because you can see both rivers.'

John nodded approvingly. 'Now that sounds very suitable. And I'll be able to watch the ships come in when I am too old to go to sea.'

'You will never be old, dear Papa, don't say such things.'

'Oh well,' John rubbed his hands enthusiastically. 'That's one little scheme completed, and it's all for you, Emma, my darling.' He hugged her affectionately.

Dolly was out in the kitchen preparing the breakfast. She heaved a deep sigh and considered how no one consulted her any more about anything.

Any spare time Ruth Anneslee had with her daughter Faith was spent in a small sitting-room on the top floor which, after all these years, was beginning to look very homely.

Faith was an excellent needlewoman, having received a good training from Alice, and she added all those homely domestic touches that Ruth had never had time for. She crocheted cushion covers, embroidered chair backs, and sewed up curtains for the windows. Everyday there were fresh flowers arranged in beautiful bouquets all around the house, and every evening Faith sat demurely sewing while Ruth worked at her accounts books. They still had little to say to each other but of late Ruth had noticed a definite change in Faith's behaviour. She was much less sullen and seemed happier. Often those dark blue eyes even flashed with humour.

Nelly had noticed it, too. 'Blimey,' she remarked to Toby, 'that Faiff is cheerin' up. Must be that Paddy teachin' 'er a few tricks.'

Toby frowned. 'Now, Nelly,' he warned, 'show some respect for your betters.'

'Well,' sniffed Nelly, 'since Faiff was a little kid I never liked 'er. And I 'appens to 'ear fings when I goes dahn the road,' she hinted.

'Well, you keep them to yourself,' warned Toby.

Adam was now deep in his studies and did not call at the Mission quite so often. But Faith never complained about this; she just sat silently sewing.

One evening Ruth remarked: 'My dear, what are you doing to that good serge dress?'

'I am taking down the neckline,' Faith said sharply. 'I intend to insert some nice lace into the bodice.'

'What on earth for?' Ruth was astonished. 'That is a fine winter gown and it will do you for several years.'

'Mother,' Faith replied icily, 'kindly allow me to know what is worn by my own generation. You are so drab, and content to be arrayed in the same shabby old dress day after day. Just don't expect me to look the same. I am a young person and wish to move with the times.'

'Well, if that is your wish,' protested Ruth, 'but I do hate waste when others are in need. Besides, such a low neckline is considered a trifle indecent in our religious society.'

'Oh Mother! Please be quiet!' cried Faith impatiently. 'Who wants to look like those drab old matrons?'

So Ruth retired from the fray but felt a little concerned for her daughter. Several times a week Faith went shopping to buy a few essentials and to collect some blooms from the flower market. These she liked to arrange around the house. They were an extravagance, Ruth was quite sure, but she did not like to be too hard on her daughter. But of late Faith would go out shopping and be missing for several hours, and on her return Ruth would survey her daughter anxiously, wondering if she had been accompanied by that very ardent medical student, Paddy. One evening, Adam dashed into the house. He looked quite irate as he rushed up the stairs to the sitting-room and confronted Faith as she sat alone. From downstairs Ruth could hear their voices raised in anger. Adam had closed the door so she hesitated to go up, but eventually she did. She knocked timidly and entered the room to see Adam and Faith sitting apart, both with unhappy expressions on their faces. She knew that the most tactful thing for her to do was say nothing.

Adam rose to his feet. 'I am just leaving, madam,' he said politely. 'I have to catch up on my work. Now I have a request of you, if you will arrange for Faith to return to Coalville to my mother until the summer vacation when I will have completed my exams.'

Faith looked coldly at him and said in a clear voice. 'Why bother, Adam? I have not promised to go.'

'Well, that is your decision,' he replied quietly.

'May I ask why?' insisted Ruth.

Both stared silently at each other and the air was thick with emotion.

'Ah! never mind,' said Ruth. 'It must only be a little quarrel. I'll leave you to patch it up.' Hastily, she made her exit feeling that something was very wrong and knowing that Faith would never confide in her.

It was Nelly who put Ruth in the picture when she returned the next morning from the hostel down the road. Several times a week Nelly would go down to take the clean linen and chat to the old chap who minded the working-man's hostel. On the way Nelly would gossip to anyone who had the time and she had to pass the big houses that accommodated the students from the hospital.

'Oh, ma'am!' she gasped that morning when she returned. 'There ain't arf bin some trouble dahn there. Irish Molly bin bashed up, some said she might die.'

Ruth was busy and was never willing to listen to Nelly's gossip.

'Oh, Nelly, who is Irish Molly and how does she concern us?'

'The cleaning women told me, those what does for the students. They found 'er outside in the alley, all bashed up an' bleedin',' gasped Nelly.

Ruth's attention was caught. 'Well, who is she?' she asked.

'Molly's a street woman,' whispered Nelly. 'She 'angs abaht dahn there.'

'Oh, poor woman,' murmured Ruth, always so compassionate for the fallen.

'Ah know,' said Nelly, 'but they do say that Paddy dun it. An' 'er bloke, what's a ponce, 'as bin to the university to complain.'

'Dear God, that young student? No, Nelly, it's a lot of gossip and nonsense,' said Ruth, feeling quite disturbed by the news.

'He ain't very nice,' announced Nelly. 'Molly turned nark on 'im 'cos she were jealous. He used to give 'er a lot o' money, 'e did.'

'Oh cease this talk, Nelly!' cried Ruth impatiently. 'Let us get on with our chores.'

'But, ma'am ...' gasped Nelly eagerly. Then she suddenly shut her mouth and no more was mentioned of the business.

It was not until the following morning that Adam arrived at the Mission and asked to talk with Ruth privately. She was busy in the kitchen but wiped her hands and smiled in welcome. 'Well you are an early bird,' she said. 'Faith is hardly risen yet.' Looking at his white, dejected face, she said: 'Something is wrong, whatever is it, Adam?'

'There is trouble down at our lodging,' Adam said. 'And I am afraid, madam, that both your daughter and I are involved.'

Ruth looked incredulous. 'Faith? Why? What has she to do with it? Please explain yourself more clearly, Adam?' she requested.

'Faith has been engaging in an illicit affair with none other than my fellow student Paddy. It breaks my heart to have to inform you,' he added weakly, as tears sprang into his eyes.

'But who or what is Paddy anyway?' Ruth asked in a dazed manner.

Adam shrugged. 'He has fled, madam, after having made a dastardly attack upon a young defenceless person and nearly killing her.'

'Irish Molly,' muttered Ruth. 'So it was all true.'

'You know about her?' Adam said in astonishment.

'Yes, Nelly brought in some gossip yesterday. But how on earth are you and Faith involved? That I don't understand,' she said.

'Because it was Irish Molly who informed me that my betrothed spent most mornings locked in a room with Paddy.'

'Oh, dear God,' cried Ruth. 'What does it all mean?'

'Well, the university authorities have taken the matter up. I might get suspended. But we are now waiting for a public enquiry. I felt that I had to warn you, and now I must talk to Faith.'

Hurriedly they ran upstairs. Ruth threw open her daughter's bedroom door and cried out aloud. The single white bed was smooth and unruffled. Faith had fled with her lover, the arrogant rogue Paddy.

Ruth was devastated by what had happened. At first she was enraged and then terribly forlorn. Her daughter whom she had cared for and brought up as best she could had now cruelly rejected her, and had so scorned those deep religious beliefs as to allow herself to be taken in by a young foolish boy. And by running off with him without one word of explanation or even repentance to Adam, her betrothed, Faith had probably ruined Adam's career and mocked the mother who had borne her. It was all too much to bear.

Late one night she knelt in the bare little schoolroom, which also served as a chapel. The altar, an old kitchen table covered with a red cloth, supported a plain polished wood crucifix and a vase of flowers. To her great Saviour Ruth poured out her heart, begging him to guide her and asking why she had failed as both wife and mother. And her Lord and master, Jesus, just for once did not respond.

Ruth got up from her knees feeling empty and confused and then went down towards the kitchen where Toby and Nelly were still preparing for the next day.

Nelly's high-pitched voice rang through the house. 'If you asks me she was mesmerised,' she said. 'That's what I fink.'

'No one has yet asked your opinion, Nelly,' returned Toby's quiet voice.

'Well, it's done, yer know. I saw it up at the fair. This fella waved a watch abaht and this 'ere girl done everyfing what 'e told 'er,' continued Nelly in a loud voice.

'Well, Nelly, I don't think that fairground magic comes into this. And you had better say your prayers, for Satan has a nasty habit of playing havoc in empty minds,' Toby warned her.

'Oo'er,' cried Nelly. 'Don't say that, Toby Jug! You knows

any mention of evil scares me out of me wits.'

'Well this is not our affair,' advised Toby, 'and it is better that we say little about it.'

Ruth stood by the door listening. For some reason what she heard made sense. Perhaps Faith had not gone entirely of her own free will, or perhaps she had gone back to Alice. If she had worries she would always confide in Alice, as she had in the past.

'Go off to bed, you two,' Ruth called to her staff.

'We were waiting for you, ma'am,' replied Nelly. 'Would you like some 'ot milk?'

'No dear, I'll retire now,' said Ruth, 'there is another long day tomorrow, God being willing.'

For many nights Ruth tossed and turned in her bed. Over and over in her mind she wondered where she had gone wrong. She had lost both husband and daughter. And just who was this man Paddy who had robbed her of her lovely daughter? What was he? Where did he come from? She had to talk to Adam again and find out if Faith could be saved from herself while there was still time. This man was a devil in disguise. He had already attacked a defenceless woman and left her almost dying, bloody and beaten in a back alley. What chance did her naive young daughter stand with such a man?

Adam was already packed to return home. But he had little solace to offer her. 'I'll go back to Coalville,' he informed her, 'because if Faith is in trouble she will certainly contact my mother.'

'What about your exams?' cried Ruth in dismay.

'Unfortunately, I'll have to drop out,' he told her. 'But at least I have been exonerated of any blame in this dastardly business so I will get a chance to return next year.'

'Why had there been no new of them? Have they contacted this Paddy's family?' cried the distracted Ruth.

Adam shook his head. 'He has none. He was brought up by an old aunt. According to a witness, both Faith and Paddy travelled together early in the morning in a hackney cab to the docks at Tilbury. It's possible they went aboard a ship.'

'Oh dear,' gasped Ruth, 'what can we do?'

'Not a lot,' returned Adam sadly, 'but I will go home and wait for her. I am sure she will regret her haste and come back to Coalville. I am confident that she will return because Paddy is not the marrying kind.'

'So, you are still prepared to forgive?' asked Ruth.

'Madam!' Adam cried. 'I love her with all my heart. She is my whole life and always has been.' His pale, good-looking face looked strained.

Ruth put her arms around him. 'Oh, my dear boy. I am deeply sorry but I pray each night and day that she will come back to you.'

After Adam had left for the Midlands, Ruth buried herself in her work and tried to forget. The evening was cold and there was a long queue of ragged children outside. From the kitchen came the nourishing aroma of the carrot, onion and marrow bones that had been put into that big soup pot. The little ones sniffed hungrily outside.

Ruth opened the doors and let them in a few at a time so that Nelly and another helper could serve the soup in to the tin cups. The little ones dunked the bread into the soup and scoffed it up. Then they went out through another door where Toby stood, handing them each a bun or an orange, or whatever had been scrounged for that particular day. As one lot of children went out, another lot was let in.

Leaning on his walking stick, Toby always kept a wary eye on any other child who misbehaved at the table, swearing, fighting or stealing another child's meal. Although the stick was never used, for Toby was the kindest and gentlest of human beings, the sight of it helped to keep order.

With a keen eye Ruth would inspect the children, always on the look-out for sickness and with a sweet smile for the regulars. There was one particular lad who caused a lot of trouble. He was not a regular, he just turned up occasionally but when he did everyone knew he was there. Dirty Dick, the other children called him. The name was quite appropriate, for he was always filthy and ragged. His bare feet were invariably caked with mud and his wild shock of hair stood up on end thick with grease. His neck and ears had clearly not touched water for a long period. Dirty Dick was an aggressive little boy. He fought and argued, and always refused to stay behind and talk with Ruth. He would just gobble up his meal and flee. Repeatedly Ruth tried to catch him but he was like a small wild kitten, as swift as the wind and positively violent towards the other boys.

'I must do something about that lad,' said Ruth to Toby one day. 'Try to catch him up.'

So this particular evening Toby grabbed and held on to Dirty Dick's ear. The urchin yelled and fought and swore as Toby marched him into the small back room which Ruth used as an office.

'Hi! hi! wot's yer game?' yelled Dick. 'Oi ain't done nuffink.'

'Now, dear, be still and I'll give you a sweet,' pleaded Ruth.

At this he quietened down and eyed the jar of sweets on the desk. Then, with his mouth full with the boiled sweet, he sucked appreciatively and watched apprehensively, alert and ready to bolt like a wild animal.

'Where do you live, Dick?' Ruth asked in a gentle, cajoling tone of voice.

'Nowhere,' sniffed Dick.

'You mean you are homeless,' she said.

'Naw, I'm a barrer boy and oi kips dahn the market.'

'You mean you sleep out in the open? Is there no one in charge of you?' Ruth asked with worried concern.

'Only me,' said Dick. 'I'm in charge o' de uvver boys see. We runs the froot barrers, we does, an' oi don't need yer bleedin' soup. Only comes up 'ere for a lark, oi does.'

Ruth endeavoured to smile and then handed him another sweet. 'How would you like to go to our hostel for a few nights? You'd have a nice warm bed and a bath. It's not the workhouse, and you don't have to stay there if you don't want to.'

Dick looked positively terrified and backed away nervously.

'Naw, oi don't need yer bleedin' doss 'ouse. Oi dosses dahn the market under the tarpaulin. Got me own spot, oi 'ave, an oi earns me own cash.'

'Well now,' said Ruth soothingly. 'That's very nice but how about you letting me give you a nice wash and I'll find a good coat for you.'

'No fanks, missus, oi don't need a wash. Oi swims in the Cut, oi do, so lemme aht o' 'ere,' he demanded.

He made for the door but Toby barred the way. Like a young ram with its head down, Dick butted poor Toby in the stomach. Toby lost his balance and fell and Dirty Dick fled, grabbing some buns from the tray in the passage as he went.

'Well, that was another disastrous failure,' said Ruth, helping Toby to his feet.

'Can't win them all,' said Toby. 'Don't distress yourself, madam. He comes from the fruit market in Spitalfields. There is a whole army of young boys living there in incredibly derelict conditions. They help with the fruit and flower barrows and sleep rough under the stalls at night.'

'Oh dear,' sighed Ruth. 'I do wish something could be done for these homeless children. We do our best and what else can we do? There are so many of them.' she said despondently.

'We will do just what we are able to do,' replied Toby. 'But it is a national problem. The government takes our taxes and it is the government that must improve the situation.'

'Yes, I know you are probably quite right, Toby,' Ruth replied.

'In the end it must be solved,' continued Toby. 'There are many reform bills waiting to go through Parliament now, so surely we must see some progress soon.'

Ruth sighed. 'Not in our lifetime, Toby, I fear. The progress is too slow.'

So the year dwindled on and Ruth, in spite of her heartbreak plodded on. Her shoulders seem to droop and the last remaining gold went from her hair. It was now a dull ash colour. Six months had passed since Faith had gone, and still Ruth had received no word from her.

Alice had sent a long letter of condolence to her friend telling her to trust in God's good grace and that she believed that Faith would eventually return to her own environment. She also told her that Adam was now working for a dispenser in the town and continuing his studies at home. George, she wrote, had won much ground for his campaign for the distressed slaves of the brick kilns, and a bill was about to be passed in Parliament preventing the employment of very young children in these industries. So all was not lost, and Ruth had to take heart and hope for the best.

Ruth was pleased to hear from Alice but the letter did little to mend her heartbreak. She thought of the long line of fallen girls that she had sent to Alice who had then trained them as seamstresses and prepared them to take a better position in life. They all seemed to have emerged, as good, industrious women. How strange that Faith, so well protected, had been the fish that escaped the net of respectability. Oh, she should have kept all her loved ones close to her! Now it was too late.

But some things in her life were good. Toby remained her staunch ally and Nelly her loyal servant. And all about her Ruth had gathered many true friends from all classes. Also, her meetings in the East End waste had become exceedingly popular. There was less disturbance and fewer outward signs of vice. But still there was the readily available drink and still the hordes of unwashed boys and girls — often the worse for drink — prowled the district picking pockets. It made Ruth very sad to see them for there was nothing she could do about these young hooligans. They were just like small animals scavenging for their own existence with no welfare or law to control or help them. For if the police picked them up, the urchin just languished in mouldy damp cells. No one ever bothered to free them and the drinking booths and brothels used them for their own peculiar kind of services.

Toby now had a job in a city barber's shop during the week and brought home plenty of the latest gossip of how this new eighteen-year-old Queen Victoria believed in total abstinence. The climate had changed since the death of the indolent licentious King George and his equally foolish brother William. More attention was being paid to the working class and much effort was being put into ridding the city of vice, gambling and prostitution.

'Well,' said Ruth hopefully, 'it is not before time. But still the very young homeless children need to be cared for and educated. And still so little is being done about them.'

But the donations poured in steadily to support her school and Mission, and many a young woman from the better class homes came to volunteer her services as a helper to Ruth. This new breed of young woman — blue-stockings, people called them — were educated, very precise and very proper but extremely concerned about the poverty they found in those back streets.

Recently the inquiry into the attack on Irish Molly had been in the news. It was already well-known that she had been well compensated by the University and the case had been dropped for the lack of evidence, as no one had as yet found Paddy.

But Toby came home one night very excited. 'Did you know that his name was not Paddy at all but Percy Amos Dell?' he asked.

'No, I was not aware of it,' she replied.

'But what is extraordinary is that he came from my hamlet in the marsh, Hollinbury, where I spent my childhood.'

Ruth looked amazed and shook her head in disbelief. 'That place haunts me. It is always cropping up.'

'Perhaps we had better talk more about this hamlet, Toby.' Ruth said. 'Alice came from the same place and has always been very secretive about it.'

'Yes, that I was sure of but when Alice did not recognise me, I held my tongue.'

'Now, dear, let us sit down and God willing we will quietly unravel the mystery of this benighted hamlet,' said Ruth. 'It may even lead us to my poor unfortunate daughter.'

So Toby told Ruth of the brick fields, the little slaves whom Larlee owned, of Alice in her youth and old Beat at the

Malted Shovel, of old Wally who had befriended him and of his brother Kit. All the while Ruth sat holding his small, well-manicured hands as she listened and allowed tears to pour down her cheeks.

'Oh, how sad,' she cried when Toby ended his story. 'That is indeed a haunted hamlet. In my heart I have always known that some day I would know all about it and now my friend I certainly intend to visit it. Something tells me I must do exactly that.'

'I shall be most happy to accompany you, madam,' said Toby.

'Thank you, my dear friend. I don't know what I shall find there but I must go. We must start to make arrangements for the Mission to carry on in our absence. We have many good helpers so it will not be so difficult to take a few days off.'

CHAPTER SEVENTEEN

The Rescue

A stranger riding from Gravesend towards the Thames marsh might pause for a moment to admire the new canal basin and the lock gates overlooked by a sturdy modern house. Then he might ride on through the more lush green meadows where the cattle grazed and the dykes buzzed with wild life activity as small rodents darted through the grasses and buzzing insects hovered lazily in the summer sun. Brilliantly coloured dragonflies flitted here and there; bullfrogs croaked their deep-toned mating songs; the blue kingfisher flashed past in pursuit of its next meal; and an abundance of wild birds filled the air with song. The stranger might then take the narrow towpath alongside the canal where the long boats passed, pulled by magnificent shire horses flexing every fine muscle as they strained to pull the heavily laden barges. Then, if he is lucky, he might see one of the Thames barges, its red sails huffed and tied down, its skipper with his face and skin tanned by the salt air, standing on the deck and cursing his luck as he wished that he had taken the sea route that would have saved him much time and money. As John Shulmead had predicted, the new canal had never been prosperous and after only seven years, plans were already afoot to convert it into a railway line.

As his barge came close, the skipper might tie up in the vicinity of the Malted Shovel, the tall half-timbered inn that stood high on the hill overlooking the canal amid the remains of what had once been a well-populated hamlet. There still remained the old church with its square Norman tower dominating the skyline and a few old cottages and wooden dwellings. But a new sight was to be seen in the vicinity — the miles and miles of hop poles surrounding it. For in these recent years hops had become the main industry of the area. Beer was no longer made from barley and the big brewers from the main towns now demanded Kentish hops to brew their beer.

The hop-picking had become an industry of its own. In late summer, as now, in between the tall poles worked the hop pickers, many of whom had migrated from London for a working holiday. They lived near the hop fields in squalid huts with hordes of their children romping about while they earned precious extra money from their labour.

Hollinbury hamlet was roused from its usual lethargy by the arrival of these hard-drinking, hard-working Cockneys. Trade picked up at the Malted Shovel where the public bar was always full as the loud-mouthed pickers squandering their hard earnings on drink and dancing to the tune of 'Knees up, Mother Brown' while their army of children ran loose pillaging the orchards and fields, leaving gates open for the cattle to roam free. This state of affairs would last for five or six weeks each year then at last peace would descend on the hamlet once more when they all returned to London. To Beat, at the bar, the money dropping into that wooden drawer was not such a great recompense as it might have been years ago. She could barely cope with the extra work it entailed, for her sister Dot had died quietly some years before.

John Shulmead would recline in the bar parlour and watch the Cockney capers in the public bar with disapproval. When they had all left, he and Beat would share a bottle and complain. 'Whatever possessed the old farmer to sell out to the brewery?' he pondered. 'It defeats me. He used to grow fine cider apples out there on that land and in my time there was plenty enough barley to make beer.'

Beatrice would sigh. 'Well, times are changing, John, but thank God it don't last long. They will all be gone before October.'

'It's too much work for you, Beat, you need help. Why did

not young Percy come home this summer vacation? He's a lazy scoundrel but at least he's an extra pair of hands.'

'I was meaning to talk to you, about young Percy,' Beat said, producing a letter. It was addressed to the old village doctor who had died last winter, and its heading bore the crest of the London University. 'The young doctor brought it in,' Beat explained. 'I can't read it but to my mind it spells trouble. The doctor tells me that Percy's been expelled. That means he's bin chucked out.'.

John looked at the letter. It was indeed addressed to the old doctor who had sponsored Percy at the medical school for a big price, and announced that they no longer wished to educate Percy Amos Dell, since he had been involved in a scandal and run away.

'After all that money I spent,' grumbled Beat. 'Bloody waste, that's what it was.'

'I am not a great reader of this high-falutin' legal jargon,' said John, 'but it seems that Percy is in plenty of trouble.'

'But why ain't he come home?' Beat asked.

'It appears he fled to avoid punishment,' John informed her.

'I thought so,' Beat shook her head. 'There's bad blood in him, and I never did like him. That Dot spoilt him just like she did Lucinda, his mother.'

'Well, I expect when he has run out of money he will turn up, so stop worrying,' John assured her.

'If he comes back here, he don't get nothin' else,' Beat sniffed. 'He can work for it like I did all me life,' she asserted. 'Bad blood will out. He's going to be a bloody pest, I feel it in me bones,' she complained.

'Well, let him work, then,' said John stoically. 'You need help and that won't hurt him.' He yawned. 'I must go now, got an early start tomorrow. Goodnight, old gel,' he said affectionately. 'I am taking Emma to the horse fair tomorrow to buy some bloodstock for her new stables. She is so happy with them it's going to be a pleasure to spend money on her.'

'Bloody fool,' groused Beat. 'Them young uns is all the same. I'll see young Percy don't get no more out of me.'

'No need to worry now that we have put out capital in Railway shares,' John said. 'It's the coming thing, investments.'

'Well, I'll keep what's left for a rainy day,' said Beat.

'Put it in the bank. It will be safer there and you will get interest,' advised John.

'No, thanks. I don't trust them buggers,' said Beat. 'It stays in sovereigns, real gold, so that I can sell it.'

'Well, it's yours to do as you wish, Beat, but you will never live long enough to spend it all.'

Pig-headed as ever, Beat drew all her money in gold and stashed it away under the floorboards in the bedroom, first pushing aside that heavy four-poster bed and then pushing it back.

Lukey knew where she hid her money since he had seen her through the key-hole. He was mostly confined to the house while the hop-pickers' children ran around for Beat did not want to take any chances with him. Lukey missed Percy and was bored. He would go up to the attic and sit on the old rocking horse, rocking back and forth hour after hour.

The inn began to take on a neglected appearance. Dust clung to the shelves, the earthenware spitoons were rarely cleaned and the sawdust on the floor did not get replaced very often. For Beat was getting too old. Much of her time was spent sitting in the kitchen dozing off. When this happened, Lukey would escape upstairs and dodge all his daily chores. So the shiny horse brasses of Aunt Dot's time had turned green and the brass coal bucket turned black. Most dwellings were now gaslit but Beat clung to the old oil-lamps and the bar looked grim and gloomy. A few regulars still congregated in the bar parlour, while the labourers and the hop-pickers cavorted in the public bar. Beatrice tried valiantly to cope with it all, but she was no longer the fiery woman of old; the fires had died down in her.

On the neighbouring hill overlooking the estuary, John Shulmead's house stood out against the skyline. The rising sun shone on those new yellow bricks, the shiny bay windows, and the red tiled roof with its tall chimneys. It was certainly the most modern and the smartest house in the vicinity. Workmen still cared for the garden laying out paths and pools. Its most dramatic features were the big round glass conservatory full of tropical plants and the round tower that contained John's telescope. John and his daughter Emma were very satisfied. The house was well worth the fortune John had invested in it, and the stables John had built for Emma were the talk of the county.

Emma herself attended the nearby young ladies' academy for the training of gentlewomen. She was very popular there and the young men fell over themselves to escort her.

John was a contented man, and very satisfied to have come so far and such a long way from that little waif who had once slaved in the brick kilns. He now owned an interest in the combined brick and cement works and spoke out on the board against employing children under thirteen years of age. He also contributed to the new school which had been built down in the village. As far as John was concerned, he had attained his dream and was a well-respected citizen in the hamlet. He had no desire to move away from the Kentish village of his roots; he only wanted to improve it.

'Riverview' was a land mark for all to see. When they had first moved in, John had put his arm about his daughter affectionately. 'This is all for you, my darling,' he said. 'It's been so very worthwhile. All I hope is that I live long enough to see you settled down happily here. And, who knows, I might be lucky enough to have a grandson. A boy in the family would please me very much.'

'Oh, Papa,' giggled Emma, 'I've no intention of getting married for a long long time.'

'Well, we will see about that,' smiled John indulgently. 'Come, let me see you put that new horse through his paces. Then I must be off.'

The new mount was a three-year-old grey stallion with strong haunches and a proud bearing. He was a gallant, lively creature that had cost a lot of money. As Emma rode it around the stableyard, his long silky grey tail swished happily and majestically.

Watching Emma sitting so upright in the side-saddle, with her cool firm hands on the reins, John felt very proud. He begrudged nothing to his lovely Emma. He could not remember the last time that he and Dolly had dined out together or when he had bought her a new gown, for he was completely eaten up by love for his lovely daughter. At seventeen Emma was coy and as skittish as her ponies.

But Emma was also a little cunning and knew exactly how to handle her doting father. Most days she would ride through the hamlet sitting bolt upright in the saddle. Her black habit fitted her perfectly, and the black silk hat, with its snow-white veil, was poised at just the correct angle. When passing the inn she would salute old Beatrice with her whip and pour a look of scorn on poor dumb Lukey huddled in the doorway.

Beatrice would sniff. 'Hoity toity, young Emma,' she would mutter. 'You are going to come a cropper one of these days.'

Later that autumn when the hoppers had returned home to London and the tall elms by the church yard had laid a golden carpet, a cold mist rose over the marsh early one morning as Emma galloped over the bridge. She was on her way to another inn — the Horseshoe and Castle at Cooling where the hunt was meeting. She wore an elegant green habit and cut a fine figure on her snorting grey stallion.

She drew in her reins and pulled her mount to one side as the old horse omnibus came rattling over the bridge and halted outside the Malted Shovel. From it, she saw a weary, dusty couple of travellers alight but she quickly rode on. She never concerned herself with the local inhabitants.

Inside the Malted Shovel, Emma's father was sitting in the bar talking to Beat. John had just finished his early morning walk along the shore and had popped in to the inn for a pint of cider. As the young couple entered, he looked at them with interest. The young woman, dressed in a shabby cloak and bonnet stood shyly at the entrance with her head down. But the young man stepped forward confidently.

John recognised him immediately, and smiled. 'Well, Percy, my lad!' he said. 'It was time you came home.'

Percy shook John's outstretched hand. 'Meet my wife Fanny,' he said. 'We have been travelling abroad for some months.'

'Well, that is a surprise.' John held out a hand to the young woman but she did not extend hers in return. She just stood passively by the door, her head dropped down in a hopeless manner.

As John relieved the young woman of her travelling bag and escorted her to a seat, Beat had watched the couple with amazement. She herself looked quite a sight, with her hair in paper curlers and her cap awry. She stared aggressively at Percy and then screeched. 'Where have you bin, you bugger?'

'Calm down, Auntie,' order Percy. 'And this is my wife.'

'Wife! What bloody wife?' yelled Beat. 'I ain't never given no permission for you to get married!'

Percy ignored her and went behind the bar to pour himself a stiff whisky.

'That's it,' complained Beatrice. 'As bloody saucy as ever and gobbling up the profits.'

At that moment, the door opened and a rough figure rushed in, hurling itself like a dog greeting its master. It was dumb Lukey, his usually pallid face flushed with excitement and he uttered inhuman sounds as he fell at Percy's feet, grabbing his legs so he could not move. Fanny stared nervously at this extraordinary sight of the imbecile welcoming his old playmate.

Percy patted Lukey on the head, just as he might a favourite dog. 'Hallo there,' he said. 'And how is our old Lukey then?'

The sight seemed too much for the young woman. A loud sob rasped in her throat.

John rose to his feet. 'Your wife is travelweary, Percy. Take her up to her room.'

But like a bullet from a gun, old Beatrice was at the bottom of the stairs and guarding them like a dragon. 'Oh, no, she don't,' she yelled. 'I ain't having none of your floosies up there.'

Percy continued to pat Lukey and swallow his drink at the same time. He turned away from Beat with a sneer.

John however forcibly moved old Beatrice away from the stairs gently but firmly. 'Madam, this lady is your guest,' he said. 'I am quite ashamed of you.' Then taking Fanny by the arm he escorted her up the stairs, carrying her case and opening the bedroom door for her. After he had left her to settle in, he went downstairs to tackle both Beat and Lukey.

'Jesus Christ,' he blasphemed as he descended into the bar. 'Are you mad, Beatrice? What a way to treat a young lady!' He turned to Percy. 'And as for you, young man. You are supposed to be a gentleman but your behaviour does not inform me so.'

Both Beat and Percy were uncharacteristically silent, acknowledging that their fiery tempers had got the better of them.

John continued: 'Whether that young lady is your legal wife or not, we still all owe her an apology after the way she's been treated.'

Beat snorted and clumped angrily into the kitchen, giving dumb Lukey a severe clout as she went and chasing him into the yard.

'I'm sorry, John,' said Percy, 'but Fanny is not actually wed to me. She is of a good background and left her home to travel with me. We are now flat broke, which is why I am back here.'

'Well, that is your affair,' said John, 'but you had better treat that young woman right. You are responsible for her whatever the legal state of affairs, and we will fall out of friendship if you don't.' With that warning, John left the inn.

Upstairs in that old cold bedroom, Faith, or Fanny, wept tears of remorse. So this was the end of the journey, the end of that ghastly trek through grimy lodgings to this grim-looking inn where everyone seemed a little crazy. Had it really been worth leaving the security of a respectable home?

Percy had been good to her even if he had not bothered to marry her and in the beginning it had all been very exciting not to know what the next day would bring. But once Percy had lost most of his money at the gaming tables, they had been forced to return to his home.

Faith looked back on that year with bitterness. They had lived in disgusting hovels and Percy had destroyed her both mentally and physically. She just no longer felt like the daughter of a strict Methodist preacher. She was just empty, void of Christian faith. Yes, Percy had certainly opened her eyes to the vice and wickedness of the world but any latent desire to improve it had left her completely. She just hung tenaciously to the little sanity she still possessed. Even her name Percy had altered.

'Faith,' he had mocked, 'sounds like a nun. I'll call you Fanny. That sounds much better.'

Yet why Faith had stayed with him was beyond her. She no longer loved him — and perhaps she never had. Perhaps it had just been a case of the devil she knew, for she had discovered that there were even worse people in that wicked world out there. Deep down she knew that only her fear of the hard life held her to him.

After a while Percy came upstairs. He had adopted his sweet, charming and cajoling manner. 'Come on, Fan,' he said. 'Come down for a meal. I realise the old gal was quite a shock to you, but come on now. You must be hungry and she's all right now.'

Without a word, Faith removed her overcoat and followed Percy down into the kitchen to meet Mistress Beatrice.

'I've told her we married in secret because your parents did not approve,' Percy grinned as they went. 'She thinks you are some society girl with pots of money to inherit.'

Faith made no comment; she was used to his subterfuge.

The meal was good, consisting of roast fowl, baked potatoes and green beans. Throughout, Beatrice fired questions at Faith, asking who she was, where she came from, and how they met. But each time Percy was ready to intervene with the answer. Beatrice seemed fairly satisfied. She sucked the meat bones loudly and drank a huge jug of wine with her meal.

Gradually Percy worked his charm on his aunt. He smooth-talked her and told her lewd jokes about London which she seemed to enjoy immensely.

'Well,' Beat said. 'I suppose it's just as well you came home. I need help behind the bar. It's all getting a bit too much for me as I ain't getting any younger. So, if you want money out of me, you had better start earning it.'

'Nothing to worry about, Auntie,' promised Percy. 'I'll take care of things here for you. Just you relax.'

'Ah, that will be the day,' jeered Beatrice. 'Rob me bloody blind, you would. But you ain't getting a penny if you don't work.

'She don't say much, does she? Cat got her tongue?' She narrowed her eyes at Faith, who shuddered.

Every morning very early, Beatrice knocked heavily on Faith's bedroom door. 'Git up, gel,' she would yell. 'Get up and make up the fire. And put the kettle on.' These had all been Lukey's normal chores but now they had become Fanny's, as they all insisted on calling her.

Percy always slept late. After breakfast, he would set out across the marshland carrying his gun and accompanied by Lukey. A few hours later, he would return carrying partridges and rabbits all still and bloody, poor little wild things that Fanny was expected to skin, pluck and cook. But she could not do it. She was simply incapable of skinning an animal. This failing caused many heated arguments between Beatrice and Percy.

'Where the bloody hell did you find her?' demanded Beat. 'And who does she think she is?'

'Oh, leave her alone, Auntie,' Percy would snap. 'She wasn't brought up to live a hard life and anyway, she is pregnant.'

'Oh, very nice, I must say,' cried Beatrice tossing her head. 'Another bloody mouth for me to feed.'

Percy continued to laze around as he always had. He played cards with the customers and drank heavily while Fanny became more silent and withdrawn and grew fat in the stomach. She took very little care of herself and spoke to no one. Through the winter into early spring poor Fanny could be seen sitting at the attic window where once Lucinda used to watch for her lover. There she would sit with a melancholy expression on her face as she stared out at the green, slimy and practically unused canal.

Dumb Lukey was intensely jealous of Fanny. His squinting eyes followed her everywhere and he would suddenly spring out at her from dim corners. His tactics worked; Fanny was so terribly afraid of him.

'Lukey won't hurt you,' said Percy. 'Try to be friends with him, he will like that.'

Fanny knew that this was not true. She now froze every time she saw Lukey and if he tried to touch her she would shriek.

Occasionally Percy got restless at the inn and rode off to town, staying away sometimes for days on end. Then Beatrice would complain loudly. 'Got some floosie in town, I'll be bound,' she would grunt. 'You get off your lazy arse, gel,' she would yell at Fanny, 'and come down here and help me. You ain't much good for aught else.'

Fanny would hump up the bottles from the musty cellar, dreading every second that she was in amongst the dust and cobwebs, with Lukey lurking in the shadows. Then one evening, as she tidied up down in the cellar, everything went dark as the heavy door slammed shut. Lukey had grabbed the lamp, run out and shut the door so that Fanny was trapped down there without a light. She stumbled about frantic and too terrified to cry out. Anyway, Beatrice would not hear her, she was too busy in the bar. So she wandered about trying to find her way to the door. The darkness was complete and she was very clumsy with her weight of pregnancy. As she tried to grope her way around, she bumped into objects in the dark causing great spider webs to fall on to her head and envelop

her. She sobbed and called and even prayed. Eventually she
fell to the floor sobbing. There she lay all night, with the cold
unearthly feeling which filled that creepy cellar chilling her
bones. She crouched close to the ground wishing only to die.
And as she sobbed it seemed that other sobs echoed all around
her as though someone else were trapped down there too.

'Oh, dear God,' cried Fanny. 'I am sorry I have forsaken
you. Please, sweet Jesus of my childhood, take me to your
bosom. I can no longer face this terrible life.'

But nothing happened. There was no relief from this terrible night as poor Fanny sat waiting to see a chink of morning light.

Upstairs Beatrice slept heavily with her stomach full of
rum, while dumb Lukey lay outside the cellar door as if to
make sure that Fanny did not escape.

Percy arrived home in the early hours of next morning
looking very seedy after his night out on the tiles. He spotted
Lukey lying fast asleep outside the cellar and gave him a good
hard kick. It was then he heard a faint whisper.

'Who's down there?' Percy demanded, but Lukey just
jumped to his feet and fled.

When Percy carried Fanny out of the cellar, she screamed
hysterically. 'Go! Go!' she cried. 'You are the devil's disciple.
Leave me to my gentle Jesus.'

She was still screaming and fighting when the doctor
strapped her to the bed. 'She will probably miscarry that
child sometime today,' he informed Percy. 'She is very
disturbed, and you must take care of her.'

Percy beat Lukey and Beatrice beat Lukey, but Lukey
seemed impervious to it all. He just sat gloating over the
trouble he had caused.

So it was that poor Fanny lost her baby. Afterwards she
was so mentally unbalanced that she was unable to leave her
room into which she was locked every day. There she would
spend her time sitting up in bed praying and crying. But no
one was duly concerned about her. Life seemed to go on as
before in the inn. 'It's a crying shame,' remarked John

Shulmead, 'that happening to a lovely young girl like that. Surely there is someone somewhere who cares about her. That blackguard Percy certainly does not.'

'Well,' said Beat, 'she has gone potty so she is no use to me any more. I've got enough on me hands with dumb Lukey. I wish she would pack up and go home.'

John was worried and tried to talk to Fanny about her folk. But now that she was out of bed and on her feet again, she just wandered about with a vacant expression on her face.

One day John spotted her small thin figure teetering at the edge of the canal. Alarmed, he strode forward quickly. 'Good morning, it's so nice to see you out walking,' he greeted her.

Fanny's sad eyes looked at him. 'Can I trust you to deliver a letter for me?' she asked.

John was amazed. He had never heard so many words from her lips before and he was astounded by the culture of her tone. 'It will be a pleasure, madam. Where do you wish it to go?'

She produced an envelope and handed it to him. It was addressed to Mrs Alice Gribbs, Spring Cottage, Coalville, Leicestershire.

'Right, I'll take it to the town to the mailing office immediately.' he promised.

'You will not tell anyone,' she whispered.

'No, indeed, not. If that is your wish, you have my word of honour,' John assured her.

Meanwhile, Ruth had managed to free herself from her duties and had completed her arrangements for the visit down to Kent.

'I don't know what I will find in this hamlet,' she said to Toby, 'but this need to visit it persists. We will travel on the Dover coach to Gravesend and then go out on the morning coach.'

'At first sight,' said Toby, 'you will find that it will all seem very beautiful, but there is hidden ugliness in those marshlands, and those dreaded brick kilns with their smoking chimneys are no sight of beauty.'

'I realise there will be sad memories for you, Toby, but so often when we go back down the road of the past it does not seem so bad after all,' Ruth said wisely.

As they sat chatting in the hall of the coaching inn waiting for a hired carriage to take them out to Hollinbury hamlet, in walked a tall soberly clad woman and a very good-looking young man.

Ruth jumped to her feet. 'Why Alice! What are you doing here?' she asked as they embraced. 'And you too, Adam!' she exclaimed excitedly.

'We have news of Faith,' said Adam eagerly. 'That is why we have come here.'

'Oh, dear God,' cried Ruth piously closing her eyes briefly. 'Thank you for guiding me in the right direction.'

'Faith has written to me and seems very distressed,' said Alice, handing Ruth the letter to read.

> Dear Alice,
>   I can only write to you as you were always a mother to me. Forgive me the unhappiness caused your son but now I need you so. I cannot go on with this life any longer? . . .

Tears poured down Ruth's cheeks as she read the letter.

'Where is she?' asked Toby.

'None other place than our own hamlet,' replied Alice gently.

Toby's face creased with emotion. At last Alice had acknowledged the past!

'She is at this moment in the inn, the Malted Shovel. Let us go quickly as she is in great need of us,' cried Alice.

So the four determined folk rode in the hired carriage to Hollinbury hamlet in search of Faith. The hop fields and orchards rolled past with the memories of their childhood.

'You did remember me, Alice,' said Toby.

'Yes,' she sighed, 'at first sight.'

'Much change has taken place in our lives since then,' said Toby. 'Yet without you I might never have survived to adult age. Even now I am only half a man.'

'You are a fine man doing God's work,' returned Alice. 'And there is no time for being bitter for past injustices.' She paused. 'I have to say that the mere thought of returning to that unhappy hamlet has always brought great fear to me but for Faith I will brave any obstacle.'

From the other side of the carriage, Ruth watched them talking intently. They looked odd together. Alice was so neat and well dressed, and her face was so scrubbed and shiny, her hands so neatly gloved. While Toby just looked odd in his square black hat and his peculiar cape. It did not seem feasible that they had started out in the same derelict cottage, living in squalor and slaving at the brickfields together so many years ago.

Throughout the journey Adam did not speak. His handsome face remained very solemn, and his hands tightly clasped the silver knobbed cane he always carried. He was clearly full of nervous tension. Would he find Faith again? How would she react to seeing him? Did he still feel the same about her? All these questions he turned over and over in his mind as they travelled along. Would he be able to control his temper if he came face to face with that scoundrel Paddy who had stolen her from him? He had never wanted to kill anyone before, but now easily he could wring that Paddy's neck!

Ruth sat surveying them all and felt sad that it was her own flesh and blood who had caused all this unhappiness.

Toby said quietly: 'It will be better when we arrive if I go into the inn alone. I am well known by old Beatrice, the proprietress, and she will give us no information if she does not wish to give it. I will be able to sound her out.'

So the carriage was halted on the other side of the bridge and Toby alighted and hobbled over to the inn.

Beatrice was busy clearing up. 'No more beer,' she yelled at him as he came in. 'We are closing for lunch.' Then giving him a quick glance, she said more kindly. 'Oh well, if you are a traveller you can sit in the bar parlour. Do you want a meal?'

'No, thank you, Madam Beatrice,' replied Toby with a smile. 'Last time I was here I could barely reach the counter and now it's still out of my reach.'

Beatrice turned and screwed up her old eyes to look more closely at him. 'Well, I'll be blowed!' she cried. 'It's little Toby Jug!'

'The same,' cried Toby, delighted by the welcome.

Beat hustled Toby into the kitchen. 'Now, whatever made you come back here?' she challenged him. 'Sit down and I'll pour you a drink.'

'No alcohol, madam, just water,' said Toby.

'Same old bible puncher,' mocked Beatrice. 'You ain't changed a bit, have you? Never thought you would ever come back to the old hamlet.'

'I am here on business,' Toby informed her. 'I'm looking for a young woman who is reported to be staying here. Her name is Faith. Do you know her?'

Beat narrowed her eyes and stared at him with some suspicion, 'We don't get no strangers here. Only the hop pickers, and they have all gone.'

'Some time last year,' Toby said. He hesitated. Was it a mistake? 'Can you recalled anyone called Faith. She is aged about twenty, with dark hair,' he continued.

'Faith? Faith?' Beat muttered. 'No, we've only had Percy's wife staying here, and she is called Fanny. Otherwise there's just me and old Lukey. You recall him, old Lukey, don't you?'

Immediately Toby knew that he had come to the right place. Leaning out of the door, he signalled to the others. As they came in to the inn, a thin figure rushed downstairs. It was Faith, already dressed in her overcoat and carrying her bag. She had seen them arrive from her seat in the window. The group of people stood and stared at each other. Ruth was trembling. She felt sure that Faith would run to Alice rather than her. She stood eyeing her fragile-looking daughter in shock. There was no doubt about it, this poor little girl, her beautiful daughter, was a mental wreck.

But it was to Ruth that Faith ran. Slowly she put down her

bag and then quickly dashed forward, clasping her arms about her mother's neck. 'Mother! Mother!' she cried, like a small child. She held her tight and rubbed her tear-stained cheek against Ruth's cheek just as she used to do as a baby.

Alice looked slightly disappointed and Adam stood shyly aside. But suddenly the silence was shattered by a torrent of abuse from Beatrice who demanded to know who they were and what they wanted with Percy's wife.

Beat's appearance made Faith cry loudly. 'Oh, Mother, please take me away from this dreadful place!'

Ruth hugged her close. 'Come, my darling,' she said, guiding her daughter outside and into the waiting carriage.

Alice stood defiantly in front of Beatrice.

'Good God!' declared Beatrice, squinting aggressively at her. 'If it ain't bloody Larlee's gel, Alice.'

'Yes, Madam Beatrice, it is!' said Alice firmly 'And we are taking Faith with us. If what I have heard is true I will send the law down on to you.'

Beat was too shrewd to deny anything. 'The best thing you can do is take her away. She is very unbalanced, she's no good to me, she ain't, nor to Percy neither. He don't want her, and I don't believe he was legally married to her, anyway,' she jeered.

'We are going,' gasped Alice as she swept out. 'You certainly have not improved with age, you old witch!'

'Yah! Yah!' yelled Beatrice after her. 'Who do you think you are? Your mother was the biggest whore about here.'

The party quickly climbed into the carriage and the driver was ordered to drive on. They could hear Beat still shouting at them from outside the Malted Shovel.

'Well,' said Toby once they were on their way, 'I certainly don't want to return there any more.'

Faith lay in her mother's arms and Adam pressed his head in his hands to avoid the tears being seen. The carriage rattled away from the haunted hamlet and the fact that none would ever return again was uppermost in their minds.

CHAPTER EIGHTEEN

The Demise of Dumb Lukey

John Shulmead's new house dominated the landscape. It stood high upon the hill overlooking the rolling green meadows which swept down to the shoreline. The tall red brick chimneys could be seen from far out on the river, as could the circular window high up in the eaves where John had set up his watchtower. With a large telescope he surveyed all the big ships that went down the river. He knew each name on sight and most of the cargoes they carried. The skippers were often his friends and gave a friendly signal as they passed by. In his heart he still longed for the deep open sea of his youth; time had given him prosperity but little freedom. It was very hard to escape from all his business interests or the affairs of the waterways of which he was now chairman. Occasionally he did manage to take a vacation and sail the old *Alianora* round the Nore Light, often docking in Sheerness where he knew a very accomodating little barmaid at a very comfortable inn. It was here he would hobnob with the old skippers and the overseas captains and gather all the news of the foreign ports and salty seas.

John would return from such trips feeling very refreshed. Life with Dolly was now very depressing. Each day she slowed down a little more and was clearly not happy. She complained all the time about the new house and the servants he had provided for her. But Emma remained the light of his life. She was still as pretty as a picture and as proud as a queen. She rode with a straight back and was as shrewd a judge of horse flesh as anyone he had ever known. Emma was all he had and all he could wish for. Deep down, he knew he would have liked a son, but it did not matter now. With a bit of luck Emma would provide him with a sturdy grandson.

He fervently hoped that he would live to see his grandchildren benefit from the fruits of his hard work. After all, that's what it was all about. Had he not slaved since he was a small boy? Had he not frozen and starved in the brick fields? Been beaten and brutalised at sea? Having surmounted all the perils of the living, his only desire now was to have descendants to whom he could leave all his wealth. Emma was yet young but perhaps next year he would look around for a suitable husband for her among the big county families with whom she mixed socially.

He thoroughly enjoyed the big parties Emma gave, and the house was always full of young folk. Emma was so pretty and vivacious, she attracted plenty of the young army officers from the camp at Chattenden, and the young naval officers of leave from Chatham Dockyard. All these visited Riverview where the food and drinks were plentiful and young Emma was an excellent hostess.

Emma still regularly rode through the hamlet with a haughty manner. It was about six months after Fanny had left him that Percy noticed her. He roamed the marshes with dumb Lukey, gun in hand, shooting the wild geese or just blasting at some unsuspecting hare or terrified rabbit. That morning he was standing with his gun over his shoulder looking down the deserted lane when Emma came riding by on her way home from a long hack. Percy watched her as she rode gracefully by, controlling her sweating horse with great skill. He noted her slim and shapely figure under the well-cut riding habit.

Lukey gesticulated wildly, as if to ask if Percy wished him to hold up her horse and pull her hair, a game which they had often played in their youth.

'No, no, Lukey,' Percy said firmly. 'That is a real fine mount she has got. If I had money I would buy myself a thoroughbred hunter and ride with the hounds.'

Lukey grinned and gibbered and jumped up and down as

though he were riding a horse.

Percy aimed a kick at him and stood for a moment watching Emma disappear down the lane. 'Come on,' he said. 'Let's go home.'

Back at the inn, Beatrice was in one of her bad moods. Naturally untidy, she had always battled with the various chores in the bar but they were becoming too much for her now and her miserly habits would not allow her to employ any staff to help her.

'Took you bloody long enough,' she yelled at Percy when he and Lukey came in. 'Get down and change them barrels in the cellar,' she shouted at dumb Lukey, who whimpered and fled immediately.

'See if you can't give me a bit of help tonight,' she complained to Percy 'instead of sitting there playing cards and losing what bit of money you have.'

Percy looked at her for a few moments with a cold, complacent expression. 'Ah, money,' he said, 'that is the question.'

Beatrice ruffled up like an angry hen. 'You will get no more out of me unless you earn it!' she cried. 'I've worked hard all me life. I wasn't brought up with a silver spoon in me mouth like you.'

Percy did not say anything. He just wandered nonchalantly up the stairs to change his clothes and then sat on his bed thinking hard. He thought about Beat's movements and how she never ever went into town to put her money in the bank these days. In fact, she had no personal contact with anyone but John Shulmead. So what did she do with the money she took from the bars? Or the money she had made from her profit on the canal shares which were not the property of the very rich railway company. While he took off his muddy boots and put on his slippers, his mind thought of all possible hiding places. He imagined his miserly aunt secretly counting out her gold coins before she went to bed at night. When he was a small boy, he remembered, she used to put the money into an old wooden chest. That he was sure of. The more he thought about it the more clearly he could recall the old chest. But where was it now?

That evening, well dressed, slick and very cool, Percy was his charming old self as he served behind the bar giving old Beatrice time to tidy herself up and regain some good humour. When John Shulmead came into the bar she was all toothless smiles to welcome him.

With his ruddy complexion and mop of thick curls, John was still good to look at, even in middle age. He retained a gentle cautious way about him. 'I'll be taking the old *Alianora* for a trip round the Nore Light,' he informed Beatrice. 'It'll be just a short trip. I won't be gone long. Is there anything you wish to consult me about before I leave?'

'No, lad, I am all right,' Beat replied. 'Now I've got rid of his fancy woman I can rely on Percy a bit more. I don't want no strangers in here. You can't trust no one these days,' she whispered, looking over her shoulder.

Percy was listening to their conversation and his lips tightened into a thin cruel line. So that's what she thinks of me, he reflected.

Late that night Percy roused Lukey from his slumbers in his old makeshift bed in the cellar. 'Money?' he whispered, showing his palm and then making a circle shape with his fingers to indicate a coin.

Lukey shook his head vehemently and pointed frantically to the ceiling to indicate that he was afraid of Beatrice.

'Not to worry,' said Percy fussing and petting him and handing him a cigarette. Lukey had a passion for cigarettes but Beatrice would never allow him to smoke. 'Does Lukey know where the money is?' he asked.

Lukey nodded excitely and put his hands over his face as if to indicate sleep.

'Ha! that's it then. It's in her bedroom,' cried Percy jubilantly. 'Lukey is a good boy,' he told him. 'Tomorrow we go and get it.'

Grinning and nodding, Lukey showed great willingness to lead Percy to Beatrice's hoard of money.

Once the bar was closed for the afternoon, Beatrice would sit beside the kitchen fire and doze off. But her ears were very sharp and the slightest sound would wake her.

Percy knew that he had to make sure that she was properly asleep. So very kind and considerate for once, he said: 'Sit down, Aunt Beat. I'll bring you a cup of tea.'

Beat was grateful for this gesture and sank back into her chair. She was feeling particularly tired. Percy watched her craftily as she sipped her tea, for he had poured in a good strong sleeping draught. It took only a few minutes. Suddenly the cup crashed to the floor and Beatrice was lost to the world.

'Come on Lukey,' whispered Percy. 'Now's the time, old fella.' He beckoned to Lukey who went upstairs on all fours like a buck rabbit with Percy behind him. In Beatrice's bedroom, Lukey tried frantically to push the heavy fourposter bed aside.

'Wait for it!' cried Percy, putting his shoulder against it. With a tremendous heave, the old bed was moved aside. They prised up the floorboards to uncover the stout heavy treasure which Beatrice had been collecting throughout her life.

Percy was most interested in the small canvas money bags filled with gold coins. 'My God,' he gasped. 'The old miser. She must have been stashing it away for years.'

'Now, Mum's the word, Lukey,' he said, as he filled his pockets with coins. Then he closed the chest and returned it to the same spot. Together they pushed back the bed and Percy said: 'Now, Lukey, be careful not to wake Beat up, and I'll bring you back a present.'

Then Percy took the old cob, hitched him to the trap and he pushed off to town. He was not to be seen for several days.

Beatrice slept through to the evening and woke up exceedingly irritable. She got very drunk, gave Lukey a good beating for no reason and went off to bed. The inn remained closed and the puzzled regulars never knew why.

It was only the first time that Percy had robbed his aunt but once his money had gone, squandered on women and gambling in town, he returned home very contrite. Beatrice seemed slightly vacant and very overworked, so Percy was charming and very considerate. As always, Beat gave in to his charm so they did not indulge in the usual screaming quarrel which followed one of Percy's absences.

When John Shulmead returned a week later, Percy asked for a word with him in private.

'Certainly,' said John affably. 'Come, let's walk over the bridge.'

'I am about to ask a favour of you,' said Percy.

'Well, I'll oblige if I can,' replied John warily. He never trusted Percy.

'I've bought a hunter with some money I won on poker,' Percy said. 'I don't want Aunt Beat to know yet because she does not like me gambling.'

'Well, that's all right, I won't let on,' said John with a smile.

'Well, I wondered if you would let me stable it up at your place — just temporarily, of course.'

'Well, I don't see why not,' returned John. 'But Emma's the girl in charge. Mind you, there's plenty of room up there. I see no reason for her to object.'

Two days later Percy rode into Riverview with his thoroughbred mount — a young chestnut gelding named Sir Galahad.

Emma examined the horse with a professional eye, and asked Percy its origin and the price he had paid.

'Well, he's a good buy,' she said approvingly when he told her.

When the groom had taken the horse into the stables, Emma looked Percy squarely in the eye. 'I would never have thought that you were a horseman. You seem like too much of a man of the town.'

Percy's coal-black eyes appraised Emma. 'Well, madam,' he said, 'one does not always abide by others' ideas of oneself.'

'All right, then,' replied Emma, with the same hard light in her eyes. She struck at her knee with her whip with some impatience. 'Let's see you ride him. I'll meet you here at eight o'clock tomorrow morning.'

Percy gave a graceful bow of acknowledgement. And so began the traumatic affair of the delinquent youth Percy Amos Dell and the beautiful wayward Emma Shulmead.

Day after day they rode over the moist marshlands racing each other like the wind. As Percy had craftily planned, Emma sponsored him with the master of the local hunt, and soon Percy was also riding with the hounds and the cream of the county set. Once more he doped old Beatrice in order to steal enough money to buy the expensive riding clothes he needed for his new mode of life. He swaggered around at hunt events inventing wild stories of his adventures in London. In no time he had become quite a sensation to the dull county set and was very popular with the ladies.

Then one night as Percy and Emma rode home through the dusk, Percy suddenly dismounted from his horse. 'He seems to be limping,' he said, running his hand down over Sir Galahad's fetlock.

Emma, fresh-skinned and bright-eyed, jumped down from her horse and stood close. In that lonely lane, the scent of the new mown hay was overpowering as Percy turned to her and took her in his arms. Emma leaned towards him and lifted her face to his. For many seconds they kissed passionately as Cupid shot his dart out there in the quiet of the misty marshy lane.

Suddenly Emma pushed Percy away from her, 'Oh, no,' she cried. She was frightened. No man had ever held her like that before, she had been too proud to let them. What was happening to her?

'I am sorry, darling,' said Percy urgently. 'But it has got to be you and me. We were meant for each other.'

But Emma had leaped back on her mount and was riding off. 'Have you forgotten that you have a wife, Percy Dell?' she called. 'Because I have not.'

Percy stood in the darkening lane and cursed his haste in case he had frightened her off after all his careful preparations.

For a while Emma avoided him, taking her riding exercise either early or later than Percy. But Percy still hung around the stables moody and nasty tempered. Then one morning Emma rode past him accompanied by Major Frederick Barrington, who was home on leave from the army. In a very casual manner Emma greeted Percy.

Percy's face blanched with temper and jealousy. Returning to the inn, he spent the rest of the day with dumb Lukey, tormenting him into such a frenzy that at eventide Lukey fell down in a fit.

Old Beat wept when she wiped the foam from Lukey's mouth as he lay thrashing about on the floor. Percy looked on horrified, for he had never seen Lukey like this before.

'Now, perhaps you are satisfied,' Beat snarled at Percy. 'For Christ's sake, why don't you go off to sea, or something? Go anywhere but get out of this inn. You are nothing but trouble around here.'

'Don't worry,' Percy snarled. 'I'll get out of here soon enough.' Then he looked at her with such intense hatred that for a second even Beatrice was afraid of him.

But once Lukey had recovered and tempers had returned to normal, things settled down and the affairs of the hamlet went on as before. That autumn, the canal had been drained and nothing remained of it but a deep chasm. Then along came the railway workmen laying long lines of gleaming rails along the track in place of the canal. Many of them dug out the earth and banked it up alongside the track.

Then came the cold winds of winter tearing over the marshlands. The horses were stabled in the warm and Emma travelled to London to stay with a friend from her academy. And all this time Percy lolled about in the bar at the Malted Shovel eaten up with jealousy at the thought of the escorts taking his beautiful Emma to dances in the brilliantly lit ballrooms of the capital.

On Christmas Eve a terrible rattling and rumbling struck the foundations of the hamlet, shaking the old timbers of the houses and scaring the wits out of their inhabitants as the first train from London to Dover came racing by.

Dressed warmly against the winter cold in a big checked cap and a red woollen scarf, dumb Lukey stood gaping at this smoky monster on wheels as it roared past.

Percy grinned and put a comforting arm about him. 'Nothing to be afraid of, Lukey, old son. It's only a puffer train.'

Percy taught Lukey how to use the level crossing with care — how to listen out for the train and to get over as quickly as possible without dawdling. But Lukey would stand in the middle of the railway lines and freeze with fright at the sight of this metal monster. Then Percy would have to reach down the bank and quickly drag him to safety.

Beat would warn Lukey to be as cautious as possible. 'Use the bridge, Lukey. Don't go over the crossing,' she would say. 'It's too dangerous.'

But dumb Lukey heard no one but Percy these days.

Beatrice was really feeling her age now and would sigh a lot. 'God help Lukey if he gets caught in the middle of the track,' she would say. 'He'll be smashed to smithereens.'

When the spring came once more, Percy decided to go up to Riverview to see his horse which had been cared for by the Shulmead's groom all winter. In the warm stable which smelled sweetly of well-groomed horses was Emma dressed in an old pair of breeches and a big jersey. She was nursing a sick mare who was about to foal. Percy and Emma stood together looking down at the unhappy animal, whose sides heaved in pain and whose soft eyes rolled in terror. Emma was very pale and subdued. 'I am waiting for the vet,' she said. 'I do hope she's going to be all right.' Tears softened the dark eyes which were usually so hard and dominating. This was a side to Emma that Percy had never seen. He moved closer to her and held her hand. Her head drooped and rested on his shoulder. 'I have missed you, Percy,' she whispered.

That same passionate feeling surged up between them and this time it was mutual. Percy knew that before long Emma would be properly his. At twilight they rode through the meadowland and stopped to rest beside an old ruined castle.

Under the shade of the ancient wall they made love. Emma allowed Percy to caress her and kiss her but when he tried to go further she pushed him aside and struck at him cruelly with her hunting crop. 'Oh no, Percy Dell, you will never roll me in the hay like some local whore,' she said firmly.

'I need you, I love you, Emma. Let us get married,' he begged. 'I'm sure you know that I was never legally married to Fanny.'

'Yes, Papa told me. But he is not too happy about our association, you know.'

'But Emma, why?' Percy looked hurt. 'He has known me all his life, and my aunt is his personal friend.'

'I am not yet eighteen, and you are twenty-five, quite frankly, a bit of a rake. You can't blame Papa for the way he feels. You are certainly no great catch.' Emma's tone was mocking and cruel.

In a flash of rage, Percy grabbed her and pressed her close to the wall, his body stiff he pushed himself between her legs. She gasped and shivered in such a way that he knew she wanted him. 'Emma, you are mine,' he whispered hoarsely. 'No other man shall have you. I swear by all that is holy I'll kill him or you.'

Their lips clung, and Percy's tongue probed her mouth as his hands held her breasts. With a deep sigh, Emma succumbed to his passion. The tightly fitting breeches she wore under her riding skirt prevented him from actually touching her flesh but both reached the pinnacle of passion almost at the same time.

'You see,' said Percy, 'you and I don't need a bed.'

'Nevertheless,' Emma replied proudly, 'you will marry me before I allow you to go any further.'

Percy grinned and fondled her well-formed thighs. 'As you wish, Emma, but now you are mine, and I will ask your father for your hand in the respectable, recognised manner.'

'In three weeks at my birthday party will be as good a time as any,' said Emma coyly. 'In the meantime, dear Percy, do try to behave yourself.'

Percy smiled in satisfaction. He was temporarily content.

So for the next week they took their morning rides together. Emma allowed him a few extra privileges but still maintained her virginity. Percy became quite frustrated and would hang about the bar all day and sometimes go fishing down at the old creek.

Dumb Lukey loved to go with him and would sneak off with Percy while Beat was having her afternoon nap. To do this they had to cross the railway line and Percy would laugh at Lukey's fear of the trains and tease him. Percy would sit on one bank and make Lukey stand on the other side of the tracks. When a train was signalled, Percy would hold up a cigarette on a piece of string and order Lukey to come and get it, crossing the tracks before the train arrived.

Percy would roar with laughter at Lukey's antics as he clambered terrified up the bank as the train swished by. But on this particular sunny afternoon something happened to Lukey. He just stopped as if in a trance in the middle of the track as the train came round the bend.

'Hurry up, Lukey,' yelled Percy. But that pathetic figure stood petrified as the train appeared with a sudden roar and ran right over him. With a loud screeching of brakes the train ground to a halt further up the line.

Percy lay on the bank looking down at the remains of what had once been his pal. Poor dumb Lukey was now severed into four separate pieces of flesh. Percy howled like a dog and vomited in shock. What had he done?

John Shulmead was walking over the bridge when he saw that the train had stopped on the line. Realising that something was wrong, he ran to have a look. He arrived on the scene just as Lukey's remains were being put into a wooden box by the railway men. The box was then carried over to the inn.

Beatrice was distraught. Her face was yellow with grief and fear as she sat crying bitterly in the kitchen. John Shulmead went to console her and gave her a good stiff tot of the rum that she was so fond of.

'He's done it,' Beat sobbed. 'That bloody devil, Percy. I

begged him to leave Lukey alone but he had to torment him.'

'It was an accident, old gal,' John assured her. 'Poor old Lukey, he never knew what hit him.'

'You can believe what you like,' snarled Beatrice, 'but I know that bloody Percy used to wait until the train was coming and then call Lukey over the tracks. Lukey loved Percy, he did, and he would do anything for him.'

John looked sad but poured her another drink. Suddenly Beat lost control and began to shriek hysterically: 'It's fate! It's time repeating itself. Poor Lukey killed his own father and now his son has killed him.'

'What are you raving about, Beatrice?' John asked sternly. 'Now calm down, old gal.'

Beat suddenly pulled herself together and stared at him with suspicion. 'Take no notice of me,' she said. 'I am just an old body, and my mind is wandering.'

There were very few folk in the hamlet who knew that the handsome prosperous John Shulmead was poor dumb Lukey's brother. It would have astonished quite a few, including Emma and Percy. But now Lukey lay in the graveyard beside the smithy who had sired him who had also met a violent end.

On the night of Emma's birthday, the lights of Riverview shone out over the estuary and the gardens were strung with bright Chinese lanterns. It was to be a very colourful affair and all the very best of the county folk had been invited. It had cost John a great deal of money but he had never begrudged anything to his beautiful Emma.

Unfortunately that night John was not quite his usual charming debonair self. He had had quite a lot on his mind since dumb Lukey's grim death and he was very concerned about the close attachment of his daughter Emma to Percy. Emma had been like a tower of strength to Percy who had really been devastated by the accident. For all the terrible things he had done to Lukey, he had still loved him in a perverse way. His grief had drawn him closer to Emma in the last few weeks.

'Why do you have to feel so guilty?' Emma asked. 'Lukey was only a poor dumb fool. He did not have a lot to live for.'

'You do not understand,' replied Percy. 'He was part of my life, he has always been there.'

'Well, you can forget him now, because you have me.' Emma snuggled close to him.

He held her tight. 'Don't ever leave me, Emma,' he cried hoarsely. 'I'll never be responsible for my own actions if you let me down.'

'Don't be such a bully!' Emma pouted. 'Now you ask Papa tonight. Don't get worried if the answer is no. I shall persuade him, I am perfectly capable of that.'

That night after the party when John relaxed in the library for a smoke, Percy joined him and broached the subject of marriage to Emma. John suddenly turned very cold, almost hostile. 'Now look here, Percy,' he said. 'You are not a bad lad, but you seem to have no aim in life except to live off your aunt. Emma is still very young and knows very little of the world. Let me see you do something worthwhile and then ask me again next year. I might consider it then, but at the moment the answer is definitely no!'

Percy turned pale but kept his temper. 'Well, it is as you wish, sir,' he said politely. 'But I hope that does not mean that you will forbid us to meet.'

'No, not necessarily, I have great faith in my daughter. She has a good head on her shoulders and will accept my advice. So be warned, Percy Dell.'

Percy bit his lip in vexation. 'It is as you wish, sir,' he said. 'Goodnight,' then he walked into the garden.

Emma was waiting for him outside in the shadows. She jumped out at him. 'Well?' she cried excitedly.

'I am afraid his answer was no, and a definite no at that,' said Percy despondently.

Emma drew herself up angrily. 'Oh it was, was it? What reason did he give?'

'Well, the fact that I have no way of making a living. But I felt there was more behind it than that.'

Emma put her arms about his neck. 'Kiss me goodnight, darling, and tomorrow I'll sort it all out. Papa has never refused me anything in all my life. I know that when I tell him how much I love you it will be sufficient.'

They began the hot passionate petting they liked to indulge in, but then Emma pulled away. 'Let me go, Percy,' she cried. 'I still have to say goodnight to my guests.'

'I'll go home,' said Percy. 'See you tomorrow.'

But Percy did not go home for the inn seemed to him to be haunted by the ghost of dumb Lukey. He hailed the passing carriage of one of the departing guests from the party. 'Mind dropping me off in town?' he asked.

Percy spent the rest of the night in his old gambling haunts and ended up in bed with a plump prostitute who robbed him of his winnings.

Once the last party guest had left Riverview, Emma went to the library and sat on her father's lap. 'Oh, why not,' she cried. 'I'm terribly in love with Percy.'

'Well, let's see if you are of the same mind when you are twenty-one,' said John rather sharply.

Emma was a little taken aback by his tone. 'Oh, don't be so cruel!' she pouted. 'But I'll not marry anyone if I can't marry Percy.'

'Well, we will see,' said John equably enough. He could not say anything but nagging at the back of his mind were the drunken ravings of old Beatrice. It was all beginning to make some sense to him now. Ever since the death of dumb Lukey, Beatrice had been drunk every night and rambled on about the past. As her old tongue had rattled on about Lucinda and Joe Lee, John had become increasingly worried. Could it really be possible that the homicidal idiot Lukey had fathered Percy? He sweated with fear. That would make Emma and Percy first cousins and the thought of the rotten seed that might produce his heir almost gave him heart failure. He could not let that evil stock produce the beautiful grandson who was to have everything, all that John had ever worked for. He would never let it happen. No, he had to part Emma from Percy if it was the last act he ever did.

CHAPTER NINETEEN

The Secret is Out

As John strolled along the shore the strong breeze swept over the saltings. It was fresh and bracing, and brought back memories of the deep sea and of his youth aboard a big warship. He had had quite a hard life but in many ways a rewarding one. His experiences had given him the confidence to cope with the hardships of the world, whether slaving in the brick fields or the bullying of a father which had utterly destroyed his early youth. Now for the first time in many years he faced a real crisis. It was not money, for he had plenty to spare. It was not love, for women still favoured him even his wife Dolly was past it. No, it was his one and only, his lovely wayward daughter, Emma, who worried him. He had set such high hopes on her and he knew that she would not deliberately disobey him. But Percy Amos Dell was another matter. That nasty business at the university had never really been cleared up, and it was obvious that Percy had inherited all the violence and cruelty of the Shulmeads. For now John believed Beat's ramblings entirely and shuddered at the memory of the way Percy had treated his so-called wife Fanny. Something drastic had to be done.

John kicked a pebble into the water and waves washed his shoes. The *Alianora* was anchored nearby, her red sails tied up, her hull in the process of being scraped. Perhaps tomorrow, when she was ready, he would sail her once more around the Nore and hobnob with the deep-sea skippers in Sheerness. The *Alianora* was getting very ancient, he thought. Perhaps it was time for *Alianora II*.

He snapped his fingers. Why, that was it! He would build a

new sea-going craft and take Emma on a long voyage. She would love that. She was so brave and courageous, and was a born sailor. Once more his cheery grin returned as John hurried home to pack his travelling bag.

Emma was out riding and Dolly was shuffling up and down the garden path with a walking stick. She had a very mournful expression on her fat face. Hurriedly John wrote a note to his beloved daughter to tell her where he had gone.

Towards evening, after John had departed, Emma swept into the house with two angry red spots on her cheeks. Impatiently she tapped her hunting crop against her thigh as Dolly's timid shape stood in her path. Her mother's passive manner always aggravated Emma and she was in a vile temper having spent the day arguing with Percy.

'There is a note for you from Papa,' murmured Dolly, eyeing the envelope on the hall table. She had never dared to open it.

Impatiently Emma tore it open and as she read the note, a grin crossed her face and a look of triumph flashed in her eyes. Dear Papa had gone away in order to avoid a quarrel with her and he would come back with presents. Then all would be well. Emma hurried past Dolly towards the stairs.

'What does he say?' asked Dolly, burning with curiosity.

'Not much. He's just gone sailing round the Nore Light. No doubt to cool his temper,' she said abruptly and the dashed upstairs.

Two large tears coursed down Dolly's cheeks. Emma had no time for her mother and sometimes she felt so lonely. She turned and went slowly back into her bedroom on the ground floor, back to her knitting and box of sweetmeats and her memories.

The next morning, a very perky young Emma met Percy in the stable yard as he led Sir Galahad out of the stable.

'I've got a lot to tell you,' whispered Emma as they rode out over the green meadowland towards the forest. Then, in a lonely glade, the couple dismounted and lay close together on a bed of dried ferns. 'Papa's gone off sailing,' said Emma. 'He will be very agreeable when he returns. I know that. I know him so well.'

'Well, what are your plans,' asked Percy. As his eyes and hands ravished her well-formed young body, the sweat rose on his brow.

'This game of possum is becoming almost unbearable,' she said. 'My plan, darling, is that we make it impossible for Papa to prevent us getting wed soon.'

'How do you propose to do that,' Percy asked a little sarcastically.

Emma stared at him and leaned back, her body stretched out langorously so that her breasts were close to his face. 'By allowing you to compromise me, darling. How about that?' she smiled slowly as Percy turned and lay half on top of her.

'You she-devil,' he said hoarsely. 'Don't torment me.'

Emma placed her arms around his neck and they clung passionately together, rolling over and over until their ardour had abated. And when those olive-green eyes, veiled by thick dark lashes, looked steadily up at Percy, they seemed to possess some sort of snake-like charm.

'Tonight, Percy Amos Dell,' she said firmly, 'you will come to me. I will open my window in readiness. She will not hear,' she added contemptuously, referring to her mother. 'And then we will make love and I'll want to be pregnant. Don't say you can't do it because I know you can.'

Percy stared at her with amazement. 'By God, Emma, do you know what you are saying?'

Emma laughed gaily. 'Oh, I am quite in my senses,' she said. 'Do not worry, darling. If you need me and want me so much, tonight I am yours!'

They remounted their horses and rode off in silence. Percy looked pale and worried but Emma rode confidently and straight-backed, a little smile playing about on her lips, a dominant light in her lovely eyes.

At midnight, a big silver pattern of moonlight danced over the smooth lawns as Percy crept silently towards the house. Emma's window was already open as Percy found himself a foothold up the creeper-covered wall. Two bare white arms helped him through the window, which was then closed, shutting out the world. Percy undid the buttons on his jacket and pressed her body close. 'Tonight, darling,' he said, 'you are really mine.'

In her room below Dolly was spending a sleepless night. She could hear strange sounds, so she got out of bed twice to look out onto the moonlit garden. What was that tapping sound she could hear? Was it a woodpecker? But it was unusual for a woodpecker to work at night.

Towards dawn when the sky was a myriad of colours and the birds had begun their dawn chorus, Dolly took another look out of the window and saw a furtive figure creeping towards the gate. Her slow mind could not decide who it was but it was most likely a poacher taking a short cut to the woodlands. Satisfied that she was right, she then retired to rest once more.

That day Emma did not go riding but stayed in bed quite late. Then after lunch, she idled her time out in the garden sitting on the swing and munching an apple, something she had not done since she was a little girl. Dolly scrutinised her from her seat in the porch and wondered if her daughter was sickening for something or simply missing her Papa.

Emma's face was pale as she closed her eyes and relived the wonder of the night before. She had no regrets. Percy was her man and her whole body ached for his love. She could hardly wait until the evening when her love was to come to her again.

But that night the sleepless Dolly heard the click of the window latch and peered out just as Percy's legs disappeared inside. With a loud gasp and a shiver, she made towards the bell to rouse the servants. A marauder had entered Emma's room. But then suddenly something stopped her pulling the bell. Dolly went to the door and looked out into the hall to listen for the sound of a cry. But there was only silence. Slowly and laboriously Dolly climbed the wide stairs and tiptoed up to Emma's bedroom door. Bending down, she peered in through the keyhole. The lamp beside the bed was still alight and Emma was lying stark naked on the bed. Percy Dell was kneeling beside the bed, his lips caressing the lower half of her body. Emma's slim hand suddenly reached out to extinguish the lamp and the picture faded. Only the unmistakeable scuffling sounds of people making love then came from the room.

Dolly was appalled. Her knees suddenly went weak and perspiration formed on her brow. A terrible fear gripped her and her mind was flooded with memories from her childhood when her mother Larlee had entertained men so freely on Saturday nights with only an old tattered curtain to shield the children from the noisy love-making. Dolly's heart almost failed her as she staggered downstairs again and fell onto her bed. 'Oh, dear God, what will John do?' she gasped.

A week later, John returned looking very bright and breezy. He had brought exotic plants for the garden to please Dolly and a little pair of love birds for Emma.

Dolly was in bed. The doctor had called and she had been ordered to stay there, the servants informed him. Emma pale and haughty greeted John with a very coy expression and sat tormenting the tiny birds with a long paper fan.

'Don't you want to know what I've been up to?' asked John jovially.

'Yes, Papa,' Emma replied. 'So long as you don't ask me what I've been up to.'

John frowned and pulled her onto his lap. 'Now, now, pet, don't be saucy with your Papa. No, because I have bought *Alianora II.*'

Emma began to show interest.

'Was a lot of money,' John continued. 'But I feel it will be worth it. She's a fine sea-going craft, an old cargo boat I am having refitted and re-christened. And you and I, my darling, will sail to the sun and blue skies this winter.'

'But, Papa, I cannot go,' Emma exclaimed. 'I cannot go because I am going to marry Percy.'

John jumped from his chair in anger, almost tipping Emma

onto the floor. 'Now cease this nonsense,' he shouted 'I have forbidden this match.'

Emma just smiled at him. 'Don't be so stubborn,' she said. 'I never meant what I said.'

But John had lost his patience and went off to see Dolly who was propped up in bed very blue in the face and short of breath.

'What's up old girl?' he asked kindly.

'Had a tumble,' said Dolly hoarsely.

'I told you not to wander around on your own. That's why I provided you with servants,' John grumbled.

But Dolly motioned him to shut the door and then beckoned him close.

'Don't be angry, John, but you ought to know that I saw Percy in Emma's room and they were, you know what ...' she nodded suggestively.

He stared at her with astonishment. 'What are you saying, Dolly? Is your mind wandering?'

But his wife had started to sob. 'No, it's true, I saw them,' she cried. 'Don't be too hard on her John, remember when we were lovers ...'

But John had already left the room and was running along the hall. He grabbed Emma just as she was leaving the house, all dressed up in her riding habit. A raging fury overpowered him. He grabbed her by the arm and struck her across the face. 'You bitch! You dirty little lying bitch. You took advantage of my absence to compromise yourself with that maniac.'

Emma lost her footing and fell down on the polished tiles. She sat there open-mouthed, unable to believe that her dear Papa had knocked her down.

'Get up! Get up!' he yelled, lashing out with his foot. For a moment his mind had blocked. This was not his daughter but some lad on the lower deck who had offended.

Emma sprang to her feet looking both shocked and scared. She ran up the stairs shouting: 'Don't, Papa! Don't hurt me!'

He ran after her trying to grab her but Emma got inside her room and locked the door before he could reach her.

When a servant girl appeared staring in shocked silence at this odd scene, John pulled himself together and calmed down. He went into the library, poured himself a drink, and then sat in his favourite chair with head in his heads, so hurt and humiliated was he that his trust in his daughter had been so flagrantly destroyed. The house seemed to breathe a deep silence, its inhabitants waited nervously for another storm to break.

At three in the afternoon just as Beat had settled down to sleep, Percy arose from bed and went out into the yard to see a strange sight. The young groom from Riverview was riding in on Percy's gelding, Sir Galahad. 'Sorry, sir,' he said, 'but the master says I got to bring the horse down here and leave him. He don't want him in his stables no more.'

'Right,' said Percy, irritably snatching the reins from him. But a frown crossed his brow. The fact that John had returned the horse like this meant that he was on the war path. This was a fair enough warning. Now what should he do? Run? Or stay and face the music? He took the horse into the old stable at the back of the inn where Beat's ancient cob spent most of his days. The cob was most annoyed to have to share his quarters with this newcomer, but Sir Galahad was not very pleased either. The animals pushed, bit and kicked out at each other until Percy lost his temper and thrashed them both with his whip.

The inn had recently become a desolate place. A few old customers still came in but most went over to the new tavern built by the railway company. And Beat became more untidy, more aggressive and more drunk each day.

Percy was fed-up. He could not make up his mind whether to rob his aunt of the rest of her savings and disappear or wait until Emma contacted him. For a while he waited day after day to hear from Emma. But she was locked in her room and unable to make contact with him.

John Shulmead was still seething and dared anyone to let Emma out of her room. Each day he said through the locked door. 'If you have changed your mind, Emma, we will talk.'

But Emma was fired by stubborn pride. 'My mind is made up,' she would call back. 'When I get out of this room I'm going to run away with Percy.'

Gradually John felt worn down by it all. He began to spend his day loading and unloading his pistol and contemplating whether to shoot Percy or himself. He felt quite down-hearted and realised that he did not care about anything any more. Dolly had already given up. She could no longer rise from her bed and was fading slowly each day.

Then one morning John marched down to the Malted Shovel and burst into the bar. Percy had seen him coming and gone out of the back door and across the marsh to avoid him. Beat was sitting in the untidy kitchen, her dung-grey hair all matted around her wrinkled face. John had not seen her for some weeks and was shocked that she had aged so much.

But Beat was pleased to see him and brightened up considerably. John Shulmead had always been her favourite.

'Can we talk in private, Beat?' he asked.

She closed the kitchen door. 'The bar's not open and Percy's gone out in the marsh. I don't bother to open in the mornings now, it's not worth it.

'You need help, it's too much work for you all alone,' John told her kindly.

'Naw! I can't stand no young folk dithering around,' replied Beat. 'It's better on me own.' She poured them both a stiff rum. 'Anything wrong, John? You look worried.'

'I am, Beatrice,' John said. 'I'm very worried about young Emma and your nephew Percy.'

'Ah, that bastard,' growled Beat. 'Mad as a bloody hatter, he is. Don't wonder, seeing as where he came from.'

'Well, Beatrice, that is exactly what I came to discuss with you. I want the truth from your own lips. We have known each other a lifetime and now it is crucial that you tell me what I want to know.'

Beat peered at him with her red-rimmed eyes. 'What about?' She hedged evasively. 'I don't know what you want to know.'

John looked at her sternly. 'Did dumb Lukey father Percy?' he demanded.

Beat stared at him for a moment and suddenly her face crumpled up as she stared to grizzle. 'How should I know,' she wailed, 'I wasn't there, was I? Who knows what happened. Poor old Lukey, poor little love.'

John twisted her wrist rather cruelly so that the veins stuck out in her old shrivelled hand. 'I don't want no performance, Beat,' he said sharply. 'I just want the truth.'

'Well, it is my opinion that he did and that Percy is a Shulmead if ever I saw one. All bloody violent bullies, they was. None of them were quite right.'

John looked quite taken aback.

'I am a Shulmead, Beat,' he said. 'Have you forgotten that?'

'No, not you, John. You are the flower of the flock, you always was.'

'Tell me all you can recall of the night that Lucinda was raped. Remember, I was out in the river being washed out to sea.'

Beat rocked back and forth in her chair, occasionally holding out her flask for John to refill. 'God forgive me but no one can hurt poor dumb Lukey now, so I'll tell you all, John,' she said. 'Well, all I know,' she paused. 'You were just a lad still slaving in the brick fields the night that the bargee Joe Lee's father was killed. No one ever found out who did it but I knew at the time that it was Lukey, so I protected him. It never occurred to me that he might do it again, and I was kind of fond of him.'

John patted her shoulder. 'I know, Beat, and you were very good to him.'

'Well,' she continued, 'then on that night your Pa was killed, Lukey was wading in the marsh all covered in blood. I knew what he was capable of so I tried to keep a wary eye on him. I did not want him put in a cage. But then again, the night Lucinda was hurt, Lukey he was out. He had found a way into the tunnel that led to your father's forge. He used to follow Lucinda and spy on her. He was getting over-sexed and used to play with himself. I used to have to keep beating him but he liked that too. So it could well have been Lukey. Lucinda played fast and loose with Joe Lee but she was no wanton and that French fella was just a friend. Another reason for my suspicions is that after the attack, whenever Lukey appeared Lucinda became hysterical.'

John looked grim. 'Well, I think you have given me my answer. That's all I wanted to know. Thank you, old gel. Now get some rest,' he added kindly. Then with determined footsteps he returned to his house and unlocked Emma's bedroom door. 'It's time we talked,' he told her.

Emma stared at him defiantly with a tear-stained face.

'I am your father who loves you dearly,' John began. 'I do not blame you for your wild ways. I am partly to blame for them because I know I have spoilt you. But also partly to blame is the blood you inherited.'

Emma looked at him quizzically. She longed to rush into her father's strong arms but a streak of stubbornness held her back.

Taking a deep breath, John went over and sat on the bed beside her and told her the long story of his father, the smithy, who had beaten him and made him a slave at the brick kilns, of dumb Lukey who had been beaten into idiocy, and of Larlee, Dolly's mother who had been the local whore. Over and over again he pointed out the unfortunate combination of genes that made family characteristics that had already passed through two generations. 'And I had only two great wishes in my life,' he said, 'and those were to see you well married and to have a strong healthy grandson. So you see, it is just a tragedy to me that you wish to tie yourself to your own first cousin, who I know has already attacked and almost killed one woman.'

As he finished, Emma began to scream, placing her hands over her face, she cried out: 'Oh, stop! Don't go on, it is all too horrible!'

John kissed her head and held her close until she had calmed down.

Emma clung to him like a baby. 'Oh, Papa, forgive me, you don't know what I did,' she sobbed in terror. 'It might be too late. I might have that terrible thing inside me already.'

'I pray to God that it will not be so,' said John gently. 'But I want you to promise me that you will not write or speak to Percy ever again. God willing, he will then leave the district. I plan to take you with me on a long sea voyage quite soon now.'

Emma bowed her proud head. 'As you wish, Papa,' she said in a broken voice. 'But you must get rid of him because I feel that I could never face Percy ever again.'

CHAPTER TWENTY

Away Down Under

Percy was beginning to get quite worried. There was only one reason why John should reject him and return his horse and that was if he had discovered that Percy had compromised his daughter. But surely that would actually make him anxious for Percy and Emma to marry. John Shulmead's silence was a complete mystery to him. For a while, he continued to hang around waiting for news from Emma. Like most bullies, he was a coward at heart and was too nervous to approach Riverview himself and find out what was going on.

As he waited for word from Emma he became extremely bad tempered and quarrelled incessantly with old Beatrice. For some reason she had begun to lock herself in her bedroom in the afternoon and once she had yelled at him: 'You keep out of my room, and don't go poking about in me belongings.'

Once Percy peeped through the key-hole, to see Beat huffing and puffing as she tried to shift that heavy bed. But she could not. She no longer had poor old Lukey to help her and she had grown too old to accomplish the task by herself. Therefore she was no longer able to continue her miserly habits of sitting and counting her money. As a result old Beat wandered around looking very jaded and weary and thoroughly disgruntled.

The fact that John Shulmead had not been to visit for a while upset her, too, and she even began to complain to Percy about the presence of his horse, Sir Galahad, 'Get that bleeding horse out of 'ere,' she would mutter. 'He upsets the old cob. He's getting on a bit, like me, and can't stand all this aggravation.'

Percy was getting desperately short of ready cash, so he

took Sir Galahad to Maidstone and sold him. Then, as usual, he went on a binge for a week, ending up almost broke with his money squandered in gambling booths, brothels and low-class bars. Every day his rage smouldered inside him as he thought with fury about Emma's cold neglect of him. He could not get her out of his mind. Then one day he was sitting at the new railway station hotel idly perusing the local papers. Inside the *Kent Post* was a picture of Miss Emma Shulmead and Major Frederick Barrington at a ball where they had just announced their engagement. Emma looked quite lovely in a blue muslin dress and with flowers in her hair. Major Barrington sported his smart guards uniform. With a cry of rage, Percy sprang to his feet and dashed out of the hotel to return to the town bars. For hours he wandered about, drinking heavily and muttering to himself: 'The bitch, the damned disloyal bitch! She has promised herself to Barrington. I was only being made a fool of.' A light swam in front of his eyes as he stared at himself in a shop window. 'I'll kill her,' he announced to his reflection. 'And him. She will never get the better of me,' he swore.

His gaze lighted on a gleaming seaman's knife in the shop-window display. It had a dragon's head design along its sharp blade. Cold steel, he thought. That was it! She would have a silent death, and then he would rape her before she got cold. Fierce erotic fancies filled his brain. His mouth worked and his hands clutched together convulsively. 'Keep calm,' he muttered to himself hoarsely. 'I must get that blade.'

Wiping the sweat from his brow, he went into the shop and bought that long gleaming knife of tempered steel. Then he got on to the next train to Hollinbury. He sat in the carriage with his head in hands as though to contain the thoughts raging within. By God he would show them! Not good enough for them, eh? With mad fury building up inside him, he stalked into the inn.

Beat looked very weary. She peered at him shortsightedly. 'Oh, come back, have yer? I thought I'd got rid of yer,' she snarled.

Silently Percy took a bottle from the shelf and sat at the corner table drinking.

'What will do yer a lot of good,' Beat jeered. 'Kicked yer out, ain't she? Good job too, stuck up little cow.'

Percy did not reply. He just sat there glowering. Suddenly he got up and made off out over the marsh. It was almost twilight; the shadows of evening were about to descend. And it was Thursday. Percy knew that the hunt meeting was that day so Emma would be on her way home from it any minute. He would catch her and force her to tell him the truth. God help her if she opposed him ...

He climbed up on the ridge and looked out over the meadows towards Riverview and the narrow lane that went out to the tavern where the hunt met. There she was! She was riding along the lane all alone. She had been riding with her friend Catherine and her escort but had passed on ahead. Percy crouched down into the shadow of a tree and waited for her as she came cantering along, anxious to get home after a long day in the saddle.

Percy was crouching down in the shadows and as Emma passed, he sprang out and grabbed her horse's bridle. With a scream, Emma tried to beat Percy off with her hunting crop but he hung on tenaciously as the horse reared in panic. Grabbing Emma's legs, he unseated her and pulled her to the ground while her mount cantered away snorting with fright. For a second Emma lay on the grass but she quickly scrambled to her feet her face red with rage. 'What the blazes do you think you are doing?' she screeched.

Percy stood in front of her and pushed her violently against the trunk of a big oak tree.

'Oh, let me go, Percy,' she begged. 'You are hurting me.'

But Percy pulled her hair back savagely and produced his long knife. 'Tell me the truth or by God I will slit your throat here and now,' he threatened her. His eyes were wild and his mouth was slavering as he held the blade up to her white neck.

'Oh, please don't, Percy, it's me, Emma,' she cried, trying to calm him.

'Yes, I know, you treacherous little bitch! Now explain.'

'I could never have married you, Percy,' she wailed. 'It's better this way.'

'Why?' he demanded.

'Because we are too closely related.'

'Liar!' he yelled. 'That's just a story cooked up by your father, no doubt. I am not good enough for you, that's the real reason, isn't it?'

'No! No! Percy, it's true,' she sobbed. 'Our fathers, yours and mine, are brothers.'

Percy looked astonished and for a moment almost let her go. But then he grabbed her tight again, shouting: 'Liar! Liar! I am a bastard. No one knew my father.'

'It was dumb Lukey,' she cried. The words seemed to echo through the wood.

'I don't believe you, you lying bitch,' snarled Percy. 'You belong to me, not that Barrington, and by God I'll have you for the last time.' He began to rip up her riding skirt and pushed her to the ground.

Emma tried desperately to push him away. 'Oh, no! Percy, for God's sake,' she pleaded. But Percy was past hearing her. He threw himself on her and raped her violently.

Having satisfied his lust, he then lay still for a moment, for Emma had collapsed in a powerless heap but now she pushed him off her with a hefty shove. Sobbing wildly, she began to crawl away. But Percy was on her again with the knife in his hand. As he grasped her around the waist, Emma gave a sudden twist. Percy lurched forward and the knife slipped into her back just next to her spine. Emma let out an eerie cry and then lay threshing and screaming in terrrible agony. Her attacker stood staring down at her for a moment. Then came the sound of voices along the lane and Percy turned and ran, panic-stricken, over the marsh, his long black hair flying in the wind.

The voices belonged to Emma's friend Catherine and her escort who were riding behind and had just heard Emma's screams.

'My goodness, Emma's had a tumble,' cried Catherine, as they came up to Emma lying now motionless on the ground.

Catherine's young man jumped from his horse and placed his coat over Emma. 'Ride quickly to Riverview and get help,' he urged Catherine.

Catherine was off like the wind while lovely Emma lay silent and crumpled in the mud, a long knife sticking out of her back, her clothes all torn and muddy, and her face bruised and bloody.

When Emma's mount had returned alone, John had set out immediately in search of her accompanied by a groom. They met Catherine along the way, who tried to tell them what had happened and led them to where Emma lay.

When John reached his daughter, he knelt beside her and pulled out the knife from her back. She was still breathing. They carried her home gently and laid her in her own bed. John's tears fell fast on to her still, white face. The doctor soon arrived. 'She will survive,' he said, 'but she has been brutally savaged and the dagger has severed the spinal cord, I fear. Whoever can have done such a dastardly thing?'

John looked bewildered and Catherine's escort said: 'I believe I saw a wild gypsy figure running over the marsh as I sat beside Emma. He had long black hair.'

John's throat had seized up with emotion. His voice was husky as he spoke. 'Someone will pay for this evening's work,' he said. 'And if it's Percy, I'll strangle him with my own bare hands. Get the men together,' he commanded the groom, 'we will get the devil, whoever he is.'

The night had fallen by then and the mist swallowed them up as John and his men rode with lanterns swinging to the inn.

Shuddering with fear and horror, Percy dashed like a mad man over the marsh, clearing the fences and dykes with superhuman strength. When he dashed into the inn, Beatrice, tipsy with drink, tried to stand her ground bravely. With his eyes flashing and his arms raised over his head in a demented manner, Percy ran straight at her and grabbed her by the throat. 'Now, you old hag,' he snarled. 'Tell me the truth or I'll knock it out of you.' He squeezed her scraggy neck tight as she gasped for breath. 'Did dumb Lukey really father me or is that one of your wicked tales you spread around? Tell me, or it's the last word you will ever utter.'

'I don't know,' Beat squawked. 'No one knows.'

Percy squeezed her neck tighter. Beat's eyes nearly popped out of her head.

'All right, then,' she gasped, 'he did and you are a bloody Shulmead if I ever saw one. All mad as bloody hatters, you are,' she squawked hoarsely.

Percy threw her from him in disgust. Beat fell and struck her head hard on the edge of the table and lay still. Without giving her a second glance, Percy proceeded to wreck the bar, picking up the heavy oak chairs and swinging them around, smashing the kegs and the glass bottles, and kicking great holes in the wooden bar panels, smashing them to smithereens. Then he dashed up the stairs, kicked open Beat's bedroom door, picked up that heavy bed as if it were a feather, pulled out the old chest and began to fill his pockets with the treasure. Dashing quickly into his own room, he pulled out an old Gladstone bag which he also filled with the money and trinkets that old Beat had collected in her long lifetime. As he snapped the bag shut, a carved bone crucifix on a blue ribbon fell to the floor. Percy looked at it for a second before putting it into his waistcoat pocket. Then, all packed, he dashed downstairs and out of the back door towards the shore, screaming: 'Black curses on you, damned evil hamlet! May all of you rot in hell!'

He ran down toward the old creek where the *Alianora* was anchored and climbed aboard the old craft. As he unfurled the barge's sails the storm winds instantly whipped them into action and within moments she was heading out to sea with Percy clinging to the wheel like some wind blown evil spirit.

When John Shulmead and his party crossed over the bridge, the inn looked quite desolate. The front door was open and no lamps were lighted. John stepped inside and shone the lantern onto the face of old Beatrice as she lay on the floor, her head all twisted, mouth agape in the throes of death. John knelt beside her weeping bitterly and then lifted her gently on to the old wooden kitchen table where she had made so many pies and bread and covered her face with his cape. Glancing at the chaos that Percy had created, he then ran upstairs to see the overturned bed and the empty chest.

'Keep your pistols handy,' he informed his men. 'We are dealing with a madman. And, by God, I'll find him. He will not escape justice,' John vowed.

All night they searched the marsh, the quarry, the caves and the sea shore but there still was no sign of Percy. By dawn the sky was rosy red. It was only then that John realised that the *Alianora* was missing from her berth.

'It's no good, lads,' he said. 'The rogue has escaped us. Let's go home now. But I swear by all that is holy that I will find him however long it takes,' he said again as they rode wearily back to Riverview.

With a fierce gale blowing wildly, Percy clung on the steering wheel of the *Alianora* as she battled her way down the estuary and out to sea. Dawn was not far away. A pearly glow crossed the horizon and exposed the storm clouds pushed along by that strong head wind. Steadfastly he hung on, actually enjoying this battle with the forces of nature. With a maniacal burst of laughter, he gave a sudden lurch and sprang upright again. 'That's it, old gel, don't let 'im beat yer,' he cried as the waves frothed along the deck and swept over him. Although he was just dressed in a thin shirt and breeches, he was quite impervious to the cold as he sailed the *Alianora* through the storm. He had lashed the heavy Gladstone bag to the mast where it now swung about with the movement of the wind-battered barge. The waves swirled and danced aboard as the storm abated but the strong cantankerous wind carried him on and on with its tide around the south coast towards the Bristol Channel. With her sails in shreds the

Alianora suddenly ground onto a hidden rock with a great shudder. Realising that the craft was ruined, Percy got the Gladstone bag down and hung it about his neck before diving overboard and heading towards the dim shadow of the shore. The water was icy cold and the huge waves kept carrying him back onto the rocks, where he hung on, exhausted and gasping for breath. Then one huge wave tore the Gladstone bag from his neck and carried it away. Desperately, Percy dived in after it but a huge roller carried him ashore where he lay half-drowned on a white Welsh beach.

Early in the morning a beachcomber found him and called for help at the big monastery on the hill. The monks came down in a long gloomy line and stood watching the old *Alianora* breaking up. The servants carried Percy into the big stone-paved hallway and put him in front of a big log fire to thaw him out. Not one word was spoken, for these were Trappist monks who had all taken vows of silence. Later in the day his clothes were handed back to him, all dry and clean. And on top of the pile of clothes were the objects found in the pockets — just a few gold coins, a couple of florins and the small carved crucifix.

With a silent gesture and a smile, the old monk picked the crucifix up and put it around Percy's neck. Then he crossed himself as though to indicate that God would like a prayer for the saving of his life. But Percy ignored him and stood staring miserably at the few coins that were now all he possessed in the world.

'Nothing else?' he asked. The old man shook his head.

'Did a bag get washed up?' he asked. 'A black Gladstone bag?'

Once more the old man moved his head from side to side.

'Oh, hell!' cried Percy, causing the old monk to raise an eyebrow.

Another old man gave Percy a bowl of oats which he took without a word of thanks and ate beside the crackling fire. Then, again without a thank you, Percy got up, put on his coat, put the money in his pocket and walked out.

Setting off down the winding, sandy road, he soon saw a signpost marked: Bristol 10 miles. His thoughts were churning over and over. What was he now going to do? He couldn't return to Hollinbury or even to London. So he had better get out of England. Once decided, his pace became quite steady. In the late afternoon, he rested at an inn, and sat outside drinking ale among the noise and babble of the dock. He drew in the smell of tarred rope, and the salt sea breeze with pleasure. He had always liked the sea and had never been afraid of it. Even after this experience, he was not afraid. What a pity he had lost the *Alianora*. If only he could have got across the Channel to France, he could have started a new life and it would be a dream fulfilled. Still, at least now they would stop looking for him. Everyone would think that he went down with the *Alianora*. That was one consolation. But where could he go now without much money and no place to live?

He wandered along the dockside watching the big ships being loaded and walked on further on to a quiet spot where a huge sailing ship lay at anchor out in the bay. Sitting on a pile of ropes on the quayside was an old sailor with a tarred pigtail and a wide-brimmed hat. He puffed a short-stemmed pipe and screwed up his eyes gazing far out into the blue ocean.

Percy came up and stood near him.

'Good evening,' said the old tar shortly. 'Take a seat.' He moved along the pile of ropes to make room for Percy. 'Waiting for a ship, mate?' he asked.

'I might be,' replied Percy warily.

'Same here, but I jest ain't sure,' the sailor answered sociably. He had a West country accent, which was slow and precise. 'See that ship out thar?' He pointed his pipe in the direction of the big sailing ship three decks high and rolling with the tide. 'Now, that there old gal just sailed in from Ireland. By the look of her she's had a heavy night.'

Percy looked at the huge ship with interest.

'Sailed aboard her. First mate I was, when she was a black birder.'

Percy turned questioningly towards him.

'Ah lad, that's when they was running the niggers from Afrikey to Amerikey. And bloody awful conditions, they was. You was lucky to get there alive but the pay was good.'

'Oh, a slave ship,' said Percy, a little disgusted.

'They died like flies, poor sods did,' said the sailor with a throaty cackle. 'But still I hain't sure I wants to go aboard her now. Not with that thar lot, I don't.'

Percy raised his brows. 'What lot?' he asked.

'Why them convicts being transported to Australia,' replied the sailor. 'Every day one sails outa here. But that being me old ship, I kinda fancy it 'cause I want to get back to Australia. But they tells me it's bloody grim. Them convicts have got lice, bugs, scurvy, the lot, 'cause they've been hanging about in prison for a year waiting for that ship. So they tell me.' He leaned over and nudged Percy. 'They say there's going to be twenty-one females aboard. How's that strike yer? When she lets out to sea there is going to be merry hell played aboard the *Paragon*, mark my word.'

'Well, don't go to sea with her then,' advised Percy. 'Choose a clean ship if you are a qualified seaman.'

'Now, that hain't so easy to do,' replied the sailor. 'Bin a bit of a devil in me time and I likes a drop o' rum. I ain't in too well with them fancy skippers on other ships but me old captain is aboard her there, so I knows he will have me. But I asks meself, can I stand it? That's what.'

'Well,' said Percy, getting bored. 'My throat is getting dry. I'm going for a drink.'

'And by glory I'll join yer,' said the sailor getting up and walking along beside him.

Over a jug of ale they got acquainted. The old sailor's name was Hunter Bent. 'It's on account that my mother had learning and me father was a poacher. They shot him in the leg, they did, them gamekeepers. It was that what finished him.' He rambled on in his slow drawl. 'The sea's in me blood,' he explained. 'I ran off when I was ten years old. I was with Nelson at Trafalgar. But call me Benjie, 'cause everyone does.'

Percy was feeling more relaxed and more cheerful. He

grinned and filled the old sailor's pewter pot with ale.

'You is a gent, even I can see that,' Benjie told Percy.

'Well, I might be but I am certainly not a wealthy one. My boat went down with all my worldly wealth. I am practically broke now, but you are welcome to a drink with me.'

Benjie's thin face screwed up shrewdly. 'Wanting to get out of the country, and quick, eh?' he challenged.

'That's right,' said Percy, impressed by the sailor's intuition.

'Well, I might be able to get you on the *Paragon.* I'll say yer me cobber,' Benjie offered. 'The skipper'll be ashore for the sails. We could wait for him.'

'Might as well,' agreed Percy.

From his greasy waistcoat pocket old Benjie produced a piece of brownish rock. 'See that?' he said waving it under Percy's nose. 'That's why I am so ready to get back to Australia.'

'What is it?' asked Percy.

'That, mate, is gold,' replied Benjie in a mysterious whisper. 'That, mate, is what blokes do murders for. I know, 'cause I've seen it all. Was out in California a few years ago. There was a big gold rush on then. They came like flies from all over the world. So I knows what gold looks like. And do yer know where I got this?' He wagged his head, shaking the big hat which balanced between two big unsightly ears.

Percy stared blearily at Benjie and wanted to laugh. Instead, he said laconically: 'California?'

'No, mate, not by a long chalk,' cried Benjie in triumph. 'Where I got that is Australia and I knows exactly where I found it,' he cackled. 'There's no gold in Australia, they say. If there was, the Queen would not let them dig it up. All convicts and ticket-of-leave men put there, they are.'

'Is that so sad?' asked Percy. He was beginning to get bored again and wondered if all this was some old sailor's tale to con him for more drinks.

'I tried to jump ship but got caught,' continued Benjie. 'I was going to stay there and get a stake and dig for gold, I was.

But now where am I? Here back on the bloody dock trying to get aboard that bloody convict transporter.'

'Do you reckon you will make it?' asked Percy. 'If so, I might as well go with you, there's nothing to hang about for in this bloody country.'

'Good, that's it, mate, see the world when you're young, that's what I say. Wait, here comes the old skipper!' Benjie winked and waggled his head furtively. ''ere 'ee comes. Take no notice. Old Stinker, they calls him 'cause his name is Tench — stench, get it?' Benjie roared with laughter.

The skipper of the *Paragon* rolled into the cramped little bar. He looked like a massive barrel, huge and shapeless in a long tunic of blue, greasy breeches and a black, straggly beard. He also wore a foreign-looking cap decorated with braid and perched on the back of his balding head. When he spoke, his voice came out in a great boom with a flat tone of the London dockside. Voices of the other customers were reduced to whispers as he entered and ordered his drink. 'Me usual, rum and strong ale.' Taking the jug, he swallowed the liquid like a thirsty stallion, puffing out his lips and blowing furiously.

Percy stared at him in fascination.

'Going out tonight?' asked one brave old fellow in the corner.

The captain turned his head slowly and stared with a hostile look in the speaker's direction. 'That's right,' he said. 'When they load them damned females from your stinking jail, I'll be off.' His voice dropped to an even more aggressive level. 'Why? Who wants to know,' he growled, glaring around the bar. His gaze stopped at Benjie who touched his forelock and grinned nervously.

'Christ!' roared the captain. 'What bloody hole have you crawled out of?'

''Tis a pleasure to see you again, Captain,' Benjie said, bowing obsequiously in the captain's direction.

'Sit down and don't keep arsin' about,' roared the captain. 'You'll want a favour of me, I'll be bound. Otherwise you be out of here like a shot.' He refilled his jug and took another great swallow.

For a while Benjie sat with the captain muttering and gesticulating and occasionally glancing over in Percy's direction. Throughout this time, the captain stared at him as if he were some repulsive insect. But then apparently an agreement seemed to have been reached. The captain got up slowly, took another bottle of rum from the barman after throwing some coins at him, and rolled clumsily out of the door.

Benjie came back over to Percy looking very excited. 'Done it,' he said triumphantly. 'I thought the old captain would. He can't get a sailor to work for him 'cos them convict ships is much worse than the black birders. So you'll have to take your life in your hands, mate, but he seemed a bit desperate so I made him a deal. We go aboard tonight afore the *Paragon* sails. There's only one snag. We don't get no pay, and you're a stockman while I'm in the galley.'

Percy was puzzled. 'A stockman on a ship?' he said. 'Of course,' replied Benjie. 'There's everything on that old hulk — sheep, pigs, and cows. And horses, lovely thoroughbreds, belonging to the gentry what's settled out there.'

At last Percy showed an interest. Horses? Well, he never minded them. 'Well, if it will get me out of this bloody country, that's all I care about.'

'Yes, I see,' Benjie nodded. 'You are in a funny position, but me, I minds me own business, 'cause when I get down under I'm going to find that gold mine if it kills me.'

At midnight the two men stood on the deck of the ancient ship watching the Redcoats come aboard with their charges. They held the lanterns high to shed light on a desolate sight as the convicts were loaded on board. There were about thirty pathetic-looking men all chained together. After months in Bristol Gaol, they were ragged, thin and dejected with filthy long beards and hair. They were weak with hunger as they struggled to climb the ladder, egged on by the butts of the Redcoats' rifles.

Percy was not one to be chicken-hearted but even he was moved by this sight.

Then came the women. There were about ten of them and

they seemed to have more life in them than the men. They
cursed and swore at the Redcoats, and pushed and jostled each
other. Certainly they looked the dregs of the Bristol brothels,
thought Percy. But one young girl caught his attention. She
had very dark wavy hair. Her figure was comely and she
looked about nineteen. Her ragged dress hung from her
shoulders exposing her small breasts and some ugly scars and
bruises on her neck and shoulders. She stood quietly, her
head up as she gazed about her with cold hatred shining out
from those beautiful blue eyes veiled with thick lashes.

Percy felt a stab of sympathy for her. He knew exactly how
she was feeling, and wanted to put out his hand and touch
that injured white shoulder. But he restrained himself and his
hand holding the lantern trembled violently.

'Hold the fucking light still!' roared a soldier. 'We can't see
what's happening. Come on, get moving, you whore!' he
yelled, shoving his gun up the skirt of one of the women and
urging them on.

Just like a herd of cows, thought Percy. How low can a
human being get? For the first time in all his selfish years,
Percy looked back at his own comfortable life in the hamlet
with a tiny amount of appreciation.

In spite of the chaotic conditions aboard the convict ship,
Percy was not put off. He decided not to take any notice of
the cruelty and the bad food. What mattered was that he was
free. No one could catch him now, and he was not going to
end up with a rope around his neck for the deaths of both
Emma and old Beatrice.

His job on board ship was to look after the livestock down
in the hold. There were two very fine thoroughbred horses
there, being sent from a big estate in Ireland to Australia.
Percy's heart was always soft for a good horse, and he looked
after them well, calming them as the ship hit heavy weather,
sleeping in their stalls and seeing that they were always well
fed and well groomed.

'Them 'orses 'as to be taken good care of,' the desolate
captain had said. 'Now yer sees yer does it well. No one else is

to go down there. They's worth a lot of money to me if I gets them safely down under, see?'

Benjie had got the job as cook, so he lorded it in the galley while the poor convicts, shut up in a big cage, were almost starved to death.

Once out to sea the women were released from their chains and put to work in the cookhouse and down among the cows and pigs. There was much competition with the Redcoats and the sailors for the women. Most of the women were whores and were obliging for they could make quite a bit of money.

The young girl who had caught Percy's eye was called Allanah. In no time she was recognised as Percy's woman and since he was quickly feared, no one interfered with Allanah. She helped with the livestock and often slept with Percy in the stalls. With the swaying of the ship they made love in unison, but there was not the terrible passion that Percy had felt for Emma. Still, Allanah was soft and gentle and so good for him.

With her big Irish blue eyes brimming with tears, Allanah told Percy of her life. She had been a servant on a grand estate in Ireland since she was a very young child. When she was sixteen, the master of the house had wanted her and had taken her brutally without feeling. When he tired of her, he got rid of her using as an excuse a childish prank she played by riding out bareback on one of his fine horses. When they caught her the master accused her of stealng the horse, so she was convicted and transported to the Welsh mines. After a year of slavery, working with the other women pulling the carts full of coal to the surface, Allanah found herself in trouble again when she attacked the overseer with a pick-axe because he was molesting a ten-year old child.

'To be sure, Paddy, that is the sad story of me loife,' Allanah said, looking up at him woefully as they lay in the straw with the horses chomping around them.

'Listen to me, Allanah,' Percy said protectively. For security reasons he had told everyone he was called Paddy Dale. 'No one on this ship or anywhere else is going to hurt you again. Certainly not while I am living.'

'I don't know what this place is they are sending me to,' said Allanah, snuggling up close. 'It's so many thousands of miles from me own dear Ireland.'

'It's a new country,' said Paddy. 'Perhaps we can all live a new life out there. At least, let's hope so. In the meantime, you are Paddy's woman and if anyone as much as looks twice at you, I'll slit his throat.'

Allanah touched his face softly. 'Ah no, not you, Paddy you are too kind and gentle. You are the only person who has treated me as a real woman for a long time. I'll always love you and I'll always be loyal to you,' she said.

The six-month voyage had been very tiring but was now at an end. Paddy stood on the deck at Sydney holding the reins of his two special thoroughbred horses. The animals were calm with Percy for he handled them so well. Their owner was pleased to see them looking so fit. He looked them over thoroughly. 'You took good care of them, I see,' he said. 'I was worried. I began to think they would not survive the voyage. Are you a convict?' he enquired.

'No,' said Percy. 'I am a free man. I worked my passage over here.'

'Perhaps you would like a job,' said the owner. 'You can continue to look after them, and I have other mounts in my stables. I need a good horseman.'

Percy hesitated as he watched the long line of chained convicts being unloaded. They were in worse condition than the cattle. They were followed by the girls who also came marching out in line. Men stood around the dock shouting out obscene remarks at them, and most of the women shouted obscenities back at them. But there was his lovely Allanah, her head bowed down low as she stood with them. The convicts were all being taken off to work in the cotton mills, slaves for the new economy.

Percy took a deep breath. 'I'll take the job if you will employ my woman as well,' he told the man.

The man looked amazed as Percy dashed forward and dragged Allanah from the line. A Redcoat came at him with his rifle butt, but then seeing the gentleman with him, he stayed his hand.

'Will you employ her too?' Percy asked.

'She is a convict,' said the man. 'It will need some consultation with the authorities. But come with me. Tether the mounts while we go and see the Army Commander.'

While the gentleman went into the wooden government house with its Union Jack flying aloft, Percy and Allanah stood patiently waiting outside holding hands in anticipation.

The gentleman reappeared half an hour later with a satisfied smile on his face. 'You are paroled into my keeping, young woman,' he said. 'Now, tell me your name.

'Allanah,' she whispered.

'Fine, from the ould countree,' he laughed approvingly. 'I'm O'Leary, Bailiff to the Lord Fitzgerald. There is nothing to worry about now. We will all get on fine just so long as your man takes good care of my horses.'

So Percy and Allanah sat in an open cart with the mounts tethered behind, followed the overseer in the smart carriage out into the wide open countryside where the Irish Lord had set up a huge estate. Without even seeing the city, they had left behind the squalor of Sydney with its shamble of shacks and its untamed population which had gathered from all parts of the world.

Allanah found peace in this new home, with a mistress who loved and cared for her and the baby girl she had with Paddy, now her husband. And even when Percy's nature got the better of him and he left his job to go gold-hunting with Benjie, Allanah was taken care of by her employers.

Percy never returned from that trip for he and Benjie got involved in a diggers' war and both died with bullets in their hearts. Thus Percy who had lived so violently died violently in a lonely spot in the outback. And Allanah and Amy were therefore to meet their respective fates on the other side of the world.

CHAPTER TWENTY ONE

Emma

For many years the village gossips related the tragedy in Hollinbury hamlet, long after progress had brought more factories and mills along the riverside and a population which had increased two-fold. The rich land had been ploughed up and modern houses built on it. There was now also a police station and a fire station, as the more affluent age began to take over.

The early Victorians were a pious lot. Even the poor working classes struggled sincerely to live to a respectable mode of life in spite of the poverty that still existed for them. The cottagers went to church or chapel with monotonous regularity. The devil drink was denounced by most vicars. Now at least little children went to school, even if it was only part-time, and no one under the age of thirteen was allowed to be employed. Yes, much had been improved. And poor George Gibbs, one of the men behind these changes, now lay in the churchyard of Coalville. He would have been extremely happy to have seen it all.

Down in Kent, the Shulmead's big house still dominated the estuary but it had a different air about it these days. Gone were the pleasant youthful activities of the young — with parties and hunt balls. The house stood looking staid and respectable. It was still windswept by the tidal breezes from the river and John still looked out towards the deep sea from his tower, but not quite so often. For he was now a deep-sea captain himself. He had grown a long red ginger beard and was rarely at home. A deep gloom hung around him, for the alert breezy personality had completely disappeared over the years when he had nursed Emma, his daughter, back to health and comforted his sick wife. But Dolly too had joined the late inhabitants of the hamlet in that churchyard beside the grimy inn. The inn itself, the Malted Shovel, lay dark and silent nowadays, its timbers old and weatherbeaten, its windows grimy, its chimneys cold. Huge trains roared under the bridge rattling the old timbers and knocking down the plasterwork from the cracked ceilings. Cobwebs decorated the wrecked bar, while rats ran around in the cellar. And the place was empty since scavengers had taken all the good furniture.

But perhaps it was not totally silent, this inn which had once been the centre of the social life in the Hollinbury hamlet. Old Amos' deep laugh sometimes echoed in the bar, as did the high-pitched screech of Beatrice, or the whine of Aunt Dot, or Lucinda's happy laugh. And often the ghost of dumb Lukey crossed the railway line and scared the wits out of the train drivers on the bend, a noted spot for railway mishaps. There had been no descendants available to inherit the property, and no one to claim the big fortune that Beatrice had accumulated in her railway shares. Everything just lay in chancery waiting for the only known relative, Percy, to turn up.

The lands of Riverview were still smooth and green and well kept, and the stables still the finest in the district. Emma Shulmead's stud farm was well known all around for breeding the purest mounts. Miss Shulmead rode through the village in a pony and chaise, driven by a groom. She was now a helpless cripple, and had to be lifted in and out of her carriage. All her days were spent in a wheelchair. Her beautiful face was set in hard lines and she looked very bitter. But still her skin remained flawless and marble white, and her olive green eyes stared haughtily out into the world.

Well known for her violent temper, Emma was also well respected by the country folk as a hard-headed business woman. Over the years she had added to the fortune that her father had nurtured by her shrewd world-wide deals with her thoroughbreds. She ran the stud farm with a rod of iron. The only time she ever relaxed was when dear Papa was home from the sea and around to love and fuss her. Then Emma would smile. They would go out together, almost like husband and wife rather than father and daughter, so devoted were they to each other.

John sailed his ship, which he had christened *Emma,* on long sea routes to Australia. *Emma* was a modern ship with steam engines and sails. He took passengers and quite often also several of Emma's stud horses which fetched good prices out there. But every time he was out on a long voyage, John would think constantly of Emma and be anxious for the return trip when he would once more see her waiting to greet him.

Several years back, when Emma was still bed-ridden and Dolly was slowly dying away, John had been unable to stand it. Still determined to find Percy and take his revenge, he had taken out his master's ticket and sailed the deep sea. At every port he stopped at he had asked and searched for Percy but no one had ever seen or heard of him. John knew that Percy had not gone down with the *Alianora,* but he remained sure that one day he would find him. After seven years of searching, John got word that Percy might have gone to Australia on a convict ship. So John sailed to Australia and spent many days amid the vice and squalor of the penal colonies of the Rocks, Sydney harbour's low district. He had no luck. It was impossible to find anyone in that screaming swarm of lost humanity. The convicts who had served their time were then released into the population of free settlers who came from depressed lands seeking sanctuary and lived cheek by jowl with the villains and murderers. But there were many like John, who kept their own counsel and made money from this squelching den of iniquity taking back home disillusioned settlers and bringing out commodities that were hard to obtain out there and getting a good price for them. Yes, contact with this new country had been good for John Shulmead financially and in fact, he rather enjoyed those long

Australian runs. Then in 1851 gold was discovered and the big Gold Rush began. There was a stampede of people to the gold fields which brought massive prosperity and on the return voyage these gold diggers brought back their findings — sewn into the hems of the ladies' dresses, or hidden in luggage, anywhere that would not be discovered by thieves. And in the hold of the ship were the heavy gold bars for consignment to the Bank of England. It was a very happy ship which brought these celebrating people home to England. Now they would not live in dire poverty, as they had previously done, but with a fair-sized stake of gold to start life anew.

It was a misty October morning when John watched the last of his passengers come aboard his ship at Sydney Harbour. He was dreaming of the Thames Estuary and its swift sweet sharp breeze away from the humid smells of Sydney in the summer. He was thinking of Emma's welcoming smile and a cool gallop on his horse over the green meadows. This was definitely his last trip. John had made his decision to retire. His daughter was lonely and she needed him more than ever. He knew that she would never marry so why should he not spend his remaining days with her, and forget about Percy Amos Dell?

As he pondered his future, he saw a rather good-looking woman struggling up the gang plank. She held a small girl by the hand who seemed reluctant to come aboard and kept looking back to her friends who were waving goodbye. John went forward to help and picked up the child. She was about seven years old with black curls hanging from under a jaunty bonnet. Her dark lashes looked at him angrily. 'Put me down!' she cried. 'I don't want to go on this big ship.'

A strange shiver ran down John's spine. He had seen that angry look and those eyes before. The child struggled and slipped from his grasp as she ran to her mother. John took the suitcases and bundles the woman carried and escorted her to the second-class cabin she had booked. Although she was good-looking, her face was hard. Although probably only in her twenties, her hair tinged with grey. But she had a sweet Irish brogue with which she thanked him.

'My good tanks to you, sor!' she said. 'Amy is a bit of a handful at times, to be sure. But she will surely settle down, I do hope so.'

'You are going home?' John asked.

'Well, not exactly,' she replied. 'My home is in Oireland but 'tis to England I'll be travelling to take my Amy to meet her father's kin.'

'Well, have a good voyage,' said John. 'If you get any problems do not be afraid to contact me.'

'Why, thank you kindly, Captain.' The woman smiled sweetly and modestly at him.

John was quite captivated and looked forward to a promising voyage.

Amy did soon settle down and proved to be a charming little girl who became a favourite with everyone on board ship. The atmosphere all around was very good and the crew and the passengers enjoyed each other's company.

John was interested in this young woman and her child and noted that on the passenger list they were listed as Mrs Allanah Dale, widow, and Amy Dale, her daughter.

In two months the best part of the voyage was over. They had rounded the Cape of Good Hope and spent a few days in Durban. John had tried to get closer to Amy's mother throughout that voyage but she had remained strangely shy and reticent, she keeping a very motherly eye on her wayward little daughter Amy and keeping her own counsel. But one day, Allanah did come to see the captain bringing with her a bundle of papers in a big leather purse.

'Will you please take care of these for me?' she asked.

'Certainly,' replied John. 'I'll put them in the safe,' he said. 'Sit yourself down now. Would you like a glass of wine?'

'No thank you, sor,' replied Allanah. 'Oi have taken the pledge.'

'Good for you. do you mind if I take a whiskey?'

Allanah smiled a lovely smile. 'No sor, my husband was a

heavy drinker so you can understand my aversion to it.'

John looked at her thoughtfully. She had certainly weathered life's storms, he thought, and he guessed, a few heavy ones at that. He was struck by the sweet mysterious strength she seemed to have. He asked her which part of England she was going to.

'To Kent,' she replied shortly.

'Why, that is my home country!' he exclaimed. 'Whereabouts in Kent?'

But Allanah evaded the question. 'You will take care of those papers, won't you?' she said timidly. Because that is my Amy's inheritance and I promised her father that when he died I would take her home. But I feel that Australia is my home. I've been there ten years. I came out on a convict ship. Does that offend you, Captain?' Her lips twisted in a sardonic grin.

John put down his glass and took her hand. 'My dear lady, indeed it does not,' he said. 'I have travelled these seas too long not to see and hear of the injustices of those bad old days.'

Allanah smiled but rose to her feet and made to go, as if regretting having disclosed so much. 'I'd better be going,' she said. 'I must find out what Amy is up to.' She smiled coyly. 'You are a very good and kind gentleman,' she added. 'It is my pleasure to meet you.' Then neatly and gracefully, she retired to her cabin.

As she left, John felt a keen sense of disappointment but he picked up the leather purse and locked it carefully in the safe. The name Dale nagged at him; did he not once know someone called Dale?

As they sailed into the Bay of Biscay the weather changed and the sea became very choppy. John was kept very busy pacifying the sick passengers and taking a turn at the wheel as the big ship ploughed through the heavy seas. When it came to manoeuvering the *Emma*, he trusted only his own judgement. As he steered the large vessel, he thought idly about the name Dale. Suddenly for no apparent reason, an image of old

Amos Dell, innkeeper of the Malted Shovel in Hollinbury,
flashed in his mind. The image was of a huge swollen shape
sitting in the bar parlour with John's father Sam Shulmead
the smithy. Amos Dell. And Beatrice Dell. Lucinda's mother,
he believed, had not married and neither had Lucinda. That
would have made Lucinda a Dell, and her son, Percy, a Dell
also. John had never actually known Percy's full name, but he
had never thought about it before having known the character all his life. He thought about it some more. Yes, Percy
probably was a Dell. Dell. Dale. It was far-fetched to think
that this passenger was in some way connected with Percy? It
would be such a concidence but not impossible — especially
since Mrs Dale said that her husband's folk came from Kent,
Also, John realised, there was something strikingly familiar
about little Amy's dark, flashing eyes.

John was stuck in a dilemma. He knew that he was
probably being ridiculous and fanciful but he could not shake
off these thoughts. His fingers itched to take the leather purse
out of the safe and read those papers he had been entrusted
with. But he was an honourable man, and he could not break
Mrs Dale's trust ...

For hours that night he struggled with his conscience. But
after a couple of drinks, he could restrain himself no more.
With a sudden impulse, he unlocked the safe and removed the
purse. Opening it up, he removed the letters and spread them
out on the desk, moving the lamp over in order to read them
in a better light. There were several letters. One was sealed
with a monogram and addressed: *To Whom it may concern.*
John put it back. Even with his current audacious boldness,
he could not break a personal seal. But there was another
document in bold, round writing. It was the last will and
testament of Percy Amos Dell.

John's heart missed a beat when he saw this. His hunch
had been right. Percy must have changed his name when he
fled the country. With trembling lips, he read on. This will
announced Percy's wish that any inheritance left to him by
his great-aunt Beatrice Dell, should, in the event of his

death, become the property of his wife, Allanah Dale, née Lehanne, and their daughter, Amy, born in Sydney, Australia. There was also a marriage certificate and a death certificate.

John finished looking through the papers and then put his head down on the table and wept. After all these years, fate had played a terrible trick on him! He had sworn revenge but what revenge could one take on a pretty comely widow and a small child? Percy had probably known that had he returned to England, he would have been arrested and hanged. Death had decided his fate for him. It was all too ironic. What could he do now?

He sat down at his desk and composed a long letter to Emma which he planned to post as soon as he reached the next port.

A storm was brewing and the ship rolled unsteadily. He should have been on deck but he knew that he had to write this letter while his mind was clear.

> My dear Emma,
> Today I received a severe shock and I want you to tell me what to do. I have at last discovered the whereabouts of our enemy but he is no more. Now there are just his widow and small daughter who are passengers aboard my ship. Now bearing the surname of Dale, they are returning to the hamlet to claim old Beatrice's fortune which has lain in chancery for so long. I beg of you, dear, advise me. I feel no hatred to this sweet little girl, whose name is Amy, particularly since I am in fact, her great uncle. What can I do but hold out my hand to them and guide them in their new land? But first, my dear, I want your opinion. I'll not take any action without your advice.
> Your ever loving father,
> John Shulmead

He sealed the envelope and placed it in his safe, the small wooden sea chest under his bunk, which travelled with him everywhere. In it, next to this letter, were Allanah Dale's precious papers. He locked up the chest and returned it to its hiding place under his bunk.

The wind was now howling into a gale force. John donned his oilskins and went on deck. He felt at peace for the first time for many years. The gale was blowing and the ship was rolling. Passengers were panicking everywhere and crowding the decks. John calmed them and told them not to worry. Once they were out of the Bay of Biscay and into the Channel, he explained, all would be well. But that night, the storm grew worse and the ship battled bravely against the heavy sea. Heavily laden with gold bars she was low in the water and the waves washed the decks. In the early hours of the morning, several sailors were swept overboard. Beginning to get worried, John wrestled valiantly at the wheel but he felt that he was fighting a losing battle all the time, particularly since they were entering some very tricky waters, near the Goodwin sands. Suddenly, the main mast broke. Passengers screamed and huddled on deck in frightened groups clutching each other and praying. Many had collected their heavy luggage complete with gold ready for their fresh starts in life; some even had parcels strapped to their waists. But the merciless sea overpowered the lot of them. As the *Emma* grounded on the Goodwin sands, it washed many of the passengers straight overboard to perish in the stormy sea.

John lashed the wheel, and went to the aid of his passengers. To his relief, he saw Allanah on the deck holding her child close to her. He called out and had almost reached them when a wave swept the woman away, leaving Amy rolling and screaming in fear about the sloping deck. Holding on to the bar of the deck, John slithered towards the child. He grasped her in his arms and managed to hand her down to the lifeboat with the other women and children as the sea carried her lovely mother away.

So many lives were lost the night the *Emma* went down. It was the worst storm of the century and the ship had been so heavily laden that there was never a chance of survival.

As all good captains do, John stayed with his ship when she went down. As the hull slipped into the water, he saw the body of the lovely Allanah floating past him, her long hair spread out on the water. He put out a hand to reach her just as the ship lurched, and they were both sucked away into the deep.

A few days later the newspapers broke the news of the shipwreck off the south coast, of the little ship carrying gold and passengers from Australia. There were grim descriptions of the shores being littered with bodies and debris. There were accounts of the brave captain who had gone down with his ship and the rescue of about twenty children in a lifeboat. The rest of the passengers had all died in their attempts to the shore, still laden with their precious gold. Many children had not been claimed and had been orphaned by the disaster. Some were still hoping that relatives would claim them, but in the meantime they were being cared for by the Seamen's Orphanage in Dover.

Emma sat stunned and read these accounts in horror. So great was her sorrow that she could not cry. Oh, her beloved father! She had lost him and now she was alone, completely alone. Life was not worth living for anything now.

After a while Emma took to her bed where she prayed for death to remove her from this meaningless world. Her medical adviser tried in vain to get her to take an interest in life but Emma ignored him. She just lay waiting for death. But death did not come. Instead, Emma gradually grew colder, harder and much more bitter.

John's body was never recovered but a month after the tragedy, a small wooden chest was delivered to Riverview having been washed up on the shore at Hollinbury. Its ownership was quickly known because it had a silver plaque on the lid spelling out the facts that it was the property of Captain John Shulmead, of Riverview, Hollinbury, Kent.

When the sea chest was delivered to Riverview, Emma's interest was aroused for the first time since the loss of her father. She asked to be lifted from her bed and be left alone with this chest. Sitting at her desk, she opened the chest and began to inspect the water-soaked papers within. They were now dried out and badly stained but it was still possible to decipher what was in them. Her hands trembled and her tears fell fast as she read her father's last letter to her. But then, quite suddenly, she went ashen white and the letter dropped to the floor as she cried out.

Her cry prompted the arrival of a small skivvy whose task it was to be always on hand when her mistress needed help. She rushed forward and retrieved the letter. Emma turned and gave her an angry slap, pointing to the bottles of smelling salts on the dressing table. She had a dependence on smelling salts and loved to buy all different kinds and line them up on her dressing table, where they sat, all gaily adorned with different coloured bows.

The child ran to get the particular bottle Emma pointed to, held it up while her mistress sniffed it, and then patted her mistress' brow with her handkerchief as Emma slowly recovered from the shock that the letter had given her.

So Percy had escaped his punishment and was now gone. That he had left a widow and brat behind was not her concern. Surely her father had not expected her to befriend them ...

'Oh, darling Papa,' she wept silently. 'Why did you have to go? Please do not leave me this decision to make. I am not like you. I hate so much that it hurts me inside.'

Emma sat reading the letters from the leather purse that Allanah had handed to John. Amongst them was a photograph of Percy with his bride on their wedding day. Percy was dressed in a checked shirt and choker and looked like a gypsy with this lovely girl with dark, waist-length dark hair beside him. The happy expressions on their faces made Emma sob bitterly.

The little skivvy was very alarmed. 'Shall I call someone ma'am?' she whispered anxiously.

'Get out!' cried Emma. 'Get out of my sight!'

The child got up and fled.

Without the slightest hesitation, Emma then broke the seal on the more official-looking envelope. It was from Allanah's mistress, Lady Fitzgerald, whose husband had saved her from the penal colony. It was a reference in which Lady Fitzgerald praised and recommended Allanah.

'Well,' muttered Emma, 'that does not concern me.' Then Emma read the newspaper clippings which had advertised for Percy Dell to come forward and claim his inheritance from his aunt Beatrice's estate. The last papers Emma read were the last letter Percy wrote and his last will and testament.

He had been so young. Emma wondered how he had died. Violently, no doubt, for that was how Percy Amos Dell had lived. She examined the photograph of Allanah and her child for some time. Then abruptly, she tied all the documents together and turned towards the fire. She would burn the lot of them. What were they to her?

Suddenly, the housekeeper came hurrying in, having heard from the skivvy that Emma was not steady on her feet.

'Is there something I can do?' the housekeeper asked.

'Yes, Mrs Mills,' said Emma coldly. 'Take the master's sea chest and place it in the library where it can't be seen. Then I'll have my tea.'

Emma thrust the papers into her desk, closed the lid and locked it. She would make up her mind about what to do with them in the morning. She could not face any decisions at the moment.

That night Emma frequently cried out in her sleep as all the horror of a distressed and thwarted mind came to haunt her. The little skivvy who slept in the annexe next door crept from her bed and crouched beside her. But Emma did not wake up. She seemed to be in a kind of half-waking sleep. Her eyes were open and her lips moved as she dreamed that she too was on board the ship that had gone down under her dear father, *Emma*, the ship that he had so proudly named after her. Emma dreamt that she could feel the waves wash over her, that she was slipping and sliding about the deck and her father was in the water endeavouring to save a child. Then suddenly a long-haired woman, her eyes turned in death, came close to Emma and grasped her arm with ice-cold hands. 'That's my little girl,' she said as Emma tried frantically to push her away from her.

As Emma woke up screaming, the skivvy ran panic-stricken from the room to get help. But Emma recovered quickly and was soon sitting in her dressing gown, in her bathchair sniffing her smelling salts and drinking coffee.

'Mrs Mills,' she said suddenly, 'I want you and your husband to come with me to Dover right now. Tell your husband to get the large carriage ready for a long trip.'

Mrs Mills, a fresh-faced country woman, looked astonished. Her mistress had never gone further than the village since she had her accident. Now she wanted to go to Dover. But she hurried to tell her husband, the groom. They were local people, both husband and wife both had been devoted to John Shulmead and had promised to take care of his beloved daughter should anything happen to him.

So after much preparation, the carriage was made comfortable. Emma was wrapped in furs and carried out to it by Mills. Mrs Mills was to sit next to Emma as they travelled. Both she and her husband were concerned about all this sudden bustle, for Mistress Emma had given them no indication of why she wished to travel all this way.

'Might have got news of the master,' ventured Mills. 'His body is not yet recovered.'

'But surely the mistress would have told us,' replied his wife.

'Well, 'tis a long drive for one so sick. We'd better get on our way,' growled her husband.

The rest of the servants watched through the windows as the carriage drove out down the drive with Emma sitting in a stately manner with her bathchair strapped to the back.

That evening they entered Dover town and stayed the night at an inn. The other customers were intrigued by the strange sight of this lovely solemn woman being carried inside, heavily wrapped in furs.

In the morning they travelled to Newhaven where they stopped at a tall, gloomy building. One wing was the work-house and the other was used to house children, mostly orphans of men who had gone down at sea, and whose keep was paid for by contributions from naval and lifeboat funds.

An aged vicar greeted the party and insisted that Emma be brought into his study.

'Well, madam,' he said. 'May I ask the reason for your visit? Do you wish to adopt or foster one of our unfortunate children?'

'I want to see all the children that were saved from the wreck of the *Emma* three months ago. My own father, the captain, went down with his ship.'

'Oh yes, most regrettable,' murmured the vicar. 'But there are only four children left here. Most have been claimed by relatives. Is the child related to you?'

'No indeed,' said Emma quite unsympathetically. 'But if she is suitable I will give her a home.'

'So you want a little girl? We have only one and that's our Amy. She is a most entertaining child but so far no one has shown any interest in her.'

'Fetch her!' commanded Emma coldly.

Minutes later, Amy stood before Emma, a small figure dressed in a snow-white pinafore and a grey cotton dress. From beneath a mop of black curls, her dark eyes scanned Emma almost in fear.

'Tell me your name,' ordered Emma.

In a clear precise voice, the child said: 'My name is Amy Dale and my home is Sydney, Australia.

'Would you like to come and live with me?' asked Emma, in the same cold tone.

'Certainly not,' said Amy. 'I am waiting here for my Mam. She will be rescued from the sea soon and take me home.'

The vicar exchanged glances with Emma. Turning to the girl, he said: 'Trot along now, Amy.'

With a toss of her proud head, Amy left the room.

'You are quite sure that she is a child from the wreck?'

asked Emma. 'Were there any other means of identification?'

'None, just a little bone cross she wears about her neck which she says was given to her by her father. But he, apparently, is dead, and no one so far has shown any interest in her. Besides, Australia is a long way off.'

'I will take her off your hands and give her a home,' said Emma. 'She comes just as a servant, you understand, but she will be well trained and taken care of. I trust a fair donation to your orphanage will settle matters.'

The vicar hesitated, this woman seemed such a cold and hard creature and Amy was such a sweet lovable child. It seemed a pity. Still, the child needed a home and money was needed for other poor children so he could not refuse this offer.

So little Amy was hurriedly packed off with a change of pinny in a paper parcel. With a tear-stained woeful face, she sat opposite Emma in the carriage on the way back to Riverview. Mrs Mills gave her an occasional warm smile.

Emma pulled down the veil of her hat over her face and closed her eyes. She did not even want to acknowledge the child.

'It beats me,' said Mrs Mills to her husband when they had returned home. 'Why should she want this child? There are plenty around here seeking a home and to go all the way to Dover and bring back memories of her lost father is all very strange.'

'Well 'tis odd, I admit,' replied her husband. 'But Miss Emma has a mind of her own and there is always a method in her madness, you can count on that.'

After the long journey Amy was very sleepy. 'Take her to the kitchen,' commanded Emma. 'And keep her out of my sight.'

Amy was puzzled by what was happening but the kitchen was warm and Mr and Mrs Mills were very kind to her. Amy became the small skivvy who got up very early to light the fires and black-lead the grates, who washed the floors and slept in the basement with another girl who became parlour maid.

Poor lonely little Amy wept floods of tears for the first few weeks before she had become used to her life. Then she would be found singing as she polished the brasses or swept the front steps. All the servants loved her and petted her. She rarely saw her mistress and certainly did not care. In fact, Amy was quite a ray of sunshine in that big gloomy house and was fond of telling everyone about her beloved mother and the big house near Sydney where she had been brought up. She was a very affectionate little girl and willing to do anything, which helped to make her life happier.

To the Mills who lived in the rooms over the stables, Amy was a very special little creature and they could not understand Emma's aversion to the child at all. When Mrs Mills suggested that the mistress might enjoy Amy as her companion now, Emma was furious.

'How dare you tell me what to do!' she bellowed. 'Remember, you may be housekeeper but you are still my servant. So keep your place.'

With tear-filled eyes Mrs Mills told her husband what had been said. 'I cannot believe it. We have always loved and trusted each other. Why should one small girl come between us?'

''Tis a strange business,' her husband agreed. 'Why, she went specially to Dover to get the child in the first place. Now Amy's been here nearly two years and the mistress has ignored her.'

'I think the mistress has been in a lot of pain lately,' said Mrs Mills. 'She is too stubborn to complain about it but her face is often tense and she sniffs at those damned bottles more and more. 'Tis a pity. Amy should have some schooling. She is ten years old now and no one bothers.'

'She can read, you know,' Mills said. 'Her father taught her. Apparently he was a Kentish man. I wonder what village he came from?'

So down in the servants' quarters they discussed the household affairs while upstairs in her parlour Emma entertained the ladies from the surrounding areas. They talked incessantly about horses and hunting. Although Emma was no longer able to compete, she still took a great interest in the local hunt and the races. Many of her best-bred mounts took part in them.

Life in the nearby hamlet went on as usual but the population continued to increase. The inn lay derelict, and the church, like its curate, was very run down and ancient. The Railway Halt was the most busy spot, in the area, as folk travelled back and forth to London on the new railway.

Still the clouds of smoke from the kilns drifted over the marsh. The clay pits and the old system of pages where little slaves worked for a moulding queen had been done away with. Nowadays children had to be thirteen before they worked and they had to attend school part-time. But quite often the children would spend the morning at school and the rest of the day until six o'clock in the brick kilns. Still they carried hot bricks by hand, and still they worked for very low wages and got plenty of kicks and cuffs from the men. But the terrible poverty of the times made it impossible to defeat this iniquitous system.

So compared with her peers, Amy was not so badly off. Her life could have been much worse. She was, after all, an orphan child in a strange land, but she was happy enough at Riverview. One day out of the blue, Amy was summoned to see the mistress. Amy was terrified. What had she done? Something must have been broken and Amy was to be blamed for it, she decided. She was often being blamed for things she never did but she had never been called to face Mistress Emma before. Her knees quaked in fright. She entered that stuffy room with its heavy drapes and smell of embrocation to see the mistress sitting very upright in her bathchair, her face pale and lined in pain.

Amy dropped the little curtsy that was expected of her and stood trembling in front of Emma, whose long shiny hair was piled high above her pallid face. Her fine white fingers fiddled with their load of rings while those olive green eyes stared at Amy with hostility. 'Do you like living here, ' Emma asked coldly.

'Oh yes, ma'am,' said Amy, bobbing another curtsy.

'Stand still, foolish child,' said the mistress irritably as she scrutinised her.

'Do you remember your father,' she asked Amy slowly and deliberately.

'Oh yes, ma'am,' gasped Amy. 'I remember him well. He gave me this,' she indicated the little bone cross she wore.

Emma lowered her eyes. She too recalled the cross, Aunt Dot at the inn had worn it always, having been given it by her dying niece Lucinda.

'Pass me one of those bottles,' she ordered. 'The one with the blue ribbon.'

Amy went to the shelf, passed her mistress the bottle and watched while Emma sniffed at it. She then replaced it.

'I wonder if you could stay here and look after me all the day,' said Emma. 'Would you like that?'

Amy stood her ground. 'I'm not sure, ma'am,' she replied.

'What do you mean? I suppose what you are trying to say is that you would not want to,' Emma eyed her with a cruel light in her eyes.

Amy swallowed hard but did not reply.

'Well,' continued Emma, 'that is just what you are going to do. You will sleep in here and stay with me all the time. Are you pleased, child? Say something,' she commanded.

Amy sighed. 'Just as you wish, ma'am,' she said.

Emma sneered contemptuously. She had rather hoped for some sort of a battle. 'Well, tell Mrs Mills to take you to town and fit you out in a suitable manner. I have also decided that you must attend the village school every morning until twelve noon before commencing your duties here as my own personal attendant. Now go, you are dismissed.'

Amy trotted off to Mrs Mills, who was pleased with what had taken place. 'Well, I'll be blessed,' she said. 'She has given in at last.'

'I'm not sure that I like her at all,' said Amy. 'She tries to belittle me. I only hope that I'll be able to keep my temper.'

'Dearie me, what words, I do declare!' cried Mrs Mills. 'We

are servants and must obey our betters.

'Why is she so much better than me?' said Amy. 'She can't even walk.'

'Oh my goodness,' cried Mrs Mills in a fluster. 'I'll have to punish you for that if you don't desist. What a forward child you are to be sure.'

Amy soon settled down at school, which she loved. She played kiss-and-chase with the village boys in the playground, took to reading and writing with ease, and her lively personality made her very popular. But she dreaded those dreary afternoons spent with Mistress Emma. She did not seem to be able to please her. Amy slept in the little annexe and there were all sorts of personal things to do, such as taking her to the water closet and helping her bathe and always being on hand with those sniffing bottes when Emma felt faint. Thus Amy spent her years from ten to fifteen in servitude to a very unpleasant and ungrateful mistress.

As Emma faded and grew more irritable with her pain, Amy grew more beautiful. Her curly hair grew long and thick and her dark eyes wide and framed by thick lashes. Her figure was small and neat and her whole demeanour very lady like. Emma's fine friends were impressed by her 'How nice is your young companion,' they would say. 'And how servile and willing. You are indeed fortunate, Emma.'

Emma would smile coldly. 'She does as she is told,' she replied. 'That is all that is needed of her.'

Always deep in her heart Emma was sure that one day she would walk again and ride freely over the meadows as she had years before. She consulted many medical men but it was always the same story. They would tell her that there was no hope. She would not believe them.

Most afternoons the young village doctor popped in for tea and a chat, Emma was generous with his fees so he liked to keep in touch, whenever the conversation veered towards the usual problem, the doctor would try to move it away again. He was certainly convinced that Emma could not be cured. But one afternoon he had just returned from a trip to

London. 'I have been staying with an old colleague of mine,' he said. 'We were at the medical college together. He is very interested in bones and has done some interestng work with disabled children. He seems to have some very interesting ideas about treating people.'

Emma's interest was aroused. Her long white dainty hands hovering like butterflies over the silver tea tray. 'Do you think he might be interested in my case,' she asked.

'Well, he may,' replied the doctor. 'I don't know much about it, it seems to have to do with the knitting of the bones, even inserting new bones. But whatever he is up to it seems to work.'

'Make me an appointment,' said Emma. 'I will go to London and consult him.'

So that spring, when Amy was fifteen, she travelled with her mistress to the great town of London. The devoted Mrs Mills also travelled with them but as Mr Mills had died, young coach and footman drove them to some lodgings in Onslow Square. They were a suite of rooms on the first floor in sumptuous surroundings.

Amy was thrilled by her first sight of London's tall buildings and ignored Mrs Mills' declarations that it was a dirty, vicious and noisy place. And Emma seemed unusually calm and peaceful. She even looked beautiful, and regal in a bright green travelling cloak and lots of fox furs. She had no time to be unpleasant, for her mind was concentrating on one thing — the day she would walk again.

CHAPTER TWENTY-TWO

The Last Love

Adam Gibbs came down the steps of his consulting-rooms in Harley Street. He had weathered the storms of life very well and was now a distinguished medical man. He was still tall and upright and had a clear, tanned skin lined with fine wrinkles from a long sojourn out east. His hair was silvery grey and his clothes were immaculate. But still there was a distant look of sadness in those steel grey eyes.

He briskly hailed a cab, put his walking cane on his arm and climbed in. 'Euston Station,' he directed the driver.

It was Friday, and he had decided to pay a brief visit to his mother. She was lonely, he knew that. She missed Aunt Ruth so much, and he felt he had better pay her a quick visit down at the cottage at Coalville. But he had to be back by Monday when he had a very important appointment with a woman with a spinal complaint. Apparently, she had plenty of money. He knew it was mercenary but he was most interested in rich patients at the moment because he was desperate for funding for a new wing in the hospital for disabled children.

His mother Alice was now in her seventies and still hale and hearty and still concerned with saving lost humanity. That weekend she and her son Adam went to the old churchyard to put flowers on the graves of Ben and Ruth Anneslee and her husband George Gibbs. If ever brave and dedicated people had lived in this world it was those three. But they had never attained any fame; only Alice and Adam remembered them. All their fine good works had amounted to very little, their true dedication had been only a drop in the ocean.

The Crimean War had devastated the working classes once

more and left many orphans and children crippled by rickets from undernourishment. Adam sighed deeply as he thought of his beloved Faith buried in a foreign land. At the battles of the Crimea they had worked together. Faith had become a nurse and had worked beside him in those terrible hospital tents on the battlefronts. They had never been married as there had never seemed to be the time. And then poor Faith had been struck down with the dreadful tropical fever. She had been the only woman Adam had ever loved and he had never felt the need for another. Now there was just Alice in his life, his mother, tall upright and very tough. But now she was missing Ruth, who had spent her last years in Coalville when her brave heart had started to give out. She had wished to stay in Coalville so that she could finally be laid to rest beside her beloved husband Ben.

After their visit to the graves, Adam took his mother's arm and they walked back to the neat little cottage beside the canal lock.

'What will you do when I am gone, Adam? You need a wife to look after you,' said Alice.

'No, mother, my work is sufficient to keep me happy,' he replied.

'Did you see Toby and Nelly?' she asked him.

'Yes, mother, they are fine. That salvationist Nelly is now in charge of the mission. She runs it like an army, so they say.'

'Oh well, God willing we did our part,' said Alice. 'Let us hope our reward will come in Heaven.'

The next day Adam travelled back to be in London. He was feeling a little depressed for his mother's pious ways had recently had that sort of effect upon him.

However, on Monday morning bright and early, he was sitting at his desk interviewing his new patient, a rich disabled woman called Emma Shulmead. She told him that she was forty years old, and that her disability was one of long standing. Adam looked down at his report and his eye caught the fact that she lived in a small country place in Kent called

Hollinbury Hamlet. Memories flashed through his brain, back down the years to when he went like a knight errant to rescue his love from the ogre who lived down there in Hollinbury. He looked up at this woman sitting before him. Her beautiful, lined face revealed many signs of hidden pain.

'As long as I could just support my own body, I would be content,' she was saying, 'but to be carried about like a child like this is quite soul-destroying.'

'Would you be prepared to stay in London for six months so that you can attend my therapeutic clinic?' Adam asked.

'I am entirely in your hands, doctor,' she answered in that highly cultured tone. 'I am a wealthy woman and I feel confident in my heart that one day I will walk once again.'

Adam nodded sympathetically at her. She was so brave and proud, and obviously a great lady. 'Well, it will be my pleasure, madam, to start treating you tomorrow. Now how will you come to the clinic? Shall I send a nurse to escort you?'

'No, I have my own companion, thank you,' replied Emma. 'Will you call her for me now?'

Adam opened the door to the adjoining office where Amy was sitting. She looked quaint, dressed in a little blue straw bonnet and a grey silk dress. Adam shot her a definite look of admiration as she wheeled Emma out of his office.

So every day Amy wheeled her mistress through the park to the Orthopaedic Hospital where Adam held his clinic and would sit waiting patiently while her mistress received her treatment. Then she would wheel her back to Onslow Square.

At first the muscular massage and various treatments she received made Emma very tired and irritable but after several weeks there was a definite change in her. She looked happier and somehow healthier. Although her joints were very stiff, she could sit up more easily than before. Emma began to make extra special preparations for her visits to her medical adviser. She would dress in her most expensive clothes and don her best jewellery. She was even a trifle more pleasant to Amy.

'My, my, I do declare! It's a miracle,' remarked Mrs Mills to the other servants.

In the afternoons, when Emma rested, Amy felt quite lonely. She would walk around the streets looking up at the tall buildings and longing for the sights and smells of the green meadows of Kent. It was on such a walk that she met Adam again, as he dashed down the steps from his Harley Street rooms. He collided with her as she was staring up in the air.

'Whoa there!' he laughed, clasping her in his arms. 'What are you doing staring into space like this?'

Amy blushed and giggled. 'I was trying to see the sky,' she said.

'Well, that is as good an occupation as any,' he jested. 'Can I escort you home?' He held out his arm and she timidly took it. Suddenly she felt safe and secure.

'You will be going home soon,' he said. 'Your mistress has made excellent progress.'

'Will she walk again?' asked Amy.

'Well, that I cannot say,' replied Adam. 'But she will need a lot of rest from all this strenuous treatment, for a while and then we will continue it again in six months' time.'

Amy knew that he was being evasive about the true prognosis, but she said nothing.

'Tell me,' Adam said, as they walked along 'about this place you live in, in Kent. Were you born there?'

'No, I was born out in Sydney, Australia,' Amy replied.

'How very unusual. Is Miss Shulmead a relative of yours?'

'No, she just fostered me. She took me from the orphanage, her father was the captain of the ship which went down with me and my mother on board coming from Australia. The ship went down in the Channel. My mother drowned,' she added sadly.

'Oh, the *Emma*,' said Adam. 'I think I recall it,' he said thoughtfully. Memories were flooding back. John Shulmead, whom he had met on that visit to the inn at Hollinbury, was Miss Emma Shulmead's father. Adam nodded. 'John Shulmead,' he said out aloud.

Amy looked startled. 'Did you know Miss Shulmead's father?' she asked.

'Well, I knew of him,' said Adam dreamily. They turned into Onslow Square. 'Goodbye little Amy,' said Adam. 'It has been very interesting getting to know you.'

'Goodnight, Dr Gibbs,' said Amy her heart beating fast.

Emma was awake and looking very annoyed. 'Well, where have you been?' she demanded as Amy crept into the room.

'Only for a walk,' Amy replied. 'I met Dr Gibbs and he walked me home.'

'Well, of all the nerve!' Emma's eyes narrowed angrily. 'You little brazen hussy! Kindly keep your place as a servant. From now on, you will not leave this house without my permission. Is that clear?'

'Yes, ma'am,' muttered Amy but her dark eyes flashed with temper. 'Damned old bitch,' she muttered as she left the room. 'She's got her eye on him herself, I expect. Still, he is nice and so clever and so distinguished. He's the kind of husband I would like for myself, even if he is a lot older than I am.'

So Amy went to bed dreaming of love and finding a man to give her a home of her own.

Once they had returned to Riverview, it was clear that Emma's health had improved considerably. Slowly but surely she sat fairly upright and then, with the aid of two sticks, began to take a few steps. Then she could manage with only one stick, leaning very heavily on tiny Amy. And as a result, Emma's temper was slightly better. Of course she still had bad days of morbid depression when she made life hell for Amy and the rest of the staff, but on the whole she was more cheerful and could actually enjoy herself entertaining her friends in the afternoons and discussing horses. Often Emma had long sleepless nights which meant that Amy had to sit up through the early hours reading out aloud from Emma's favourite novels.

Emma wrote long letters to Dr Gibbs describing her progress and she was very secretive about them. Once they were signed and sealed, she would trust only Amy to post them.

'The mistress is certainly much improved,' remarked Mrs Mills. 'But I've never known her to be so moody or, I might say, broody.'

'What do you mean?' asked Amy.

'Well, I think she has become enamoured of that good-looking doctor.'

Young Amy's face went pale. 'But why? She has always hated men. I can't believe that.'

'Well, that's how I see it,' asserted Mrs Mills, her long chin wagging as she sat with her feet propped up on a kitchen chair enjoying a natter. 'A lot of women can be funny that way,' she explained. 'Lots of them hate the thought of dying old maids, so they suddenly chuck their lives away by marrying rogues and bullies. And they are all the more likely to do that when they are rich.'

Amy listened to this piece of wordly wisdom with a sad expression on her face. 'I'll probably remain a spinster,' she said wistfully. 'What prospects are there for me? I have no family and no money and Miss Shulmead hates me.'

'Oh, I would not say she hates you,' said Mrs Mills kindly. 'She's probably just very jealous of you. After all, you're a very pretty presentable young woman, and very popular. Someone is going to snap you up and get a good bargain.'

Amy smiled. 'You are such a comfort to me,' she said, kissing the grey wrinkled face of the only real friend she knew. But the thought of remaining at Riverview, always to be at Emma's beck and call made her seethe with anger. She could just walk out, she supposed, but where would she go? And no one would employ her without a reference. Deep despondency overcame her. Amy then thought of the tall distinguished Dr Gibbs and how kind he had been to her.

Each day Amy walked down to the bridge to post Emma's mail. She would often cross over the railway bridge and sand looking towards that old derelict inn, The Malted Shovel, which stood high up on the other bank, with its black-and-white beams flaking, its chimneys slightly slanting. It was quite an impressive building, Amy thought, and she wondered why it had been left to rot away.

Amy felt drawn to the old inn in a strange way. She wished that she had the courage to go nearer but somehow it always failed her. According to the post mistress, who was from the north country, someone had told her that the old inn was haunted. An old woman was robbed and murdered in there, she informed Amy. But most of the old inhabitants had left the hamlet now, and the new houses were inhabited by folk who had moved out from the overcrowded towns.

'That is where there used to be brick fields, down there on the marsh,' the station master told Amy. 'They are closed now. They make cement now, they do.'

Amy stared out over the marshland which was now very green and yellow with marsh marigolds. A herd of black-and-white cows grazed peacefully knee-deep in the grass. She was not sure what a brick field was but that tall remaining chimney looked quite sinister. Nevertheless, she did like it here. There was something in that fresh salty breeze blowing over the marshland that excited her.

When she thought she had been out for long enough, Amy would hurry back to Riverview, with her cheeks glowing and a wild light in her eyes, and Emma would stare at her suspiciously.

Mrs Mills said one day: 'Don't go prying and poking about that old inn, because I can tell you, my dear, what I have heard of old Mistress Beatrice, she never lies easy in her grave.'

'Whoever is Mistress Beatrice?' cried Amy.

'Well, when I was courting Mills, he used to go drinking in there,' replied Mrs Mills. 'I lived in another village, and the inn was on his route to my home. Many a weird story he has told me about that place.'

Amy was eager to hear more but Mrs Mills got tired quickly and began to doze. 'They's all buried in that old churchyard,' she muttered. 'A long line of them ...'

Amy was intrigued by Mrs Mills' ramblings and on her next trip to the mail, she carried on into the old churchyard under the mossy lych-gate, along a weed-ridden red-brick path and on to the ancient Norman church which now only opened on Sundays because the young curate, who lived in the village, had to service the village church as well.

Amy paused by the massive walnut tree that had scattered its fruit among the gravestones. Then she sat on the stone wall and looked down towards the shore, just catching a glimpse of the river as it wound its way to the sea. Jumping down to her feet, she gently pulled the ivy away from the nearest gravestone. The lettering was already worn down by the salt breezes from the sea but it could be deciphered. 'Here lies Amos Dell,' Amy read. 'Inn-keeper of this parish. Also his daughters Dulcie Dell, aged 17, Dorothy Dell, aged 56, and Beatrice Dell aged 72.' Amy was astonished. These people held her own name. Her mother had told her that her father had originally been called Dell but had changed his name to Dale when he sailed to Australia. What an extraordinary coincidence! How could this be? A little further on was a fairly well-kept grave. The stone was marked clearly: Here lies Luke Shulmead who met his death on the railway track on Christmas Eve 1850. Shulmead? Well, he must be related to Emma, she thought. That was not so strange. The next grave she moved to was a big one with a large, overpowering stone angel that spread its wings to caste a shadow over the grave. 'Here,' she read, 'is buried Sam Shulmead. Blacksmith of this hamlet.' It also mentioned his wife and his two sons Mark and Matthew, who died in the battle of Waterloo in 1815.

Amy was enthralled. Next she discovered a very smart tomb with a big stone cross. This was the family vault of John Shulmead, drowned at sea, and his beloved wife, Dolly, who lay buried here. 'Emma's parents,' Amy murmured.

The name of Dell on the first tombstone nagged at her mind. Could this be the very place that her mother had been bound for when they set off from Sydney? Could this Dell family be her father's? Her own? How could she find out? There was really only one way of being sure, and that was to ask Emma herself.

One afternoon, when Emma seemed to be in a good mood, Amy ventured forth. 'I've visited the local church,' she said timidly. 'I was interested to see that your family vault is there, too.'

Emma's apparent good mood had disappeared. Her eyes flashed with rage. 'You did what?' Emma cried sharply, trying to get to her feet, her lips compressed and blue.

'Don't fuss yourself. I was all right,' Amy assured her. 'Indeed, I found a grave with my own family name on it.'

'How dare you!' screeched Emma. 'What right have you to go prying into my family affairs? Stay away from the church-yard. If I ever hear you have crossed over that bridge again, I'll send you packing back into the streets where you belong.'

'I am sorry,' stuttered Amy, completely confused.

'Get out of my sight,' shouted Emma. 'Then get Mrs Mills,' she gasped and had become quite breathless. Emma was shocked to discover that Amy was aware of her real surname.

Mrs Mills came hurrying in on her old thin legs to comfort her, as Emma sobbed and screamed wildly. After a while, she quietened down enough for Mrs Mills to send for the local doctor.

Later in the kitchen, Mrs Mills quizzed Amy.

'Whatever did you do to her?' she asked.

Amy shook her head. 'Nothing. I told her that I had been to the churchyard and seen her family vault. After all, Mrs Mills, you did suggest it.'

'Oh dear,' gasped Mrs Mills, 'so I did. My old head must be losing its power. Miss Emma does not like the past brought up. There is a lot of tragedy in her life, poor dear, so don't ever mention it again, my dear.'

'I won't,' said Amy, 'but please tell me who Amos Dell was. I am interested because it happens to be my father's true surname.'

An odd look came over Mrs Mills' face. 'He was the old innkeeper,' she murmured. 'That's all I know,' she added quickly and turned away. It was obvious that she did not want to say anything that might lead to more trouble.

Amy bit her lip, feeling both hurt and resentful. It was obvious that there was some significance to her being in this hamlet where the graves carried her father's true name. But why would no one tell her anything and give her the sense of heritage that she longed for so much?

CHAPTER TWENTY-THREE

The Death of a Birthday Party

That summer Emma seemed to become unusually content. She wheeled herself about the garden in her bathchair, humming to herself and collecting the lovely roses to arrange in big earthenware jars ready for Amy to place around the house. Occasionally Emma would get attacks of breathlessness and then Mrs Mills would come slowly upstairs to attend to her, giving her the pills that Adam Gibbs had prescribed for her.

She was not very friendly to Amy who was feeling increasingly unhappy, lonely and frustrated. She never felt able to please Emma, no matter how she tried. One morning would stay in her memory forever it caused her such anguish.

Amy had carried huge jars of flowers into the library and tried to put them on the shelf, as Emma had asked her to. But as she did so Amy's elbow knocked the old white ivory elephant from the mantelpiece down into the marble fireplace. When she retrieved it, the trunk had broken off.

Emma heard the crash and within seconds had appeared in the doorway, like a raging screeching virago. 'Oh, you clumsy hussy!' she cried. 'That belonged to my father. He had that ivory elephant all of his married life.'

Shaking with fear, Amy picked up the elephant and ruefully tried to stick on its broken trunk.

'Leave it alone!' Emma screamed. 'My father was very superstitious about that elephant. You will bring bad luck on us all, you evil child!'

Emma's harsh voice suddenly seemed to die down and a white haze drifted in front of Amy's eyes as something snapped inside. 'Oh, you horrid old hag!' With a yell of fury, she threw the elephant at Emma's head. It just missed and crashed through the window to land in the middle of the lawn.

Emma's mouth opened in an effort to scream but instead she passed out in a dead faint.

Amy was terrified by what she had done, and ran for the new housemaid. She asked her to stay with Emma while she went to get Mrs Mills.

All that day, the house was hushed and silent. Amy lurked in her room partly remorseful but also nursing a kind of defiant feeling that kept surging up inside her. Now Emma would surely turn her out, and a good job too. She would be free to go to London then. Yes, whatever happened to her, she no longer cared.

At eventide, Emma had recovered. She was up and dressed and down to dinner where she stared coldly at Amy across the table. There was no mention of the morning's dreadful scene.

Mrs Mills was very worried. 'I don't know what brought on that attack,' she said to Amy. 'But it was not one of her usual turns. According to the doctor, it was definitely a mild heart attack. Miss Shulmead must contact Dr Gibbs about those pills.'

Amy stared miserably at Mrs Mills, who was so wrapped up in her mistress's health condition that she failed to notice Amy's unhappy face.

That night Emma called for Amy at three o'clock in the morning and ordered her to read out loud to her from the final chapter of *The Mayor of Casterbridge* by Thomas Hardy.

When Amy had finished reading the novel, Emma sat up, her face like a cold mask. 'Stay there,' she said. 'I am not sleepy yet.' Then she suddenly began to talk. 'When I was eighteen, my father gave me a lovely birthday party. The house was new then and the gardens were strung with coloured lanterns. Everyone who was anyone all over the county came to the party. That was the night he asked Papa for my hand.' As she spoke, her voice seemed to have an eerie tone to it which matched the faraway look in her eyes.

Amy stared at her with dark gypsy eyes. She had never seen Emma like this, seeming so vulnerable and fragile.

Emma had come out of her trance-like state. She tightened her lips and narrowed her eyes. 'So, you do want to harm me,' she said triumphantly. 'I've always thought you did.'

Amy lowered her head in shame. She had not been aware of thinking that way but now it was said, she knew it to be true.

'That's right,' Emma sneered. 'You need to feel ashamed because you are born to be a murderess, I am quite sure of that.'

'Oh, ma'am,' she cried. 'I never did anything. Release me! Let me go! I'll get a situation somewhere if you will only give me some sort of reference.'

'Yes! You would like that, wouldn't you?' Emma jeered, 'after I have fed and clothed you all these years.'

'I'll repay you if you will allow me to go my own way,' begged Amy.

'Oh, no, my lady!' ranted Emma. 'You will stay here and serve me. That is your duty. You are a penniless orphan. What would your chances be out there in that cold world? I'll forget what you did. That's generous of me when I could call the police and have you locked in jail.'

'Now I am going to have a birthday party. Fetch me my stationery book and then you will help me write the invitations ...'

So there followed days of endless fetching and carrying as Emma planned a big garden party to celebrate her fortieth birthday. A large marquee was erected in the garden and row upon row of chinese lanterns was strung out among the trees. Many cooks were employed to create rich exotic dishes and there were crates of champagne. It seemed that Emma was sparing no expense in order to recreate the famous birthday party of twenty-two years ago.

There were trips to the dressmaker for numerous fittings. Emma was determined to look stunning. She ordered an emerald green silk evening gown with an off-the-shoulder design which showed off her perfect white skin.

Amy was quite worn down with orders. Day after day she trotted here and there and bore the brunt of Emma's tempers.

Two days before the party, Adam appeared. It was a Friday evening and Amy had watched the coachman go off to meet the train and wondered who was coming so early. When she later saw Adam's tall figure alighting from the coach, her heart missed a beat. He seemed so smart and clean with that soft silver hair and dark tanned skin. Oh, how she wished he were her man! But no, that would never be possible. Amy felt like a wild bird trapped in a cage.

'I don't need you at dinner tonight, Amy,' Emma said. 'So keep out of sight and out of mischief.' She clearly wanted Adam all to herself.

Amy lay on her bed listening to the sounds of their voices and tinkle of laughter as Emma did her act for the handsome doctor, while outside in the garden, the footmen were putting the finishing touches to the elaborate display for the next day.

Later, as Adam stood outside on the terrace to smoke a cigar, Amy could not resist peeping at him as he stood there alone. Adam sensed that he was being watched and looked up. Seeing Amy, he stepped down into the middle of the lawn and called up in a loud whisper. 'Is that you at the window, my sweet Amy? What is the matter? Are you poorly?

'No,' replied Amy in a tremulous voice. 'I am quite well but just having an early night.'

'Oh yes, the festivities on Sunday. I look forward to seeing you there,' he called. 'Well, goodnight, Amy.'

'Goodnight, Dr Gibbs,' Amy replied, her voice choked with tears.

Early the next morning Amy crept out of the house. It was a beautiful summer morning and the sky was still rose coloured from the sunrise. A white soft mist obscured the marshland as Amy walked forlornly along keeping carefully in the shadows so that no one from the house would see her.

She was not sure of where she was going but she found herself drawn towards the old railway bridge and the inn beside. They had both haunted her dreams the night before. Now she knew that she wanted to walk down and take another look at it before anyone else had risen.

She stood with her arms on the small gate that led to the level-crossing, not daring to cross the line. When she looked down, a creepy feeling gripped her. Suddenly a gentle arm linked into hers and a kind voice said: 'Why, little Amy taking the morning air. May I join you?'

Amy almost jumped out of her skin. Looking up, she saw Adam Gibbs in an old tweed jacket and a shooting cap on his silvery hair. She gasped for breath as she looked at him.

'Come,' he said. 'Let's cross. Nothing is coming down the track and I want to take a good look at that deserted inn.' He took her arm and helped her through the gate down the back and over the crossing where they stood outside the old Malted Shovel and stood looking up at its crumbling timbers.

'I know that inn could tell a strange story,' he said.

Amy looked up at him timidly. 'How do you know, sir? It's strange but I have the same impression of it.'

Adam kept his arm linked in hers and fondled her finger tips. This sent thrilling shivers down her spine.

'Oh, it's a long story,' he said. 'But that inn is linked with my past.'

'Oh, please tell me,' Amy pleaded. 'I find this place so fascinating but I can never find out what it is I am searching for.'

'Come, let us sit on the churchyard wall,' Adam said. 'I want to be with you, Amy. That is what I came out here, when I saw you leave the house.'

Amy stared at him in disbelief.

'Well, never mind,' he said. 'Let us discuss the inn.' He looked amused. 'Don't be nervous of me, Amy, will you?' he asked earnestly.

Amy shook her head. 'No. In fact I feel very comfortable with you, Dr Gibbs.'

'The name is Adam,' he replied, putting the tips of her fingers to his lips. This caused Amy almost to faint with ecstasy and love for him.

'I first came to this inn a long time ago,' he told her. 'Twenty-five years ago at least. I was very young and very much in love with my betrothed. Her name was Faith and she was staying there. It was peopled by the strangest characters — an old woman called Beatrice and a village idiot called dumb Lukey. It was the most unhappy period of my life, yet I've never forgotten that inn or this strange hamlet. I am quite thrilled to make contact with it again.'

'Did you marry your Faith,' asked Amy seriously.

'No, my dear, but we were as close as two human beings ever could be.' He sighed. 'Unfortunately, she died of the fever out in the Crimea. It seems that there was not time to marry. And then, until I met you, no other woman has ever interested me.'

Amy blushed. 'Oh, please, don't toy with me,' she said in a low whisper.

'Amy look at me, straight into my eyes and tell me what you see.' Adam turned her chin up to his face and looked at her. Slowly their heads moved close and their lips met. Then they clung passionately together as they stood by the ancient churchyard wall.

'Amy, darling, I am in love with you,' continued Adam. 'I came here because I could not forget you. Something tells me that fate has drawn us together, and so I will not leave until you have promised to marry me.'

Amy drew so close to him and that deep dark inherited passion almost overwhelmed her. 'Oh, my dear! I simply can't believe it.' Suddenly, she felt self-conscious. 'Please let us walk on, dear Adam, for someone might see us.'

'I don't care,' cried Adam, gaily tossing his cap up in the air and catching Amy in his gentle grasp. 'I am a lot older than you, Amy, and you are so young and innocent. Tell me, do you feel that I have now taken advantage of that fact?'

'No, Adam,' replied Amy. 'It was just the same with me as

soon as we met. But I am so afraid of Miss Shulmead,' she added, her lower lip trembling.

Adam looked very sober. 'Yes,' he said. 'And after last night I know that she is a very strange woman. She offered to make out her will in my favour and support my new hospital wing for poor children if I would consent to marry her.'

They were walking along side by side and Adam laughed out loud at the idea again. But Amy stopped in her track. 'She will never let me marry you,' she said in a hushed voice.

'Why not, Amy? What has she against you?'

'She hates me,' sobbed Amy. 'I don't know why but she really hates me.'

Adam held her close as Amy wept bitter tears. 'Then that's all the more reason for me to take you away,' he said reassuringly. 'Miss Shulmead will not need you later on. I am afraid that she has a very weak heart. That is why we thought it unwise for her to continue with the treatment.'

'Oh, so that's why she has those fainting attacks when she is distressed,' said Amy. 'Oh, I feel almost sorry for her. She gets so little out of life.'

'Well, my darling,' said Adam, 'now we have each other. I will insist that she allows you to go to my mother in Coalville until I make our final wedding arrangements.'

Amy shook her head with amazement. 'I still can't believe it,' she cried.

Forgetting that they were now in sight of the house Adam swept her into his arms and they stood clasped together in a long lingering kiss as they pledged their beating hearts to each other.

But another heart was beating fast and furious at that moment, as Emma Shulmead looked out through her father's telescope at the scene below. What she saw made her scream and stamp and foam at the mouth. Emma had been unable to find Amy and had asked to be carried up to the small room where her father used to spend so much of his time. It had become Emma's favourite room too, as she enjoyed looking through the telescope to survey the estate, and spying on the

activities of her estate workers. However, she was not surveying the estate today, she was looking for that hussy Amy. And
now she had seen more than she had bargained for. There,
through the lens, she could see Adam and Amy standing on
the path in a close embrace. With a cry of rage, she threw the
telescope from its stand, and staggered wildly about on her
two walking sticks. Then she lost her balance completely and
suddenly crashed to the floor.

A servant heard the crash and came running. Emma's frail
body was carried back to her bedroom but by now her head
lolled back and her eyes had turned upwards. It seemed that
Emma Shulmead had left this world.

When Adam and Amy arrived at the house the place was in
an uproar. A groom was on his way to call for the local
doctor. 'The mistress is taken bad, doctor,' he called. 'Hurry!'

Adam dashed upstairs, leaving a bewildered Amy behind in
the hall.

For nearly an hour the two doctors worked to resuscitate
Emma but to no avail. Adam came wearily out of the
bedchamber and Amy stood trying to comfort poor old Mrs
Mills as he announced that the mistress of the house was
dead.

The following week was a strange one for Amy. Everyone
seemed to depend on her, coming to her for their orders, now
that the mistress was gone. The first thing that had to be
done was to take down the marquee and dismantle the fabu-
lous decorations. Messages had to be sent to the guests
cancelling the invitations to the big birthday party and
inviting them instead to Emma's funeral.

Amy coped with her sudden responsibilities with admirable
strength and competence but she always felt a little odd. At
times she even expected her tyrannical mistress to walk into
the room and bark out orders.

Adam had to sort out his own affairs. 'I must return to
London, Amy,' he said, 'but I will be back for the funeral.
After that I will want you to come away with me to meet my
mother. She will be very pleased that I have found myself

such a sweet little woman.'

'But I am a pauper without any background,' replied Amy dolefully.

'Oh dear, little Amy, such dramatics!' Adam mocked. 'I love you for yourself, Amy, and I also am poor, I give most of my services to charity and I only wish I could do more. So you can assist me in this and I am sure we will be very happy together.'

Amy smiled and kissed him goodbye. 'I'll always love you,' she said, 'and I'll always belong to you.'

Now Adam had gone and Amy was kept busy in the house. Then one morning two legal men arrived at the house, to go over Miss Shulmead's papers. They rummaged about for the whole day in that precious bureau that Emma had always kept locked.

The lawyer took off his spectacles and looked shrewdly at Amy. 'Now, tell me, ma'am, you were Miss Shulmead's personal attendant and companion. Can you tell us if she made a will recently? We have no record of one in the office.'

'I was not in her confidence,' replied Amy. 'Perhaps you should ask the housekeeper, Mrs Mills.'

But old Mrs Mills was so very distressed at the loss of her young mistress that her mind had gone very vague. 'She did talk about leaving all her money to some animal society at one time,' she said, 'but I have no knowledge that she ever did make that will.'

'Do you know of any distant relatives,' asked the lawyer.

Mrs Mills shook her head. 'A strange lonely one, was my mistress. Her life was beset by tragedy. Poor dear, to die so young.' She began to weep and Amy put her arms about her to comfort her.

'Please leave her alone,' Amy begged the men. 'She was devoted to Miss Shulmead, and has been here most of her life.'

'Well, there is a great deal of money and property at stake,' the lawyer explained. 'Did Miss Shulmead ever promise you a legacy?' he asked Amy.

Amy gave a wry grin and shook her head. 'Miss Shulmead hated me,' she said.

Then the solicitor produced an old leather purse and some papers. 'Is this your property?' he asked.

'No, I've never seen it before,' Amy replied.

The lawyer looked perplexed. 'Your name is Amy Dale and you were born in Sydney, Australia?'

'Yes,' Amy nodded dumbly.

'Well, among other items of interest in here is your birth certificate. It seems that your father changed his name from Dell to Dale at some point in his life.'

Amy looked astonished to see such papers.

The lawyer put all the papers into his case. 'We had better go back to town and get more advice. This seems to be developing into a tricky situation,' he said.

'How did Emma get my birth certificate?' Amy asked Mrs Mills. 'I thought that my mother lost all her possessions when she drowned.'

'Well, you can't be sure of that,' said Mrs Mills. 'Perhaps the orphanage gave Miss Shulmead all your papers. Oh, dear, I'll be glad when this business is all over and my lovely mistress is laid to rest.'

So it followed that Emma was laid in state in the old church surrounded by flowers and candles. All the villagers came to look at her body and exclaim her beautiful she was and how sad her life had been. The funeral was attended by the best of the county society.

When it was all over Adam said, 'Get your case packed, Amy. I'll not go and leave you in this gloomy old house. I'm taking you with me to Coalville to my mother.'

Amy was not going to hesitate. She put her belongings together and then went down into the drawing-room to listen to the reading of the will amongst the black-clad ladies, the last of Emma's friends. They were very anxious to know just what was to happen to the property, the huge stables, the brood mares and the stallions. Emma had collected all the best bloodstocks. Would they all be auctioned off?

The lawyer cleared his throat. 'My late client did not leave a will,' he said, 'and it was necessary to locate her next of kin. That next of kin is Miss Amy Dale, resident of the house and constant companion of Miss Shulmead.'

The lawyer continued. 'Miss Shulmead was unmarried and left no offspring. Amy Dale is the daughter of Miss Shulmead's first cousin, Percy Amos Dell, now deceased, who died out in Australia. He was the great-nephew of the late Beatrice Dell, resident of this hamlet, and owner of the Malted Shovel inn. Miss Beatrice Dell also left a sizeable estate which is now in chancery. This will also come to Miss Dale. Miss Dale you are indeed a very fortunate young woman.'

Amy had leaped up from her seat and ran out into the garden weeping madly. Adam followed her and held her in his arms until she was calm.

'Well, that was indeed quite a shock for you. You had no idea at all.'

'Oh, that is the terrible part of it. Emma hid from me my true heritage and reminded me constantly that I was a pauper and because of that she could keep me for all those years in a virtual prison. How could she have been so cruel? I don't want that money. It is evil. Let them give it to the poor.' Tears flowed down her cheeks.

'But why did she hate me so? That I will never understand.'

Adam shook his head. 'That I do not know, my darling. But if you wish to relinquish your fortune that is your decision. I'll not marry you for money.'

Amy panicked. 'Oh, darling!' she cried. 'Do not let the money change our lives. I love you. I would die if you deserted me.'

'Now calm down, my love,' he said. 'The money can do good if you use it well. Think of all the disabled children who spend their lives in pain, as Emma did, born with deformed limbs or suffering as a result of malnutrition. Yes, that money could work miracles.'

Amy smiled. It was like a ray of sun through the clouds.

'Yes,' she whispered, 'you are right, it is God's will. That is what we will do with the money.'

They sat holding hands. 'With you beside me, Amy, what more could a man want?'

'It's strange,' said Amy thoughtfully 'when I think of how angry Emma got when once I asked her who had owned the tavern. And how very strange it is that this hamlet brought us together,' she looked at Adam. 'I have often thought that this hamlet is full of ghosts.'

Adam said nothing. All he could think was how extraordinary it was that Percy, the homicidal pervert who had destroyed his Faith, had fathered this sweet lovely Amy. Bad seeds did not have to go on forever.

Adam took her hand and rested his chin on her soft hair. 'The hamlet has brought us together,' he said, 'but I feel that we should leave it and its ghosts behind and not return. We can carry our own banner of salvation out into the world together.'

Amy smiled and squeezed his hand. She turned to look at the house she had just inherited and then back over the roofs of the little hamlet of Hollinbury. It seemed to have brought so much unhappiness to so many people yet in the end it had brought her ecstasy. Yes, Adam was right. They had to leave it and never return. They had a whole life of happiness before them and she did not want it jeopardized. For the sake of the future she would cut herself off from the past forever.

All Futura Books are available at your bookshop or
newsagent, or can be ordered from the following address:
Futura Books, Cash Sales Department,
P.O. Box 11, Falmouth, Cornwall TR10 9EN.

Please send cheque or postal order (no currency), and
allow 60p for postage and packing for the first book
plus 25p for the second book and 15p for each additional
book ordered up to a maximum charge of £1.90 in U.K.

B.F.P.O. customers please allow 60p for
the first book, 25p for the second book plus 15p per
copy for the next 7 books, thereafter 9p per book

Overseas customers, including Eire, please allow £1.25
for postage and packing for the first book, 75p for the
second book and 28p for each subsequent title ordered.